THE LIES BENEATH

LUCY O'CALLAGHAN

POOLBEG CRIMSON

This book is a work of fiction. References to real people, events, establishments, organisations, or locales are intended only to provide a sense of authenticity, and are used fictitiously. All other characters, and all incidents and dialogue, are drawn from the author's imagination and are not to be construed as real.

Published 2024 by Crimson,
an imprint of Poolbeg Press Ltd.
123 Grange Hill, Baldoyle,
Dublin 13, Ireland
Email: poolbeg@poolbeg.com

A catalogue record for this book is available from the British Library.

ISBN 978-1-78199-699-7

www.poolbeg.com

Printed and bound by CPI (UK) Ltd, Croydon CR0 4YY

About the Author

Lucy penned her first story, 'Arthur's Arm', with her father, at the ripe old age of eight. When her children were young, she wrote stories for them and they subsequently illustrated them. A self-confessed people-watcher, stories that happen to real people have always fascinated her and this motivated her move to writing contemporary women's fiction.

Lucy writes a weekly 'Really Useful Links' column for writing.ie, aimed at helping writers with various aspects of writing. She also writes regular feature interviews with literary agents. When not writing, Lucy can be found rearranging her purple pens and purple notebooks, lining up her collection of elephants (not real ones), or walking the beaches and hills of the west of Ireland with her husband and dog Zouma. Her three almost grown-up children have long since come up with excuses not to go.

The Lies Beneath is her first novel.

About the Author

To Niall, for everything

PROLOGUE

DAWN

June

She just has to get in and out, that's all. It'll take two minutes.

Dawn pauses for a neighbour's car to pass before crossing the road of the quiet cul-de-sac, her heart thumping. Her mother's blue Fiesta is still in the driveway; she must have cycled to work. That explains why Dawn hasn't heard anything – she's always in a rush when she's not driving. It'll be this evening before she feels her mother's wrath.

Her heart calms a little as she approaches the neat semi-detached house. Unlocking the door, she steps in, pushes the keys into her hoodie pocket, and leans firmly against the stiff door to shut it.

Dawn turns and freezes. Her mum hasn't gone anywhere. She's lying in a twisted mess at the bottom of the stairs.

Rushing forward, Dawn drops to her knees, barely aware of her legs nudging into a pool of blood, the stickiness seeping quickly through the thin material of her black leggings.

Blood is clotted in her mum's thick, curly, blonde hair, and a congealed puddle surrounds the back of her head, soaked into the collar of her pink fluffy dressing gown, which is half off, exposing her shoulder.

"*Mum,*" Dawn whispers, her breath catching at the back of her throat as she puts a hand on her mum's bare shoulder before quickly taking it away, gasping. The skin is cold to the touch. Lowering her head to her mum's mouth, she can't feel any breath and, pulling back, she sees the slight blue tinge on her lips.

"*Oh my God, oh my God!*" Dawn rocks back on her knees, feeling the perspiration prickle on her forehead. Bile surges into her throat and she swallows it down, the acidic taste lingering. She opens her mouth to take a breath and inhales the tangy iron scent of the blood in the air.

Running her fingers into the roots of her hair, she tries to think. What should she do? What does she *need* to do? Her whole body is convulsed by shudders, and she tries to steady her shaking shoulders. Shuffling back, the blood stuck to her knees smears across the tiles.

Shit. The blood is on her. Dawn has touched her mum. She shouldn't have. Now she *has* to stay.

1

GALWAY

April 2019

Carla zips her black Chelsea boots and checks her watch as she looks in the mirror in the hallway. Thomas usually rings if he's running late. She applies her lipstick and gently pushes her lips together. She loves the opportunity to wear lipstick. It's a Chanel tinted nude colour, subtle yet still makes her feel like she's dressed up. It's only a parent association meeting but it's nice to make the effort. The only other adults she's seen today were at the school drop-off and collection times. She glances into the living room on her way into the kitchen – Ben and Daniel are sitting on the rug in their pyjamas, playing Lego.

She has everything organised since earlier this evening so she could slip out to the meeting. Chicken curry is ready for Thomas along with the lemon mousse she made this morning – his favourite. She's bathed the kids. He'll only have to read them a story before putting them to bed. And they'll probably play for a while before that, giving Thomas the chance to catch up on the news, as he likes to after his dinner.

Carla turns to the breakfast bar, sliding a sheet of paper out of her folder, and scanning the agenda for tonight's meeting. They've got a lot to get through and she doesn't want to be late. She's determined to make 2019 the school's best fair ever.

The headlights from Thomas's car flash through the double doors of the living room and reflect off the cream units in the kitchen as he pulls onto the driveway. *At last.* Pushing the agenda back into the folder, she slips a blazer over her slender frame and runs her fingertips through her straight blonde hair.

"I'm going soon, boys – make sure you're good for Daddy. He'll be tired."

"Hi, babe! You look great, have you been somewhere nice?" Thomas comes into the kitchen, hangs his sports jacket on the back of a stool at the breakfast bar, and kisses her. "Sorry I'm late. It's been a mad busy day. I'm heading out again. Just back to get showered and –"

"I've got a PA meeting at half past. Remember, I reminded you this morning. Your dinner's ready." She nods at the countertop, gripping the folder, anticipating how this is going to play out.

"Oh shit, sorry. I completely forgot. You don't mind missing it, do you?"

"It's an important meeting. There's only a few weeks before the fundraiser –"

"Babe, this is a client thing. It pays the bills. I can't get out of it." He turns to go. "You'll be able to catch up at the school gates tomorrow morning, won't you?"

He shouts a quick hello to the boys as he goes upstairs.

Carla drops the folder heavily on the breakfast bar. She does mind actually. She's worked hard preparing for this meeting and there's still lots of organising to do before the event. Why does being a mum and supportive wife always have to exclude everything else?

She sighs, reaches for her phone and sits down on a high stool. Carla likes being part of the planning. It's given her a focus, and she's enjoyed the adult company. It can be lonely being a stay-at-home mum.

Taking a photo of the agenda, she texts it to Emily. Although it's already been emailed to the committee, she knows no one will have printed it out and the 4G in the school is terrible. Emily will definitely be going; her kids are at their dad's tonight. Her best friend seems to have the best of both worlds lately, back at work part-time and she gets time off to do things.

Replacing her phone on the breakfast bar, she lines it up with the corner. She shouldn't think like that; it's wrong. Emily's had an awful couple of years with her shock separation from her husband, and she didn't go back to work because she wanted to – she loved being a full-time mum – but she had to. Still, Carla can't help feeling a bit jealous that her friend is carving out a new life for herself, moving forward, while she's still stuck in the same routine. And, now that her youngest, Ben, has started school, her days feel even longer and emptier.

Her phone beeps a text from Emily: **Aw shit. Was looking forward to catching up. How about we do coffee tomorrow afternoon? I finish at 1 pm.**

She replies: **Perfect**

It was pure luck that after meeting in secondary school in Limerick and going to college together in Galway she and Emily ended up living in the same village in Galway. It was visiting Emily and Chris in their new house in a cosy estate in Dunroe that alerted Carla and Thomas to a brand-new sprawling development of large houses set in a horseshoe shape near woodland walks on the other side of the village. Having their children around the same time was another blessing and meant they were stay-at-home mums together. Carla has never tried too hard to make friends with the other mothers. She has them to go to Pilates with and for a coffee, but none of them are as close to her as her childhood friend.

"*Has Lena ironed my blue striped shirt yet?*" Thomas shouts downstairs.

"*No, it's only just been washed. Will you eat your dinner before you go?*"

"*No, I'm eating out. Can you run an iron over it while I shower, please?*"

Why can't he pick one of his other already ironed shirts? She takes a deep breath as she plugs in the iron and turns back to her phone to send her apologies to the committee group. She hates letting them down. Surely, as the boss, Thomas could send someone else to the dinner? He needs to start delegating. There's no point in being successful in life if you can't enjoy it.

She irons the shirt.

"You're the best," Thomas says, walking into the kitchen bare-chested. He leans over the ironing board and kisses her firmly. "I don't know what I'd do without you."

His newly sprayed aftershave envelops her and she welcomes its familiarity. It was the one she'd bought him for Christmas, the one she loves.

"I'm meeting Philip O'Connor – do you remember him? He took a shine to you, he always asks after you." Thomas collapses the ironing board and stores it in the utility room. "Maybe we should have sorted a babysitter and you could have joined me."

"I'd need a bit of notice to organise that. You do know you're working too hard. Surely you can start to pass on some of the workload?"

"*Mm*, maybe, things have been busy lately." He fastens the buttons on his shirt and runs his hands through his dark floppy hair, pushing it back off his forehead. "And I've got that golf event on Saturday."

She'd forgotten about that. That's another day gone with her on her own with the kids.

"Why don't we go out for dinner after, just us?" she suggests, thinking that she could mention the idea of her going back to teaching then. It has been circling her mind ever since Ben started school.

"Let's see. You know how I love just chilling with you at home after a busy week." He puts his sports jacket on, pulling the cuffs of his shirt down.

She sighs. Thomas is often out wining and dining, building his business. She, on the other hand, would love to go out for dinner. It's been a while. She can picture the dress she'd wear: the cobalt-blue one. She's only worn it once before which is a shame because it wasn't cheap.

"How do I look?"

"Gorgeous." She smiles. "As always."

"Right. I'm off. I love you." He kisses her again. "Don't wait up, it could be a late one. Bye, boys, be good for your mother."

She walks with him into the hall and he blows her a kiss from the front door.

"I'll be home early tomorrow night, I promise."

Shrugging off her jacket and boots, she sits down. She puts a reminder into her phone to order some more of those shirts he likes, in different colours – they fit him well. Staring at the time on her locked screen, she sighs. Yet another evening on her own to fill.

She turns her attention back to the PA folder and begins to make a list of things not on the agenda that might need following up on for the fundraiser. Once she's put the kids to bed, she'll research print-design companies for the tickets.

2

"It's horrendous, the things they say, the photos – it's all so fake. You'd think men our age would be a bit more mature and have some experience chatting up women, but they're disastrous. Dating in 2019 is not too different to 1999!" Emily pushes her auburn hair over her shoulder before reaching to cut another slice of Carla's lemon cake. *Two small slices only count as one.*

Carla nudges the raspberry coulis towards her before topping up their cups from the cafetière. "It must be exciting though, seeing all that choice lined up for you to swipe left or right." She passes the sugar bowl. "No need to waste an entire evening with a guy in a pub or nightclub, only to find out he's an idiot."

The grass is always greener. Emily spoons three sugars into her cup. She hates all of this venturing back into the world of dating. It's changed so much in the years since she was married. Shuffling on the stool, she pulls the fabric of her jeggings from the inside of her thighs where they are bunching.

The washing machine beeps, signalling it's finished its cycle and Emily watches as Carla walks across the kitchen. Its cream units and black granite top twinkle in the light shining through the huge windows. How does she keep it so neat? Everything is in its intended place and the family photos on the mahogany cabinet add to the homely feel. Not to mention the walk-in pantry that Emily has long since envied. Even though she knows that if it was in her house half the things on the shelves would probably be out of date. She thinks of her own kitchen with the breakfast pots still in the sink and the net bag of mouldy oranges she threw out this morning.

"You'd think it would be exciting but, god, Galway is so small I'm terrified to match with someone we actually know. Can you imagine how embarrassing it would be if they were from Dunroe and I bumped into them in the village shop!"

Carla comes back to the breakfast bar, her willowy figure looking like it's never tasted cake, and sits down.

"Wait till I tell you, one guy actually asked me for a photo of my boobs last night!"

"What?" A look of shock flashes across Carla's face.

"Yep, straight up. We'd exchanged a few basic 'how are you' kind of messages and then he shoots straight in with his request."

"You didn't, did you?"

"Of course I bloody didn't! I mean, god, seriously, it's no wonder some of these men are single at forty."

"Ah, you shouldn't say that! They might just have had a bit of bad luck like you."

"You're ever the romantic, Carla, always looking for the best in people." Emily takes another forkful of cake. "I can't be that great if I turned my husband gay."

"Don't be daft – you didn't turn Chris gay! He *was* gay. He was just in denial about it for all those years."

"You're too nice. He was a dick who lived a lie, and betrayed me and our kids."

"Well, that's true. But it's time you got on with this dating business. You deserve a decent man."

It's all right for Carla to say that from her cosy life vantage point. She's not the one having to go back out there.

A lawnmower starts up outside and Carla stands to close the Victorian sash window over the sink and clicks the lock across. Her hair hangs neatly down her back, with not a kink to be seen. Emily's given up straightening hers lately, she doesn't have the time. She's embracing the wave instead.

"How's the new gardener working out?" Emily asks.

"Okay. He comes midweek which Thomas prefers. He didn't like seeing him working in the garden at the weekend. It made him feel bad."

"What, having de help? De inner-city boy done good?" Emily mimics Thomas's Dublin accent which he tries so hard to hide. "He's allowed to pay for help, isn't he?"

Going over to the window, she peeks out. The garden looks fabulous. She really must tackle her own at the weekend. Her ex may have left her the house, but he took the sit-and-ride lawnmower with him. She looks at the portly, balding man zooming around the half-acre site on a lawnmower.

"He's not exactly Desperate Housewife gardener material, is he?"

"No, unfortunately not."

Sitting back at the breakfast bar, Emily finishes the last mouthful of her lemon cake. "Maybe I shouldn't have had that second slice. I'm going on a date this weekend." She twists her eternity ring around the full circle.

"*Ooo* … who with? Tell me more."

Emily shows Carla his profile on her phone. "He's called Joe. I'm not sure if his photo is an old one though. Do you think he looks forty-two?"

"Maybe. He says he likes walking, sightseeing and is into his food. He seems nice, doesn't he?"

"He does, and he hasn't asked to see a photo of my boobs yet either, so maybe he's a keeper!" Emily can feel the laughter bubbling inside her. "Remember our first boyfriends? James – and what was the other guy called?"

"The other guy." Carla laughs. "You mean the guy you practically forced me to go out with because you fancied James so much?"

"Yeah. Didn't we have some sort of notebook with his information in it?"

"And quizzes stuck in. Can you remember those love quizzes that we were obsessed with from *Just Seventeen* mag?"

The two of them burst out laughing at the absurdity of their teenage love life.

"I had to convince you to double-date," Emily says.

"You pretty much forced me! You said something like 'We're going to the cinema, we won't need to talk to them, we can just snog the face off them!'"

"God, maybe I did say that!" Emily holds her sides as she laughs. "Oh, to be seventeen again!"

They finish the last of their coffees and Emily stands. "Who'd have thought I'd be doing it all over again twenty years later." She hitches her high-waisted jeggings up over her stomach and stacks their cake plates. "God. That sounds so depressing."

"At least you know how to kiss men now. And, think positive, this date might turn out to be the one." Carla takes the cafetière to the sink and rinses it through.

"Maybe." Emily doesn't hold out much hope though. This dating business is a nightmare.

"Right. Come on, school pick-up time!" Carla grabs her phone off the windowsill.

Emily follows her friend's jeep down the road. Carla is being overly optimistic – the guy on the app is only okay – nothing *wow* about him. But then, what's *wow* about her? A single mother trying to juggle her house, childcare, job, and now trying to find a new life partner. She is struggling to keep everything going. It's all right for Carla with her lovely house, garden 'help', and a husband who doesn't want her to go out to work, to look at Emily's dating life as a bit of fun.

"*Think positive*," Emily mutters under her breath as she indicates right for the school.

3

"Hold this." Dawn passes a paper grocery bag to Ruth and reaches for her keys as they approach the front door. Her eyes land briefly on the CCTV camera affixed above the entrance, but she reassures herself it's not working. She'd seen to that, loosened the battery earlier. She hasn't told her mum she was bringing friends over. There was no need. They would be gone before she was due home.

Dawn drops her keys into the green porcelain dish on the side table, her college bag on the floor, and kicks her trainers off. "Take your shoes off, Mum's a bit particular about it." This was the first time her friends were coming past the front door.

"Here, hold my books." Samantha dumps the heavy pile into Dawn's arms.

"Really, Sam, do you need to bring every book home from the library?" Dawn says, and Ruth laughs.

"It *is* open on weekends too, you know." Ruth unlaces her green Doc Martens.

"Yeah, but this saves me going all the way back into town. It's not like there is a library in Moycullen, is there?"

The girls follow Dawn into the kitchen-living area, and she's conscious of seeing it through their eyes. It's not too small but it's cosy. Enough space for her and her mum, and it is clean, very clean.

"You could relax a bit on the weekend, Sam."

"Dawn, our exams are in less than a month. It's you two who need to think about studying."

"We have ages yet." Ruth moves around the kitchen, opening cupboards. "Where do I find the plates?"

Dawn points above Ruth's head. "You might need to stand on tiptoes."

"Hey, I'm not that short!"

Samantha puts her books at the end of the kitchen table and takes her denim jacket off. "Right, nacho time. I'm starving." She takes a scrunchie from her wrist and ties her dark-red hair up.

"Me too," Dawn says.

"You should always be starving. I swear I never see you eat. You're all skin and bone."

"I am not!" Dawn says, "And I love nachos so pile them up."

"I, on the other hand, should be eating a big dish of fruit instead but, hey, the diet starts Monday." Samantha unpacks the groceries.

"You don't need to diet, Sam. You're curvy, that's all."

"Yeah, well, I only have time just to snack between study and lectures."

"*Sam!*" Ruth and Dawn say in unison.

"We're only in first year, Sam. Chill out." Ruth puts a large plate on the table and twists open the jalapenos.

"My brother makes these nearly every weekend. Once you start on them, you can't stop." Sam spreads a layer of Doritos on the plate and then sprinkles the grated cheese.

Ruth is at her side, dropping jalapenos over the pile.

Dawn looks into the paper bag. "Did you forget the ingredients for the guacamole?"

"Ingredients? No, I cheated, obviously!" Sam nods at the ready-made dip next to her.

"Seriously? You're always raving about your brother's homemade guacamole. I thought we were making it." Dawn takes the carton from her friend, removing the lid and plastic film.

Samantha reaches over and dips her finger in, scooping up a small dollop and tasting it. "It is, but by the time you buy all the ingredients it's cheaper to buy it ready-made. I'm saving for next year's rent, remember. Galway rentals aren't cheap. Living out in second year is worth skimping on guacamole!"

Dawn grabs spoons for the ice cream and, as she turns back to her friends, a warm glow spreads through her. This is lovely, having them here in her home. They are an odd trio, she thinks, listening to her friends nattering about whether to put the guacamole on the side of the plate or in the layers of Doritos. They couldn't be more different. Samantha is ultra-studious, Ruth is a fly-by-her-pants, last-minute kind of student, and Dawn fits in between them. Ruth's obsessed with keeping fit, carrying textbooks is Samantha's only exercise, and Dawn, although naturally slim, does just enough to keep her fitness-fanatic mum's mean comments at bay.

Dawn can't remember the last time she had friends over, not since primary school anyway. It wasn't like she didn't have any friends, just that it was better if she visited their homes instead. She was probably about ten when she realised her home life was different, that her mum was different from other mums – clingy, needy, and claustrophobic. Maybe it would have been different if she'd had siblings.

"It must be nice to have an older brother," Dawn says, looking over at the photos of just her and her mum, decorating the kitchen wall.

"No, it isn't," Samantha says. "He's the most annoying person ninety-five per cent of the time."

"And younger siblings are annoying one hundred per cent of the time," Ruth says.

"Yeah, well, Dad never wanted more kids anyway." Dawn puts the nachos under the grill. "He didn't want kids full stop."

"I bet he's glad he has you now, though," Ruth says. "I'm so jealous you're going to New York. Imagine seeing the Empire State Building and the Statue of Liberty!"

"Central Park, the shopping. Oh my god, you're so lucky!" Samantha says.

"I can't wait. It's going to be a real adventure. Imagine my Insta story!"

"I wish my dad lived in some place amazing like New York instead of the same house as me! He might not wreck my head as much then. I swear he treats me like I'm eight." Ruth makes for the coffee table with three cans of Coke.

Dawn rushes around the couch, grabs the wooden drinks coasters from the holder and places them underneath each can and glass.

"Yeah, but your dad is your dad. Mine left when I was three, and him living in Limerick meant he was just a weekend dad. And then he moved back to the States when I was eight after Granny had her stroke. I don't even remember him living with us. To me, he's always been Brad, the dad I see once or twice a year. It's almost like having another uncle. I don't think I know him any better than my Uncle Michael in Australia."

The three of them plonk themselves down on the couch and dig into the nachos. Dawn glances back towards the kitchen area – they really should be using napkins. Leaning across the armchair, she reaches for the tissue box and passes one each to her friends.

"How is everyone's savings going?" Ruth asks. "I reckon I have almost the deposit and three months' rent saved."

Dawn smiles. They have this conversation regularly. "Me too. I'm banking my tips every week as well to stop me from spending them."

Samantha scoops up a blob of melted cheese. "I'm almost there and I've got my birthday coming up so any money I get will go straight into the bank. It's going to be so good living in town instead of Moycullen – no more long bus journeys to the library. We'll actually be like proper students."

"We'll be able to spend days like this." Ruth leans back on the couch.

Dawn examines her nails, nibbled short, and red-raw. She hasn't mentioned she's yet to tell her mum she's moving out.

"We'll have thirty hours of lectures every week in second year. We won't have much time to lounge about." Samantha puts her empty plate on the coffee table. "You two might even have to find where the library is!"

Giggling, Dawn reties her brown wavy hair into a high ponytail. "Right. Movie time!"

She reaches for the TV control and switches on Netflix, scrolling through the recently added while the others give their opinions on each movie.

Dawn doesn't hear the front door opening until it clicks shut.

She stands up – terrified. *Shit!* She can feel Samantha's eyes on her as she stares at the living-room door. Taking two steps forward, away from the couch, she hears someone in the hall.

Dawn's mum, Amanda, bustles into the living room and stops abruptly.

"What's going on here? I didn't realise you were having friends over, Dawn."

"Oh, it was a last-minute decision. I thought you were out for the evening. We were just going to watch a movie." Dawn's voice is a mousey-mumble yet her heart is thumping loudly. Her shoulders hunch and she keeps her eyes firmly on the floor as she silently prays her mother doesn't erupt.

"Hi, Amanda!" Ruth and Samantha say.

"Hello, girls, how are you? First year of college nearly over." Amanda smiles brightly but then turns back to Dawn. "My plans changed. I would have expected you to ask me beforehand."

The stern voice coming from the figure, tiny despite the high heels, causes Samantha and Ruth to make eye contact and Dawn catches it.

"Sorry, I should have asked," she says meekly.

"We can watch the movie in your bedroom on your laptop if it suits better." Ruth looks from Dawn to Amanda.

Amanda ignores the suggestion completely. "You made a fine mess of the kitchen." She nods over to the table where the left-over ingredients sit.

"Sorry. I was going to tidy it up. I'll do it now." Dawn scurries into the kitchen area.

"We'll help," Samantha says.

The girls tidy in silence. Both Ruth and Samantha try to catch Dawn's eye, but she stays determinedly focused on the task of tidying up.

Dawn can feel the tension across the kitchen. Her mum is fuming, Her hands shake as she washes the cloth and takes out the kitchen spray.

"Not that one, the yellow one." Amanda puts her handbag on the armchair and takes off her cropped black jacket, watching them all the while.

Dawn replaces the spray and takes out the yellow one. Her friends stand awkwardly, watching her.

"You know I always like to watch the *Late, Late Show* on a Friday night," Amanda says.

"Maybe we should go," Samantha says, and both Ruth and Samantha look at Dawn who raises her head slightly to meet their eyes and gives an imperceptible nod.

They gather their jackets and Samantha collects her pile of library books, hugging them to her chest.

"See you on Monday, Dawn," Ruth says.

Dawn is silently raging but relieved her friends left before her mum could say anything else. She goes into the downstairs bathroom and stands staring into the oval-shaped mirror, her hands tightly grasping either side of the sink. She should have been more careful. They should have met at Ruth or Samantha's house. There was always going to be the chance that her mum would come home early.

Ruth and Samantha's voices float in through the open window. Dawn strains to hear them.

"What was all that about?" Ruth says.

"She was like Miss Trunchbull from *Matilda*, only a tiny and really skinny version!"

"What's the problem with us watching a movie?"

"I don't know – you'd think she'd walked in on us having a house party."

"They must have had a row earlier – she's usually so nice."

The voices fade as they walk away.

Stepping quietly back into the kitchen, Dawn sees her mum sitting on the couch watching the news while scrolling through her phone, acting as if nothing has happened. Dawn wants to scream at her, but she won't. There's no point. Dawn resigned herself to that a long time ago. It's not worth the grief. She should have been more careful.

She goes upstairs to her bedroom without saying anything and, even though it's still early, she puts her pyjamas on, cleans her teeth, and snuggles into bed. Staring at the ceiling, she focuses on the marks left by the CCTV camera that used to be installed there. Her mum had agreed to take it down when Dawn hit puberty, on the condition that any Skype calls with her dad were taken downstairs. Dawn had asked once, when she was younger, why they had to be supervised and her mum said she didn't want her to be upset by her dad.

Dawn half-heartedly scrolls through her phone for a while.

Ruth texts her: **Hiya. Hope everything's okay with your mum.**

She answers: **Sorry about earlier. She wasn't feeling too well.**

She feels awful lying to Ruth, but she can hardly say that's just the way her mum is, can she?

The sooner we move out the better. Think of the freedom we'll have!

Yeah, I can't wait … freedom.

Dawn doesn't know how she's going to bring that topic up with her mum. She switches off the phone before Ruth comes back with anything else.

4

Emily smokes the cigarette in quick, sharp puffs. She hasn't smoked in ages, but she had to escape him for a few minutes. She'd bummed a cigarette off the gaggle of women in the smoking area. Stubbing it out with her gold stiletto, she turns back into the Italian restaurant, trying her best not to waddle – these shoes are killing her. He isn't there when she reaches the table, so she continues to the bathroom.

Leaning against the sink, she takes off a stiletto and rubs the sole of her foot. She should have worn them in before the date. Why were stilettos so high these days? Of course, that's why young women carried flats in their handbags. Still, they looked better than the navy court shoes she was going to wear which were a bit mumsy.

Turning around to face the mirror, she scrunches her hair. She'd thought this navy dress was flattering. It isn't too tight across her thighs, is it? Joe's comment that she looked well for her age was cutting. The cheeky git. She was only thirty-seven! She'd nearly spat her wine at him. She should have poured the bottle over him, only that would have been a waste. Who was he to judge her anyway? There had been no sign of his thinning hair or paunchy stomach on his profile picture. Not to mention his annoying knee-jiggling and habit of clearing his throat every five minutes. His listed interest of cooking seemed to stretch to sampling different takeaways and going to his mum's for his dinner. This was one guy not getting a second date.

She reapplies her lip gloss and runs her finger under her bottom eyelashes to remove a smudge of mascara. Right, she'd better go back out there. She'll be polite, split the bill, get a taxi home and watch something funny on Netflix, maybe start the next series of *Good Girls*.

She puts a smile on her face and leaves the bathroom. It's nice to be nice, she thinks, as she makes her way back to the table.

He isn't there. He must still be in the bathroom. She finishes her wine and calls for the bill. Five minutes pass, and Emily twiddles her eternity ring, looking around awkwardly. Turning back to the table, she realises his jacket isn't on the back of his chair. He's gone. The cheeky fucker. He didn't even have the decency to say thanks but no thanks. He's done a runner, and without paying his half of the bill. She almost laughs out loud at his brazenness.

The waiter hovers patiently, waiting for her to put money or a card on the bill dish. Did he see her date go? Are the staff sniggering in the back, watching to see her reaction? Emily calmly takes out her credit card and places it on the tray. She regrets not ordering the steak now – she's still kind of hungry after the salad.

Walking slowly in her heels, Emily keeps her eyes down and makes her way through the usual Saturday-night crowds of couples and groups to the taxi rank at the top of Eyre Square. She joins the queue, adjusts the length of her dress, and hugs her clutch bag. Pressing her lips tightly together, she squeezes her eyes shut for a moment. *Why is it so difficult?* She opens them to see three couples pass her by. She doesn't think she's that fussy, she just wants someone genuine, good company, up for a laugh, and is accepting of her being a single mother. And who is not gay.

The people in the queue seem so young to her or, maybe, Emily smirks to herself, she's getting old. She wills the taxi to hurry up; she wants to get into her comfy pyjamas.

A familiar deep booming laugh catches her attention, and she looks up to see Carla's husband, Thomas, in the middle of a group of people walking towards her. She drops her chin to her chest, letting her hair flop down in front of her face, hoping he won't notice her. But he does.

"Hey, Emily, how are you?" Thomas asks as he brushes his hand through his thick brown hair. It flops back into place.

He must have product in it, she thinks. Carla always jokes that he spends nearly as long getting ready for a night out as she does. He's looking smart in a polka-dot navy shirt, with the top few buttons open, and dark inky-blue jeans with a brown belt and shoes.

"Grand," she says. "You having a good night?"

"Yeah, we were at that new tapas place on Dominic Street. The food was amazing, real melt-in-your-mouth stuff. Where are you coming from?"

"Don't ask." She looks at her stilettos. "Another disastrous date."

Thomas glances down the road, to where his friends are waiting for him. "What happened?" he asks, lowering his voice.

"He ran out on me when I was in the loo!" She laughs awkwardly.

Thomas laughs gently. "Not meant to be so." He squeezes her shoulder.

"He wasn't going to be getting a second date anyway. I'm happy to be going home without him."

"No need to spoil your night out – why don't you come along with us? I'm with a gang from work – we're off to a cocktail bar around the corner." He grins, scratching his neat stubble. "Apparently it's eighties night."

Emily is at the top of the taxi queue now. She smiles at Thomas's inner-city Dublin accent emerging after he's had a few drinks.

"Thanks, but my feet are killing me. I don't think I'd be up for dancing. Netflix is calling."

"Don't be daft, you're all dressed up and you love eighties music. I *know* a bit of cheesy Wham will cheer you up. Come on. This crowd is a great laugh. You won't feel your feet hurting you at all – it'll be your sides from laughing when you see Max and Sarah on the dancefloor. Come on."

She looks at the taxi pulling up. Why shouldn't she have a bit of fun? She has all weekend to watch *Good Girls*. "Okay so, just for a while."

They join the others and walk to the cocktail bar. The group Thomas is with *are* good fun and Emily has met some of them before. They've already had a few drinks and are up for a laugh and a dance.

The neon-clad DJ soon has them all in stitches and gets them bopping on the dancefloor to Wham, Yazz, Duran Duran and many more.

Emily has a brilliant night, and maybe one too many mojitos but who cares?

A few of them share a taxi home and when it arrives at Emily's house, Thomas refuses to take any money for it. "I told you, it's *mytaxi*, it's already paid for."

Telling the driver to wait, they get out of the car and walk up the narrow garden path, stepping on the weeds growing between the stepping stones. She can hear the others singing in the taxi as she puts the key in the door.

"Thanks for making me stay out. I haven't laughed like that in ages or danced. I'd say my feet will be in agony tomorrow."

"I'm glad you had fun and, listen, don't worry about that runaway guy – it was his loss. See you soon." He squeezes her shoulder and turns back to the taxi.

Emily unlocks the peeling blue door and steps into the quiet darkness of the house. Letting out a sigh, she kicks off her shoes. She doesn't think she'll ever adjust to being in the house when the kids are at their dad's.

She switches a lamp on before going upstairs and changing into her pyjamas. Back downstairs, she ignores the kids' breakfast pots in the sink, makes tea and toast and grabs a sharing bag of Maltesers before flopping onto the settee. She flicks through her phone, deleting Joe from her dating matches. She'd like to text Carla to tell her about her evening, but it's too late, she'll be fast asleep. No doubt Thomas will fill her in tomorrow. They'll laugh at the ridiculousness of it and then Carla will go all solemn and pity her. Her poor friend who can't get a man, who can't keep a man. Emily blinks away the tears forming.

She fills the kettle again and makes a hot-water bottle. It's not cold but she misses the warmth of someone next to her in the bed. Why is it so hard to find a decent man?

5

Rolling over in bed, Carla stretches her arm over Thomas's bare chest.

"Morning, gorgeous," he says, moving his arms from behind his head to pull her closer.

"How was your night? I don't think I heard you come in."

"It was a late one. I didn't want to wake you. We bumped into Emily."

"*Oo*, really? What was her date like? Did she look like she was having a good time?"

"They'd already gone their separate ways. She was in the taxi queue. It was early enough too."

"That's a shame. He seemed okay on the app. I'd better text her."

"I'd give her a while yet, it's only early." Thomas shuffles himself to a sitting position. "I dragged her with us to an eighties bar. She had more than a few cocktails."

"That was good of you." Her finger trails across his chest, following the line just under his nipples where the hair stopped. "She'll have a sore head today so. I hope you made sure she got home okay."

"Of course I did, I'm a gentleman." He kisses the top of her head, "And, because I am such a gentleman, I'm going to make my wonderful wife breakfast. You look after me so well all week, I'm going to look after you this morning. How does a Thomas Special sound?"

Carla reaches up and kisses him. "That sounds perfect. Does it come with coffee too?"

"For you, anything." He smiles, getting out of bed.

The bedroom door opens a fraction and two sets of eyes peek in.

"Come on, you two, how about you help me make Mummy some breakfast?" Thomas says, leading Ben and Daniel downstairs before they can bound into the room.

Carla shuffles to sit against the headboard and reaches for her phone, clicking on Emily's WhatsApp. She was last online at four am. Her fingers hover over the keypad. What can she say to cheer her friend up?

Emily seemed to think when she'd first signed up on Tinder that the right man was only a click away. She'd become quite disheartened after a few crappy dates. Carla doesn't doubt that she'll have plenty of admirers, Emily always has, but it's sifting through these to find a good one, a keeper, that is the problem. It has taken her a long time to come around to the idea of dating again after the heartbreak of her marriage, Carla doesn't want to see her friend go back into despair about men.

She puts her phone on the bedside table and swings her legs out of bed, looking at her reflection in the mirror on the wardrobe door. She runs her fingers through her blonde bed-hair, pulling through the tangles, and thinks how nice it would be to get dressed up, go dancing, and drink cocktails. She'd hoped that she and Thomas would go out for dinner last night, but their babysitter cancelled at the last minute so instead Thomas went out with friends and work colleagues whom he'd played golf with earlier in the day. Carla had been left to spend the evening sitting on the settee, in a tracksuit, sorting out the donations and sponsorship for the school fundraiser while watching rubbish TV.

She must organise a girly night out for herself and Emily – they haven't been out in ages either. Smiling, she remembers when they made their own cocktails in college – they were so disastrous that both of them spent the next day sick in bed.

Pulling on her dressing gown, she resolves to encourage Emily to keep looking. Maybe she could ask Thomas if there are any suitable single men in his workplace. She'll leave Emily to her lie-in and contact her later.

6

"Oh *wow*, that looks amazing." Ruth exclaims as Dawn emerges from the changing room wearing an emerald-green mermaid gown, with a low sweeping back.

"It fits you perfectly. The best one yet," Samantha says.

Dawn does a twirl in front of the mirror.

"Hold your hair up," Samantha says.

Dawn lifts her hair from the back of her neck and turns to the girls.

"Definitely wear your hair up. You could even have a couple of strands curled and framing your face," Ruth says.

"Add a pair of drop earrings, and your outfit will be complete," Samantha says.

"I think you have found your law society ball gown." Ruth smiles.

Dawn beams in delight. "I think so too. I love it. It could be the one." She turns back to the mirror. At five foot eight, she has the height and the figure to carry off this design.

Her friends are sitting on navy velvet chairs inside the spacious changing room. They'd surprised her by turning up at the restaurant just as she was finishing her shift, to take her shopping. The law society ball is on Saturday and Dawn still didn't have a dress. Her mum kept putting off going shopping with her, and her friends knew she'd resigned herself to wearing the dress she'd worn to her end-of-school Debs a year ago.

"You're so lucky that you fit into a size ten. My boobs are a size fourteen and my hips are a twelve – it was a nightmare finding my dress." Samantha reaches into her thick red hair held up in a messy bun and takes out a black pen stuck there, slipping it into her college bag at her feet.

"No, you're lucky. Your body has a shape. I am all straight up and down." Dawn laughs.

Ruth moves to the small display of shoes at the entrance to the changing rooms. "What do you think about ruby-red shoes? Or nude?" She turns, holding a pair of nude patent heels.

"I'd prefer red."

"Yeah, I agree. The red would complement the green nicely. You should ring your mum. Ask her to transfer the money now before someone else chooses it," Samantha says as Dawn walks back into the changing cubicle.

"Ah no. I'll bring her to see it. She'd like that." Dawn closes the curtain and looks into the mirror. What will her mum say about this dress? She turns from side to side. What would she criticise? It's a fabulous dress – surely her mum will think so too?

She can hear the girls chatting about handbags and other accessories as she gets changed. This law society ball is important to her. She is the secretary of the society and she's worked hard with the committee in organising the event. She knows she'll have to tread carefully with her mum if she's to get this dress. She sighs. She already has a feeling her mum has been trying to manipulate the situation by putting off going shopping and cancelling at the last minute. Placing the dress on the hanger, she runs her hand over the delicate satin material once more. It's beautiful. Carefully, she zips it into its plastic cover and decides to ask the owner to put it on hold for her.

"Right. Who's joining me for a spin class?" Ruth asks, bouncing along the pavement outside the dress shop.

Dawn and Samantha groan.

"I've got an assignment to work on."

"Me too." Dawn laughs.

"Lightweights," Ruth says.

Dawn is buzzing with excitement when she gets home that evening, going straight into the kitchen where her mum is emptying the dishwasher.

"You went without me? You planned this behind my back!" her mum snaps.

"I didn't plan anything, the girls surprised me after work. I've been asking you to go with me for weeks, but you keep cancelling."

"I can't believe you would do that to your own mother. I wanted to be with you."

"I told you, the girls turned up after work, I could hardly say no." Dawn lowers her voice. "I'm sorry – I didn't think I would find the perfect one so quickly."

Amanda turns her back to the dishwasher.

"Don't you want to know what it's like?" Dawn asks. "It's emerald-green satin with a low sweeping back and it fits perfectly. I can't wait to show you." She hesitates. "Can we go tomorrow?"

There is no answer from Amanda.

"Mum?"

Her mum turns around. "Okay. We can go for a look but don't get your hopes up. I'm not sure that green will suit you."

Dawn eagerly leads Amanda into the dress shop the next day. This dress is definitely the one, she's even surer trying it on again today. She can't stop grinning as she looks at herself from different angles in the mirror. The material feels divine on her skin, and the mermaid fit of the dress makes her feel as if it's made especially for her.

She comes out of the changing room and says "Well, what do you think?" She twirls.

Amanda doesn't look up from her phone screen, her blonde curls hanging in front of her face.

Dawn looks expectantly at her. "Mum?"

The shop assistant looks awkwardly between them. "It is very flattering, don't you think?" she says, more loudly than is necessary.

Amanda still doesn't look up and Dawn shifts her weight from one foot to another, feeling the heat rush to her face.

The assistant continues, "The deep hue of the emerald green really complements your skin tone. What colour shoes do you think you'll go for?"

"I'm not sure. Ruby-red maybe."

Dawn turns back to the mirror, blinking away the tears, her heart sinking at her mum's blatant rudeness. She knows she's being punished because she came here with friends first.

"What colour do you think, Mum, for the shoes?" She looks at Amanda in the mirror.

"Hang on a second. I have to reply to Jane's text."

"Okay," Dawn says, trying to avoid the shop assistant's look.

Amanda glances up, putting the phone on the arm of the chair, her eyes narrowing as Dawn turns to face her.

"What colour shoes do you think I should wear?"

"Oh, I don't know. Are you really sure about the colour of the dress? I'm not sure it's right for your skin tone. It makes you look a bit green yourself."

Dawn's face falls. Does it? She swirls around again on her tippy toes, scrutinising herself in the mirror, seeing her mum smile behind her.

"I love it. My friends liked it too. Does it sit too low on my back?" She turns to the shop assistant.

"Not at all," the shop assistant says, watching this exchange in astonishment. The dress is perfect for Dawn.

"Well, if you're sure," her mum says noncommittally, picking her phone up again.

7

"How's Aunt Mary? Is her Alzheimer's getting worse?" Michael asks, his adopted Australian accent creeping in.

Amanda glances at the clock as she moves towards the kitchen window to get a better phone signal. It must be late in Sydney.

"No change really," she says, watching the birds twittering around the bird bath in the back garden. She makes a mental note to ring the nursing home to get an update before her brother arrives for his visit in two weeks. She hasn't been for a while – it's easier not to. Mary, their father's sister, is mostly living in the past now and that's too painful.

"Aunt Mary's solicitor sent on a pile of Uncle Seán's old paperwork."

Amanda frowns. "What kind of paperwork? Uncle Seán died a year ago – why are you getting them now and why didn't she have them sent to me?"

She hears Michael's sharp intake of breath down the phone line.

"Bank statements from Mum and Dad's accounts. There were strange transactions in the couple of weeks before the fire. Can you remember someone called Deborah Phelan?"

"No," she murmurs. But she did know who Deborah Phelan was.

"Seán said in the note that he'd tried to show the statements to you years ago. There's more as well –"

"Michael," she cuts him off, "Uncle Seán was always trying to find someone to blame, that's why I wasn't interested. There's no point in digging up the past, it isn't going to change anything. It was an accident." Her hand clenches on the phone. Closing her eyes for a moment, she can see the flames licking the stairs as she led Michael to safety.

"I think we should take a look at the statements together when I'm over, see if we can make any sense of them. Maybe try and talk to Mary too."

Amanda opens her eyes and begins to pace the small kitchen. She hears him take a drink, ice cubes clinking in the glass and against his teeth. He must be drinking whiskey. She hopes he hasn't developed a fondness for spirits like their parents had.

"There's no point talking to Mary – she doesn't even remember who's who at this stage." She clears her throat. "What time does your flight arrive? Will I tell Supermac to have the curry chips at the ready?"

"Yes, do. I can't wait for the taste of home. My flight gets in around four, I think, but I'll hire a car. I'll be doing some visiting around the country, catching up with college friends."

"Hire one from Galway. Sure you won't be going too far for the first few days, no point wasting your money. I'll be waiting at the airport. Not sure if Dawn will be with me – she'll only be back from New York the day before. Speaking of Dawn, I better let you go, I have to collect her." That's a lie but she wants to end the call.

Putting the phone on the kitchen table, she sinks into the chair, stretching her hands in front of her. Talking about the past always brings her back to the night of the fire. She breathes in deeply, closing her eyes, the memory returning of the smoke at the back of her throat, in her nostrils, her skin prickling in the heat, and her eyes stinging. She exhales slowly, opening her eyes and staring at her hands lying flat on the table, reassuring herself the past is better left in the past.

8

"Goodnight, boys," Carla says.

"Goodnight, Mummy!" they chorous.

She comes downstairs to find Thomas sitting at the breakfast bar tapping away on his laptop. He's late home again but at least he made it before the boys went to bed.

"Will I serve dinner there if you're working?"

"Not at all, babe. We can eat at the table. I added the water to the couscous a couple of minutes ago."

"Okay, great." Carla goes and begins to fluff it with a fork. "Have you got much more to do tonight? I thought we could relax and watch some more of *Ozark*. Even though," she laughs, "it's not exactly relaxing watching, is it? I kind of just want to race through the series to find out what happens." She spoons the couscous onto plates, and adds the lamb tagine.

Thomas shuts down the laptop and hops down from the stool. "I'm done. I was just checking money stuff. I'm going to start looking for a bigger office premises."

"Really?" Carla brings the plates to the table. "I thought the offices were perfect. They're in a great location."

"Yes, but they're cramped and dark, and there's hardly any parking around the back. It's not the right vibe for investors." Thomas reaches for the jug and pauses as the ice clatters into it from the ice-maker in the fridge door. "We need to look like we have money if we're going to make it for them."

"Surely it's your reputation and proven investment history that gets you clients?"

"You'd think so, but our clients want more, and I'm willing to invest money to make money. We're on a roll, my love, business is booming." He sits down. "This smells amazing."

"I think I added a bit too much cumin, I hope it tastes okay," Carla says, watching as he takes a mouthful.

"It's delicious."

"So, does the business have the money to buy new premises?"

"Well," he hesitates, "kind of."

"Do we need to dip into our savings?"

"No, no, not at all. I have a plan. I have money coming in but, in the meantime, I'll use funds to tide a sale over."

Carla sips at her water, frowning. "What do you mean – funds?"

"Just client funds we have," Thomas says and, seeing her worried expression, adds, "Don't worry, it's standard practice – everyone does it."

"Do they? Why don't you just wait until the expected money comes in? There's no rush surely."

"Business moves quickly, my love. If I find a suitable premises, I'll have to move fast."

Carla fidgets with the saltshaker. "Just use our savings. I don't mind if it's only for a while."

"Look, babe, you're worrying about things that haven't even happened or might never happen. I have to find the right place first. That in itself could take some time." He reaches across the table and takes her hand. "Enough about work, I'm glad I got home early enough to spend some time with the boys this evening." He pours her some more water. "Tell me about your day – how's the planning going for the fundraiser? Is Julia still wrecking everyone's head?"

Carla shifts in her seat. Standard practice, he'd said. She wonders if he's allowed to do that. She sips her water and smiles at him. "Oh, you won't believe what she's suggesting this time."

They snuggle up on the settee later on, watching the latest season of *Ozark*, their feet intertwined, stretched out on the pouffe. Carla tries not to jump at the violent parts of the show.

She smiles to herself. At least Thomas isn't money-laundering, she thinks. Now that would be stressful. He leans into her, and she reaches over to run her fingers through his hair, gently massaging his head.

9

"*Hiya!*" Emily calls as she opens Carla's front door. "*Are you all set?*"

"*Hang on, just taking the Bakewell out of the oven!*"

"*God, doesn't that kind of defeat the purpose of our walk?*"

"No. It's a treat for our effort." Carla comes out of the kitchen to meet her, slipping her toned arms into her sky-blue walking coat. She adjusts her baseball hat, pulling a few strands of her blonde fringe down.

Emily smiles at her friend as they turn to leave. "I suppose it'll be an incentive to walk faster, to get back for cake and coffee."

"Exactly. Hang on a sec." Carla stands at the bottom of the stairs. "*Lena, I'm just popping out for a while! I left the ironing pile on the kitchen chair! Thank you!*"

"Do you think your cleaner would do my ironing now and again?" Emily asks as they walk down the drive. "I'm so wrecked by the time I've got the kids into bed and tidied up that I just don't have the energy to start doing chores."

"Of course, just drop a bag to mine when she comes next week, and she'll do it."

"Maybe next month. I've got to pay the house insurance this month."

"I'm sure she won't mind waiting to be paid. Just drop a bag over."

Detecting Carla's sympathetic tone creeping in, Emily shuts it down. "'*Neither a borrower nor a lender be*,' as Shakespeare says and my grandad used to quote. I'll wait until I can afford it, but thanks for the offer. My car loan will be paid off next month, so I might have a bit of spare cash."

"Oh, that's great. You'll be glad to trade in that car, it certainly doesn't owe you anything. What are you thinking of upgrading to?"

"I won't be upgrading. The car is grand – gets me from A to B, doesn't it? That's all I need. Besides, it'll be nice not to be paying a huge sum out every month."

They turn out of Carla's estate and along a narrow farm track with grass growing up the middle and Emily drops a step behind, watching Carla's ponytail sticking out of her baseball cap, swishing from side to side. Her eyes fall to her friend's toned legs, picking up the pace. She can't believe Carla just said that about the car. It was like a punch in the gut to remind Emily of the life she doesn't have anymore. She knows Carla didn't mean it that way, but she should have thought before she spoke. Just because Carla and Thomas change their cars every two years for top-of-the-range BMWs doesn't mean to say she can. Not anymore anyway.

They climb the wooden stile across the wall, and jump down onto the path, walking side by side again.

"Tell me about this date anyway. Thomas said he bumped into you afterwards."

"Yeah, he delayed me going home to my sad and lonely life of Netflix. Have you seen his friends, Max and Sarah, on the dancefloor? They're hilarious with their crazy dance routines."

"I've not been out with them in years," Carla says, stepping around a puddle. "It's a shame they aren't together. I always thought they'd make a good couple."

Emily follows her around the edge of the puddle. "We must go to that cocktail bar. We haven't had a girly night in ages."

"I haven't had a night out in ages, girly or with Thomas."

"You need nights out too. God, you're too nice, Carla! You should be more assertive with him."

"He's busy with work stuff and entertaining clients – he's even talking of moving to bigger offices. He works so hard I don't have the heart to deny him a night out to relax with friends."

They turn onto a narrow path leading deeper into the woods, inhaling the spruce pine scent and picking up their pace, walking in single file until the path widens.

"So, tell me about the date. What was so disastrous about it?" Carla says as Emily walks by her side once more.

"Well, where will I start? He told me I looked good for my age!"

"*Ouch!* Really? The cheeky sod."

"I know, so that was a real confidence boost. And then, when I went to the bathroom, he did a runner and left me with the bill!"

"What a gentleman! Is there a review section on Tinder where you can rate him and let others know what he's like?"

"Do you mean like Trip Advisor?"

"Yeah, you could score his manners, conversational skills out of ten, let others know what to expect."

"No, there isn't – but that wouldn't be a bad idea." Emily laughs. "Anyway, he wouldn't have got a second date – he was boring, balding and paunchy."

"But you were just too polite to say it to his face, I suppose."

"God, maybe I should speak more directly to them. That could be where I'm going wrong."

"Or hand them a scorecard at the end of the date!" Carla takes a wide step to avoid protruding tree roots.

"That could work too. Why is it so difficult to find a nice, decent guy? Am I really that fussy?"

"You? Fussy? You aren't fussy at all! Think of all those awful boyfriends you had in your twenties."

"You cheeky cow!" Emily shoves Carla's arm playfully. "That was careful research to find out what I did and didn't like. Those days were great fun, we used to be out all the time."

"I can't remember what going out is like anymore. Getting dressed up these days is not wearing sporty clothes and wearing jeans instead."

"God, don't be daft, you're the envy of all the mums at the school gate. Some of your casual outfits cost more than my entire wardrobe."

"I just wish I had a reason to dress well. If I was to go back to work, even part-time, I might have a reason to."

"You sound bored, Carla."

They pass the small stone gatehouse and stop to kick the wall at their turning point, a strange ritual they always perform, as do other walkers.

"It's not that I'm bored. I love being with the kids, and I know how lucky I am to have the opportunity to be at home."

"But?" Carla doesn't realise how easy she has it, living in her posh Paddock's estate. Emily sucks in her breath through clenched teeth. She'd love to have a cleaner, a gardener, and a loving husband who spoils her and doesn't want her to go out to work.

"I really would like to go back to teaching. I miss being Carla, not just a mum or wife – but Carla."

"You're Carla to me." Emily links arms with her friend and they step over tree roots and puddles in sync together. "Have you tried talking to Thomas about it?"

"You know what he's like. It's all 'I earn enough for both of us so you don't need to go out to work'. He goes on about how his mum struggled to work several jobs to provide for the family and he's adamant that no wife of his will have to do that. He doesn't seem to realise that I actually want to go out to work. That I love teaching."

"You need to tell him that."

"I should never have agreed to stay out of teaching for so long but you know how persuasive Thomas can be. Every January when it came to filling out the career break forms, he'd talk me round to taking yet another year."

"Tell him that you're thinking of going back part-time now that the boys are getting older."

"I know, I should," Carla says.

They walk on in companionable silence, greeting a couple of other walkers on their path.

"You should tell him you want a date night too. I'll babysit for you if you want."

"I know, but he's out a lot and when he is home he's all about us being together as a family. He says snuggling on the couch is his favourite place to be."

There is a pulling sensation in Emily's gut and her ribs squeeze tight. She has to stop herself from saying how lucky Carla is. God knows, Carla has listened to her problems enough over recent years.

They arrive back at the start of the farm track and wipe their trainers on the grass before turning back onto Carla's estate.

"God, I'm out of breath. I must get myself back into going to the gym. Though where I'd find the time, I don't know."

"You should make time for you, Em."

"We need to take control, Carla – you and me against the world. You need to start by being more assertive."

"And you need to be patient. The right man will come along and see you for your wonderful self. It'll be worth the wait."

"But first, let's have coffee and some of your yummy Bakewell tart," Emily says with a laugh.

10

As Dawn leans against the stiff front door to click it shut, she hears her mother start humming loudly, and the 'Oompa Loompa Song' from *Charlie and the Chocolate Factory* floats into the hallway. She sighs, her shoulders sagging. Her mother has been humming this since Dawn came home with a spray tan yesterday.

Looking into the mirror above the side table, she feels so elegant. Her hair is perfect and she's delighted with the salon's make-up application. Smiling, she uses her fingertip to wipe a smudge of lipstick from her tooth. She has the ball, the holiday to visit her dad, and then she's going to move out. She just has to get through these next couple of months and she'll be free of her mother.

The humming stops.

"How did you get on?" Her mum comes into the hallway, wearing gym gear, her hair scraped back into a tight ponytail, and her forehead shiny with sweat.

Dawn turns from the mirror to face her.

"Oh, love!" Her mother laughs, more of a guffaw than a laugh. "Who's done up like a dog's dinner? It's a bit much, all that foundation and lipstick caked on."

Don't react, you are about to have a great night. Don't rise to her.

"I like it," Dawn says, desperately willing the tears forming to go away as she walks past her mother and upstairs to get ready.

"Are you sure about the lipstick? It's a bit bright and full-on. Why don't you wash it off and try again? I could help you."

Dawn tries to block out her voice and blinks furiously. Reaching the sanctuary of her bedroom, she closes the door, careful not to slam it. That would only invite her mother upstairs to continue.

Sitting on the edge of the bed, she stares into the full-length mirror opposite her. She had liked the lipstick at the beautician's, and she'd been happy with the make-up. She leans closer to the mirror. Is it too much? It is a lot more than she'd usually wear. She has time to wash it off and start again. Her phone pings. It's Ruth.

How did the make-up session go? Send photos.

She face-times the girls at Ruth's house.

"*Wow*, you look amazing! What do you think about mine? Is my foundation too dark? Do you think I should tone it down a bit?" Ruth asks, her words rushing out in the excitement of the night ahead.

"No, it's perfect," Dawn says, breathing a little easier. "Does mine really look okay?"

Samantha's face comes onto the screen. "Absolutely. What do you think of my fake eyelashes – is one a bit wonky?"

Laughing, Dawn says "Your head is a bit wonky! Straighten up, let me see. No, they're fine. Are they heavy, do they feel weird?"

"Not at all," Samantha says "I just hope I don't lose one during the evening! Your hair is fab, I knew an up-style would be perfect."

The call gives Dawn the boost she needs. "See you in a while, girls."

"Yep, we'll be there soon. Party time!"

Dawn slips into the dress and looks in the mirror. It does look nice, she reassures herself. Sure, it would be great if she had bigger boobs, if she had more curves to her body but she is happy with the fit and feel of it on her skin. She hears the murmur of the fitness instructor on YouTube telling her mum to hold her position for five as she tiptoes down the stairs in her ruby-red stilettos. Her mum counts down from five and then exhales.

Dawn's stilettos tip-tap on the tiles in the hallway, and her mum pauses the TV and comes to meet her. Dawn is sure she hears an intake of breath, and she smiles brightly. Her mum is going to be nice, how could she not?

"Come here, into the light, let me look at you properly." Her mum leads her into the kitchen.

Dawn puts her bag on the table and holds out her arms, twirling around.

"Oh, Dawn!" Her mum tilts her head. "You really should have tried it on again when you brought it home. Those shop mirrors can be deceiving." She pats her own toned stomach. "It's a bit tight across your tummy – you can see the material stretch. It's a shame."

Alarmed, Dawn looks down at her stomach. Her hip bones are slightly visible against the green satin but she doesn't think that her stomach is protruding. Although she is looking at it from a different angle. Maybe it is. Going into the hallway, she switches on the main light and stands in front of the mirror scrutinising herself. She turns to each side, her eyes fixed on her stomach. She thinks it looks fine. She turns to the side again and holds her stomach in.

Lights shine in the frosted windows on either side of the front door as a car pulls into the driveway.

"Who's that?" her mum snaps.

"Oh, that must be Ruth." She totters into the kitchen and grabs her red-sequinned clutch bag.

Her mum follows and stands in the doorway. "What? I thought I was dropping you off later. I just have to finish this toning class and shower. I'll be ready in no time."

"Well, she was going to be passing and her mum thought it would save you the journey," Dawn lies. She'd asked Ruth to collect her, although she didn't think it would be quite so early. She knew that her mum would have stalled her with excuses and made her late, and she didn't want to miss a thing this evening.

"That's not on, Dawn. I want to take you."

"She's here now – I didn't think you'd mind."

"You're not going with her now."

Her mum stands blocking the doorway.

"I am, Mum, she's waiting for me outside."

"I don't care." She grabs Dawn's chin between her thumb and forefinger. "This is not what we'd planned."

Dawn can feel the sweat from her mum's hands on her chin. "Stop it, Mum. Please don't spoil my big night."

Her mum takes a small step closer. Her nose is almost touching Dawn's and she squeezes her chin harder. Dawn can see the perspiration dotted across her mum's nose.

"You'll have an awful night, you look terrible – no one will want to dance with you."

The doorbell rings. Her mum lets go and steps back. Dawn hurries past her to the front door, rubbing her chin. It's Ruth's mum.

The mums exchange pleasantries and Dawn checks in the mirror that the foundation on her chin is okay.

"You look fabulous, Dawn!" Ruth's mum exclaims.

"Doesn't she?" Her mother agrees. "The green is beautiful on her. Oh, to be young again!"

Ruth's mum laughs. "Yes, the excitement of it all."

"Bye," Dawn says, as she turns to leave.

"Have a wonderful night, my love – give me a hug."

All Dawn can do with Ruth's mum watching is hug her mum who pulls her in close and whispers in her ear. "Don't forget to hold your stomach in, especially for the photos."

11

Amanda closes the door as the car reverses out of the driveway and waits until she can't hear the engine anymore. She shouldn't have been so mean.

Admittedly, she was shocked when she saw Dawn all dolled up – she looked so grown-up and elegant. No longer a gawky teenager but a beautiful young woman. It felt like a sucker-punch reminder that her daughter is growing up and away from her.

Anxiety knots in her stomach, and she rolls her shoulders and twists her neck from side to side. Taking out her hair bobble, she scrapes her fingertips through her hair, pulling the curls back tight against her head and refastening the bobble. She moves into the living room and, ignoring the fitness class on the TV, sits in the armchair and focuses on slowing her breathing.

Ever since Dawn started college last year the foreboding consciousness that her time with her is ticking away is overwhelming at times. She probably only has three years until Dawn finishes college, finds a job and moves out seeking independence. And then she will be alone. She has been fearful of this happening for years, ever since Michael moved to Australia and her ex, Brad, abandoned her after only four years of marriage. Dawn is all she has left. Well, she glances at her phone on the arm of the chair – the only person who's all hers.

Picking up the phone, she opens her messages with Thomas. She hasn't seen him since Thursday but, then, it is the weekend – she wouldn't expect to. Weekends are generally off-limits. She knows the rules: weekends are his family time. He belongs to his wife and children then. Amanda learnt very early on in this relationship that she has to follow his rules. It was worth it to be loved by him.

Amanda rests her head back on the armchair and closes her eyes. They've been together now for six months. Long enough to know that he loves her. Thomas is so demonstrative of his love, in his words and actions. She doesn't doubt that they'll be together properly soon. She knows she must be patient; they have to bide their time. She opens her eyes and looks around the quiet house. She hopes that by the time Dawn finishes college, Thomas will be hers. Then, she won't be alone.

Only, she isn't so sure it will work out like that. She'd met Dawn's friend Ruth's mum in the library last week, and she'd mentioned that Ruth was thinking of moving into town to be closer to college after the summer. She doesn't think Dawn is considering it. She hasn't said anything and, besides, she has everything she needs at home. She surely won't want to leave her mother on her own?

Walking into the kitchen area, she reaches into her handbag for her tablets, pops two out of the blister pack and crunches them slowly. She can't be left alone.

Pouring a glass of water, she swirls a mouthful around her teeth, flushing out the residue of the anti-depressants, and swallows, turning to face the kitchen table.

Scattered across the table are folds of felt material, in blue, red and green. She glances at the clock on the wall. She has the whole evening ahead of her. She'll complete her toning exercises and then go for a run before sitting down to make these story sacks for the library. She smiles as she walks into the living area. She doesn't mind bringing her work home with her. The children at the library are going to love them – she can't wait to see their faces.

Unpausing her YouTube class, she stands feet apart awaiting the next instruction, thinking it's a shame children have to grow up. Their sense of wonder, enthusiasm and, above all, their neediness and dependence on you, as an adult, is so fulfilling.

12

"What about trying the last three on the subs list? I know they are based in Clare, but we are desperate. Even if they can only make it for the afternoon, it would be something," the Principal is saying as Carla steps inside the school office. He's standing at the secretary's shoulder, as she looks at her computer.

"I've already rung them. No one is available this week." The secretary sighs, taking off her glasses and cleaning them with the edge of her cream jumper.

The Principal looks up. "Sorry, Carla, we won't keep you. We're having a logistical nightmare with substitute teachers."

"It's tricky to get them sometimes, isn't it?" Carla takes out her PA folder and shuffles through the poly-pockets.

"To be honest, I've never seen it so bad. We are really stuck this week."

"Can't you get anyone?" Carla puts a pile of flyers and posters on the desk.

"Nope, and I need three!"

"Three! Look, I'm a qualified teacher, I'm just on a career break. I can help out if you're stuck." The words are out of her mouth before she realises and a tiny bubble of excitement begins to bounce around in her stomach.

"Are you? Would you mind?" His face breaks into a huge smile. "It would be wonderful if you could – even if it was just for today and tomorrow."

"Today?" Carla says, looking down at the gym leggings she's wearing, ready for Pilates at ten o'clock. "Can I pop home and sort myself out?"

"Of course, take your time. Mr Griffin will be delighted to hear he won't have half of another class in with him. He looked like he was going to have heart failure when I told him this morning." He laughs. "Thank you so much for this – you're a godsend, I really appreciate it. Bring your teaching number in if you have it to hand."

Carla rushes out to her car, feeling dazed and excited. It's only when she's rifling through the filing cabinet ten minutes later, looking for the teaching number, that she realises she never even asked which class she'll be teaching.

The buzz stays with her all day as she teaches a class of ten-year-olds. Daniel and Ben get a bit of a shock when they see her in the school corridor but, from the smile Daniel gives her when she explains, she thinks he's secretly proud that his mum's teaching in the school.

At lunchtime, she makes a point of avoiding sitting too near to Daniel and Ben's teachers in the staffroom. She knows there's nothing worse than being stuck with a parent. The secretary comes in with the school fair posters and flyers, and Carla talks her through the latest fair details and school permissions needed.

By the time three o'clock comes, she's tired but still on a happy high. Her calf muscles are aching from wearing heels all day and her ears are ringing from the constant noise of thirty children, but she has a grin on her face.

"Thank you so much for stepping in," the Principal says. "I hope you haven't been put off for tomorrow."

"No. Definitely not. Although I will wear lower shoes! It's been great, teaching again. I'd forgotten just how much I enjoy it."

She's at home with the boys before she even thinks to look at her phone. Two missed calls from Thomas. She rings back but he doesn't answer.

The boys are starving as usual, so she lets them have some snacks, fruit and a few crackers while she supervises their homework. She'd usually have dinner ready for them when they get home from school. She had planned to make a casserole for tonight but that would take too long. Listening to Ben sound out the tricky words in his reading book, she decides to make a quick stir-fry.

While the boys play Lego in the living room, she makes a start on dinner. Her mind wanders to the classroom and she starts to plan what activities they might do tomorrow to support the *BFG* novel they are currently reading. This could be the start of something good for her. She smiles to herself, tossing the veg into the frying pan with the chicken, it could be a pathway back into teaching.

She hears Thomas's car pull onto the driveway just as she puts the noodles on. That's good timing. She is bursting to tell him all about her day. The boys beat her to it, abandoning their Lego and rushing to meet him in the hallway.

"*Daddy, Daddy, Mummy was teaching in our school today!*"

"What?" Thomas says, hugging them and half-laughing at their excitement. "Has your school-fair planning taken over the school already?" He leans forward to kiss her.

"No, I was actually teaching." She beams at him. She has so much to tell him.

"What? You're joking. Why?" He looks confused as he takes off his jacket and hangs it over one of the breakfast bar stools.

"They were desperately short-staffed, and I happened to be in the school office, so I offered to help out. It was brilliant." She turns to adjust the heat on the noodle pan.

"Are you having a laugh? They just take random people off the street to teach the kids now, do they? Surely they have a list of subs to use?"

Carla's heart sinks a little at the tone of his voice. Keeping her back to him as she adds the sweet chilli sauce to the stir-fry, she says, "They were down three teachers – there's some stomach bug going around, and they couldn't get a sub. And, I am a teacher, not just some random person." She forces a small laugh, as she lines the plates along the countertop.

Turning, she finds Thomas leaning against the breakfast bar, his arms folded, a stony expression on his face.

"It was fantastic to be in the classroom again. I had fourth class and, to be fair, they were quite well behaved considering I was a sub teacher."

"I'm sure they'd have found someone. I bet the Principal thought you were desperate for money or something, offering to teach like that. You haven't taught in years!"

"No, of course he didn't. He was relieved to have someone to help out. I'm going in again tomorrow."

Thomas stares at her for a moment before she turns to serve up the dinner.

"Boys, wash your hands, dinner's ready," she says.

All through dinner, Thomas chats away to the boys about their day, and about a Tesla he saw parked in town, telling them these cars are going to take over the world. Carla knows he's making a very obvious point of not asking her about the teaching, and her stomach dips in disappointment. Pushing her food around her plate, she can't understand why he isn't happy for her. Maybe she should have rung and told him about it this morning when she'd popped home to get changed.

After dinner, she rinses the plates and begins to stack the

dishwasher. "Aren't you going to ask me about my day?"

"No, Carla. To be honest, I'm embarrassed you got yourself into that situation. What must people think?"

"*What?*" She turns around to face him.

"Well, people are going to be thinking you are desperate for money, aren't they? That I can't provide for you."

"Thomas, that's ridiculous. I wasn't begging on the side of the street, I was teaching," she says, her voice dropping.

"Well, you don't need to. We discussed this when Daniel was born – there's no need for you to go out to work. I provide enough for this family."

She sighs at Thomas's old-fashioned mantra of providing for his family. She knows it stems from his mother struggling, working three jobs at a time to provide for her family while his father drank away his dole. But why can't he see she liked her day teaching?

"It wasn't as if I planned it. I was just helping out. They were stuck *and* I enjoyed it."

"Still, I don't want people thinking you need to work. I don't think you should offer again."

Carla's stomach clenches. She'd enjoyed today and she was looking forward to tomorrow. "What about tomorrow? I promised I would cover the same class."

"Can't you get out of it?" he says, staring her straight in the eyes, his forehead creased.

"No, I can't let them down."

"Okay, well, do tomorrow then." He turns his back. "I think I'll go to the gym for an hour."

Carla's shoulders hunch over the sink as she crashes the pans into it and squirts washing-up liquid over them.

"*Five minutes to bath time, boys!*" she calls into the living room.

13

Emily isn't surprised when Thomas contacts the estate agent's where she works about viewing offices. Carla had mentioned his business was looking for bigger premises. She is a little surprised when he asks specifically for her. But then, he knows her, he probably thinks she's more likely to be honest on prices and offers.

"I want to stay close to Galway city," he says. "If I was to specify then I'd like a nice view. And not Parkmore. The traffic in and out of there is a nightmare."

"I'd say we have a few of the kind of size you are looking for. I'll put a list together."

"When do you think we can view them?"

"I'll try to line up a few for tomorrow afternoon if that suits you. Say around one o'clock?"

"Perfect. And it will be you, Emily, won't it, showing me around? You know I can't stand all that bullshit from estate agents."

Emily laughs. "I am a senior estate agent, you know. I have plenty of bullshit ready to impart to you."

"I know you won't bother with all that. Just show me the properties, get me a good price and we'll have a deal. I'll be happy and so will you."

"I'll see what I can do. I have a few other viewings lined up for the morning but, providing they don't overrun, I should be able to meet you."

"Great, thanks."

* * *

When they meet the next afternoon, Emily is determined to keep it professional. He may be married to her best friend, but these office spaces can be quite lucrative in commission, and she has bills to pay. She has all the information on the properties in folders for him. It's already been emailed to him, but she likes her clients to have the information there in front of them.

Following him upstairs to the first floor in the third premises, she finds herself focusing on the way his crisp white shirt fits snugly yet perfectly across his back and arms. She has to stop doing this, she berates herself. Since she started online dating, she is increasingly finding herself like this with all men, even in the most banal situations. Last week, she found herself staring at a man in the post office queue, appraising his physical attributes and daydreaming about the sort of films they might watch together. She'd been caught out when the queue had moved forward, and she didn't. A lady in the opposite queue had smirked and raised her eyebrows, and Emily blushed from her chest to her face.

She watches him pace out the office and look at the views. His freshly tousled hairstyle, which he's had since he met Carla, seems different today – softer, floppier. She talks him through some of the information about the office and he comes to stand next to her, looking at the floor plan in her hands. His fingers run along the page as he repeats the measurements she's mentioned. His aftershave permeates her nose, and she finds herself inhaling it a little more with each breath. Taking a step back, she corrects herself and clicks back into professionalism.

"Do we have many more to see?" Thomas asks, checking his watch.

"Two more, both down by the docks."

"Have you had lunch?"

"Eh ... no."

"Do you want to have lunch now? I didn't get to eat yet and I'm starving."

"I've some paperwork to do when I get back to the office, so *erm* ..." she looks at her phone, "I have to be finished with you by four. But okay."

"Perfect. Follow my car. I know just the place."

Their lunch is very relaxed. He orders them a half bottle of Chardonnay to share and tells her about his plans to expand his business. As he pours the wine, her attention is caught by the tiny dark hairs sprouting from just below the knuckles of his thumb and forefinger.

When their food arrives, she looks at her seafood linguine and regrets ordering something so messy to eat. Glancing over at Thomas's steak sandwich and chips, she reminds herself that this is Thomas, Carla's husband, whom she has known for years, who knew what wine to order for her without asking. She's comfortable in his company. This online dating is sending her a bit crazy, she thinks, as she tucks into her food.

It is three o'clock before she realises.

"*Shit.* Come on, we better get to those last two places. I'll never get that paperwork done now. I'll have to go straight to collect the kids after this."

"Sorry, I didn't realise we'd been yapping for so long." He calls for the bill. "It was nice though. Let me get this, it's the least I can do, keeping you here, delaying you like this."

The next office space is on the fourth floor and it's Thomas's favourite so far. Emily is aware of the time ticking and of needing to collect the kids from afterschool club. She tries to subtly hurry him on, but he loves the place and he takes his time walking about the floor space talking out loud, planning where everything would go, which department where. They talk prices and she negotiates the best she can. She can tell he wants her to go lower but she can't without first checking with the developer. While he goes to the toilet, she makes a list of the extra information he's requested.

Turning, Emily stares out of the floor-to-ceiling windows, across the docks. She can see Nimmo's Pier from here, but no sign of the dolphin that frequents that area.

"Not a bad view, is it?" he says, coming up behind her.

He's so close she can smell the shower gel he used that morning, under his layer of aftershave, and she's flooded with a sense of warmth.

"Not bad at all! It could be difficult to get any work done staring out from this window."

"Thanks a million for this, Emily." He touches her arm, and she turns around.

He's standing very close. She tries to take a step back, but she is almost up against the window. She's aware of her thumping heartbeat and wonders if he can hear it too.

"Just doing my job."

He leans in and without warning kisses her. Softly on the lips at first, then he quickly parts her lips and kisses her hard, his tongue probing her, his hands on her face. Her face tingles with pleasure and her mouth responds until her brain kicks into gear, and she realises what she's doing. She pulls back quickly, putting her hands on his chest to push him away.

"*Thomas, what the fuck?*"

Thomas's warm blue eyes are looking into hers. His reaction takes a second or two and he steps back. "God. Emily, I'm so sorry. I don't know what came over me." He stands staring intently at her.

Emily looks at the ground.

"You were just so close, and you smell so good. I don't know what happened. I needed to kiss you."

"You're married, Thomas. To my best friend." She lifts her head, looking directly into his eyes. The intensity of them forces her to look down at the floor again. Her whole body is throbbing and a flushed feeling is sweeping through it. What is happening to her? She clenches and unclenches her hands.

"I know. I'm sorry." He looks out of the window and then says, "You did kiss me back."

"I … I …" She falters. "It was wrong. Very wrong. Carla is my best friend and your wife."

"I know. I've said I'm sorry."

"You need to leave. Now."

"Okay. I understand." He touches her arm briefly and she flinches. He walks across the office floor. At the door he hesitates. "Bye, Emily."

She doesn't answer but turns away, looking out of the window again, her eyes filling with tears and her nails digging into the palms of her hands. She wants to thump the glass. She wanted that kiss; she can't deny it. All afternoon she's been tingling for him. Why? Why, after all these years of knowing him, is Thomas suddenly having that effect on her?

Emily drives straight to collect the children. She's half-expecting her boss to call looking for a follow-up to the appointments today. She knows Thomas is interested in that last office space and she'll have to put some calls in to the developer to negotiate the price, but she can't face it this afternoon. She'll do it in the morning, or better still pass it on to Martha. Emily doesn't care if she loses the commission on it. It's tainted with her betrayal now.

As she drives, she realises she's clenching the steering wheel and loosens her grip. How could she? Her stomach grumbles with disgust. Why didn't she turn her head immediately and push him away? And who did he think he was, kissing her like that? He's a married man. Married to her best friend. She tries to direct her anger towards him, but she can't. As much as she wants to blame him, she knows it's just as much her fault. She had responded. She kissed him back and, worse, she wanted to.

She turns into the school carpark. How is she ever going to face Carla again?

14

"*Mum, do we have a medium-sized suitcase? I can find the large one and two small, but not a medium!*" Dawn shouts down the stairs.

"*It might be in my wardrobe, hang on.*"

"*Okay. I'll check.*"

"*No. I'll do it. Wait a minute!*" her mum barks.

Walking back into her bedroom, Dawn looks at the piles of clothes neatly laid out on her bed. Is she packing too much? She picks up her new American passport from the desk. Her dad, Brad, said it would make visiting easier. She flicks through it. It feels strange to be the owner of a passport issued from a country she's never visited. Brad is American and has lived there since she was eight. She's never been to his home place. He's always travelled to visit her in Ireland or collected her en route to a European destination.

Hearing her mum's footsteps on the stairs, she replaces the passport on her desk and moves the piles of clothes so that there's space to fit the suitcase on the bed. She goes across the landing and, from the doorway of her mother's bedroom, she sees her mother looking into the suitcase lying on the bed.

"You found it."

Her mother slams the lid shut as Dawn glimpses something black inside. "*Get out! I'll bring it in to you in a minute!*"

"Okay, okay." Dawn holds her hands up. *Calm down,* she thinks, as she backs out of the doorway, going into her ensuite and packing some toiletries.

"Here you go." Her mother dumps the dusty suitcase not in the space ready but on top of the clothes Dawn has just moved.

She tries not to react. Today is not the day to fight.

"Do you really want to take that kind of stuff? Don't you know New York is a stylish city" Her mother nods towards the bed, her hands resting on the slim hips of her black skinny jeans. "You're going to stand out as a pale, pasty Irish girl over there anyway." Her thick blonde curls bounce as she picks up an oversized T-shirt. "The people over there are all slim and beautiful – you don't want to go drawing attention to yourself wearing such things. You'll feel self-conscious in no time." She tosses the T-shirt on top of the suitcase.

Dawn has to close her dropped jaw; no words will come out. She turns away from her mother's icy blue eyes and stares at the suitcase.

"Have you even checked what the fashion is like over there? Really, Dawn, you should make more effort."

Dawn feels a stab in her gut as her mum turns to leave the room. Why do her insults never get any less painful? She really should be used to them by now.

"You'll have to get the bus to the airport tomorrow, I'm busy," her mum says, closing the door behind her.

Dawn's heart sinks as she lifts the suitcase off her clothes and sits down on the bed. Why can't her mum be happy for her? She's going on a big adventure to see her dad's home for the first time. She unfolds and refolds her clothes before packing them into the suitcase, trying to push the negativity out of her mind. She wants to focus on her excitement about going away but her mum's comments have dulled it.

Despite Dawn being almost twenty, Amanda has been dead against her going, protesting that it's too far to go alone. Dawn had begged her dad to speak to her mum, to help convince her. She only heard one-sided snippets of their telephone conversation as she sat at the top of the stairs. 'Don't tell me how to raise my daughter – you haven't exactly been involved so far – you're not much of a father from over there.' But her dad somehow convinced her mum in the end.

She holds up a cropped tie-dye T-shirt, pinks, blues, and purples all merged, and refolds it. She loves this top; she, Ruth, and Samantha had all bought one at the same time. Putting it in the suitcase, she glances at the pile of clothes, and nibbles at the skin around her thumbnail. Maybe her mum is right. She hadn't thought to check the fashion in the States. She should throw in her smart jeans and a couple of dresses. She doesn't want to stand out.

She sits on the carpet, and leans against the bed, inspecting her nails. They're bitten to the quick, the skin around them red and raw. She makes a promise to herself to leave them alone while she's away. They have to heal.

"*I'm off to athletics club!*" her mum calls up the stairs. "*I'll be back by eight!*"

Dawn hears the front door slam. Perfect, she thinks, I'll be able to lie on the couch with the guidebook and read up on everywhere Dad has talked about taking me to. No sarcastic comments or put-downs from Mum.

She'll finish packing first. She reaches for her passport on the desk but it's not there. Her eyes dart around the room. She lifts her laptop and looks underneath. Where is it? She had it only a few minutes ago. Where is it?

She drops to her hands and knees, scans the floor and looks under the bed. No sign. She empties the small backpack she's using for hand luggage, checking each pocket. Still no sign. She turns to the suitcase, her heartbeat pulsing in her ears. *It has to be here somewhere.* She methodically goes through every item of clothing. Running her hands through her hair, she curses under her breath. *Where did I leave it?*

She perches on the edge of the bed, looking at the clothes strewn around her. She was sure she'd put it back on her desk. She lets out an exasperated groan and falls back onto the bed. *Mum.* Of course her mum would take this opportunity to spoil things. It has to be her. She was standing right next to the desk when she'd been insulting her choice of clothes. Dawn's face reddens as the blood rushes to her head, and she wipes away a layer of perspiration forming above her top lip. How dare she? Is Mum actually going to let her get this close to visiting Dad, and then hide the passport from her?

"*Bitch!*" Dawn whispers as a tear escapes from the corner of her eye and drips down the side of her face and onto the bed cover. Inhaling deeply, she holds the air in her lungs for a few moments, then exhales and sits up. She will find this passport if she has to tear the house apart. Grabbing a scrunchie, she scrapes her hair back into a ponytail and wipes the tears away with the back of her hand. *I will find it. She won't stop me from going.*

She leaves her messy bedroom and crosses over to her mum's. She shakes the bedcovers and looks under the rose-decorated pillowcases. She lifts the mattress on both sides and doesn't think twice about pulling open the drawers on the oak bedside table and rifling through, pushing aside medicine bottles, receipts, and perfume samples. *Where is it?* Through the open window, Dawn can hear children's laughter out on the green in the middle of the cul-de-sac. The purple-and-red curtains ripple slightly on the breeze coming in. Looking out, she sees the car has gone. Back by eight, she'd said. A wisp of wavy hair escapes the scrunchie and dangles down in front of her eyes. Tucking it behind her ear she glances at the clock on the bedside table: five o'clock. Three hours. *Where could she have put it?*

Staring at the oak-fitted wardrobe lining the wall, a memory comes to her of searching for Christmas presents as an eleven-year-old. Her first year of not believing in Santa and searching for tell-tale presents in her mum's room before she came home from work. She'd found a shoebox full of unopened letters and cards to her from her dad shoved to the back of the wardrobe. Her mum had come home to find Dawn sitting against the bed, opened letters and cards scattered on the rug around her. That was probably the first time she realised how manipulative her mother could be. She was old enough to know it was wrong to have these things withheld from her.

Dawn stares at the wardrobe. Her mum has taken her passport to stop her from going; she never had any intention of letting her go. She's been standing in the way of Dawn having a relationship with her dad her whole life: checking letters, supervising Skype calls, reading emails. This was going to be no exception and Dawn shouldn't have dared to hope it would be. She pulls at a loose thread of an embroidered red rose on the quilt cover and wraps it around her thumb until it hurts. She pulls until it snaps. She unwinds the thread and rubs the thin red marks left behind.

What is she going to do? She could call Dad. Would he think she's crazy saying her mum's taken her passport? She's never told him how her mum can be. *How could she?* She examines the red marks left on her thumb. How could she even begin to explain it? Her mum is so nice to everyone else that she probably wouldn't be believed. Plus, her dad never wanted kids in the first place so he certainly wouldn't have wanted to deal with her complaining about her mum when they had their one-week holidays together.

No, Dawn has to find this passport and finish packing. She pulls open the wardrobe doors and drops to her knees to search through the bags and boxes stored at the bottom. A musty, stale smell escapes from a soft black plastic parcel at her knees. Is this what her mum had been taking out of the suitcase earlier? She picks it up and reads the label addressed to her mum.

Tipping out the contents, her forehead creases. Two body bumps fall onto the rug and an invoice note. Picking up one, she inspects it: a flesh-coloured mound attached to a belt. Taking up the other, she sees it's the same only bigger and firmer. What the hell? She drops them both and reads the invoice note.

1 x 5-month bump

1 x 8-month bump

2 x scan black-and-white

It is dated 21.2.2000.

Dawn stares at the piece of paper. Fake pregnancy bumps. She was almost two years old then. Why was her mum faking a pregnancy? Is this why Dad left? Did she do this to get rid of him? She's always said he didn't want children.

Pushing everything back into the black plastic parcel, she sits on her knees on the deep-pile purple rug, staring at the package, until the tune from an ice-cream van, driving into the cul de sac, drifts in through the open window.

After searching the kitchen and the living room, Dawn resigns herself to the fact that her mum must have taken the passport with her.

She has to talk to her dad. It's early morning in New York – she might catch him before work.

"My passport's gone, Dad. I don't think I'm going to be able to fly." Saying it out loud makes it seem more real and her voice catches in her throat.

"Hang on, calm down, honey," her dad says. "What do you mean it's gone?"

"It was on my desk in my room and now it's gone." She hesitates. "I think Mum took it and hid it."

He doesn't say anything for a few seconds and then, "Are you sure, sweetie? It's probably under something or you've packed it already without realising it. Have you double-checked everywhere?"

"Yes. I've gone through everything. Mum was in my room, and then it disappeared. She must have taken it – there isn't any other explanation." She tries and fails to stifle her sobs.

"I'm sure she hasn't. She probably just put it somewhere for safe keeping."

"No. She's hidden it on purpose."

He sighs, says "Amanda," quietly under his breath. "Look, don't get too worried. She'll be minding it for you. Have you asked her?"

"No, she's gone to her running club."

"Okay." He pauses. "Well, when she comes home, ask her, just ask her straight out."

Dawn nibbles the skin around her thumb. "What if she doesn't give it back?"

"She will. Look, Dawn, honey, she used to hide things from me too but if you confront her, she will back down."

The air in Dawn's lungs is sucked out like there was a sharp, quick drop in altitude. Her mum did this kind of thing to her dad. What? So, it's not just her?

"She can't legally stop you from going. I can call her if you like."

"No. I'll wait for her to come back and ask her. Did she, did Mum do that sort of thing to you much?"

She hears her dad take a breath before he says, "Ah, sweetie, let's not go there. Let's get your passport back and get you over here. I'm so excited about seeing you."

A tiny bit of skin is hanging off her thumb near the base of the nail. She tears it off with her teeth and is stung by the soreness of it.

"Dad …" She wasn't going to say anything but now after he's told her this … "I found something strange while I was searching for my passport. Fake pregnancy bumps – two of them."

Dawn can hear him breathing down the phone. Maybe she shouldn't have mentioned them.

"Dad? Did you know about these?"

"Yes. Yes, I did. It was a long time ago."

"Oh my God, what happened? Did Mum actually fake a pregnancy?"

"She did. Not quite the peak of her manipulative tactics but pretty close."

Dawn sits down on the arm of the settee, stunned. Mum treated Dad the way she does her?

"What? What happened? And what do you mean not the peak of her tactics?"

"We can talk about it while you're here. It's not really a conversation for the phone. I'd better get to work. It's my last day in the office for a week. If you have trouble getting the passport from your mum, send me a text and I'll call."

"Okay. I'll let you know. See you tomorrow, hopefully."

Dawn puts the phone down and flops back onto the settee. Why did her mum pretend to be pregnant? She always told her that her dad left them, abandoned them, because he wasn't interested in family life. Did she do this to push him away? And Dad didn't seem surprised by her mum taking the passport. Such behaviour wasn't new to him. Taking the scrunchie out of her hair, Dawn twists it over and back between her fingers. She has a lot of questions for her dad when she gets to New York.

15

Amanda pulls up the handbrake and looks at the red front door of her house expectantly. She counts slowly to thirty. Nothing happens. She was sure that Dawn would come rushing out, her face puffy, eyes rimmed red from crying, her words falling out in a sobbing stutter as she explains the missing passport, and that she needs her help to find it.

Amanda sits waiting patiently. Waiting to be needed. But Dawn doesn't come out.

She reaches into the side pocket of the car door for the passport and pushes it into the waistband of her running leggings, pulling her T-shirt down over it.

"*I'm home!*" she calls out, closing the front door.

There's no answer but she can hear movement upstairs. Dawn must have her AirPods in.

Amanda goes into the kitchen and refills her water bottle. She takes big gulps before resting it on the countertop and allows herself a little smile. Dawn is going to need her help to find the passport, and she'll be so relieved and thankful when she finds it for her. She'll head to New York tomorrow knowing that her mum saved the day and saved the trip.

Hearing Dawn on the stairs, Amanda turns to face the kitchen door. Dawn comes in, not with tear-stained cheeks as Amanda expected, but with a pale, stony look.

"Hi, are you all set?" Amanda asks. The cold stare she gets in return surprises her and she takes a small step backward.

"Have you taken my passport?" Dawn asks, her hands gripping the back of a kitchen chair.

Amanda is so shocked by Dawn's direct question that it takes her a second or two to process her answer. This isn't how she'd expected the evening to go. Gathering herself together, she breaks into a wide smile.

"I did, my love. I didn't want you to misplace it. Your room was such a mess with clothes strewn everywhere while you were packing." She laughs. "You know what you're like – you were bound to lose it!" She laughs again.

Dawn's face doesn't soften, she doesn't smile in relief. She hardly seems to breathe.

"Right, well, can I have it back now?" She loosens her grip on the chair. "I'm going to put it in my carry-on bag ready for tomorrow."

Amanda pulls open a drawer and shuffles through some bills and papers, pretending to get the passport. She's taken aback by Dawn's directness – it's unlike her. Carefully, with her body blocking Dawn's view, she pulls the passport from the waistband of her leggings and spins around, smiling brightly at her daughter. 'Here you go!' She steps forward, placing it on the table between them.

Dawn snatches it up and turns to go.

"Aren't you going to say thank you?" Amanda asks, annoyance clear in her voice.

"I'm going to bed." Dawn stands in the doorway.

"It's not even nine o'clock. I thought we could watch something together. I'm not going to see you for over a week." Amanda moves across the room.

"I've got to be up early," Dawn says. "Goodnight," she adds quietly as she leaves.

Shit! Amanda slaps the back of the chair. That did not go to plan. She'd pictured a movie night. Eating popcorn and Minstrels, curled up on the settee with her daughter. Instead, here she was at nine o'clock, alone, with a week of being alone ahead of her.

Staring into the fridge after her shower, Amanda tells herself to make a cup of tea, watch the news and go to bed early. She tries to ignore the bottle of white wine lying on the bottom shelf. She shouldn't, she knows she shouldn't. It's a Tuesday – a work night. She closes the fridge door. *This is not what I do. I am a health-conscious woman who takes care of my body.* She should just go to bed but her body is already turning back to the fridge. The wine comforts her. It numbs the loneliness and, when her daughter is about to abandon her for a week, she deserves a glass of wine.

Amanda pours a large glass, puts the bottle in the cooler, and reaches into her handbag for her tablets. One more should do it, she reassures herself. Everything will be easier to deal with.

16

Dawn's eyes widen as she makes her way down the aisle to her seat. The plane is huge. On the seat are a blanket, a headset and a little pack. She stores her hand luggage at her feet and sits down. There's a TV on the back of the chair in front and a control that sits in the armrest. Taking out the control, she examines it – a TV control on one side and a game remote on the other.

Looking around, a wide grins spreads across her face. Her first big adventure on her own. Off to New York City.

She thought she'd be nervous, but she isn't. She's excited to see her dad and explore New York, and relieved to be escaping Mum for a while.

She flicks through the inflight magazine to see the menus and movies offered before settling back in her aisle seat and people-watching as passengers board and look for their seats. A pregnant lady with a toddler passes and Dawn's reminded of the fake pregnancy bumps she found last night. She'd been ready to explode. It had only been when Dad had reminded her that Mum couldn't legally stop her from going that she'd calmed down. He'd also been right about confronting Mum – she'd handed the passport over straight away. She watches as the lady and toddler manoeuvre themselves into the middle of the row of seats in front of her. The lady reaches into a small *Toy Story* rucksack and takes out some storybooks. Dad's words from last night echo around Dawn's mind. '*Yes, I did know.*' Her mum faked a pregnancy. Why? What for? Hiding letters meant for your daughter is one thing but, crikey, faking a pregnancy!

"Excuse me."

A man in his forties, wearing chinos and a navy jumper, is standing at the end of her row. She stands and he passes her to sit in the window seat. Pulling down the little table as soon as he puts his seatbelt on, he takes his laptop out of his bag and opens it. No one has taken the seat between them yet which Dawn is rather relieved about as she's a bit wary of falling asleep on a stranger's shoulder .

Resting her head back, she watches the safety demonstration and tries to relax for take-off. Her mind wanders back to her dad. Not the "peak", he'd said – *what did that mean?* Opening the blanket packet, she unfolds it over her lap. It definitely means that her mum has at some point treated Dad the way she does her. She yawns. Although it's only lunchtime, she's shattered – a combination of an early start to get the airport bus and the drama of yesterday. She flicks through the movie channels until she finds *A Star Is Born* with Lady Gaga and the gorgeous Bradley Cooper.

17

Guilt thumps Emily in the chest almost as soon as she opens her eyes and everything comes flooding back. Her dreams, during the brief sleep she managed, had flicked between Carla finding out, and kissing Thomas in various scenarios. Emily detests herself. Why was she dreaming about kissing him? It had been a mistake; she should never have kissed him.

Sitting at the breakfast table, she cradles her coffee cup and stares out of the patio doors into the overgrown garden. The kids chatter away while eating their cereals. Their voices floating over her like wispy clouds. What has she done?

"Mummy, Mummy …. Mummy!" Rosie says.

"What, love, sorry, I didn't hear you."

"Where's my helmet? It's Wednesday. We've got camogie training today."

"Oh right, yes. I'll get it."

She clicks back into reality. Ignoring the breakfast dishes on the table, she hurries the kids upstairs to clean their teeth, digs out the helmet and football boots, and lines their schoolbags up at the front door.

"Where's my lunch bag?" Theo asks, zipping his coat up.

"Lunches, shoot." Emily races back into the kitchen. "You can have croissants today as a midweek treat," she says, throwing pre-wrapped croissants into their lunch bags alongside cereal bars, and a banana each.

"That'll do." She fills their drinks bottles with water. "Into the car, kids, we're going to be late."

The front door is open, and Theo climbs into the back seat. Rosie is sitting on the bottom step of the stairs, putting her shoes on.

"Come on, hurry up, Rosie!" Emily snaps.

"I'm trying to go as fast as I can, Mummy – these laces are tricky." Her voice wobbles.

Emily stops at the front door, her hand on the doorframe, and closes her eyes to take a deep, pained breath. "Okay, lovey, take your time. You're doing really well with your laces."

On the drive to school, Theo talks animatedly about the volcano experiment they are doing at school today but Emily's not really listening. She is willing the tightness in her chest to ease. Approaching the school, her chin starts to quiver. She pulls into the drop-off area instead of the carpark. She can't face Carla this morning. She is afraid that her friend will see the betrayal written all over her face.

"Why aren't you coming to the gate, Mummy?"

"Sorry, lovey, I have to get to work a little earlier today. I'll be waiting at the gate for you this afternoon."

She watches from the car as her children meet Carla's boys just inside the school gate and run into the playground together. Emily swallows the lump in her throat but the pain is still there. Carla turns from the other side of the gate, looking, expecting to see Emily walking towards her. Emily flashes her lights, points at her watch, waves, and pulls away.

That was awful. Her face is still grimaced in the fake smile as she pulls out of the school drop-off area. She is being such a bitch to her best friend. Joining the steady stream of slow-moving traffic, she curses and throws her hands into the air, beeping when a driver tries to push his way into her lane. How is she ever going to meet Carla face to face again? There is no way to undo what she has done.

At work, she immediately gives Martha the task of negotiating a price for Thomas with the developer, making it clear that she stands to get a decent commission if she can close the deal. She updates her boss and says that as her morning client from yesterday wants her to research some other properties, she has handed the office interest to Martha. Her boss is a little surprised but only because she knows what the commission is on these offices.

Emily tries to busy herself all morning. Today is one of her short days so she doesn't have long to fill. The guilt sits inside her head knocking at her brain and she works hard to ignore it. At eleven, the receptionist buzzes through to say that Thomas is on the phone. Emily directs the call to Martha. Martha gestures back across her desk that Thomas wants to speak to her. Emily shakes her head frantically and mimes that she is busy. She can feel a layer of sweat forming at the base of her spine. Trying to focus on her computer screen, her lips move silently as she reads the words, but nothing is registering. She reads them again but her attention has gone. The walls are closing in on her and she needs space.

She picks up some paperwork and heads to the filing room. In her mind, all eyes in the office are on her as she walks across the floor – all of them wondering why she's avoiding talking to a client. She toes the door-wedge out of place and the door swings closed behind her. Resting the paperwork and her hands on top of the photocopier, she closes her eyes and exhales.

Why is he ringing? Surely he must be as embarrassed as she is by the situation? She can't talk to him, what would she say? With her eyes still closed, she pictures Carla and Thomas smiling at her, welcoming her into their home. The guilt is too much and she opens her eyes.

She busies herself photocopying and then filing away the originals. She has put two folders in the wrong place before she realises and swops them over. Adjusting her black pencil skirt, she perches on the table and closes her eyes again. Thomas's dark-blue eyes and his lips come into view; she can smell his aftershave. She raises her lips to meet him leaning towards her.

She blinks furiously. What the fuck? Why is she daydreaming about kissing him? She hates herself for what she has done.

The door swings open and Martha comes in. Emily stands up and quickly begins gathering and sorting her photocopies.

"I'll just be a minute," she mutters.

Martha waits for her to move away from the photocopier before stepping forward.

"Did you manage to sort out Thomas's O'Reilly's call?" Emily tries to keep her voice as professional as she can and keeps her eyes on the sorting that she's pretending to do. She's sure Martha can hear the wavering noise in her throat as she speaks.

"Yes. He had lots of questions and was quite insistent he needed to speak to you, but I was able to answer most of his queries. I think he might go for the offices at the docks. He was raving about how important it was for him to have a view."

"Good. Good. Those offices have a great vantage point. You don't realise it until you are up that high." Her words try to chant over the reoccurring image in her mind of Thomas kissing her in front of that view, of his tongue probing her mouth. They fail. "Right. I'd better get back to my desk. I have that marketing meeting this afternoon and must focus on delivering that presentation."

Emily is glad when the meeting runs over time. It means she can leave straight away to collect the children.

Martha appears at her desk as she's packing her laptop away. "Listen, Thomas O'Reilly has been back on the phone. He wants a second viewing on that office space. We've arranged tomorrow at noon."

Emily nods at Martha and puts on her jacket. "That's good, he must be almost ready to sign."

"Yeah, but the thing is, he's adamant he wants you to do the viewing. He says you're a friend of the family and he trusts you not to mess him around. Which I thought was a bit rude of him. I mean, what was he implying I was doing?"

Emily's face falls but she quickly puts on her professional mask. "He's probably a bit wary of paying more than he should, but he is getting a good deal there." She looks at her phone. "That's the reason I handed it to you, Martha. It is a good commission, but I had to pass it on. He's a family friend so it could be seen as unethical for me to be involved."

Martha nods and Emily zips her laptop bag.

"It would be better for you to see it through at this stage. You meet him. Don't worry – he won't bite! I'm sure you'll have it in the bag by tomorrow afternoon. I have to go, I've got to collect the kids."

The cheek of him! Why in the world is he ringing asking to speak to her, to see her? How obvious does he want to be?

Emily starts the car in gear, and it jerks forward and stalls.

"*Fuck!*" Tears spring to her eyes and she blinks them away. How the hell did she let herself get into this mess?

She has finally got her life back on track after the disastrous end of her marriage. Who doesn't notice that their husband is gay? She hadn't even had an inkling. It has taken her a long time to sort herself out emotionally, and she's only getting back into the dating scene now.

She had never even looked at Thomas in that way before. She didn't even like him much when Carla started dating him back in college. Yes, he was good-looking but in an arrogant way, she'd always thought. She had actually been a bit wary of him. He seemed to be such a flirt with everyone. Anyway, she got used to him and his ways over the years. His total, obvious love for Carla had won her over in the end. And now this.

Why has this happened to her, and why can't she stop thinking about him? He's Carla's husband. He's not an option.

The news comes on the radio and she starts the engine again. She's going to be late if she doesn't get a move on. She tries to swallow and clear the thickness building at the back of her throat but it won't go away. She listens to the news as she drives but nothing sinks in. All she can think of is Carla. Thank goodness they won't meet at the school gates – her children have swimming lessons today and share lifts with Julia. But very soon she is going to have to meet her.

18

Standing back from the mirror, Amanda turns to the side. Yes, this dress is perfect. Not too dressy but dressy enough. It's a V-neck midi dress that shows off her tiny waist perfectly.

She knows Thomas will want to take it off her as soon as he sees her in it, but he'll have to wait, because today they are going out for a late lunch. Out-out. Not room service in a hotel that they hardly ever eat because they're too busy devouring each other, but lunch in a restaurant. She loves it when they go out like this, like a proper couple. It doesn't happen often but when it does they have a brilliant time, non-stop conversation, and lots of laughter. Being with Thomas brings out the best in her – she relaxes with him and lets herself just enjoy the moment.

She sits on the edge of the bed, and slips her feet into her sandal wedges, pulling the elastic straps around her heels. She's been very guarded when it comes to affairs of the heart, afraid of being let down again like with her ex-husband, Brad, and with her brother Michael moving to the other side of the world. Thomas, however, has managed to wheedle his way in and she's welcomed him. He loves her, of that she's sure. He tells her all the time. She just has to be patient and he'll be all hers. It's only a matter of time before he leaves his wife.

Standing up, she turns from side to side again, patting her stomach. 'Perfect.' She smiles at her reflection.

Her phone beeps a text. It's Thomas.

I'm so, so sorry to do this but I have to cancel. Something's come up at work. Promise I'll make it up to you xx

"*Shit!*" She throws the phone on the bed. "*Shit, shit, shit!*"

She'd been looking forward to this. She'd even swopped a shift at the library which meant that now she was going to be off for three days in a row. With nothing to do and no one to see. She sinks onto the bed, reaching for make-up wipes from the packet on her bedside table. Wiping one across her face, she rubs it over and over the brown eye shadow on her lids.

Three days. What the hell is she going to do?

She has running club tomorrow evening but that's just show-up-and-run, with maybe a bit of small talk on the way around the track. No one really hangs around afterwards. They all have busy lives and families to go home to. All except her. Well, she has Dawn, but she's growing further and further away from her with each new step of independence.

Kicking off her wedges, Amanda lies back on the bed and wonders what Dawn's doing in New York. No doubt she's having a fantastic time. Brad will be showing her all the sights and she'll be amazed by it all. How could she not be – it's New York? She feels a thickness in her throat, and swallows, ignoring the tears welling in her eyes. Trying to hold on to Dawn feels so hopeless. She's going to leave eventually. Turning on to her side, she curls up just as the tears spill out. She tastes the lavender scent of the make-up wipes as the tears make their way past her mouth and drip off her chin.

Her phone beeps again.

We'll do something soon. I promise xx

She types **No problem at all. Maybe tomorrow??**

19

Arriving at JFK, Dawn is overwhelmed by the stifling amount of people all around her waiting for luggage. It puts her in a bit of a fluster, and she pauses at the entrance to the arrivals to put her passport away and adjust her denim jacket. Taking a deep breath before grabbing a firm hold of her suitcase handle, she walks towards the automatic doors. It's been seven months since she's seen her dad. Her eyes dart around looking for his familiar face until she sees him waving, his face lighting up as he approaches. He embraces her in a warm hug. She had forgotten his scent yet his voice greeting her is as comforting as velvet.

"Welcome to New York! How was your flight?" He guides her to the side before the crowd swallows them up.

"Grand. I slept most of the journey. I thought I'd be watching lots of movies, but I only saw one."

"It's so good to see you. Come on, this way, sweetie, we'll get the train into the city."

He takes her case and Dawn follows him across the concourse. She watches her tall, dark-haired dad with his broad-shouldered frame stride purposefully forward, and wonders how her mum managed to manipulate and lie to him. She bounces on her tiptoes and takes a step and a half to his every one as she tries to keep up.

Announcements bellow through the speakers in the station. People are everywhere. Dawn sticks close to Brad as he confidently navigates their way to the correct platform. The noise and bustle of people make Dawn pull her jacket tightly around her. You wouldn't get these crowds in Galway, she thinks, unless it was for the St Patrick's Day parade or race week.

Getting on the train, Brad finds seats and stores her suitcase next to them. The questions about her mum are bubbling around in her gut but she doesn't want the topic to consume their holiday. They've never spoken about her together before. Can she tell him how her mum treats her, and how desperate she is to escape and move out? Their eyes meet and he smiles brightly. Will he understand, she wonders, smiling back at him and listening as he begins to tell her, over the rattle of the train moving, what he has planned for them in the Big Apple.

"So, to get to my house in Winchester, we have to go into the city and change trains. If you aren't too tired, we could have a little walk around the sights but, if you are, we can go home and rest. I have a full day of sightseeing planned for us tomorrow anyway."

"Yes to a look around." She beams at him. "I can't wait to see everything. I'm not tired, not at all."

They change at Howard Beach Station and catch the A train into the centre. The people move as a colony of ants, a long line moving from one area to another and onto the next train. Dawn's heart races as they emerge from the station. She feels like she's walking onto a TV set, it feels so surreal, like a dream. Everything is familiar yet strange to her. Buildings and a skyline that she's seen thousands of times yet never experienced. She cranes her neck at the silhouette created by Manhattan's buildings racing each other in a quest to touch the soft blue sky, the sun glimmering off the glass of the skyscrapers.

The smell of hot car exhausts is trapped between the buildings and catches at the back of her throat. The city is dense and loud. Everything and everyone seem to be moving in a perpetual rhythm and motion. Dawn can't stop her head from turning to watch it all happening around her. But the people here don't like to be slowed down so she grabs on to her dad's arm and tries to keep up with him.

It is certainly very different to sauntering down Shop Street in Galway.

20

That woman is so annoying, Carla thinks, walking away from the school gates. Emily would have had some quick-fire response if she'd been there, but Carla had been so shocked she'd barely been able to speak. She flops into the car, slamming her door, and rams the key into the ignition. She texts Emily,

Guess what Miss La-de-dah wants for the fundraiser now? She makes my blood boil. All ideas but never wants to actually do anything!

Exhaling loudly, she sits and waits for the car park to empty. She knows she'll be laughing it off with Emily as soon as she's been able to vent about it.

An hour later and no response from Emily. Carla sits at the breakfast table, putting the raffle-ticket envelopes into class groups, ready to drop into the school office later. Emily is usually quick to reply with some sarky comment to pick her up when the PA people vex her.

All the best responses seem to come into her head now that she is away from the school. All the things she could and should have said. She knows she shouldn't let that woman get to her. The fundraiser is coming together nicely. She sips her coffee. That's the problem, though – they expect her to do everything.

Her phone beeps with a time confirmation for the bouncy castle for Daniel and Theo's birthday party this weekend. They are hosting a joint party at Carla's house. It makes more sense to have it here. Emily's garden is in a bit of a state lately, and she's busy juggling work and the children – she'd never have it organised in time. Carla takes out her notebook and checks the list of jobs for the party before sending Emily a text.

Bouncy castle confirmed for Saturday. All coming together now. Picking up decorations later.

Pushing her phone aside, Carla runs her fingers through her hair and wonders if Emily's ex, Chris, will come to the party. She hopes not. It was so awkward last year; she couldn't look at him. She sighs and steps down from the stool. She'd better get on with making the chicken-and-ham pie for dinner. Thomas mentioned the other day that they hadn't had it in ages – it's one of his mother's recipes. Carla doesn't make it often because the pastry never turns out quite right for her.

It's only after dropping the raffle tickets into the school office that afternoon, before collecting the kids from music, that she thinks of Emily again. One of the dads texted to say he'd be doing the party drop-off at the weekend for his son. He's Spanish, handsome and divorced. Carla smiles to herself – maybe she could invite him in and subtly leave him alone with Emily for a while. She stands to the side of the entrance to the music room, hearing the clattering of cymbals interspersed with the tinkling of children playing the triangle, and checks her phone. Still no response from Emily. She's seen both texts. In fact, she hasn't heard from her since Monday which is unlike Emily. She must be busy in work. Thursday is her long day. Knowing this message will put a smile on Emily's face if she's having a stressful day, Carla texts:

Handsome Spanish Juan, coming to the party!

"Mum, Mum, I got a turn on the drums today, the real drum kit, not just the bongos!" Ben says as he dashes out from the classroom.

"Wow, that sounds amazing, and loud!" She laughs as Daniel joins them and they walk over to the car.

The boys eat their dinner and rush outside to get in the last play of the day before bath time. Carla puts a plate aside for Thomas and cleans up before reaching for her phone. Emily is online. It's so unusual for her not to reply. Carla looks out of the kitchen window, watching the boys bounce on the trampoline. She'd better check in on her.

You're very quiet, are you okay?

The grey double ticks turn blue as Emily opens it. *Emily is typing* flashes across the top of Carla's screen, but no reply comes. Leaving the phone on the countertop, Carla wipes down the table, scooping the crumbs into the bin. Her mind wanders to Emily's Tinder app – she hopes this dating business isn't getting to her friend.

Her phone beeps.

Just a busy day. Sorry. Chat at the party on Saturday.

Carla's relieved, not Tinder then, she's just busy with work stuff. Her eyes settle on her notebook and she opens to the page of things to do for the party. Resolving to take on more of the tasks, she takes her pen and draws a star next to the extra ones she'll do. She has the time and she doesn't mind. Emily has a lot on her plate.

21

After a full day of sightseeing and a garden BBQ, Dawn, her dad and his wife, Maria, are sitting on the decking at the back of his house in Winchester. Dawn pushes her plate to one side and sits back in her seat, sipping her ice-cold water. Her eyelids flutter briefly, and she raises her face to feel the last of the day's warmth.

"You looked shattered, Dawn," Maria says.

"I'm okay." Dawn yawns. "I think the jet lag might be catching up with me."

"You've had a busy day." Maria stands up to stack their plates and Dawn moves to stand too.

"No, no, you stay there. Relax. We've got this, haven't we, dear?" Maria says, looking at Brad.

"What, oh yes, of course." He laughs, collecting up the salad dishes.

Dawn listens to them laughing and chatting in the kitchen and smiles at the easy banter between them. It makes her wonder what her parents' relationship was like. She can't imagine them interacting like that. But then, Dawn can't imagine her mum being like that with anyone.

Brad settles himself back into his chair and reaches for a beer from the cooler.

"Do you want one?" he offers.

"No, thanks," Dawn says.

Maria appears behind her and puts her hands on Dawn's shoulders. "If you'll excuse me, I have a bit of work to do so I'll leave you guys to it."

Brad nods at his wife and Dawn realises that Maria's subtly leaving them to have father-daughter time.

Dawn waits a while before she clears her throat. "Can I ask you something?"

"Of course, sweetie, what is it?"

"What happened with the baby bumps? Did you leave because you thought Mum was pregnant?"

"*What?* No. Although we weren't getting on too well. We'd married so young, you know, but I was delighted about having another baby. I thought it might help us reconnect." Brad shifts in his seat. "Do you remember the rows?"

"No, I don't remember much of the three of us together." Dawn sips her drink, gripping the glass in both hands to stop herself from fidgeting, from biting her nails.

"I suppose three is too young to be aware of these things. Which is probably a good thing." Brad stares across the garden at the mountain range in the distance. "Amanda used to be very controlling. Ever since Michael moved to Australia, she wanted to close our life to just the three of us. I think that she felt let down by him moving so far away. They were very close. I started to feel suffocated by her control. I didn't feel I could be myself."

Dawn puts her glass on the table and begins to twist the napkin in her lap. What he's describing is very familiar, but how can she tell him?

He takes a long drink of his beer and looks across at her. "Sorry, I shouldn't be telling you this. This is your mum, she raised you single-handedly. I know she's better now – that she got some help."

The napkin tears in Dawn's hands. Mum got help – that can't be true, she thinks. She's still behaving like that, only now it's me she's trying to control. I have to tell him – this is my chance.

She sits up straight and turns to her dad. "I know what you mean about being suffocated by her. That's exactly how I feel. It's like she has to be in control all of the time. I knew no different when I was younger, but now I've realised it's not normal behaviour."

"I'm sure she's trying to be a good parent to you. I suppose every young adult feels a bit suffocated by their parents."

He doesn't get it. She looks down at the tiny pieces of the torn-up napkin in her lap. *I have to make him see.*

"No, it's more than that. She used to hide all the letters you sent me. And then, after I found a stash of them, she moved on to opening them as they arrived and telling me snippets of what was in them but withholding the actual letters. And, you know those earrings you sent me to wear for my Leaving Cert Debs? I had to hide them in a pair of boots so she wouldn't confiscate them."

"*What?*"

"She has access to my email account – she's in the background of any Skype calls we have."

"*What?* Are you serious?" His face pales, and he reaches across the table to grasp her hand. "Why didn't you ever tell me? Oh, honey, I feel so bad!" He squeezes her hand.

Dawn's eyes brim with tears and her voice catches in her throat. "I thought it was just me. She is so nice to everyone else that I didn't think for a minute she did it to you."

Brad comes around the table and pulls her to her feet. "I thought she'd got past behaving like this." He takes her in his arms. "When I left and moved to Limerick, she'd assured me she was getting help – counselling. I watched you so carefully when we met up for signs that she was manipulating you. But, you seemed such a happy-go-lucky kid." He rubs her back. "I'm so sorry. I never thought for a moment that she would do this to you. I feel awful. I wouldn't have moved back to the States if I'd have known. I stupidly assumed it was just me she manipulated. That we just had a bad relationship."

"Granny had the stroke. You had to go back to care for her. Look, I don't blame you." Dawn stands back and her eyes drop to the table, focusing on a splodge of spilled BBQ sauce. She sits back down, and Brad pulls up a chair next to her. "I thought you left us because you didn't want children, that's what Mum said," she says, using the back of her hand to wipe away her tears.

"*What? No!* I love kids. I would have loved to have more but Maria and I, well, we can't, it hasn't worked out for us." Now it was his turn to look down at the table.

"I'm sorry to hear that." She pauses. "Why did you leave then?"

"I'm not sure you need to know the whole story. She is your mum after all."

"Yes, but I need to escape her control. I'm going into my second year of college, and I want to move out, live with friends, but I know she'll freak out. Yet, if I stay, the manipulation will continue. She can be really nasty."

"I know."

"I have a summer job so I'm hoping to pay for my accommodation. I'm not asking her for money."

"I'll pay for your accommodation. I'd be more than happy to."

"Thanks, Dad! That would be great. But what happened between you? What's the story with the bumps?"

Brad drinks the last of his beer and puts the bottle down on the table between them.

"Do you want another one?" Dawn asks, looking at the cooler at her feet.

He shakes his head. "Look, sweetie, I can help you financially to move out, so you can escape her manipulating you, but I'm not sure you need to know all this." He stares out over the garden. The sky has grown dark and tiny stars are visible, scattered across the night sky.

"I do. I need to know what she's capable of."

"You do." Brad sighs. "But not tonight. You look shattered, the jet lag must be setting in. This has been a lot for both of us to take in, sweetie." He grips her hand. "My head is pretty wrecked knowing she treated you this way. I'm so, so sorry, Dawn."

"I'm sorry too. I wish I'd told you sooner. It's like she's stood between us all these years."

"She certainly has. I can't believe she told you I never wanted you. You're the best thing that ever happened to me, you have to believe that."

He stands and takes her in his arms again. She rests her head on his shoulder, her feelings so much lighter now that they have shared tonight.

"We can talk some more tomorrow. Go on, bed for you." He turns to collect the empty bottles.

Dawn climbs into bed, pulling the covers up. Despite all the revelations tonight, a warmth spreads across her chest. She goes over and over everything in her head. She *was* wanted. Her dad *did* want her. How could her mum have been that devious and cruel?

22

Emily has convinced herself Thomas was probably only trying to contact her to apologise. So, when he walks into the estate agent's later that morning and asks to speak to her, she stays calm. It's an open-plan office; she can't pretend not to be there. Plus, it is Martha's day off so she can't avoid him.

She concentrates hard on trying to look normal as she walks across the office to meet him at the reception desk. But as soon as he puts his hand out to shake hers, the heat spreads from her chest, up her neck, and onto her face. She's sure her cheeks must be on fire, although neither the receptionist nor Thomas reacts. Returning his firm yet gentle handshake, she silently prays her hand doesn't feel as clammy as she thinks it is.

"Hi, Emily. I totally forgot that Martha was off today – she did tell me. I wanted to sign the paperwork, get the ball rolling on the office space at the docks."

"Yes, of course. Come over to my desk and I'll see if I can locate it," she says, trying to keep her voice steady. He's standing so close that it feels like his aftershave is flooding her senses and all she can think of, as she walks back to the desk, is how he tasted when he kissed her. He follows her and sits opposite. "Just a moment. I'll give Martha a quick ring and find out where she's put the paperwork."

She lifts the phone but before she can press any numbers, Thomas reaches over, puts his hand over hers, and says quietly, "I need to talk to you. That's why I've been ringing. That's why I'm here today. We need to talk."

Emily pulls her hand away and glances around her. "Not here. Go to the wine bar on the corner of High and Middle Street, and I'll meet you there in a few minutes."

A wine bar, what was she thinking? She tuts to herself as she watches him leave, his fitted, red-striped shirt showing off his strong shoulders. It was the nearest place she could think of where they're unlikely to bump into anyone they know. She shuts down her laptop. He'll want to apologise about what happened and so do I, she thinks. It was down to both of us. She stands up and straightens her skirt. He may have made the first move but I kissed him back, I'm as responsible for this as he is.

Going to the bathroom, she reapplies her candyfloss lipstick in the mirror. He's probably worried I will tell Carla, and I won't, why would I? She would be crushed. Her husband and her best friend. It meant nothing. It was an accident. It definitely won't happen again. She's avoided contact with Carla so far, despite the thump of guilt with every text she's received from her. She can't pretend to be busy for much longer, not with the joint birthday party this weekend. She wipes a bit of mascara from under her eye and squirts a quick spray of perfume. On her way out, she tells the receptionist that she is taking an early lunch while it's quiet.

At the entrance to the wine bar, Emily hesitates, and peers in the window slit in the door to see if she recognises anyone. Thomas is sitting in a booth, with two glasses of white wine in front of him, looking at a menu. *Wine? Really.* Wine is not needed here. Strong coffee only. She isn't sure whether she should go in. She has to, she tells herself, she has to deal with this so that they can regret it, forget it, and move on.

Determined, she pulls open the door to the wine bar and walks inside.

As soon as Thomas sees her, he stands up. "I was beginning to think you weren't coming."

"I had to finish a few things before I left," she says, sliding into the opposite side of the booth.

"I ordered you some wine – Chardonnay."

"Thanks, but I think I'll have coffee. I have to go back to work after this."

A silence descends between them. She looks around the wine bar and he reads the menu.

"Look," she begins just as Thomas says, "What do you fancy eating?"

"A coffee will be fine for me. I don't think we should be having lunch together."

"Don't be daft, Emily, we're friends. We aren't doing anything wrong."

His hands are clasped together on the table between them, and Emily looks away from the tiny hairs on his fingers and stares instead at the salt and pepper pots before looking back at him.

"But we have done wrong, Thomas. Carla would be devastated. You know she would be. I can't believe we did this to her."

"I know. I feel awful too." He looks down at his menu again. "I didn't intend it to happen, it just happened."

She can't help herself from staring at his eyebrows as he reads the menu. They are so perfectly shaped, she is convinced he must get them waxed.

The waitress appears at their table. "What can I get you?"

"I'll have the toasted BLT, please, with sweet potato fries," Thomas answers.

"And for yourself?"

Emily quickly scans the menu. "I'll have the Caesar salad, please, and an americano. Thanks."

Thomas smiles at Emily and passes the menus to the waitress. He reaches for his wine glass. "Cheers. To a successful office move, I hope."

Emily touches her glass to his and takes a sip. This feels wrong, so wrong. She shouldn't be here. This is a betrayal of Carla. "We shouldn't be doing this."

"We're just having lunch. If what happened hadn't happened you wouldn't be thinking anything of us having lunch together, celebrating a deal, would you?"

"Well, no but…"

"So, let's just forget it ever happened."

The waitress returns with the americano and a small milk jug.

"Thanks," Emily says, adding four sugar cubes.

"Don't four sugar cubes kind of cancel out the Caesar salad?" Thomas says with a raised eyebrow and a cheeky smile.

"Yep, but hey, who's looking?" She laughs, relaxing. It's only Thomas, she reassures herself, and they can move on from their mistake.

They chat easily over their lunch, laughing about the night in the eighties bar and that crazy neon-clad DJ. She puts aside her guilt; it's not going to happen again.

"I'm glad you stayed out that night, it was good to see you relax. You've had a tough year or so."

Looking down at the table, she twiddles her thumbs. "It was a good night. Dating is pretty crap at the minute. I suppose it's difficult to trust again. If I didn't realise my own husband was gay, what chance do I have of trusting a stranger?"

"I'm not surprised." He moves to put his hand over hers, but she pulls away and rests her hands on her lap. "It must have been such a shock finding out. To be fair, we were all blind to it. I know Carla couldn't believe it. Anyway, you're well rid of him."

Emily convinces herself that all is okay between her and Thomas, that what happened was a mistake and everything is sorted now. They can move on. She gets the bill while Thomas is in the bathroom, and she's putting her coat on when he returns.

"Well, that was nice. I'm glad we cleared the air," he says.

"I'll get Martha to sort that paperwork for you to sign when she's back in the office tomorrow."

"Okay, great. See you soon."

He leans in to kiss her on the cheek, but Emily reacts quickly and backs away. Walking off towards Eyre Square, she can feel his eyes on her every step.

23

Dawn wakes early. Her body has finally started to adjust to the time difference. The last few days have been a buzz of excitement, a whirlwind of tourist sights and tours. New York is amazing. She can't wait to explore more.

Yet, staring at the light fitting above her head, she can't stop her mind from wandering back to her mum. How could she have lied about something like a baby? How low can you go? She shuffles herself into a sitting position. Her mum has always led her to believe that her dad didn't want children, as if Dawn was in some way responsible for them splitting up, as if her very existence had driven a wedge between her parents. It had all been a lie.

Dawn's fists clench. Part of her wants to phone her mum and shout at her that she knows the truth, and another part of her feels nothing, just empty. She wants to have nothing more to do with her. But that, she knows, is impossible.

"Morning," Dawn says, walking into the open-plan kitchen and living area, its huge windows framing the garden and mountains in the distance.

Maria smiles at her from the hob.

"Pancakes will be ready in two minutes."

"Morning, Dawn. Coffee?" Brad says, filling the cafetière with water from the kettle.

"Yes, please." She goes over to the fridge to take out some orange juice.

A photo of her smirking teenage self looks back at her, standing in front of the Eiffel Tower. Another photo stuck to the fridge shows her in her primary school uniform grinning a toothless smile; her front baby teeth are missing. Dawn turns and looks around the kitchen, noticing for the first time that she is part of this family, that she has never been an inconvenience. Evidence of her dad's love is all around her. A fat penguin chick, made out of a grey glove, that she made in third class and sent them for Christmas, sits on the windowsill. The needlework she did for her Leaving Cert is framed and hanging on the wall by the oven. It's weird to think that she exists in this house that she's only visiting for the first time. Dawn smiles to herself. She was always wanted by her dad; she was always loved. Everything her mum has told her is a lie, designed to keep her and her dad apart, to stop them from developing a close father-daughter relationship. To stop them from finding out how she has treated them both.

"I make the best pancakes!" Brad says, putting the plates on the table.

"You didn't make the pancakes, I did." Maria laughs. "You only flipped them!"

"I call it teamwork."

Laughing, the three of them sit down for breakfast.

After breakfast, Maria disappears to run some errands.

"Look," Brad says, refilling the coffee pot and bringing it down to the table, "I really don't want this stuff about Amanda to be hanging over us all holiday. Our time together is precious."

"I agree. It would be nice to be about just us. But …"

"I know you want to know what happened." He pours more coffee for both of them. "There is a train into the city in half an hour – will we go and do some more exploring and sightseeing, and talk later? Or would you prefer to talk first?"

Dawn smiles brightly. "Let's go and have fun."

Walking in Central Park later that afternoon, Dawn can't stop her head from swivelling to look at everything. The park is huge. So big that you don't feel like you are in the middle of a massive city. The air feels fresher too. She welcomes this relaxing haven within all the noise of the city. Her ears had been starting to ring.

"Maria has booked an Italian restaurant for dinner tonight if that's okay with you?" Dad says.

Dawn sidesteps out of the way of a family of cyclists coming her way. "That sounds great. The restaurant I work in back in Galway is Italian. I'll have to compare!"

A companionable silence descends between them, mainly because Dawn is taking everything in. This park is a lively, green lung of the city. People are strolling, jogging, cycling, roller skating. There are picnics, games of Frisbee, and kids feeding the birds. It's different from the crowds in the city, all hurrying along the sidewalk. Here, everyone seems calmer, more relaxed.

They stop for a few minutes to watch a man with dreadlocks playing the saxophone. Brad drops a ten-dollar bill into the hat on the pavement. Dawn links his arm, and they walk on.

A pregnant lady pushing a double buggy with toddler twins passes them and Dawn looks up at Brad, wanting to ask him to tell her more about Mum.

She is about to speak when he says "You're thinking of the fake pregnancy bumps, aren't you?"

"Why would Mum fake a pregnancy?"

"I think it was to try and repair the relationship," he says, veering off to another path. "Come on, let's head up this way to the Bethesda Fountain. This is called Literary Walk. See the statues of literary figures. There's Shakespeare up ahead."

Dawn takes a selfie with the Shakespeare statue before turning back to Brad.

"Go on, Dad," she prompts.

"The marriage was breaking down. Amanda had to be in control of everything. She was manipulating all areas of our life. I couldn't take it. I told her I couldn't live in a relationship like that any more, that I thought we should separate. Amanda said she was hormonal because she was pregnant again. Dawn takes a sharp intake of breath. "So you wouldn't leave," she murmurs.

"I was gobsmacked. She'd told me she didn't want to have another child. She was young having you and was quite an anxious mother. Everything had to be done by the book. Hitting your milestones, feeding, sleeping. She needed to be in control of all those." He sighs. "I naively thought that a new baby could be the bridge to bring us closer together again."

"How cruel of her!"

Dawn sees the fountain up ahead.

At the Bethesda Fountain where crowds of people are milling around, the path opens out into a terrace and Dawn steps closer to the water, looking at the eight-foot statue of a female winged angel in the centre. She takes some photos and pulls her dad in for a selfie.

"This place is huge," she says, spinning around.

"Come on, let's go up to the upper terrace and see the lake." Brad leads her to the grand staircase.

They stand on the bridge, looking out at the crowds strolling about. Dawn watches a young family feed the ducks at the edge of the lake.

"How did she manage to trick you?" she asks.

"Quite easily as it turned out. The date for the twelve-week scan clashed with a visit home to the States. Your granny was going through some health problems. This was before her stroke but, as you know, she only had me since my dad died. I had to be with her. I asked Amanda to reschedule, just by a few days, but she wouldn't. She said it was important to have it as close as possible to twelve weeks. When I came back from the States, the scan was stuck to the fridge door. I was excited about being a father again."

"I can't believe she did that to you." Dawn stares at him in horror. She'd been worried about how her mum would react if she moved out, but she had no idea just how devious she could be. This was awful. "But what about the body bumps?"

"That came later."

They walk down the far staircase and follow the path around, coming to a food stand.

"Do you want to get hot chocolate and pretzels? We can sit down for a while."

They get a selection of pretzels, and sit on a bench on the grass. Sipping their hot chocolate, Dawn watches as a crowded rickshaw comes trundling by, full of tourists taking in the park, the poor driver huffing and puffing as he cycles them along.

Brad hands her a pretzel. "This one's cinnamon."

Taking a bite, she says, "*Mmm*, this is definitely the best so far. I'm not that mad about the salted ones."

"What? Salted are the best!" he says, laughing. Wiping his mouth on a tissue, he leans back on the bench, one arm stretching along its back.

"How did you find out she was lying?"

"There were a couple of times when I questioned myself as to whether she was telling the truth. She didn't want our friends to know or Michael, which I thought was strange as they were very close. Another time, I found a receipt for a spa day when I thought she had a doctor's appointment."

Brad shakes out their paper pretzel bag so that all the salt, sugar, and cinnamon crumbs tumble onto the grass. She stares at the grass, at the crowd of pigeons flocking to peck at the crumbs.

She actually feels a little bit sick at the thought of her mum lying like that.

"I was going to paint the garden fence one weekend and I went rummaging around in the attic for my old painting clothes. I found a parcel hidden at the back of one of the shelves."

Dawn holds her breath; she knows what is coming next.

"I was fuming, thinking she'd had gone back to hiding my post. But it was addressed to her. I couldn't help myself – I wondered why she'd hidden it." He pauses and looks at Dawn. "There were two body bumps inside: two different sizes. Fake pregnancy bumps and a 20-week scan photo."

"The ones I saw. What did you do?"

"I confronted her. She tried to talk her way out of it, saying she'd had a miscarriage but that she hadn't told me because she didn't want to upset me. She thought she'd be able to conceive again quickly. She said she'd only ordered them so that she could get the first scan picture so I'd believe she was pregnant again. She got herself tangled up in her own lies though. I was done with her then."

"I'm not surprised the marriage broke down. That was unforgivable," Dawn says, staring at the red and broken skin around her fingernails. *Just like it was unforgivable that Mum had led me to believe that Dad never wanted me.*

"Yes." He looks over at Dawn. "I didn't want to leave you. I moved to Limerick so there was a safe distance between myself and Amanda.

She did all sorts of weird stuff when we broke up but then she calmed down. She told me she was getting help. That her counsellor had said her neediness was down to losing her parents in the house fire when she was younger. It made sense. I believed she was getting better." He sighs, folding the empty pretzel bag in half and half again. "I didn't want to leave you. We saw each other every other weekend, and I always made sure I was at your school plays and sports days. Do you remember?"

"Yes, I do."

"But when your Granny had the stroke, I had to move back to the States. I hated leaving you. I'm sorry I wasn't there for you. "

Dawn swallows and turns to look at him. "I need to get away from her, don't I? Your story has shown me that, reinforced it."

"Why don't you come over here, to the States, for college? I'll support you."

Dawn is shocked. It's not something she has ever thought of. "I don't know about that," she says. "I've already a year done of my degree. I want to finish it." Looking up, she can see the cityscape and it's mind-blowing. "But I definitely want to come back here. It's amazing."

"I can try to talk to your mum and make her understand that it's important for you to move out. Legally, she can't stop you," he says, as they stand, ready to walk on.

"No," Dawn says quickly. "I'll talk to her. It'll be better coming from me."

She knows it won't be better coming from either of them. Her mum will go crazy. But, after everything she's learned, she is even more determined to move out.

24

"Amazing!" Theo says as he steps inside Carla's house and sees the space bunting weaving in and out of the stair banisters. Stuck on the door leading into the kitchen, a huge astronaut is holding a sign saying, '*Welcome to Theo and Daniel's Birthday Party!*' A solar system hangs from the light fitting over the breakfast bar above all the food.

"Why don't you two run out and join the boys on the bouncy castle?" Carla says.

"My God, Carla, this is fantastic! I am blessed to have a child that was born within a week of yours. Look at all of this!" Emily nods at the rocket-shaped sandwiches under clingfilm and planet cookies. She silently wished she'd said she would do the sandwiches. It would have been cheaper than buying the cakes. But it was the least she could do. Carla had gone to so much trouble, hosting and organising the party. "You've outdone yourself this year."

"It was good fun to organise. You know me, I love to have an event to plan for."

Emily catches herself dragging her teeth along her bottom lip and stops. *Act normal,* she screams internally. She'd been dreading today. She puts the two cake tins on the breakfast bar, taking the lids off and Carla comes over for a peek. One is a rocket, the other a space helmet.

"*Wow!* They look great."

"It's the least I could do."

"I can't believe our boys are eight!" Carla pulls Emily into a tight hug and whispers into her wavy hair, "Thomas freaked at me for doing those couple of days subbing so I'm not sure me bringing up going back to teaching is a good idea. Please don't shout at me!"

"I won't but you should stand firm about it, if you really want to do it."

Carla shrugs as she stands back. "Look at you, all dressed up. I love your dress, very summery, is it new?"

Emily does an exaggerated twirl, the baby-blue dress sprinkled with pink flamingos flutters around her knees. "No, not new, last year's. I've only worn it once before. If I can't dress up for my son's birthday party, when can I?" Her voice wavers a little with nerves and she adds more loudly, "I mean, it's the social event of my summer." She laughs.

"Is this effort for the Spaniard?" Carla smiles.

"Who?"

"Don't act all coy! You know! Peter's dad, the handsome, divorced one. Juan! He said he'd be dropping Peter off."

"What, god no! I wore it because it's warm and it's a party. Although, I'll admit," she looks out of the window, "it's not very practical for a bouncy castle."

"What's not practical for a bouncy castle?" Thomas asks, coming in through the French doors.

"Emily's dress." Carla laughs.

Emily feels his eyes on her, and her cheeks burn red-hot. She quickly looks away.

"I think we should have some jugs of water for the kids – they're likely to dehydrate out there," Thomas says.

He looks amazing, his white, short-sleeved, fitted shirt shows off his tan and his biceps. Emily turns and reaches for the plastic cups in the cupboard next to the sink. If Emily was on a night out with Carla, she'd only have to give her a certain look at this point and Carla would know Emily had spotted a hottie. She can't do that now. This is Carla's man, Carla's husband.

She stacks the cups in two piles on the tray Thomas is holding, resisting eye contact even though she can feel his on her.

"Will Chris be showing his face this afternoon?" he asks.

"No, he's best man at his friend's wedding so he has a valid excuse, and he got Theo tickets to Tayto Park for next weekend, so I think Theo is okay with him not being here."

"I think we're all okay with him not being here, aren't we?" Thomas nods at Carla, whose forehead creases as she turns away.

Emily looks quizzically at both of them.

"Well, I'd better take this outside before they die of thirst," Thomas says and leaves.

"What did he mean by that?" Emily carefully lifts the cakes out of their tins.

"Just that it might have been a bit awkward, I suppose. Remember last year's silences."

"Yeah, well, that was probably the first time you guys had seen him properly since we split. Anyway, the main thing is Theo's okay with it, and Chris is a good dad to them. He's mad about the kids – he wouldn't be missing it if he didn't have the wedding, you know that."

The doorbell rings with the first party guests.

"*Theo, Daniel, come and greet your guests!*" Carla calls to the boys.

The afternoon is busy. Thank goodness the weather is fine, Emily thinks. Having this giant mass of energy stuck inside would be too much even if it isn't her house. Emily stays well away from Thomas and she feels he is doing the same. Occasionally their eyes meet, or they're left alone in the garden supervising the children. The images of them kissing flash fleetingly across her mind. It must be the effect of the glass of wine in the sunshine.

Putting down her glass, she starts to walk inside to get a drink of water.

"Can you bring out the lighter with you, please?" Carla calls. "We'll do the cakes outside." She bends to help a crying boy. "Actually, will you bring out a plaster as well? Peter here has got a burn on his foot." She lifts Peter to sit on the table of the picnic bench. "You must have been going lightning fast down that slide." She glances at Emily. "It was a shame Juan had to drop and go."

Iniside, Emily fills a glass of cold water and drinks it in one go. She refills it and puts it on the countertop while she gets the lighter from the living room. In the kitchen, she looks in the usual drawer for the first aid box. No sign of it. She tries the drawers below it.

"She's moved it to the walk-in pantry," Thomas says, stepping into the kitchen. "Random, I know."

Emily raises her eyebrows and moves across the kitchen to the pantry. This pantry is like something out of Downton Abbey, another room almost. She switches the light on and steps in, her eyes wandering along the organised shelves, herbs and spices, tinned food, the baking section.

Thomas comes in behind her. "You look so sexy in that dress," he says, and half pulls the door closed behind him.

"Thomas, I don't think …"

Moving in closer, he kisses her before she can finish speaking. She kisses him back forcefully. Her hands are on his arms feeling the tightness of him. He pulls her towards him, his hands under her dress, on her bottom. He kisses her hard, pushes her against the pantry shelves, their tongues darting into each other.

"*No. Stop,*" Emily says, coming to her senses and pushing him away, even though her body aches for him.

Pushing past him into the kitchen, she grabs her glass of water and goes back into the garden. She stares at the bouncy castle full of kids, laughing and jumping, but she doesn't see them.

"Well, did you get the plaster?" Carla calls from across the garden.

Inside, Emily looks up to see her sitting with young Peter on the picnic bench.

"I, *er*, I couldn't find the first aid box." Her voice wobbles and she stares straight at Peter to avoid seeing Carla. She can still feel Thomas's hands on her, and she pulls her dress down behind her.

"Oh lord, I should have told you, I moved it to the high shelf in the pantry."

"I have it, don't worry," Thomas says, smiling as he strides out of the house, holding up the first aid box. "Now, let's have a look, Peter – what size plaster do we need?" He kneels and inspects Peter's foot.

Emily looks over at Carla. "I'll get the lighter, I think I left it next to the sink."

Going back inside the house, she pulls the door behind her. The sound of the children recedes and Thomas' sing-song voice to Peter is muffled. Emily focuses on breathing steadily. In and out, in and out. What the hell just happened? She didn't turn him away, not until something clicked in her brain and alarm bells rang. She runs her fingers along her lips, where only minutes before his tongue was parting them. She really wanted him. What the hell is going on with her?

25

Amanda wakes with a start, nightshirt sticking to her chest and her throat dry. She reaches for the glass of water on the bedside locker and gulps it down. She hasn't dreamt about the fire for months. The nightmares always intensify before a visit from her brother, Michael. Peeling the nightshirt off, she uses it to wipe her sweaty chest, before wrapping her dressing gown around herself and padding across the landing to the spare room.

The bed would look better pulled out from the wall, she thinks, pulling out one end and standing at the other to line it up. It would be nice if there were two bedside lockers, but it's only Michael so it'll be fine. On alternate years, he brings his Australian wife, Sally, and their two children, but Amanda prefers it when it's just her and Michael. They can bond and catch up properly then.

She turns to the pine chest of drawers and, reaching down to the bottom drawer, feels around under the folded pillowcases until her fingertips touch the small, black velvet box and, beneath that, the photo frame. Smoothing out the duck-egg blue bedding, she sits down, placing the photo frame face down beside her, and opens the box. She lifts out the gold Celtic heart locket and chain, running her fingers over the intricate pattern on the locket. She opens the clasp. The locket is empty, it always was. It had been a fourteenth birthday present from her parents and she'd never known what to put in it.

She'd taken it off shortly after the night of the fire, and only wears it now when Michael comes to visit. It's part of their shared history, their childhood, their family. It's important to keep that alive for Michael, for his memories. She fastens it around her neck, feeling the Celtic design of the locket facing outwards and the polished underside resting between her collar bones.

Turning over the photo frame, she rests it on her legs, staring at the four beaming faces looking up at her. Their parents have their arms around each other and one hand resting on each child's shoulder. She's glad she took this from the snug, as they used to call the small cosy sitting room off the living room. All the ones Aunt Mary gave them were stiff, formal photos from events like christenings and family weddings. It's nice to have a natural-looking one. Tracing her fingers over their faces, she wonders if they were ever really as happy as they look in this photo?

She twiddles her thumbs around each other, her forehead creasing in a frown. She knows she can't help Michael with whatever questions he's coming over with. She was only fourteen at the time of the fire, so how could she have known about their parents' finances? She's tried over the years to keep their family memories alive and happy for him. She knows she probably wrapped him too tightly in cotton wool after the fire but he was all she had left. When he became a doctor, she was so proud of him, but then she felt abandoned all over again when he moved to Australia to take up a surgeon's post. She rolls her neck until it cracks, and sighs.

Looking at her watch, she stands up. She'd better get on with things. The towels need to be sorted for Michael and she has to make pavlova, his favourite. She'll whip the cream and add the fruit in the morning before she collects him from the airport. She can pick up the pavlova base in town later after her lunch with Thomas. She has always told Michael she uses their mother's recipe and that it had been his favourite as a small boy. In reality, their mother had never been much of a baker, there had been caterers for that sort of thing, but Amanda thought it was good for him to have impressions of a happy loving family.

Right, she thinks, what is she going to wear for lunch with Thomas? Not the midi dress. Lunch with Thomas ended up being cancelled the day she was wearing that dress. Going back into her bedroom, she opens the wardrobe and looks through her dresses. She stops at the blue-and-yellow fitted one Thomas bought her. She'd arrived home one evening after work to a Brown Thomas parcel. The dress was gorgeous, and fitted her like a glove, showing off her slim figure. She would never spend that much on a dress for herself. Maybe I could introduce Thomas to Michael when he arrives, she thinks, running her hand across the satin material. She pictures the three of them in conversation, sitting in a cosy snug of a pub. What about Dawn? She reminds herself that, if she's going to introduce Michael to Thomas, she'll have to introduce Dawn too. Will Dawn be okay with the idea of her having a partner? She lifts the hanger off the rack and lays the dress on the bed. She's never brought another man home to meet Dawn. There's never been anyone that she thought was going to be around long enough. She's had a few flings and a couple of short-term relationships but nothing too serious.

Going into the bathroom, she switches the shower on and hangs her dressing gown on the back of the door. Six months isn't really that long, she thinks, but it feels right to introduce them. Thomas will think so too, she's sure of it. She'll mention it to him at lunch and they can plan it together. Amanda steps into the steam.

26

Emily's right, Carla thinks as she sets the table. I just need to tell Thomas that I want to go back to teaching, and stand firm.

Emily had always been more assertive and assured of herself than Carla, but her ex's revelation had shaken her to the core. Carla's delighted she's regaining her confidence and dating again. She wishes she could be more like her. Placing a small bunch of grapes between the cheeses, her inner voice tells her not to be too hard on herself, she's only being sensitive to Thomas's childhood. The fact that his mother worked two or three jobs at a time trying to provide for her family, while his father drank away his dole and spent his time with other women has made Thomas adamant that Carla and the kids would be provided for.

It's not that she isn't happy, but she wants to be Carla again, not just a mum or wife. She wants some of her independence back now the kids are getting older. Seeing Emily going back to work after her ex left, seeing her thrive in her newfound independence, having work colleagues and new friends, seeing the world opening up wider than parenting to her, Carla wants a taste of that. She doesn't think she's being unreasonable.

Hearing Thomas on the stairs, she reaches for the bottle of red he'd left breathing on the countertop, and turns, smiling as he comes into the kitchen.

"This looks lovely," he says as they sit down.

Thomas pours the wine and passes a glass across the table to Carla. The nose of the wine, sweet spice and vanilla, catches at the back of her throat. She'd prefer the white wine resting in the fridge, but there's no point opening two different bottles. She'll just have the one glass of red, to be sociable, any more gives her a headache.

"I can't wait to show you the view from the new office. You can see right over to Nimmo's Pier," he says.

Smiling, she watches his eyebrows dance as he describes the view from the office he's buying and how wonderful it'll be to have the extra space. Her heart flutters a little faster; she loves seeing him so enthusiastic. Their boys are just like him when they're describing their Lego ideas and superhero battles.

"How did you get the money for it in the end?"

"Like I said before, I used some client money. They won't even notice. By the time they want to look at figures or withdraw their profits, I'll have put the money back. No one will be any the wiser." Seeing the concern on her face, Thomas smiles. "Don't worry about it, babe, it's all normal in the investing world. We'll be the only ones that know and that's because it'll bring us way more money in, in the long run." His hair flops forward as he spoons chutney onto his cracker.

Now is a good time to bring up the teaching idea. She rubs her hands down her trouser legs. "The boys are getting on really well at school, their parent-teacher meetings were brilliant."

"That's all down to you, babe – you're so good with them. Look at all this extra work you do." He nods at the project table she's set up inside the French doors. It's all about Australia; books, pictures, a boomerang, aborigine art, and small native animal figures line the table. "You're fantastic with them." He smiles, raising his glass and toasting, "To our family!"

Carla raises her glass and sips the red wine, barely tasting it. Here goes, she thinks, taking a deep breath. "I know you weren't happy when I did the couple of days subbing, but I've been thinking about it again and I really do want to go back to teaching." She reaches for another cracker. "And, well, the boys are getting older." She raises her eyes to meet his.

He takes a mouthful of wine, swirling it around his mouth before swallowing, and says with almost a half-laugh, "Why would you want to? You don't need to."

"I like teaching. I think it would be good for me now that the boys are in school."

"The boys still need you. I mean, look at all this." His arm sweeps around the room. "They're thriving because you're at home." He smiles.

"They would still thrive if I worked, I'd still be able to do all this. I'd be finished at almost the same time as them and I'd be off during the school holidays."

"You'd be rushing, it'd be stressful for you. Unnecessary stress – working, the kids and their activities, household management. I wouldn't be able to help. You know the business takes up too much of my time as it is. The kids flourish, I flourish, with you here."

"I could cover a maternity leave, or go part-time, look for a job share. It could alleviate the pressure of moving funds for the new premises too."

"I doubt a few teaching hours will do that!" he scoffs. "Besides, I have that under control. Babe, look at any family you know with two working parents – they are racing around, trying to keep on top of things. We're lucky, we don't need you to work. I thought we'd agreed on this when you gave up teaching. I provide enough for us. You don't need to work and the children need you, *I* need you." He reaches across the table for her hand and rubs his thumb along her skin. "Maybe when they're older."

"I suppose you're right," she says, remembering how she thought she'd be back at her teaching role a lot sooner, and that it was Thomas who dissuaded her every year when it came to filling out the form for yet another career-break year. But maybe he is right. She sees how Emily struggles to keep on top of things and she only works part-time. But still the disappointment sits deep in her stomach.

He picks up the wine bottle with his free hand and fills his glass. The spicy aroma floats over to her and she tries not to gag. She pulls her hand gently away from his and reaches for a glass of water.

"Anyway, did I tell you I heard a chef from that hotel in Waterford on the radio?" he says. "You know, the one we're always saying we must go to. He was launching a new tasting menu. It sounded amazing. I was salivating just listening to him."

"It's Michelin-starred, isn't it?"

"Yes. Why don't you book it for a weekend early next month? We could do with having some me-and-you time."

"That'd be brilliant. I'll give them a ring tomorrow." She beams at him, distracted from the subject of teaching. Some much-needed time for her and Thomas would be wonderful. "We'll have to get dressed up."

Thomas takes their plates to the kitchen countertop, leaving them next to the dishwasher. Carla puts the crackers back in their box and stands to put the cheeses in the fridge.

"You should buy yourself some new dresses. Spoil yourself." He grins as she turns from the fridge, taking her hands and pulling her close, kissing her. "In fact, you should buy yourself a treat."

Lifting her eyes to his, she says, "What do you mean, a treat?"

"Some sexy underwear maybe, something we can both enjoy." He kisses her again before pulling away. "I'm going to put the news on, are you coming in?"

"Yes, I'll follow you in. I'll just clean up first."

Carla tries to push the teaching out of her mind as she tidies up. He's only looking out for what's best for our family. He's probably right, it would be stressful, rushing to drop the kids off and be back again. And, with her extra workload, the kids might not be able to take part in all of their activities. It might be best to leave the teaching for a few years. Maybe when the boys are in secondary school.

27

"Well, that's me all packed." Dawn pulls her suitcase into the kitchen.

Brad looks downcast. "Honey, I don't feel comfortable with you flying home to your mum, knowing how she treats you." He carries the coffee pot out onto the deck and Dawn follows him. "I know you want to tell her yourself about moving out, but maybe if I speak to her she'll know I know, and she'll back off."

"No, Dad. That could make things worse. I'm on the lookout for a rental house with the girls. I'll wait until I'm sorted with that before I tell her. I'll have somewhere to go then. Say it and go."

"Are you sure, sweetie?"

Dawn reaches for the sugar. She isn't sure at all but if her mum knows that she's been talking about her to her dad, she'll make her life hell. She can't say anything until everything is in place. "Yes. It'll be better coming from me."

"Remember that I can be on the next flight if you need me." Brad smiles across at her as she sips her coffee. "In fact, Maria and I were talking – she's never been to Ireland. We were thinking of visiting in the fall. Would you care to show her the sights?"

Dawn puts her cup down. "I'd love that. Galway is gorgeous in autumn."

"I remember." Their eyes meet. "Everything's going to be okay, honey. I'm so glad we've had this time together."

"Me too."

Dawn begins to nibble the skin around her thumbnail before realising what's she's doing and stopping herself. It's not as easy to stop the knot forming in the pit of her stomach though, as she stares at the mountains in the distance. All she can do is hope that her scheme works. That she can escape her mum.

28

Emily's phone pings just as she's saying goodbye to Carla at the school gates. The preview flashes across the top of the screen.

I need to see you. Can we meet? X

Emily pushes the phone into her pocket and looks behind her quickly to check where Carla is. She is talking to the chairperson of the parents' association. *Phew!*

Sitting in her car, Emily opens the message from Thomas. No sooner has she opened it than another pops up.

Meet me at the g at 12pm? X

The g? The luxurious five-star hotel in Galway city? Staring at the kisses, she is startled by rapping on her window and drops her phone into her lap. Looking up, she sees Carla grinning at her. Emily puts the key into the ignition and lowers the window, tucking her hair behind an ear.

"You'll never believe this. She only wants to go and ask every teacher to take turns manning stalls. As if they all will, and wait until you hear this, she wants to put it in writing from the parents' association."

"What*? Er*, right, does she? She's crazy, she can't expect all the teachers to be able to give up their free time." Emily glances down to her knees, pushing the phone between them.

"Exactly what I said. And, well, she didn't like me saying that."

Emily's phone pings again and she jumps in shock.

"Are you okay, Em? You nearly jumped out of your skin then."

"Oh, it's just the phone." Emily smiles. "Ignore her. Once she puts it to the whole PA, it'll get dismissed."

"Yeah, I suppose. She just rubs me up the wrong way. Who's texting you anyway, some hot hunk from your dating app?"

"I wish. My mum nagging me to bring the kids for a visit no doubt."

"Right, well, I better go, I've got Pilates in half an hour. See you later," Carla says.

Emily starts the engine straight away, driving out of the school car park and home, not picking up her phone until she pulls the handbrake up in her driveway.

Does that suit, Em? X

Her fingers hover over the keypad. The tingling spreads across her body, remembering his touch in the pantry.

Yes okay. See you there.

She sends it before she can change her mind.

Three hours later, she parks in the underground car park and takes the lift up to the hotel. She adjusts her lilac flowered summer dress under her white bolero, and checks her lipstick in the mirrored wall of the lift. Stepping out of the lift, she nods to the receptionist, passes the huge tropical fish tank, and walks along the soft pink carpet runner that links the three lounges, looking for Thomas.

Reaching the gentleman's lounge with the cocktail bar, there's no sign of him. She glances at her phone; no text. She is a little late herself so she expected him to be here by now. Should she wait at the bar? Twisting her ring around her finger with her thumb, she looks around. Maybe he's waiting in Gigi's restaurant beyond the bar; it is a more private setting.

She walks towards the entrance, tucking her hair behind her ear, and greets the maitre d'.

"Hello. Reservation for Thomas O'Reilly?"

She watches as his finger runs down the list of reservations and wonders if he can hear her heart pounding. She adjusts her dress again with one hand and holds her clutch bag tightly to her chest.

"I don't see a reservation here for Mr O'Reilly, madam."

"Oh, okay." She glances around her. "I'll wait for him in the lounge." Turning quickly, she walks back the way she came.

On reaching the first lounge, she makes her way over to the window and sinks down into a plush red-velvet chair. Thomas is never late for anything; it's a pet hate of his. Has he stood her up?

"Can I get you a drink, madam?" A waiter appears beside her.

"Not yet. I'm waiting for a friend,'" she says at the same time as her phone beeps in her bag.

Are you here yet? X

Yes. I'm in the velvet lounge.

I'm in Room 203. There's a key card at reception for you x

A room. He has booked a room.

Emily stares at her phone. A room. Looking out of the window, she watches a swan glide on Lough Atalia. From the reeds at the edge, another emerges and meets its mate. A room. Of course, she allows a smile, they have to be careful. She puts her phone back in her bag and makes her way to reception.

As soon as the lift doors close, she tucks her bag under her arm, closes her eyes and takes a calming breath, before clasping her hands together tightly. She is about to adjust her dress again when the doors open on level one and a member of staff steps in, nodding politely at her.

The lift arrives at the second floor and Emily steps out. Her knees feel weak and her hands are shaking yet tingly at the same time. Slowing her step, she wiggles her fingers, stretching and closing them. She reaches Room 203 more quickly than she's prepared for. Taking a deep breath, she steadies her hand on the handle, puts the key card in, and pushes in the door.

There he is, sitting in the chair by the window. He folds his newspaper and stands, running his fingers through his hair, pushing it back over his forehead. He grins at her, his dark eyes meeting hers.

"Hey, you." He moves towards her.

"Hi," she says in barely a whisper as the full enormity of her nerves renders her unable to move forward.

Reaching her, he puts his hands on her cheeks. "You took your time." He smiles, kissing her softly and gently.

Dropping her bag onto the sideboard, she kisses him back hungrily, knowing that with the urgency of their kisses, the afternoon tea sitting on the side table will not be eaten. Thomas pushes the bolero over her shoulders and down her arms, dropping it onto a chair as he manoeuvres her closer to the bed.

29

Taking the ham and cheese out of the fridge, Dawn taps the kettle on. She needs caffeine. Her body doesn't know if it's morning or afternoon since she returned from New York two days ago.

Uncle Michael arrived from Australia yesterday. Her mum collected him from the airport, then they'd done their usual and driven straight for a Supermac's. Dawn used to laugh at this when she was younger. Collecting him from Dublin airport and not stopping until they had crossed the River Shannon. Only then stopping for a Supermac's, when they were back on Galway soil. Dawn used finishing an essay for college as an excuse not to go with Amanda. She couldn't remember the last time she'd gone to collect Uncle Michael. The thought of spending hours in the car together on the way to the airport was too much.

"Anyone want coffee?" she asks Michael and Amanda, who are sitting in the living area.

"Not for me, thanks. I had some with brekky," Michael says.

Amanda doesn't answer. Dawn glances over. Her mother is perched on the edge of the armchair seat, twiddling her thumbs and looking at Michael, her face pale and blank. It's as if she hasn't heard Dawn speak.

Dawn layers ham and cheese on the bread in the toastie machine. Mum has been moodier than usual since Dawn returned from the

States. At first, she'd asked about the trip, then the snide comments had slipped in, making derogatory remarks about Brad and his lack of involvement in parenting. Dawn didn't want her mum to put any kind of damper on her trip, especially after everything she'd learnt while she was over there. So, she'd kept her answers neutral, non-descriptive, and focused hard on not rising to the taunts or put-downs. It was tough and she'd had to bite her lip on more than one occasion.

What was even stranger was that her mum didn't seem as excited as usual about Michael being here. Normally, she would have been planning day trips and meals with her brother but Dawn keeps coming across her sitting at the kitchen table, staring into space. At first, Dawn thought it was directed at her. Did she somehow know what she and her dad had been talking about in New York? Did she know that she had found the pregnancy bumps?

The kettle boils and Dawn makes coffee while trying to zone in on what Michael is saying to her mum.

"I just reckon it might help to give us some clarity."

"Michael, I've already told you. Aunt Mary doesn't know what day it is half the time, she's not going to remember all those years ago."

"Sometimes they live in the past. She might remember clear as day thirty years ago but not yesterday."

"Well, if she does, she's going to get the fright of her life seeing you – she'll think you're Dad."

"I'm not that like him."

"You're like him enough to give her a fright." Amanda stands and turns to the mantelpiece. She rearranges the candles and peels off the dried wax dripping down the sides, her back to Michael. "I'm not going. There's no point going over it all. The past is the past."

"It's our past though, Amanda, it's important. I want to know the truth, *don't you?*" Michael's voice has become louder.

"No, it won't change anything now," Amanda says, turning around to face him. She glances towards the kitchen area at Dawn hovering next to the kettle. "I'm not going. And neither should you. Leave the poor old lady alone." She marches past Michael and comes into the kitchen area. "Are you keeping an eye on that sandwich or just snooping?" she snaps at Dawn.

Turning to the toastie machine, Dawn quickly lifts the sandwich out, the bubbling cheese dripping out of the side and over her fingers. "*Ouch!*" She drops the sandwich onto the plate and puts her two fingers into her mouth.

"Serves you right for being nosey," Amanda says quietly, taking the bag out of the pedestal bin.

Michael stands up and hitches up his navy chinos, tucking in the back of his maroon checked shirt. "Right, I'm going to head into town. I'll probably call into Barry on the way home so don't count me in for dinner. I'd say we'll go for a few pints."

Taking her sandwich and coffee to her room, Dawn makes herself scarce. She is far too jetlagged to trust herself not to react to any more snide comments.

On her return from the college library that evening, Dawn closes the front door and smells spaghetti bolognese. Yawning as she kicks off her shoes, she leaves her bag and college books on the stairs and goes into the kitchen. She just wants to eat and fall into bed, and hopefully not wake up in the middle of the night on American time.

Her mum is washing up, clattering pans and cutlery. "Your dinner's on the countertop," she says without turning around.

"Thanks. Have you already eaten?"

"Yes."

No explanation is offered as to why she didn't wait for Dawn. No

'How was your day?' or 'Was the library busy?' chat was forthcoming either. She checks her watch; she isn't late home. This is the time she was expected. Mum must be still annoyed with Michael.

Putting her plate in the microwave, she asks, "Are you going out tonight?"

"No."

Right, okay, Dawn thinks, so that's the kind of mood she's in. That's fine.

She is too tired to care. Taking a glass of orange squash, she sits at the table with her dinner. She has taken maybe four or five mouthfuls when her mum slaps an envelope down in front of her.

"Are you going to explain this?" she demands.

"What is it?"

Turning the envelope over she sees her name on it. She pulls out the official-looking paper and sees the bank logo at the top of the page. Her eyes narrow. *Shit!* She never thought about bank statements coming to the house when she opened the savings account a few months ago.

"You never told me you'd opened a bank account. I thought your wages were paid into the Credit Union account we opened together."

"Why have you opened my bank statement?" Dawn asks.

"I have a right to know what my daughter is doing with her money, make sure she isn't frittering it away." Amanda stands with her hands on her hips.

"No, you don't. I'm over eighteen. I'm pretty sure that it's against the law for you to open my post."

"I'm your mother, Dawn, I have every right. And it's a good job I did. Why do you have a second bank account? And who made that large donation?"

Dawn pushes her plate away and takes a gulp of her squash before answering, hoping the drink will cool her mounting anger.

"It's my bank account, my finances are private. I don't go nosing around your private bank statements."

"Of course you don't, you're only a child. I am your mother. I need to keep an eye on you."

"I'm almost twenty. That money is my savings to rent a student house," she says quietly, watching as her mum's face at first pales and then her eyebrows curl over in a frown.

"How have you got this money? Have you been prostituting yourself, have you got a Sugar Daddy? Is that how you're thinking of financing your move? You are not moving out, you know, we've already discussed this."

Standing up, Dawn pushes back from the table, planting her hands on either side of her placemat so that her mum can't see them shaking. Her voice wavers at first. "*How dare you say that?* The money, not that it is any of your business, is the money I've saved from working in the restaurant, tips I've banked, and money that Dad gave me to pay for my accommodation because *I am* moving out!"

For a brief second her mother is silenced, flabbergasted by Dawn's outburst. "Well, of course you don't have a Sugar Daddy – who'd want you?"

Dawn doesn't react. Amanda continues. "And, Brad giving you money, buying his way into your affections. How lovely when he's played no part in raising you. And now he shows up to steal you from me, to turn you against me."

"He isn't turning me against you, he just understands that I'm not a child anymore. I have to be allowed to live my life." As soon as the words are out of her mouth, she regrets them – she should have kept quiet.

Her mother's eyes draw inwards, her lips purse, venom ready to be spat out.

"I've raised you single-handedly and a simple donation from him is enough to turn you against me. You can't leave. You can't move out. *No way!*" Her eyes are now white with anger.

Stepping forward, she grabs Dawn's arms. Squeezing them tightly, she begins to shake her. Dawn tries to wriggle free but her mum is holding her tight.

"*You can't leave! You can't leave me!*" she screams into Dawn's face.

Wriggling harder to break free, Dawn steps back, trying to push her arms against her mum's. Amanda lets go and retreats to the other side of the kitchen, leaning against the countertop. She hasn't finished, Dawn knows that, but she doesn't have any intention of hanging around for more assaults and insults.

Grabbing her bank statement, she storms up to her bedroom.

With tears dripping down her face, she sits on the window seat overlooking the back garden, watching the birds chittering and chattering, flittering from the bird box to the fence, down to the ground, and back up to the bird box. She envies them their freedom.

Mum wasn't always like this, she used to be fun. Dawn remembers the two of them singing at the tops of their voices in the car, going on day trips. She can't remember the last time she heard her mum singing. She lets her mind wander as she watches the birds. Her mum's possessiveness and manipulation seem to have intensified as Dawn's grown up and become more independent. Wiping her tears on the back of her hand, she sighs. Will she ever escape her mother's clutches? Biting her fingernails, she then starts on the skin around them. It tears easily. A piece strips from her thumb and blood oozes. She sucks it; the tangy iron taste assaults her tongue.

She's so annoyed with herself for losing it and yelling back. She should have kept her cool, waited until she had accommodation found before she told her. She definitely shouldn't have let it slip that her dad had given her the money. But, what could she have done? She had been so furious and her mum was throwing insults at her. She still can't believe she opened her bank statement.

Dawn watches as a magpie swoops down from the pergola and frightens two sparrows. They fly back to the safety of the birdhouse. Why is she surprised at her mum? She shouldn't be, not after everything she's found out. Dawn needs to talk to her dad, explain before her mum does. Before she tries to poison him with lies.

She hears the door to the kitchen open, followed by footsteps on the stairs, the second-to-top step creaks, and a key is put into her bedroom door. It turns and clicks. Dawn isn't surprised or angry. No, if she is honest, she'd half expected it. Although it's been a long time since she last did it, it was what her mum did to make her point. Dawn doesn't jump up or hammer on the door, screaming and pleading. No, tonight the wind has changed. Dawn has the means to escape. She just has to plan how. This cycle is never going to end unless she ends it. She has to get out. Besides, she knows she won't be locked in overnight. Her mum always unlocks it eventually before going to bed herself.

Putting on her pyjamas, she snuggles down into bed, pulling the covers up over her shoulders, and rubs her tender arms. Closing her eyes, her mind is racing. How is she going to escape?

30

Tracing a finger around Emily's nipple, Thomas looks deeply into her brown eyes. "You are so perfect, just delicious."

Emily cups his cheeks with her hands and leans in to kiss him. Her phone's alarm beeps loudly. "*Errgghh*. I've got to go. Office appointment in half an hour."

She rolls over and out of the bed. Thomas puts her pillow on top of his and shuffles up the bed, watching her get dressed. "Don't put them away. Leave them with me!" he groans as she fastens her black lacy bra.

She laughs and slips her arms into her navy silk blouse. They've met up a few times now, usually in show houses Emily can get the keys for, but in the odd hotel too.

"Can I ask you something?" he says. "Did you really have no inkling about Chris being gay?"

"What?"

"Just, I mean, were there ever any doubts? I know Carla was gobsmacked when she saw Chris with that guy – but you were married to him – did you see any gay tendencies? Looking back on it."

"No. I was completely blindsided. I'd no idea at all." Sitting on the bed, she pulls on a pop sock and then stops. "Wait, what did you say?" Slowly she turned around to him. "What do you mean? Carla saw Chris?"

Thomas shifts uncomfortably on the bed and runs his hands through his hair. "You know, with the guy he went off with? I mean, seeing them together was shocking. Sorry, I shouldn't have mentioned it. I'm sure it still grates, even after all this time."

Standing up, Emily slips on her kitten heels and takes her jacket from the back of the chair. "God, no, I'm well over Chris."

Thomas gets up and retrieves his boxer shorts from the floor. He walks over, pulls her close, and kisses her gently.

Emily doesn't feel his lips on hers. Her mind is racing. Carla saw Chris with a guy, and was gobsmacked – and didn't tell her? Pushing him away, she says, "I've got to go. I'm late. Text me soon."

The lift pings as she approaches but she ignores it and takes the stairs; her pulse is pounding in her eardrums, she can't stand still, she has to keep moving. *Did Carla know? What the fuck?* Pushing open the door to the reception area of the hotel, she walks straight across the foyer without checking left and right. It doesn't matter if anyone spots her. She is a single woman; she can be in a hotel with a man if she wants to.

How fast Thomas's words came out, after she asked him, niggles her. Emily can't think straight. It's only when she reaches her car that she allows herself to exhale. Fastening her seatbelt, she reapplies her lipstick in the rear-view mirror. Her heart calms. She has overreacted. Carla must have seen Chris after he told her. There is no way that Carla would have seen him and not told her.

Driving back to the office, Thomas's sudden change of expression keeps flashing across her mind and now that she thinks about it, there was that funny look Carla gave Thomas at the birthday party. Was that connected? Did Carla know about Chris before she did?

Filling the dishwasher that evening after she's tucked the kids into bed, it's still hovering in Emily's mind. She racks her brains to remember

Carla's reaction to their marriage break-up. Emily had been in a complete fog of disbelief and devastation and Carla had been a rock to her. She'd been sure Carla was just as shocked as she was.

Opening the fridge, she pours herself a glass of white wine, grabs a sharing bag of salt-and-vinegar crisps, and takes them into the living room. She definitely misunderstood; Carla must have spotted Chris *after* he'd told her. If Carla had seen Chris with a man, then she would have told her straight away, of course she would have.

Surely your best friend knowing and not saying is betrayal?

She sips her wine, and the cold stings her throat. Betrayal, isn't that what she, herself, is doing? Sleeping with her best friend's husband. And worse, she thinks, falling in love with him.

31

Dawn listens for movement downstairs. Her mum is usually up and about early; she strains her ears but the house is quiet. Sitting up in bed, she rests back against the wall, drawing her knees to her chest. Maybe her mum is still asleep. *Could I escape now, pack a few bags and leave?* No, even if she loosened the battery in the CCTV camera on the front door like she did last time, her mum might wake to the alert on the door sensor. And, if Dawn tries to move out later, her mum will get the door alert while she's at work. She might check the CCTV and be home in minutes. She's done it before when Dawn's shift at the restaurant finished early and when a lecture was cancelled last semester.

If she was to collect some things up and pack a bag, what would she take? She'd need her laptop and some clothes. Her college bag sitting against her desk is way too small. She'd have to pack as much as she could. Dawn is in no doubt that, if she did leave, her mum would make a drama out of the belongings left behind. There might be no coming back. She needs to plan and be organised.

Dawn tries to think of solutions while she showers. She could pack a few things every day, take them with her when she goes to the college library, leave them in a locker. Nothing too noticeable. The small bag wouldn't raise suspicion surely. Even if she has to make a hundred runs like this she's determined. She has to escape her mum's control.

She notices two hoodies hanging on the back of the bathroom door as she dries herself. Let's start with these, she thinks, bringing them into her bedroom, tightly rolling them, and pushing them into the base of her bag. She adds some underwear and T-shirts, squashing them all down.

Small amounts like this aren't going to be noticeable even if her mum was to have a nosy around her bedroom. Going back into the ensuite, she brushes her teeth, takes out an old make-up bag from the cabinet above the sink and starts adding in things she has double of or can do without. Mascara, lip gloss, eyeliner, Tampax, cleanser – she didn't realise she had accumulated so much stuff. In the bottom of her make-up bag are a box of tablets. She inspects the packet. Sleeping tablets. Her mum had given them to her last year in the run-up to her exams when she was stressed and not sleeping well. Dawn had been so wary of sleeping through the exams that she hadn't used them at all. Instead, she used some meditation guidance her friend Ruth gave her – it helped with her anxiety too.

Looking at this packet, she can't stop the idea that comes to her. Could these help me to escape? Give them to Mum? All I need is an evening to clear things out – a few uninterrupted hours, without the threat of Mum waking up. Sitting on the edge of the bed, she reads the back of the box. **Take two tablets with water twenty minutes before bed.** Would this be enough to keep Mum out of the way? She' has no idea how quickly they work, or how drowsy they make you. Should she up the dose a bit, just to be sure? And how would she get her to take them?

A door clicks shut and she quickly pushes the tablets under her quilt. Hearing her mum going downstairs, she exhales, realising that she can't plan this now. She has to think this through carefully. She might only get one chance to do this. It has to work.

She dresses in her work uniform of black trousers and a black T-shirt, and adds a few more things to her bag. She rolls up leggings with the box of tablets inside and pushes them down the side of the bag to the bottom. She places two heavy college library books, her apron, notepad, and name badge for the restaurant at the top. Before going downstairs, she stands in front of the mirror and whispers to herself. "This could work."

She goes into the kitchen, having left her bag in the hallway near the front door, wary of what the atmosphere will be like after last night's argument.

"Morning, Mum," she says pleasantly, going straight to the breadbin and putting two slices into the toaster.

"Morning, my love. Is it half-past ten that you're starting today?"

"Yes. We have a big group coming in for brunch. I'll go straight to the college library after the lunch shift so no need to count me in for dinner. I'll eat at the restaurant."

It is as if last night's row never happened, but then it's always like that, she thinks as the toast pops. Squeezing honey onto the slices, she cuts them in half. It doesn't mean it won't happen again.

"Do you want a top-up?" Dawn asks, pouring hot water into her mug. She's trying so hard to behave normally that she's sure her mum will notice something different about her.

"No, thanks." Amanda stands up, taking her cycle helmet from the back of the chair. "I'm going to cycle to work so I'd better get going. Can you put your rota for next week on the fridge, and WhatsApp it to me? I don't seem to have it yet."

"Okay. Will do."

Amanda goes into the hallway and Dawn hears her pause in front of the mirror. She holds her breath. Keep going, she urges her, don't notice the bag. *Please.* Dawn perches on the edge of her chair, a knot slowly tightening in her stomach as she pulls apart her toast. The front door opens and closes. Dawn exhales. *Phew!* Thank God.

Familiar insecurities sneak into her mind as she walks to the bus stop and she begins to doubt herself. Is using sleeping tablets a bit extreme? Could there be another way? But she has to get out, otherwise she is going to be suffocated. Seeing the bus trundling along the road towards her, she takes out her bus pass.

Settling herself into a seat halfway down the aisle, she connects her headphones. She needs to make a decision but is she brave enough?

The bus stops for passengers on High Street. It always waits here for about five minutes. Dawn's stop is next. In theory, she could get off here, it's only a ten-minute walk to the restaurant, but she likes to people-watch from this vantage point. She watches a lady push a buggy. The infant is trying to take his socks off. A little girl is close by but she has stopped walking. The lady turns back and speaks to the child. Dawn watches as the little girl's face slowly contorts into a cross expression. She's standing her ground and refusing to walk any further. The mother reverses the buggy until she is in line with the little girl, then crouches down to her level. Dawn sees the change in the girl's face and the relaxation of her frown. The girl takes her mother's offered hand and together they walk on.

Dawn turns her attention to a young teenager and her mother emerging from a clothes shop. By the look of their bags, they've been to a few more. They are laughing as they walk. Resting her head back against the seat, Dawn knows she will never have that kind of relationship with her mum, no matter how much she craves it. Slipping her a few sleeping tablets so she can move out of the house is a good option. It might even work to both of their advantages. Her mum might change her ways and the distance between them might serve as a start to rebuilding their relationship.

Starting the engine, the bus driver closes the doors and drives around the square in the direction of the restaurant.

She reaches out and presses the bell for her stop. She needs to experiment. She'll add a few tablets into her mum's dinner sometime soon and watch how they affect her, how quickly she falls asleep, how long she stays asleep.

32

"Hi, Amanda!"

Amanda looks up from behind the library counter to see one of the story-time mothers arriving early, two young children in tow. "Hello there, and how are Sarah and Matthew today?" She walks around the counter and perches on the other side.

"They were nagging me all morning 'Is it time to go yet?' They love it."

"That's great. Well, I'm delighted you're here too." Amanda smiles at the children. "Are these the books you're returning?" She nods at Matthew who's holding the books. "I'll check them in and then you'll be able to pick some new ones."

Matthew gives her the books and Sarah grabs him by the hand and leads him to the children's section.

"Thanks for the recommendations. They loved *The Monkey with the Bright Blue Bottom*. I had to read every single night," the mother says, reaching into her pocket and taking out her vape before realising where she is and putting it back.

"That's brilliant. It's great to be settling them with a story before bedtime. It relaxes them." Amanda zaps the barcodes on the books before putting them on the trolley. "And, it's nice to snuggle up with them too."

Looking up, she sees little Sarah sitting down at one of the children's tables and reaching for a colouring page. “Let me get Sarah the crayons. She goes straight for the colouring every time, doesn’t she?”

“She does, yeah. I should get them some but, to be honest, I’d be scared they’d draw all over the house. I’d be in trouble with the council then.” The mother laughs. “I bought them some of that playdoh stuff once and, God above, it got everywhere, and all the colours were mixed up until they were dirty-looking. I swear, I threw the whole lot out the same day.”

Amanda crouches down next to the girl, putting the crayons on the little table. “Here you go, let me know if you need another page and, remember, we only do our colouring when we’re sitting at the table. No wandering about with the colours.”

Matthew comes over to Amanda. “Can you read this one?” He thrusts a book into Amanda’s hands.

“I’m just going to set things up for everyone arriving for story-time, but I can read this one first when we’re ready to start if you like,” Amanda says gently and Matthew beams back at her.

Glancing at the mother, she sees she has her back turned to the children and is scrolling through her phone. Amanda spreads out the little chairs and giant beanbags in a semicircle. She loves doing story-time. It’s the children’s enthusiasm that spurs her on, and their dependence on her to give them half an hour of dedicated time. Something a lot of children in the Westside area don’t get at home. Amanda, along with the rest of the staff, run story-time, and offer extra assistance to the parents, trying to support literacy from a young age. Even something small, like with this family, encouraging a parent to read a bedtime story, or giving the children the space and materials to colour or do some craft is very much needed in this area. She’s worked hard with her colleagues to set up this support system and she enjoys feeling needed.

Looking up, she sees her colleague coming back from lunch. He smiles, holding up a brown-paper bag. "I got you a salad pot. I know you said you were fine," he holds his other hand up to protest, "but I can't let you starve, can I? I'll put it in the back."

"Thank you." She smiles back at him.

She'd been so disappointed when Thomas cancelled their lunch yet again that her appetite had disappeared. She reaches for some picture books, and thumbs through a couple, trying to recall his physical reaction last week when she'd mentioned introducing him to Michael and Dawn.

They'd been in bed in the House Hotel, which was becoming a regular of theirs even though Thomas usually liked to meet out of the city – in hotels you'd never even know existed. She'd been telling him about Michael's visit and what they've been up to, when she just came out with it.

"Why don't I introduce you to him? I think the two of you would really hit it off. And Dawn too. My daughter. It would be lovely to introduce you."

He hadn't even hesitated, of that she'd been sure, but smiled, kissed her on the forehead, and said, "Yes, I'd love to meet your people."

She'd been convinced by his words, but had she been so carried away with this 'next stage' of their relationship that she'd missed something? That behind his polite words, he didn't want to meet them, didn't want to move to that stage? The last thing she'd wanted to do was put him under pressure. The thing that she likes about their relationship is that there's no pressure. They both enjoy each other's company and she's confident that, in time, they will have more.

Amanda selects two picture books, *A Squash and a Squeeze*, and *Mog and Bunny*, and takes them over to the counter for a moment while she waits for other parents and children to arrive. She watches little Sarah concentrating on her colouring and lets her mind drift. Dawn loved arts and crafts when she was younger. The tight fear of losing Dawn had become so much more real last night.

She'd been surprised by her daughter's headstrong reaction when she confronted her with the bank statement. As for Dawn moving out so soon, she can't allow it. But, how can she stop her? Dawn is an adult now, plus she obviously has the funds. She is going to have to up her game, she thinks, putting a smile on her face as she greets more parents. She is going to have to pull on Dawn's heartstrings. Surely her daughter has to see how cruel it would be to abandon her mother?

33

"Just the person we need to speak to," Julia, one of the PA mums, says as Carla approaches the school gates. "We were wondering if all the raffle tickets have been collected yet."

"I don't know." Carla glances at the schoolyard. No sign of any children coming out yet. "I know plenty have been sent back in, but I can't remember off the top of my head who's responsible for collecting them and counting what monies they've raised."

"It isn't any of us." Julia looks at the two other women with her.

"Hang on, I can check." Carla takes out her phone, scrolling through her documents until she finds the jobs list. "Oh, it's Emily actually."

"That's who I thought it was and, well, to be honest, we haven't seen much of her, either at the meetings or the school gates lately."

Carla can imagine what kind of sarcastic comment Emily would have in reply, if she was here in person, and she allows herself a little smile. Looking at the three expectant faces, she says, "I'll chase it up with her. I know she's been very busy with work lately so they may have escaped her mind."

"We all have busy lives, Carla, but we're managing to stay on top of the jobs for this event."

Yes, but you aren't trying to work a job and raise two children alone, are you, she wants to snap. Instead, she says, "I can call into the school office and check."

Carla examines her shellac-painted nails; one of her thumbnails has chipped. Using her fingernail, she gently teases the shellac off, deciding not to bother Emily with the raffle ticket job. She'll talk directly to the school secretary tomorrow morning and find out where any tickets are outstanding. She can total up the money in the afternoon. Emily has enough on her plate. She tunes back into the women's chatter which has moved on to Julia's divorced brother.

"It sounds like a cattle market on those dating apps. He says it's awful and so, so fake. He'd much rather meet someone naturally you know, like in a pub or at a party, but how does that happen at our age?"

The bell shrills, signalling the end of school.

Carla has to stop herself from saying how tough Emily's finding it too. The instant noise of two hundred children all exiting school at the same time bursts into the silence. Chatter, laughter, and shouts float over the children as they swarm out and across the schoolyard. Carla spots Ben coming across the schoolyard towards her, and Daniel a couple of steps behind, deep in conversation with a friend. Maybe Julia could introduce her brother to Emily – Carla could mention it to her. In fact, she should invite Emily around next Friday – her kids will be at their dad's, and Thomas is going out for a client dinner. They could get a takeaway. It's been ages since they had a proper catch-up.

34

Dawn cracks the eggs and drops them into the poaching pods. "Mum will have the granary bread," she says to Michael. "She doesn't eat white."

"Okay," Michael says. "I'll wait until the eggs are nearly done. I don't imagine Amanda will be too long in the shower. I can't believe she ran ten kilometres already, and I'm only after getting out of bed!"

"I know – she makes me feel so lazy sometimes." Dawn reaches for the salt and pepper.

"Don't forget the honey." Michael smiles at her.

"Honey on poached eggs?" She raises her eyebrows at him, tilting her head.

"For sure. I reckon it should be always served with eggs, especially for brekky."

"Weirdo!" She laughs, reaching for the honey. "Who has honey with poached eggs? Is this a random thing Australians eat?"

"Not that I know of. I think it's just my random thing." He puts the bread into the toaster. "So, how's the college course going?"

"First year's been interesting but tough going. I just hope I pass the exams."

"I'm sure you will. Your mum told me about your first semester results – they were super."

"Did she? That's not what she said to me at the time." Dawn turns away.

"What do you mean? She seemed delighted."

Dawn nudges the eggs to see if they're firm. "She said with those results it was unlikely I'd get through the four years."

"Ah, she was probably just saying that to make sure you didn't take your foot off the pedal. She used to be like that with me when I was studying medicine – always pushing me to work harder. It used to drive me crazy but, looking back, she was just mothering me, encouraging me onwards."

"Was your Aunt Mary like that too?"

"No, Amanda was more of a mother to me after the fire. Don't get me wrong, Mary and Seán were very kind to both of us, but they didn't have any children of their own, you see, so they didn't really have any experience. We were shipped off to boarding school quite quickly." The toast pops and Michael slides them into the toast stand.

"That must have been difficult, so soon after losing your parents."

"I suppose it was. But the busy routine provided a distraction. Once I settled, I really enjoyed it. Sure, some of the people I met there I'm still friends with today."

"I never really hear mum talking about her time at boarding school." Dawn spoons the eggs out of their pouches and put them in a dish on the table.

"I don't think she really liked it. Everything after the fire was very tough for her. I mean, she was a hero; she saved my life. Battling the flames to get to my room and then get us out of the house. We had to climb out of her bedroom window and onto the flat roof and then drop down to the garden. The smoke, the heat, it was so intense. She was so brave. But I think she struggled with survivor's guilt. That's why I want to visit Aunt Mary, to try and find out more about the fire. Make Amanda realise there was nothing more she could have done." Michael pulls out a chair and sits down, reaching for the butter.

"I don't think Aunt Mary is very present these days."

"Who's not present?" her mum says, coming into the kitchen, her curls hanging damp on her shoulders.

"You are present now, my dear sister, and breakfast is served. Would you like honey with your eggs?"

"*Ergh!*" Dawn laughs, reaching for a slice of toast as they sit down.

"So, do you think you'll move out for college next year?" Michael looks across the table at Dawn.

"I'd like to –" Dawn begins.

"She'll live at home," her mother says. "She can't go abandoning her mum now, can she?"

Dawn's hair falls in front of her as her eyes drop to her toast. She butters it in silence and wonders if Michael ever felt suffocated by his sister. Did she try to control everything then too? Knowing what she knows from her dad, Dawn thinks it's quite likely.

"Maybe you'll get the chance in your third year," he says.

"Accommodation is very expensive," Amanda says, passing the milk jug to Michael.

"I have some money saved and Dad said he'd –"

"So, what do you fancy doing today, Michael?" Amanda says, talking over her. "I've the whole day off and the sun is definitely thinking of shining for us. How about the Flaggy Shore?"

Dawn keeps her eyes focused on her breakfast. She hears Michael exhale loudly.

"The weatherman wasn't so sure," he says. "I'm meeting some of the lads from boarding school tonight in Dublin so I'll need to leave late arvo, around four o'clock. I'm going to stay at Joseph's – he's just moved into what is apparently a fabulous new house near St Stephen's Green."

"Thanks for telling me! I've got fish in for dinner. I was planning on making that fish pie you loved as a child." Amanda puts her knife and fork together noisily on her plate.

"I thought I'd mentioned Dublin to you when we were talking dates in our emails before I came over." He reaches for the pepper pot, lining it up neatly next to the salt.

Dawn stands to clear the table and Michael follows suit. There is an awkward silence as they tiptoe around each other tidying up. Dawn knows she'll be the one having to put up with her mum's annoyance later.

"Are you going to join us for the walk, Dawn?" Michael asks.

"No, I have an assignment due on Monday. I need to finish doing the references for it. Enjoy the walk, and Dublin. I hope Joseph has some honey in!" She smiles at him.

35

The first thought that comes to Emily that morning is '*I need to know*', as she lies in bed listening to Rosie and Theo chatter in the next bedroom. Did Carla know Chris was gay and not tell her? The sensible side of her brain tries to tell her it doesn't matter. It's all water under the bridge now.

"Mum, can we have pancakes for breakfast?" Rosie asks as both children come bounding into the room and leap onto her bed.

"Okay. But you have to put your slippers and dressing gowns on first."

"*Yippeee!*" Theo starts bouncing on the bed.

"Theo! Help, Rosie, he's going to squash me!"

Rosie climbs under the covers with her as Theo jumps and lands on both of them.

"Now I have you both trapped and I'm not letting you go until you let us have Nutella on our pancakes!"

"Oh, really?" Emily sneaks an arm out from under the covers. "Well, what if I tickle you?"

Theo rolls off them giggling.

"Come on, you two, let's get some breakfast."

"Are we seeing Ben and Daniel today?" Rosie asks.

"Yes, we'll meet Carla and the boys at the park this morning."

"Can we bring some bread to feed the ducks?"

"Of course." And I can throw a few crumbs to Carla about Chris, and see if she bites, Emily thinks, reaching for her dressing gown.

She is dreading the thought of seeing Carla. She knows she's been avoiding her and it must be becoming noticeable.

"Please, Mummy, it's been ages." Rosie had protested yesterday at the school gate.

"It has been a while, Em." Carla had looked over at her with raised eyebrows. "Why don't we meet up at the park tomorrow morning?"

"God, no, not on a Saturday, Carla, that's your family time. I don't want to intrude on that."

Having to spend time watching Thomas and Carla playing happy families would be excruciating. The birthday party had been bad enough and that was before anything major had happened between herself and Thomas.

"Thomas is playing golf in the morning, so we'll only be looking for entertainment," Carla said.

Carla is there ahead of her, standing at her car boot, her hair tied in a neat French plait. She's wearing bright-blue jeans, a cream jumper, and a sky-blue body warmer. By the look of the bag she's taking out of the boot, she has made a picnic. No doubt it is full of delicious homemade goodies.

Emily looks over to her passenger seat where an eight pack of brioches, a box of Jaffa Cakes and half a loaf of bread sit. Oh, well, at least she has some bread for the ducks; she doubts the ducks will mind shop-bought bread.

Emily isn't thinking of her own betrayal as she parks next to her friend but of the possibility that Carla betrayed her. Had she kept this information to herself all this time? There was only one way to find out. Emily pulls her hair back with a banana clip and tucks the stray strands behind her ear.

She takes a deep breath and swallows, "Okay, kids, watch out for cars as you get out."

"Hiya! It feels like ages. They must be working you too hard." Carla comes over and hugs her at the car. "Thank God we'd this planned for today. The boys have been driving me crazy all morning. They're like little balls of energy bouncing off the walls."

"Well, at least it's dry for now." Emily looks at the grey, muggy sky, knowing how bland and hollow her words sound. "Let's go and feed the ducks first," she says brightly and a little over-enthusiastically to the children.

Out of the corner of her eye, she sees Carla watching her. *Be normal,* Emily urges herself. The kids run on ahead of them, stopping to pick up twigs to play Pooh sticks at the bridge. They follow the path through the woods, passing the entrance to the Fairy Trail, which the kids ignore, racing on ahead. The smell of wild garlic is all around them, the plants scattered on either side of the path. A tall, gangly man runs past with his black Labrador running in front, attached to his owner by his lead fastened to the man's belt.

"Slow down, will you? I didn't realise we were doing a power walk," Carla says.

"Sorry, just automatic."

"Are you okay, Emily?"

"I'm grand. Just had a hectic week." I can't keep anything from this woman, she knows me too well. She's going to see straight through to my betrayal if I am not careful. She slows her pace and swings the half loaf of bread in one hand, and the bag of brioches and Jaffa Cakes in the other. The bread reminds her of her plan to reel Carla in.

"Any news on your Tinder lately?" Carla asks.

"Not really. Just un-datables."

"Julia at school was saying her brother is divorced and doesn't like these dating sites either. Maybe we should set the two of you up on a date."

"Two people aren't going to automatically get together just because they are both divorced and have a dislike of dating apps," Emily says, a little too harshly. "That's like saying two men who are single and gay will get together."

"Okay. Sorry. I just thought you might like him. From what Julia was saying, he sounds like a nice guy."

Emily doesn't respond. She shouldn't have snapped; she knows Carla means well. She's only trying to be nice. Her friend always sees the best in people. Emily knows she has no right to question Carla, not when she herself is betraying her best friend in the worst way possible.

But what did Carla know about Chris? How is she going to broach the subject? She can't say that Thomas let it slip; she has no way to explain that.

"Are all the mums at the school gate talking about me dating again?" She glances over at Carla as they walk alongside each other.

"Not that I've heard of. It's not as if you've been talking about it with them, is it?"

"No, but God, I'd hate to think they're pitying me, gossiping about me dating."

"Not at all, and I obviously didn't say anything to Julia about you going on a date with her brother. It was just my random thought, that's all." Carla links Emily's arm.

Rosie runs back towards them with an almost perfect heart-shaped stone and Emily takes the opportunity to unlink from Carla and admire it. Putting it into her pocket for safekeeping, she watches as Rosie runs ahead to the others.

"Do you think any of the other mums knew Chris was gay?" Emily asks.

Carla hesitates in her step for no more than a millisecond but Emily notices it straight away.

"What do you mean? Why would they?"

"Well, they might have heard rumours or seen him."

"I doubt it, Em. *Ben, wait, don't go too far ahead!*" Carla shouts and picks up her pace.

Emily's face stings like she's been slapped. Carla knew something. Feeling her face redden as the anger rises, she calls out "*Carla, hang on!*"

Catching up, she puts her hand on Carla's shoulder. Carla half turns back to her.

"Did you know about Chris?" Emily stares into Carla's eyes, willing the answer to be no.

Carla looks down at the ground.

"Oh my God!" Emily takes a step back. "You knew!"

Carla lifts her eyes to meet Emily's and they are pooled with tears. Emily's own well up.

"Please tell me you didn't."

"Look, I didn't know, not really. I just saw him. Once."

"What do you mean you saw him? Doing what?" Emily asks slowly, her eyes wide.

Carla looks down again.

"*Answer me, Carla!*" Emily almost hisses.

"He was ..." she hesitates, "he was in your car, your old one. I thought it was you and him so I went over. But it was Chris with a man. I didn't recognise the other man. They were – I don't know – dishevelled." Carla stays staring at the ground.

"*What the fuck?*"

"I wasn't one hundred percent sure of what I saw, and I didn't want to come running to you on a whim. What if I'd misread it?"

"You're my best friend. How could you not tell me?"

"Let's sit down for a minute," Carla says, nodding at a nearby picnic table.

"No. I don't want to sit down. *Why didn't you tell me?*"

Two children come scootering past with their parents following them. Standing to one side of the path, both Emily and Carla avert their eyes.

Looking back at her friend, Emily repeats, "Why didn't you tell me?"

"I was confused. I was trying to make sense of what I saw. Honestly, I didn't sleep for two days worrying about what I'd say to you."

"But you didn't tell me." Turning away, Emily stifles the sobs that are threatening to overcome her, willing herself to hold up the dam. She takes a deep breath and spins back around, glaring.

Carla steps backward.

"I can't believe you didn't tell me straight away. You're supposed to be my best friend."

"Emily, please, hear me out. He told you before I had a chance. Maybe he was always planning on telling you or maybe me seeing him made him tell you. I don't know. I really don't." She takes a deep breath. "You came to me devastated, and it just wasn't important to tell you then."

Taking a tissue from the pocket of her light jacket, Emily wipes her eyes and sniffs. "How can I believe you? Did you challenge him when you saw him?"

"No … I … I … I didn't know what to do. He said he was dropping a friend off and …"

"God, I can't do this. I have to go. Drop the kids to mine later, will you?" She thrusts the bread bag into Carla's hands and turns to walk away.

"*Em, don't go! Please don't walk away!*"

Emily increases her pace. The vein at her temple throbs as she mutters to herself all the way back to her car, not caring what a mess she looks with her tear-stained mascara-streaked face.

She tosses the brioches and biscuits onto the passenger seat, and slumps into her seat, letting out a vent of noise, thumping the steering wheel with both hands. She has worked so hard to heal herself over the last couple of years yet now she feels thrust back into the vortex of pain.

The rain starts plinking on her windscreen as she starts the engine and drives out of the carpark.

36

Stepping out of the car, the wind takes her breath and Amanda instantly regrets not bringing a hat. She zips her coat up to her chin. This is not the weather she'd expected for Michael's visit. It's May, for God's sake, and she'd hoped for some sunshine.

The horizon is dull and grey, the Burren hills are hidden by low clouds and a fine mist lurks around them, dampness without the rain. She ties her bushy curls back with a scrunchie, knowing that the wind will no doubt free them soon enough.

Fresh air is good for you, she'd reiterated to Michael this morning, when he'd hesitated about the forecasted weather. That was before he'd taken Dawn's side about moving out. He'd said 'maybe next year'. He hadn't even thought before opening his mouth. What about her? What would she do if Dawn moved out? She'd be all alone. Michael won't be thinking of that when he's back on the other side of the world with his family. It'll be just her sitting on her own in the house, waiting for Dawn or Thomas to visit her.

She'd insisted on the walk, playing the favourite-family-walks card like she used to do during their holidays from boarding school. Pretending it was what they did with their parents. She would pack a picnic and they'd get the bus out from Galway. Refusing their Aunt Mary and Uncle Seán's offers to drive them and accompany them. Amanda always wanted it to be just her and Michael. He'd no interest in walks of any sort unless it was on a computer game to get to a battlefield, but he would go with her the moment she mentioned their parents.

Now, staring out over the limestone pavement along the Flaggy Shore, seeing the inky grey clouds scudding across the ocean towards them, she can't prevent her irritation from coming to the surface.

"I was surprised you weren't in my corner earlier about Dawn moving out," she says as they walk.

"Don't you think it's important for her to experience living away from home?" Michael says. "Can't you remember when you lived in halls in UCD and how independent you felt? A grown-up at last, freedom away from boarding school."

She turns to him, twisting her hair bobble tighter, tucking strands of her curls into it. "She'll have plenty of time for that when she graduates and gets a job. Let me have these last few years."

"It's difficult to let our kids go but that's our role as parents. Raise them and set them free to find their way in the world."

Amanda walks a few paces ahead, before half-turning back. "It's all right for you to say. If Dawn goes, I have no one else."

"If you let her go, she'll come back to you. Forcing her to stay might make her resent you."

"With all due respect, Michael, your kids are young, you haven't had to deal with the things that I have yet."

"All I'm saying is that it's completely normal for a young person to want to move out. You did it, I did it, we turned out okay."

She stops and stares at him, her icy blue eyes boring into him. "We didn't have parents, Michael. We didn't have people who loved us. Dawn does, there's absolutely no reason for her to move out."

"Maybe for her independence."

Amanda turns her back and stares out to sea, her tiny frame buffeted by the wind. Her breath cloud hovers in the mist in front of her. The drizzle is turning to spotting now. "It's going to pour down, come on," she says, turning and walking on past him.

"Amanda, can we talk about Dad?" Michael says, stepping faster to catch up with her. The sky darkens above them.

"Not now," she says, and the wind takes her voice.

The clouds empty themselves of small sharp hailstones and, bracing herself, she lowers her head and increases her pace, knowing that she's not going to be able to brush his questions aside forever.

After a lunch of sweet potato soup and sandwiches back at the house, they take their coffees into the living area. Amanda looks at her phone; she hasn't heard from Thomas in a few days. They don't usually go too long between meet-ups and texts. She'd asked him straight out again about meeting Michael and Dawn, and this time she'd spotted his unease. She'd brushed off her disappointment and reassured him it wasn't the end of the world if they didn't meet, and she understood. Thomas told her that maybe next time Michael was over, they could meet. So, is he avoiding her now because her brother is over? Because he thinks she'll force the situation? She reaches for her coffee. She'll have to wait patiently. She won't text him; she knows the rules.

Out of the corner of her eye, she sees Michael cradling his coffee mug and staring at the photo on the little table next to the fireplace. The photo of Michael, Amanda, and their parents on a ski trip, the year before the fire. It's such a natural photo, she smiles to herself, their grinning faces, the sun on them, the ski slope in the background.

"Where did you get that photo from?" he asks, nodding at it.

Looking up briefly from her phone, she says, "Don't know, probably from Aunt Mary. We were so happy, weren't we? We look like a family from a magazine shoot, it's just perfect." Her calm words surprise her.

Michael pushes his glasses up his nose and puts his coffee down. "No family is perfect. You've always painted them as perfect parents. They weren't. Can you remember that holiday?"

Amanda opens her mouth to speak, but he continues. "We barely saw our parents all week. They were full of promises about doing things as a family, yet I remember poor Charlotte, the au pair, never got a night off because our parents were so busy partying with their friends."

"That's not true, Michael – we had a great holiday."

"We didn't, we were shunted out of the way. Dressed up and brought to dinner and then sent away afterward as inconveniences. I know you've always tried to relive nice memories of them with me but I don't ever remember being read a bedtime story, playing board games, or going for walks at the sea. I do remember lots of shouting, lots of making up quiet games in our bedrooms because our parents were entertaining downstairs. I remember waiting outside school because they'd forgotten to pick me up. Usually when we were in between au pairs. Did you ever question why we went through so many of them? Can you remember Mum, who always seemed to have a glass of something in her hand no matter what time of day it was, roaring at some poor girl who was probably not much older than Dawn is now?"

"That's nonsense. Mum and Dad worked hard to provide for us. They needed help to mind us, that's all. They left us with enough to go to fancy boarding schools and to put us through college, you through years of medicine. They worked hard for that. For us."

"No, Amanda, you're wrong. Uncle Seán paid for that. Our parents barely had anything left. The house was all they had and it was remortgaged to the hilt," Michael pauses, putting his coffee down. "From the paperwork I saw, the fire could have been started deliberately."

She feels the colour drain from her face and tries desperately to widen her eyes as she looks at him. Words won't come.

"Dad had big money problems, he was a gambler, and not a lucky one," Michael says. "He might have staged the fire to get the house insurance. But it went wrong."

Amanda stands up, feeling the heat rushing to her face. "*That's bullshit!* Dad wouldn't do that. He wouldn't risk our lives for money. And, he died in it, he hardly staged that."

"The signs are there. It might have gone wrong – maybe he'd drunk too much. It wouldn't be the first time."

"*Stop it, just stop it.* You shouldn't speak ill of the dead."

Grabbing their coffee mugs, she crashes them into the kitchen sink, and stands staring out into the garden, shoulders hunched, her hands holding on to the sink to keep them from shaking. She can't look at him, she doesn't trust herself. Willing her breathing to calm, she says nothing. Hearing him move towards her, she turns.

"Amanda, please. I don't want to upset you. I just want to try and get to the truth."

"Enough. I don't want to hear any more." She glares at him until he breaks eye contact. "I'm going to get some milk," she says as she walks past him into the hallway and slams the front door shut behind her.

37

"Emily, can we talk? Let's not leave it like this," Carla says at the door when she drops Emily's kids off later that morning.

"I've nothing else to say to you. Thanks for dropping the kids home." Emily closes the door, ignoring the hurt and shock in Carla's eyes.

All afternoon the anger bubbles away in Emily's gut. It's only when she is sitting on the side of the bath, washing Rosie's hair, that she begins to see sense.

"Mummy, did you and Carla have a fight?" Rosie asks.

"No, lovey, why do you ask that?"

"Well, you just disappeared at the park, and Carla looked sad without you. She didn't even hear Ben when he said he was bursting for the toilet. He had to say it three times and by then he was so desperate he had to go in the bushes."

"I just forgot I had a meeting for work, that's all."

"That's okay then. You've been friends forever with Carla, haven't you?"

"Well, for a long time, yes," Emily says. "Put your head back and I'll rinse out your shampoo."

As the soap suds wash down Rosie's back, it hits Emily, a great big punch in the stomach. She doesn't have any justification for being cross with Carla. She is sleeping with Carla's husband, for fuck's sake, and that's a billion times worse.

* * *

Later, when the kids are tucked up in bed, and Emily is nursing a cup of tea feeling sorry for herself, the doorbell rings. She knows it's Carla, even before she answers.

"Please let me explain," Carla says, standing on the doorstep with red puffy eyes and hurt etched across her face.

Emily opens the door wider and Carla steps in.

"Come here!" Emily's eyes well up as she pulls her friend into an embrace.

Leading Carla into the living room, she feels a thickness in her throat as the guilt punishes her.

"Do you want a cup of tea?"

"Have you got anything stronger?" Carla asks, blowing her nose.

Emily returns with two glasses of Chardonnay and sits at the opposite end of the settee.

"Look, I couldn't have told you straight away. I wasn't sure what I'd seen. I did intend to confront him though. I promise you that."

"Let's just forget about it, shall we? Water under the bridge." *And what I am doing to you is way, way worse.*

"No, I need to explain. It's stayed with me for a long time. It was the weekend Grace was up from Kinsale visiting and we went for dinner in that Italian restaurant – you know, the one on Bridge Street, in the old mill." Carla gulps at her wine before continuing, "When we went back to the carpark, I saw your car. I could see heads in it so I thought it was you and I went towards it. It was only afterwards that it dawned on me the windows were all steamy. When I reached the front of the car, Chris saw me and opened his window." She takes a deep breath. "His hair was sticking up and both of their shirts were undone a bit. He tried to remonstrate with me but I just backed off and left. I was shocked."

"Right, well, like I said, it's over and done with now." Emily fidgets with the drinks coaster. "I'm not cross about it anymore. It was just a shock." *What I'm doing to you is way worse.* Reaching out, she takes her friend's hand and squeezes it. I need to stop this deceit, it can't continue. Like Rosie said earlier, our friendship has lasted forever. If Carla finds out about Thomas and me, it will be over in a second. Our friendship is surely worth more than that.

"I was going to ring him in work on Monday and have it out with him. But he told you on the Sunday evening," Carla says, the tears dripping off her nose as she speaks. She reaches for her tissue again.

Emily dries her own eyes. "Look, if you hadn't seen him, he might not have told me at all. I might still be in that lie of a marriage." She pulls Carla into a hug again. Will *you* ever forgive *me?* The question echoes around her head.

She needs to stop this betrayal; she knows she does. The tightness in her chest moves downwards to knot her stomach, leaving behind it a feeling of heaviness. What is she going to do?

38

Standing at the sink in her ensuite, Dawn reads the instructions on the box for the third time: **Take two tablets with water twenty minutes before you go to bed**. Her mum is a notoriously light sleeper; Dawn often hears her going downstairs during the night for a glass of water or to watch TV for a while. She needs her to stay asleep all night if she is going to be able to move out.

Tonight is the perfect night to trial the tablets. Her mum is making fish pie and Michael is staying over in Dublin for the night. If she could somehow put them into her mum's dinner and then observe her for the evening. It might take a few trials to see what will work.

Is she really going to do this? Give sleeping tablets to her mum? If she's going to escape her clutches, her manipulation, then she has to leave. It is not like she's a child running away. She must push Ruth and Samantha along in looking for a rental house too. Time is of the essence now.

Slipping two tablets into the back pocket of her jeans, she hesitates and puts another one in. *Is this too much? Her mum is a very slim build.* Putting a tissue between the tablets and her pocket so the outline of them can't be seen, she reassures herself that she doesn't have to use all of them. Now, she just has to work out how to feed them to her.

The acrid aroma of fish rises to greet her as she comes down the stairs. Seeing the potatoes simmering on the hob along with the fish pan, and the oven already preheating, she asks, "Can I help?"

"You can set the table. Just the two of us seeing as Michael has ditched us for his friends."

Dawn takes out the placemats and arranges the cutlery on the table, noticing the half glass of wine on the countertop.

"I have had to put the mushroom starters in too. They won't keep. I don't see why he can't meet up with his friends during the days I have to be at work. He's only here for a short time. You'd think he'd prioritise his family."

"I suppose he only has a small window of opportunity to catch up with everyone, and his friends are probably working during the day too."

Her mum swings around. "It doesn't surprise me that you are defending him. I should have expected it." She takes a swig from her glass.

Dawn doesn't answer, doesn't react. It was the wrong thing to say. She doesn't want to invite a row tonight. Filling a water jug, she puts it on the table with two glasses, her mind turning back to the tablets. Amanda pours herself another glass of wine and puts the bottle on the table. Checking the potatoes, Dawn strains and mashes them. Her mum adds the cream and mustard to the sauce. They work alongside each other in an awkward yet acceptable silence. Dawn is used to it; it doesn't usually bother her but tonight she's a bundle of nerves. She sprinkles the herbs into the sauce and stirs, wishing they were the tablets. When Amanda goes to the bathroom, Dawn waits for the lock to click before taking out the tablets and crushing them in a small dish with the back of a spoon.

She could put them in the fish pie – if she grinds them her mum mightn't taste them at all. But then she couldn't eat any herself. No, that's wouldn't work.

The toilet flushes.

Shit, what is she going to do with these crushed tablets now? She can't put them back in the pocket of her jeans. The lock on the bathroom door unclicks. Opening the cupboard, she quickly puts the dish underneath four others at the back of the shelf.

Her mum comes into the kitchen just as Dawn's jittery hands are pouring the sauce over the fish in the pie dish. Her heartbeat thumps in her ears as she spoons the mashed potato over the fish. She needs to think fast if she is going to get the opportunity to do this tonight. Taking the dish, her mum puts it into the oven, taking out the starter.

"You're very quiet. How's the restaurant doing?"

"It's grand. Busy enough most shifts. Brendan has us polishing glasses and cutlery any time it's quiet. The chef, Stuart, is a head case – he gets so shouty." She rattles on while frantically trying to work out in her mind how she's going to do this. She could slip the crushed tablets into the wine but what if the powder doesn't dissolve or if Mum notices a difference in the taste.

They eat roasted and filled mushrooms for starters and Dawn resigns herself to leaving it for another night.

Amanda takes the fish pie out of the oven just as the doorbell rings. She turns around with a puzzled look and then her face breaks into a smile. "That might be Michael coming back to join us after all."

Dawn listens for voices. It isn't Michael, and whoever it is hasn't been invited in. Now is her chance. She scoops out a portion of fish pie onto a plate, takes out the dish with the crushed tablets, and sprinkles them in the fishy bit of the pie. Using the end of a teaspoon to stir it in, she adds a bit more from the pie dish. *There.* She stands back from it; yes, that looks like a completely normal serving. Spooning some out for herself, she puts the two plates on the table just as she hears her mum saying goodbye and closing the door.

"Who was it?" she asks as they both sit down, and she clicks the timer on her Fitbit.

"One of Martyn's kids from around the corner looking for sponsorship for some charity cycle."

Dawn's stomach churns with nerves and she pushes her food around her plate, taking small mouthfuls. It doesn't go unnoticed by her mum.

"Don't you like it?"

"It's yummy." Dawn forces herself to eat everything on her plate.

Watching her mum carefully as they clear up after dinner, Dawn washes the pans while Amanda stacks the dishwasher before taking her glass of wine and sitting down in the living area.

"Do you know, I've been hit with a belt of tiredness all of a sudden," she says.

"I'll get you a glass of water," Dawn says as she puts the last of the pans away.

"Maybe I've had too much wine."

She puts the glass of water on the coffee table next to her mum. "Here you go. Do you want some of the chocolates that Michael brought?"

"No, thanks."

Dawn puts the empty wine glass next to the sink and wonders how the tablets might interact with wine; her mum must have had two glasses between preparing dinner and eating it. She takes the box of chocolates and folds herself into the armchair, tucking her legs under her. The knot forming in her churned stomach is twisting tighter and tighter every minute. The timer on her Fitbit seems to be edging along so slowly as she watches Amanda out of the corner of her eye. Fifty minutes have passed now. She's watching *A Place in the Sun* but Dawn can see her eyes closing, her head starting to loll. Amanda jars herself awake and then a few seconds later the lolling starts again.

Dawn yawns exaggeratedly. "I'm shattered. I think I might have an early night," she says. "Why don't you do the same, Mum? You looked wrecked."

"Yes, I think I might." Stretching her legs out, her mum yawns and then stands up. Wavering a little, she sinks back onto the settee.

"Are you okay?" Dawn asks.

"Just feel a bit dizzy. That wine must have gone to my head." She stands up again. "Will you lock up? Michael's staying out so you can put the deadlock on the front door when you go up."

Dawn listens to her plodding up the stairs before she checks the timer on her Fitbit: an hour since Mum ate the fish pie.

Flicking through the TV channels, she bites the skin around her fingernails. She can't concentrate on anything. Keeping an eye on her Fitbit, she scrolls through her phone and Netflix, without watching anything, and picks at the chocolates in the box. Time seems to be passing so slowly.

Putting her head around Amanda's bedroom door an hour later, she calls, "*Mum, Mum, are you okay?*"

No response. Not a stir. Standing inside the room, Dawn shuts the door loudly behind her, watching carefully for some sort of reaction. Nothing. Mum doesn't even flinch to the bang.

Dawn starts to sing, quietly at first then louder. "*I know a song that will get on your nerves, get on your nerves . . .*"

Still no movement. *These tablets really do work.* Dawn smiles. *I can do this. I can escape. This can actually happen.* She has proved it tonight. Should she begin to pack? Get some stuff out now while she can? No. She calms herself. This is only a trial. She must be patient. This has to work properly.

39

Amanda turns over, opens her eyes and winces at the light through the gap in the middle of the curtains. It's ten o'clock, how did she manage to sleep so late? Sitting up, her head feels like a fuzzy whirl. She sips at the glass of water and she tells herself it has to stop. Stop drinking wine during the week and stop taking the extra anti-depressants. This is not who she is. If there's one thing she has always been in control of, the only thing that sometimes she felt she could control, it is her body. She's kept herself trim and fit. If anything, it's been a bit of an obsession for her over the years: how toned she is, how far she can push herself to run. She *has* to stay in control. Wine and pills aren't going to help her.

Lately, everything has become too much: Michael asking questions, bringing back memories of the fire and Dawn wanting to move out. The loneliness hits her in the gut, and the wine helps to numb it. But she's taking more and more tablets too, and that's not good. The prescribed dosage doesn't seem to be as effective anymore. It barely takes the edge off. She must make an appointment with the doctor and get it sorted. Becoming reliant on them is not an option, she thinks, going into the ensuite. Switching the shower on, she glances into the mirror, horrified by the tired, lined face looking back at her. She cannot be this person.

The shower doesn't do much to improve how she's feeling. She's exhausted. Downstairs, she takes a couple of paracetamol and puts the kettle on before switching it off straight away.

I'll make a superfood smoothie instead, and then go for a run, she thinks. That'll sort me out. No doubt Michael will be back by then and we can do something for the day.

She has to stay in control, she reminds herself, taking out the blender.

Amanda's legs are heavy and sluggish as she runs through the woods. She feels herself getting annoyed with dog-walkers hogging the path, her slow pace and the fact that her head is banging as if she'd drunk two bottles of wine last night.

She stops and puts her hand on a tree to steady herself and waits for her breathing to calm. Two men run by, and Amanda recognises one from her running club. He nods and says hello, and then turns, jogging slowly backwards.

"Are you okay?"

"Yep, fine. Just taking a breather."

The men run on and Amanda walks along the path until she comes to a bench. She sits, willing the pounding in her head to stop. Staring at the tall trees around her, she zones in on one. It has a strong, thick trunk. The branches shoot off it, reaching for the light in the canopy of the wood. She's tried to be the trunk for her family, the strong supportive one for Michael and Dawn, letting their branches grow. But what thanks does she get for it? Dawn arguing with her and Michael digging around in the past, wanting her to accompany him to the nursing home to visit Aunt Mary. She doesn't want to go. God knows what it would drag up.

Is the way she's feeling a direct response to the pressure her family are putting her under lately? It's difficult to be the supportive one all of the time. It's like they never think of her needs. How it will affect her if Dawn moves out? How dredging through the details of the past, bringing up memories of the fire, will throw her back into that memory of pain? Amanda rubs her temples and leans back on the bench.

Maybe if she accompanied Michael to visit Aunt Mary, she could have some control over the situation. Steer the conversation and Michael's line of questioning somehow.

Aunt Mary was good to them growing up after their parents died. Having two children thrust upon you when you're in a happily childless marriage must have been a big shock. Especially when these children had survived a house fire that killed their parents. Looking back, Amanda can see it must have been full on for Aunt Mary and Uncle Seán and that's probably why Michael and herself were quickly shunted off to boarding school. Aunt Mary was always kind, and they wanted for nothing but at the same time she was never a mother figure.

Amanda tries to imagine Dawn attending a boarding school when she was younger. She would have hated to have been separated from her daughter and not known what was going on in her life on a day-to-day basis, and, worse, not be able to control it. It was bad enough that Brad had left her, and Michael moved to Australia. She could never have coped with losing Dawn too.

She's cooling down from her run now and starting to feel a chill, so she begins to jog lightly back to her car. She decides, as she reaches the car park, if Michael wants to go to visit Aunt Mary, she'll go with him. She needs to stay in control.

40

"Mum, can I have two euros to get some brownies?" Daniel asks.

"Wait a moment." Carla lifts the little drawer out of the money box and places the bundle of notes underneath. Closing the box, she reaches into her jeans pocket for a few coins. "Here you go." She looks around the school hall for Thomas. "Have you seen Dad anywhere?" Thomas had gone for another game of golf early this morning, the second day of a competition with clients. He'd said he had to keep this client happy, he was a big money guy and right now Thomas needed his money for the new offices. Nevertheless, she'd expected him home before they left the house. Now, an hour later, she could really do with him here, keeping an eye on the boys while she's busy sorting out the money for all the stalls.

"No, not yet."

Carla sighs. "Okay, I'm sure he'll be here soon. Don't leave the hall and keep an eye on Ben, will you? Stay together."

Watching as he dashes over to the cake stall, she looks over people's heads, searching for Thomas's height above the crowd.

"Carla, the tombola stall is looking for change."

"On my way." She hugs the cash box and makes her way across the hall, smiling and saying hello to parents and teachers of the school as she goes.

The fundraiser is a great success so far. They've already taken in a lot of money from the raffle tickets, the silent auction, and sponsorship. The crowds are here and the weather for the outside games is great. Carla would feel happier if Thomas was here to mind the boys. She can't concentrate on helping to deal with problems and sorting out the cash flow properly if her head is jerking around looking for the children.

And where's Emily? She glances at the auction stand. Isn't she supposed to be manning it with Julia? Julia is frantically pacing between customers, trying to keep her voice light, cheerful and encouraging. Her darting eyes don't escape Carla's notice. She hopes Emily isn't avoiding her after yesterday. She's always felt guilty about not telling Emily about seeing Chris. She's kind of relieved it's out in the open now.

After sorting out the change for the tombola, she checks her watch again. Where is Thomas? As Carla reaches for her phone, Julia catches her eye and waves her over.

"Carla, where's Emily? I'm run off my feet here."

"I haven't seen her, maybe she's taking a break. To be honest, I've been racing around so much, I've not had much chance to see anyone."

"She's not on a break. She hasn't turned up yet. I haven't seen her all morning. There's nothing on the WhatsApp group. Has she contacted you? Maybe one of her kids is sick or something?"

Carla unlocks her phone. No message from Emily, or Thomas for that matter. She scans the crowd until she sees Daniel and Ben at the G*uess How Many Sweets* stand. Julia clears her throat and Carla looks back at her.

"No, no message from Emily. I know she was dropping the kids at their dad's today, it's their granny's birthday. I'll text her. Maybe she's running late."

Julia's going cracked, where are you?

She checks if Thomas is online. If he'd got home from golf and seen they'd already left, he would have rung her. Work surely can't have distracted him on the weekend. Seeing he was online five minutes ago, she calls him.

"Hi, babe," he answers, "sorry I'm running late, I'll be there in a minute, I'm just pulling onto the school road now."

"I was expecting you nearly two hours ago. Where were you?"

"I got distracted at the golf, keeping the clients happy, you know how it is. The fair completely slipped my mind. I'm sorry."

"Right, well see you in a minute then." She hangs up, looking up to see one of the teachers walking towards her.

"Do you have change for a fifty? We're running low."

"Yes, no problem," Carla says, smiling, and opens the cash box.

As the teacher goes back to her stand, Carla sees Thomas striding into the hall. Daniel and Ben run to him, showing off what they've bought. Thomas looks up and their eyes meet. She can't help but smile at his apologetic look.

Right, she thinks, turning around, back to it. She wants this fundraiser to be successful, this extension to the grounds won't come cheap. Looking across the hall, she sees Emily behind the auction stand, arms aloft as she's apologising and gesturing in conversation with Julia.

41

Emily steps inside the back door and fills a glass of cold water from the tap. Leaning against the countertop, she sighs. This is hopeless. She'd been determined to get stuck into some household jobs she'd been neglecting and, after dropping the kids at school, she'd finished a pile of ironing, scrubbed the bathrooms, and is now trying to mow the lawn. But the bloody lawn mower won't start. She wipes her brow with the back of her dirty hand and drinks the water. She's tried everything she can think of – checked for blockages, topped up the petrol, and sprayed WD40 on pretty much everything. Turning, she stares out at the overgrown garden. She'd been worried she'd left too much time between cuts, that the grass would be too long for the mower. She hadn't counted on the mower not starting.

The doorbell rings. Emily sighs again. Probably another misdirected parcel for across the road. It's a neighbour's 60th today and delivery vans have been arriving all morning. One called here earlier by mistake. They are having a party at the weekend to which all the neighbours have been invited. Emily's invite had a subtle plus one on it. She doesn't really fancy going. A party full of sixty-year-olds – she can't imagine it being much fun. She hasn't had much of a social life herself lately but there are limits.

Glancing in the hallway mirror, she smirks at the dirt streaked across her face and her hair looking like she's been rolling in the garden. Pulling her hair tighter in her bobble, she tucks the strands dangling down behind her ear before opening the door. On seeing the bouquet, she says "Oh, you'll be looking for Miriam. You're not the first today. She's directly across the road, green door."

A short man peers around the flowers, his red cap with the florist's logo on it rising to meet her eyes.

"I'm looking for an Emily …"

"Oh." She takes a step back. "That's me then. Thank you."

Taking the bouquet and closing the door, she dips her nose into the floral arrangement, inhaling the beautiful scent. *Wow.* She knows they're from Thomas without reading the card. Who else would they be from?

Sliding the card out from the tiny purple envelope, she reads: **You blow my mind. Can't wait to be with you again.**

She wishes it was in his handwriting so she could run her finger along it, imagining him leaning on the florist's countertop, thinking and writing it, his dark hair hanging down over his face, his smiling eyes meeting the florist's as he lifts his head and hands her the card. But it isn't. The florist has written this. Still, Emily knows she'll save it and keep it somewhere safe, probably in her bedside drawer.

Beaming, she goes into the kitchen and finds her best vase. She resigns herself to not getting any further with the lawnmower today, makes a cup of coffee and sits on the settee, admiring the flowers. A warm feeling spreads throughout her body. This isn't just an affair, Thomas cares about her. She's sure he does. She lets her head rest back on the settee. Although they don't have much time together when they meet, he always asks about her day, and he never rushes her when she talks about her kids or stuff at work. And the things he says to her in bed, well, that blows *her* mind. She smiles thinking of his words on the card.

She can't stop thinking about him. They are falling in love; she has no doubt about this. The constant thinking about each other, checking phones, daydreaming. He is like a drug that she can't get enough of. Staring at the mantelpiece and the photos of her and the kids, she lets herself imagine a picture of herself and Thomas up there: faces pressed together, eyes alight with love, sun-kissed faces – after a holiday maybe. An excited *eek* flutters in her chest as she pictures their life together.

Looking around her house, she pictures beautiful velvet couches instead of her tired leather ones. She sees a long elegant mahogany dining table, set with the finest of glassware and cutlery, perfect for entertaining guests.

She takes her coffee cup into the kitchen and looks out of the window, imagining a neat garden bursting with flowers, a BBQ in the corner, and a fabulous rattan garden set. She sees Thomas sitting next to her in the sunshine, clinking glasses of rose prosecco, holding hands and chatting. Him telling her to stop rushing around, to give up her job, that he'll take care of her.

The clock chiming in the living room echoes through to Emily and jolts her back to reality. She has to collect the kids soon; she'd better have a shower.

She parks at the school and glances around looking for Carla's white jeep before remembering her kids do art class after school today. The guilt doesn't hit Emily like it usually does. Today, a defiant pang is in her gut. Carla doesn't appreciate Thomas; she isn't grateful to him like Emily would be if she had Carla's life. She takes him for granted. Emily would never do that. She sends him a text.

Thanks for the beautiful flowers. You brightened up my day. I thought of you in the shower xx

He replies straight away.

Xx What did you think of the other parcel? I thought you might show me tomorrow xx

Other parcel? There's more to come. Thomas is spoiling her; she could get used to this. Smiling, she gets out of the car as she sees Rosie and Theo cross the schoolyard.

At home, the parcel is waiting for her, half pushed through the letterbox. Emily ushers the kids into the kitchen and gives them a snack before slowly tearing the Sellotape from one end of the package and peeking inside. Stepping into the living room, she pulls out a royal-blue bra and thong set. The designer label leaves her in no doubt as to the cost of these tiny items. She hugs them to her chest, and allows the thought of Thomas peeling them from her body to linger in her mind.

42

"Do you know where would be lovely? Kai. The food there is divine." Julia stirs her americano. "If we could get a booking, that is."

"I can organise it," Carla offers. "I'll set up a separate WhatsApp group so that it's a surprise. Throw a few dates out there and see what suits."

"That'd be great," Sarah says. "What about a collection for a voucher?"

"Good thinking." Julia smiles. "Add that in with the WhatsApp message."

"Great. We could get her a voucher for BT's or that seaweed spa. I can pick it up." Carla reaches for her phone.

"Sinéad's going to love this. It's not every day you turn forty." Julia sips her coffee.

Carla taps in a reminder and list of names into her phone just as Thomas texts.

I'm outside.

OK. I'm on my way, just finishing coffee with Pilates girls. Will I bring you a takeaway coffee?

I'll come in and get one

Carla reaches for her lipstick and gently applies it, smiling to herself. Thomas is collecting her from Pilates class because she left her car in for a service this morning. He'd suggested lunch before they collect the car in time for the school run. Lunch together, without children, is an absolute luxury and she's really looking forward to it. She slips the lipstick back into her gym bag and tunes back to the girls' chatter.

Her heart does a little dance as she sees Thomas walk into the coffee dock and engage the barista in conversation. The barista throws her head back and her brown plaits jiggle as she laughs at something he's said. Thomas half turns and catches Carla looking at him, flashes her one of his wide grins, and turns back to pay for his coffee.

"See you later, girls, I've got a date with a tall, dark, handsome man," Carla laughs, walking over to join him, kissing him on the cheek and linking his arm as they leave the coffee dock.

Bumping into the Pilates teacher, Carla introduces her to Thomas.

"How's the Pilates business doing?" he asks.

"Very well, too well in fact," she says, as they walk through the leisure centre alongside each other, "I don't suppose you know of anyone who'd like to get involved in helping me for a few hours a week?" She looks at Carla.

"I don't, sorry," said Thomas.

"What about yourself, Carla? Would you be interested?"

"Oh, I'm not qualified. All I know is what I've learnt from you." Carla glances at Thomas, who's looking straight ahead, as they walk through the double doors and out into the car park.

"You wouldn't need any qualifications – you'd be assisting me, not leading a class."

Thomas pings the car open. "Nice to meet you," he says brightly, before climbing into the car.

"I'll have a think if I know of anyone," Carla says. "Thanks for a great class, see you next week."

She throws her gym bag on the back seat and hasn't even fastened her seatbelt when Thomas bursts out laughing.

"How did you keep a straight face? You teaching Pilates! As if we'd sink to that!"

"Don't be so rude," Carla says. "She's a brilliant teacher – plus, I enjoy the classes. I might like helping her out for a few hours a week."

Thomas drives out of the car park, joining the main road before speaking again. "Don't be daft, you'd only get paid a pittance. You don't need to anyway." He switches the radio on, changing the station to the one she loves, the classics of the eighties and nineties.

"It's not all about money," she says. "I'd be happy to do it, I might enjoy it."

Reaching over, he takes her hand. "Sorry, I shouldn't have laughed. I know you like her. I just want you to enjoy taking part in the class, relaxing or whatever it is you do in them. I want you to take some time for yourself while the boys are at school."

"She's a lovely lady. I'd hate to see her stuck."

"She'll find someone, don't you worry. Now, my darling wife, lunch. Where do you fancy? I'm starving."

43

Emily parks on Carla's drive, removes the keys and twists her eternity ring around her finger. The deeper she is falling in love with Thomas, the more awkward it is meeting Carla.

Carla had bounded over to Emily earlier this morning at the school gate. "You're not working until eleven today, are you?" she'd said and without waiting for an answer said, "Come straight over for coffee. I need you."

And, with that, she'd waved goodbye to Ben who was lining up for class and walked back to her car. Emily didn't have a chance to reply, never mind back out.

Emily has been seeing Thomas for a few weeks now and is in the midst of teenage-like highs and lows of love. Although, unlike when she was a teenager, she can't confide in Carla. She's trying her best to compartmentalise her affair and her friendship with Carla. At first, she found herself subconsciously avoiding Carla, and that, she realised, was acting too suspiciously. So, in her head, she has put Thomas, Carla's husband, into a space with Carla, and Thomas, her lover, into a separate space. Emily tries her best to keep them apart.

"*Hiya.*" Emily knocks lightly on Carla's front door and lets herself in, a habit they've had since their college days.

"*I'm in here!*" Carla shouts from the kitchen.

The sweet-smelling scent of the hyacinths and tulips sitting in the Galway crystal vase on the dining table hits Emily's nose as she enters the room. She glances at them, remembering the intimate touch of Thomas yesterday. Carla is spooning coffee into the cafetière.

Emily puts her handbag on a stool at the breakfast bar. When Carla turns around, Emily sees her whole face is beaming. Her deep-brown eyes are lit up like fairy lights and her smile streaks across her face in a wide grin.

"You look delighted with yourself. Did we beat last year's fundraising total?"

"No. Better than that. Way better!"

"*Ooo*, I'm intrigued!" Emily pulls out a high stool and sits down at the breakfast bar, tucking her hair behind an ear.

"Well, I'm going to need my suitcase and I might even borrow your new stilettos."

"Girly night away?"

"No, silly, Thomas and I are off for a romantic weekend. We've been talking about going to this hotel for ages, the restaurant is supposed to be ..."

Emily doesn't hear anymore. It's as if someone has slipped noise-cancelling headphones over her ears. She's smiling at Carla, she knows she is, her cheeks are aching with her fake smile. But inside, she is hollow. Carla's words are echoing around Emily's being. The compartments she's been so carefully managing come colliding together. She's grateful that she's sitting down.

"That's great," she half mumbles, trying to sound positive. It sounds false to her.

Carla turns back to the kitchen counter and takes out cups and the milk. A buzzer sounds on the oven and Emily has a few seconds to right herself while her friend is busy taking out the cherry scones.

Emily is winded, sore in her heart. *Thomas is taking Carla away for a romantic weekend. What the fuck is going on?* Only yesterday he was inside her and whispering the most amazing things in her ear and, yet, all along he'd planned to take his wife away for the weekend.

Carla places the cafetière, scones, cream, and jam across the breakfast bar and turns back for the cups and milk jug. Emily hasn't spoken since 'That's great' and she knows she needs to, and quick, but she can't push the colliding compartments aside, she can't separate them now. She wants to leave. To grab her handbag, feign illness, and go. But, she can't. She knows she can't. This is her best friend, who is excited about a long wished-for, long-deserved, romantic weekend away. A busy couple who want to spend some alone time together. This is also about Emily's lover, the man who is tugging at her heartstrings, whom she is falling in love with. What does she say? Emily takes a deep breath to compose herself.

"Where are you off to?"

Carla looks at her strangely.

Of course, she's told me already, only I had zoned out.

"I mean, where did you say it was?"

"Waterford. The Cliff Hotel. You know, the five-star one. It has cliff-top walks, a Michelin-starred restaurant, a spa – we can have afternoon tea."

"God, I can't see Thomas going for afternoon tea," Emily says, a little more sharply than she intends.

Carla's brows curl slightly but then she smiles again. "We might just spend the afternoon lounging in the spa, having a massage, relaxing in the sauna. No running around after the boys, no half-finished conversations. I want to be able to talk properly about me going back to teaching, convince him that it'll be good for me, for us. We'll have plenty of time to chat and relax."

And plenty of sex, Emily thinks to herself, as she pushes down the plunger on the cafetière. She tries to push that thought out of her mind. This is her best friend. She has to focus on being pleased for her. *Compartmentalise!* she inwardly yells to herself.

"Do you need me to take the boys for the weekend for you?"

"Thanks for the offer but my parents are going to come and stay. It's all arranged. They'll stay a night either side of the weekend too."

Emily pours the coffee. Carla takes a scone and passes the plate to Emily. There is no way Emily can eat a scone. She is struggling to talk normally, never mind eat. She wraps her hands around her coffee cup to steady them.

"Not for me thanks, I had a big breakfast."

"You, eat a big breakfast? When did that start happening? I thought coffee was all you have before midday."

"Yeah, well, Rosie wanted scrambled eggs so I ended up doing some for all of us." Emily lies, twisting her eternity ring around her finger.

"Gosh, you're organised. I feel like a sergeant major here most mornings, trying to get them ready and out on time for school." Carla butters her scone. "You can take some home with you." She nods at the scones.

"Thanks," Emily says, wondering how soon she can leave this awkward situation. "So, what are you planning on wearing on this weekend away? I'm sure with it being a five-star hotel, the evening meal will be a super-dressy affair."

"Exactly. That's why I need your advice. I have it down to a choice between three dresses. Hang on, I'll go and get them."

Carla's straight hair flicks behind her as she jumps down from the stool and goes upstairs. Emily looks around. *Is this really happening?* She reaches into her handbag for her phone. No new notifications. No text from Thomas. Is he not texting her because he knows she'll be finding out from Carla about the weekend away? Does he even feel bad for organising this with his wife when he is sleeping with her best friend? Emily shivers. She thought they had something special between them. What will she say to him when he contacts her? Should she mention that she has heard he's off on a romantic weekend or should she ignore it; pretend it's not happening? Continue to keep them in two separate compartments. Hearing Carla's footsteps on the stairs, she closes her phone case and slides it back into her handbag, trying to blank her mind of Thomas.

"Well, what do you think? The black and gold?" Carla swirls it around. "The navy and red, or this purple one?"

"*Wow!* They're all gorgeous. Are they new?"

"Yes, they arrived yesterday from Brown Thomas."

Yesterday. Emily stumbles through the dawning realisation that this weekend wasn't a last-minute idea, booked last night. It had been booked earlier, and definitely before she met Thomas yesterday lunchtime. She feels sick. *Focus on Carla*, she urges herself.

She steps down from the stool and takes the navy and red dress. "This is fab. I bet it's stunning on you."

"It's quite tightly fitted. I won't be able to eat much of the eight-course dinner," Carla laughs. "But I'm happy with the fit of it. It'll look good with your new stilettos."

Emily notices the price tag. Six hundred euros. No doubt the other two are around the same price. Very nice, if you can afford it.

"Will you keep all three, or are you trying to decide on one?"

"I'll keep two, I think. Friday and Saturday night. And wait, I have these too."

Carla dips back into the hallway and reaches for something on the stairs. A fuchsia-pink bra and knickers set come into focus as she comes back into the kitchen.

"What do you think? For the late evening entertainment," she giggles.

"They'll be perfect," Emily says, turning away quickly. She starts to clear away her coffee cup and concentrates on keeping her voice light and cheery. "I think they are all gorgeous and you'll look stunning in all three. I think the navy one and the purple are the nicest two." She rinses her cup in the sink. "I can't stay, I have a painter calling sometime before half ten and I don't want to miss him. You'll have to try the dresses on for me next time." She picks up her handbag.

"Oh right. What room are you getting painted?"

"The outside of the house. I'm only at the estimate stage so far."

Emily surprises herself with how easily the lie slips out, and how Carla swallows it without questioning. Her trusting friend. Emily feels a surge of disgust with herself and steps towards Carla to hug her. She pulls her into a tight embrace.

"What time do you leave on Friday?"

"Oh, it's not this weekend, it's next weekend. We're not that spontaneous!"

"See you later," Emily says, smiling back at Carla as relief washes over her. It's not this weekend. She closes the door quietly behind her and gets into her car. Maybe they won't go. Maybe Thomas was planning on coming up with an excuse all along but didn't have the heart to refuse Carla. He'll probably use work as a reason not to go.

She clicks her phone into the car holder and waits for the speaker to inform her of any messages.

There aren't any.

44

Emily checks her phone for the umpteenth time this morning. She hasn't heard from Thomas and after the intensity of the last couple of weeks radio silence feels strange, especially after she's learnt about his planned weekend away with Carla. She's sure he'll come up with an excuse not to go but she can't exactly ask him. She's the lover, not the wife so she must be patient and wait for him.

She is desperate to see him, to feel his touch, to smell him. This is falling in love, and all the better because it isn't like falling in love with a stranger. She knows Thomas. She's known him for years. She knows all his good bits and his flaws. They can skip all that awkward stage at the beginning of a relationship. Theirs can and will evolve quicker. Does he feel the same? She needs to see him and suss him out, without being too obvious.

Leaning back in her office chair, she reviews the house specs she has just completed before sending them to the printer. She closes her laptop, puts her jacket on, and grabs her phone and bag.

"Martha, would you mind displaying these in the window and entering the info on the website, please. I have to pop out for a while. Be back soon."

It's warmer outside than she expected. She takes off her navy suit jacket and rummages around in her bag for her sunglasses. She was going to drive around to Thomas's offices but, seeing as it's so nice, she decides to walk. The heat is lovely. Summer is here. People are sitting outside coffee shops and old people are chatting on benches. The sunshine puts a smile on everyone's face.

She tries to think through various scenarios with Thomas as she walks. Will she tell him that she is falling in love with him? They don't seem to have much time when they meet up. It doesn't worry her too much. As time goes on, they'll have more time for chat and normal couple stuff. For now, they have to be patient. Emily can be patient.

She is more than halfway there now and she is glad she is wearing the navy kitten heels and not those stupid stilettos that she bought for the date with the baldy guy. She can't even remember his name but she regrets putting in as much effort as she did. She's sure Thomas wouldn't care if she was wearing kitten heels or trainers.

Passing the recently refurbished House hotel, she glances in the window and comes to a complete standstill. Thomas is standing at the reception counter. She only has a side view but she's certain it's him. He is standing very close to a woman, a woman who is not Carla. A man with a pram tries to pass on the pavement and Emily turns and has to push in against the window, her bottom almost resting on the ledge. Turning back to peek through the mullioned window again, she notices people sitting in the lounge area just inside and moves slightly to the side so she's not peering in on top of them. Who is this blonde curly-haired petite woman beside Thomas? He must have had a business meeting or lunch here with a client.

Watching as they turn away from the counter and walk towards the back of the hotel where the car park is located, she decides she'll wait for Thomas to say goodbye to his client. Then she'll have the perfect opportunity to catch him and have a chat. She walks around the side of the hotel before hesitating. It would be more natural, she thinks, if he was to drive out of the carpark and happen to see her on the pavement nearby. She waits for a second or two until curiosity gets the better of her. She spots his car as soon as she rounds the corner. He isn't in it. Her eyes dart around the carpark until she sees Thomas's back. His light-blue shirt stretched across his shoulders, the arms of the woman's lilac blouse around him, their heads tilted into each other.

Emily stands frozen to the spot. What is going on? This is no business meeting. Wincing, she steps back and swallows the lump in her throat. Retreating around the corner, she leans against the cool, hard wall. She's lightheaded. Did she just see what she thought she saw? Was Thomas kissing another woman? *Her* Thomas. Another woman who wasn't his wife and wasn't her? What is going on?

She hears a car door slam and then another. She needs to move quickly. Her legs wobble as she half walks, half runs back to the street, one hand gripping the handbag on her shoulder. Ducking into a bakery next door to the hotel, she stands staring out of the window. She watches as first the woman and then Thomas drive out of the carpark, indicate opposite ways, and drive off.

A weakness comes over her, the world turns blurry and she puts a hand on the window to steady herself.

"Are you okay, love?" the lady behind the counter asks.

Emily turns to her blankly.

"You're very pale. Here, come and sit down a minute." The lady takes her arm and leads her to a chair and table. "Sit down here. I'll get you a glass of water."

"Thank you," Emily mumbles.

She stares at the ground. They were kissing, weren't they?

"There you go, love, take a few sips of that. Are you okay? Is there someone I can call for you?"

Emily shakes her head. "No. Thank you. I'll be all right in a minute. I just came over all weak."

Who could she call? Carla is the only person she could call in a situation like this and she can't call her because it's her flipping husband. If Emily had spotted any boyfriend in that situation, it would be Carla she'd ring first. Together, they'd bitch and moan about it. When she'd found out her ex-husband, Chris, was gay, it was Carla who was there for her throughout. And now, here she is, devastated over the sighting of Thomas kissing another woman, not because of the injustice it is to Carla, his wife, but because, she, herself, is in love with him.

Sipping her water, she looks out of the window onto the street bustling with people. How can Thomas be so stupid? Anyone could have seen him and told Carla. Why was he acting so carelessly? Is he actually having two affairs? She had been under the impression what she and Thomas have is special. That they aren't having an affair for the sake of it but because they can't help themselves. They love each other and have no choice but to be together. They don't want to hurt anyone, least of all Carla. But now this, what is going on?

"Are you feeling any better?" the lady asks from behind the counter. "Would you like an iced bun? A bit of sugar might do you the world of good."

Emily smiles. "Thanks, but I'm okay. I don't know what came over me. I didn't eat much for breakfast, that might have been it." She stands up and takes her glass over to the counter. "Thank you for being so kind."

She turns to go but then turns back.

"Do you know what? I will take some buns. Will you make me up a selection box with four of your nicest, please?"

Walking slowly back to her workplace, Emma tries to simplify everything in her mind, to see a road forward. What should she do now?

45

The blue folder nudges Amanda's leg as Michael turns into the driveway of the nursing home. She ignores it. She'd shoved it there, out of the way, when Michael asked her to hold it on the way over. She doesn't know exactly what's in there, and she doesn't want to. As she keeps telling him, the past is in the past and that's where it should be left.

She chews at her inner cheek, folding her arms across her stomach. She doesn't want to be here. But, although dread sits in the pit of her empty stomach at what Mary might say and remember, she will at least be more in control of the situation by being here.

Michael reverses the hire car under the trees and, turning the engine off, stares at Little Willow Nursing Home. Glancing at him, Amanda knows he's having doubts about going in.

"You don't have to do this, you know. It will be very upsetting for you and we really don't want to confuse Mary any further."

"I want to give it a try. Aunt Mary might be able to shed some light on it all." He reaches for the folder, and they get out.

They walk the lavender-scented path to the entrance. A nurse meets them at the door and leads the way down a carpeted corridor to Mary's room. An earthy old-people smell accompanies them. Amanda walks behind Michael, repeatedly trying to swallow the lump in her throat, saying silent prayers that Mary will be asleep.

Glancing into the large living area as they pass, she sees elderly people doing jigsaws. Two are staring at a game show on the large widescreen TV. At a table in the corner, some are painting, a staff member hovering around them. Other residents are just sitting in their chairs, staring at nothing. Amanda falters in her step. Is this the sort of place where her parents would be now, had they lived?

"Does Mary interact much with the activities provided?" Michael asks the nurse as they walk.

"A little, yes. Some days more than others. She loves to listen to music and take part in the dancing class. Here we are. Visitors for you, Mary, love."

Mary is sitting in a high-backed armchair, overlooking the garden. Amanda sees a hint of recognition in her eyes as Michael approaches, and her heart deflates. She was hoping Mary would be the same as last time she saw her and then he might put all this digging in the past to bed.

"Hello, Paul. How are you?" Mary says brightly.

Amanda sees the disappointment flicker across Michael's face as Mary says their father's name. He settles himself into the chair next to Mary. Her eyes reach Amanda next and try to place her. She can't and she looks back at Michael. Amanda hovers. Not sure what to do or say. Feeling awkward, she perches on the edge of the high bed, clasping her hands on her lap.

Mary stares at Michael intently and he smiles.

"How are you, Mary?" he asks.

"I'm well. My garden's looking lovely, isn't it?" She nods at the window. "I have my bird table out there. I like to watch the birds feeding and fluttering."

Michael leans forward in his chair and reaches for her hand. Her thin-skinned hand grasps his in return. "Do you see the butterflies around the sweet peas? Two cabbage whites chasing each other?" he asks.

"Yes, yes, I do."

They sit together watching the birds and the butterflies.

Amanda zones in on his thumb stroking the bumps of Mary's veiny hands. He seems so comfortable in this strange situation. Amanda hasn't spoken yet; no words will come. The dread has climbed into her mouth and holds her tongue.

"Have you told Sarah about losing the money yet?" Mary asks.

Amanda's fingernails press sharply into her palms. She watches Michael straighten in his chair at the mention of their mother's name, and the realisation again that Mary thinks he is his father.

Clearing his throat, he says "No, not yet."

"You must. There shouldn't be any secrets in a marriage, Paul."

Amanda stares around the room, a little relieved. Her shoulders relax as she realises it'll be difficult for Michael to ask questions about the fire if Mary believes him to be their father, who died in it. She zones in on a photo on the sideboard of Michael and herself in their youth, standing on a boat going out to the Aran Islands. Ignoring their chatter about the garden, she picks it up, studying their grinning faces, and their yellow waterproof jackets, Amanda's hair blowing across her face, the waves churning in the background, and Michael's damp hair from sea spray.

"Is that the boat trip?" Michael asks. "Let's have a look."

She passes it to him and sits back on the bed. Glancing at the wall clock, she's glad she delayed them at home this morning. It's almost lunchtime. They won't be able to stay much longer.

"This was a great day, wasn't it, Mary? Remember how Seán's hat blew off into the sea on the return trip?"

"Oh yes." She smiles. "The red one, he loved that hat." She takes the photo frame and holds it in her hands. "Michael and Amanda laughed so much at it bobbing in the sea." She looks up at Michael, a confused look passes across her face, and she looks back at the photo again. "It was good to see Amanda laugh. It didn't happen very often."

Amanda tenses, sitting up straight on the bed. "What did you do on the island, did you cycle around?" Her words rush out, trying to focus Mary on the happy times, the ones she's tried to focus Michael on for so many years.

Michael looks over at her, annoyance flashing across his face. She knows he wants to let Mary talk about the past, but Amanda needs to steer the conversation to safer waters.

Mary reaches for her hankie in her cardigan pocket and rubs her nose. "She was a ball of pent-up anger bouncing around the house," she says as if she hasn't heard Amanda.

"Was she?" Michael asks.

"Yes. She used to sleepwalk too. I'd try to lead her back to bed, and she'd cry, 'I'm sorry, I didn't mean to!'. I don't know why she always said that – sure she was only sleepwalking."

"She was probably sorry for disturbing you during the night." Amanda's words come out louder than she intended.

Mary frowns and looks down at her hands. "I don't know why she was staying in our house, why wasn't she in yours?"

"What? Oh, we must have gone away for the weekend. You must have been minding the kids for us," Michael says.

"Oh yes, probably." Mary twiddles her thumbs. "I forget things, you know, sometimes. That's what they tell me. Some things are gone from me now." Her voice quietens to a whisper. "I suppose that's what happens."

A bell rings down the hallway and Amanda jumps up. "That must be the lunch bell. We should go, leave Mary to eat."

Michael and Mary ignore her, both staring out of the window, watching sparrows on the bird table pecking at the seeds.

Amanda stands, watching as a grey squirrel scurries out from under the bushes and shimmies up the pole of the bird table, frightening the sparrows away.

"Look, Mary, see the squirrel," Michael says.

"Oh yes. He comes every day, bullying his way in to get some food. We have to put extra out, you know – they're very greedy, squirrels are."

Michael glances at the folder next to him and Amanda holds her breath. Surely, he's not thinking about questioning Mary.

She perches back on the bed, hearing the nursing staff coming down the corridor, talking to other residents, and she knows she only has to fill a few more minutes.

"Can you remember the ice-cream shop on the island?" she says. "I don't think we'd seen quite so many flavours before. Michael got a cone with two scoops, and can you remember, Mary, the top one, raspberry I think, fell off as soon as he stepped out of the shop!" She forces a laugh.

Mary laughs too, but her eyes cloud over as she stares at Amanda, still trying to place her. Michael gently squeezes her hand as the nurse arrives to see if she wants to have lunch in the dining room.

"You'll have to come earlier next time," the nurse tells them.

Amanda allows her relief to creep out in a small smile as they walk back through the nursing home. "I hope we didn't confuse her too much. She's quite far gone into her own world, isn't she?"

46

The sun is shining through the mullioned windows, highlighting rectangles on the cabinets, making them gleam. Carla puts her handbag on the stool at the breakfast bar and takes out her phone. It's a shame none of the ladies were free after Pilates; she could have done with a coffee and a chat for an hour. Julia can be annoying at times, but she is okay for small chunks of time, and Sarah always has some funny story about the young girls at the clothes shop where she works two days a week. Carla glances at her phone screen. It's only eleven o'clock. No new notifications.

She looks around the spotless kitchen and outside at the washing hanging on the line, blowing gently in the breeze. Maybe she could make a start on dinner. No, it's too early; the potatoes for the shepherd's pie would go soggy. The washing basket sits just inside the door of the utility room, there are only two things in it. It's hardly worth taking the ironing board out. Lena did the rest yesterday. Carla taps the kettle on and leans against the countertop, reaching for her pendant and rolling it between her fingers. She exhales long and slowly. Four hours until the boys finish school. Three hours until she needs to start prepping dinner. She could bake. Reaching for *Cake*, her latest favourite recipe book, she flicks through the pages, looking for inspiration. She made muffins a couple of days ago – maybe she could make orange shortbread this time. Hang on – she turns to the cake tin sitting at the end of the countertop – did the muffins get finished? Nope, still six left. She sighs. No point baking today then. She clicks the lid back into place.

The house is so quiet without the boys in it; everything seems to echo. She remembers how she used to love coming home to a quiet house after a day of teaching in school. Her head would be ringing from the constant noise of the classroom. Just to have peace was heavenly.

Making a cup of coffee, Carla decides to tackle the playroom, get rid of some old toys and fill a box or two for the charity shop. She's learnt it's always best to do these jobs when the kids aren't around. Otherwise, they remember the fun they had with long-forgotten toys, and suddenly they're interested in them again and can't bear to part with them.

Her laptop catches her eye as she moves to leave the kitchen and she hesitates in the doorway. It wouldn't hurt to have a quick look for teaching jobs, would it? Just to see what's out there and what the demand is? If not for now, then just to keep an eye out for the future. She places her coffee mug next to the laptop and keys in her password, perching on the stool.

An hour and a half later, Carla has three tabs open: A list of subbing jobs, longer-term positions like maternity covers, and Google maps. In a separate document, Carla has made a spreadsheet with the names of the school, opening hours, the position, the distance, and the time to get there from both the house and the boys' school. She moves the sections around so that she has the nearest schools at the top, whether or not they have a position available. Leaning back on her stool, she glances at the clock at the far end of the kitchen; she still has plenty of time.

Looking at the list of primary schools within a forty-minute radius from her, she sees there are plenty and even though most of them aren't advertising, she could still send in a CV for subbing. Her old school is at the bottom of the list. It's exactly forty-three minutes from this house and probably too far to be able to work around the kids. Carla had liked the distance when she was teaching – it kept her home and work life separate; she was less likely to bump into families from the school. Now though, it would suit her better if she did teach somewhere locally. It would make the logistics much easier.

Carla lifts her pendant to her mouth, holding it gently between her lips, staring at the list of schools. She'd never planned to take so much time out from teaching. When she was pregnant, so many people told her what a great career teaching was to be in when you had a young family: short days, school holidays, and all of that. She'd smiled, thinking mainly about how annoying it was that most people thought the job finished for the day when the children went home from school. Her maternity leave had been extended to a year off and then another. The great thing about teaching in Ireland was that you could take up to ten years of career break and still come back to your job. So, why had she been happy to step away completely, to agree with Thomas that it was better if she stayed at home? Was it the fog and busyness of two small children that made her go along with it then or is it that the shine has gone off being a stay-at-home mum now? She sips her coffee and pushes it to one side. It went cold a long time ago. Her eyes land on the project table in the corner of the kitchen. She loves being with her boys but they're at school all day now and she could be teaching during that time.

Clicking into Google maps again, she sees there are plenty of schools close by that she could sub at. Subbing could be her way of finding out if she could work around their family life. Her way to prove to Thomas that it could work. She could pick and choose her days. Moving the mouse over a school, she clicks on it and a street-view photo comes into view, of the school sign and building in the background. She could prep the dinner in the mornings or batch-cook at the weekends. Maybe even Thomas could help occasionally. They used to cook together regularly before they had kids. And, would it be so bad, Carla thinks, typing in her own kids' school website and clicking on the afterschool club, if the boys went to afterschool now and again? It would only be for an hour at the very most. Emily's kids love it. Emily calls it a glorified play date but without the mess and hassle of hosting it yourself.

Her phone rings, making her jump. Thomas's face lights up the screen and a flash of guilt courses through her. She closes the internet browser and answers.

"Hello you, what are you up to?" Thomas says.

"Just about to start on dinner." She snaps the laptop shut.

"Well, I'm glad I caught you then. Forget about dinner. I'm heading to a meeting in the west end of town and it's quite near to that Thai restaurant we used to go to near your rental house. I thought I'd collect us a takeaway and we could reminisce about me and you being young and carefree again."

"Remember their dumplings? You used to be obsessed with them!"

"And you with their green curry. I don't think you ever ordered anything different!" he says, laughing.

"Well, we've never found a green curry quite as good as there, have we?"

"Right, that's sorted then. I'll be home around six. Something sweet and sour will do the boys, won't it?"

"Yes, sounds great."

"Now you won't have to make dinner, you'll have some extra time for yourself. What will you do?" he asks.

"Oh, I'll probably tackle the playroom. I've been meaning to do it for a while."

"Leave it. Relax. Set the table and choose a bottle of wine for later. I think there's a nice Pinot Noir on the rack. See you later. Love you, babe."

"You too."

Carla puts the phone down and lifts the lid of the laptop, her spreadsheet lighting up as she does. She could make going back to teaching work, couldn't she? Her biggest stumbling block, she clicks to save the spreadsheet, is going to be Thomas.

Carla types in the name of the hotel she's booked for next weekend. She needs Thomas to be as relaxed as possible, for the weekend to run smoothly. Clicking into the spa, she books a couple's massage package with complimentary fizz. Hopefully, they'll have time to chat properly about it. They won't be disturbed by his work or the kids, and she will have the chance to explain her reasoning and somehow convince him that her going back to work is going to be good for them all.

47

Thomas sent a few texts yesterday about meeting up at lunchtime at a hotel – about how he was missing her. Emily ignored them at first, still processing what she'd seen at the hotel. Eventually, though, she'd replied and said she couldn't make it and maybe tomorrow.

She couldn't get what she had seen in the car park out of her head. Was it a kiss? Was it a hug? Had she overreacted? Is she allowed to react even? She isn't the wife after all.

Today, he'd texted early.

How about we meet for lunch today? Can you find a place?

Lunch was different. It would be a good opportunity to suss him out.

That would be nice. There's is a nice Italian on Dominick Street.

A bit dangerous, I think. Is there a property we can 'view'?

Oh right. Her heart deflates a little. So, not lunch then. She doesn't reply. Fifteen minutes later, he texts.

I'll bring the food.

Lunch at a showhouse. That makes sense. They have to be careful. She texts him the address of a place they can use.

Waiting at the show house for him two hours later, she checks her hair three times in the bathroom mirror, and adjusts her emerald silk blouse. Making sure just enough buttons are undone, but not too many to be obvious. Her stomach churns with nerves and a sense of betrayal. What was Thomas up to, and how can she ask him? Is she being used or did her suspicious mind see more to the exchange in the carpark than it actually was?

Hearing a car drive into the new estate, she tucks her hair behind one ear. Her phone rings.

"Which house is it? None of them have numbers," he asks.

"It's the one with curtains, the show house."

"That's what I thought, but your car isn't there."

"No, I parked around the corner."

"Okay, hang on. I hope you're planning on answering the door naked."

Laughing, she hangs up, and opens the front door, jokingly hiding behind the door, pretending she's naked.

"You spoilsport!" he says, kissing her hard as the door closes behind them.

He drops the Tesco bag, a wine bottle clinks as it hits the floor, and a tiny part of her brain hopes it hasn't smashed on the brown tweed-effect carpet inside the front door. The rest of her brain does not give a damn. She wants his lips, his hands, his body on her.

Pulling her blouse from her skirt, his fingers find the buttons.

"Slow down, you promised me lunch," she says.

"You don't really want lunch, do you? You want me, inside you," he whispers in her ear.

Gasping, she pulls away.

"Did you bring wine?" She straightens her blouse and turns towards the kitchen.

He sighs and picks up the shopping bag, following her.

The dining table is set for dinner for four, and Emily moves a couple of the place settings to one side as Thomas takes out mushroom pasta, meats, and a couple of cheeses. Only tumbler Ikea glasses are on the table, so Thomas pours wine into them.

"*Woah!* That's loads. I have to drive and go back to work after this."

"We'll be fine after this lunch."

Reaching for her glass, Emily swallows the cold Sicilian white wine and welcomes the relief to her dry mouth. Should she bring up the other day? She focuses on his clean, manicured fingernails as he opens the cheese and cuts into it. The way he greeted her at the door, that wasn't just passion, that was love, wasn't it? She must have read too much into what she saw at the hotel.

"Here, try this Parmigiano, you'll love it." Balancing a piece on the knife, he passes it across the table to her.

"*Mmm*, yummy."

"You're yummy." He smirks at her and she tries not to melt. "Are you nearly finished?"

She laughs. "We've only just sat down. How are the plans for the new office refurbishment going?"

"Slowly. I have great ideas. It's such a big, open space, I really want to maximise it," he says, his hands gesturing in the space between them as he tells her about his plans.

She nods and *ahhs* at the right moments, all the while having an internal argument with herself over whether to mention the hotel or the weekend away with Carla.

As he pours more wine, she tucks her hair behind her ear and says, "The House hotel has apparently had a very fancy refurbishment recently, bright-coloured furniture, lots of mirrors and the lighting is supposed to be fabulous. I haven't seen it myself, but Marcia in the office was telling me about it." She studies him carefully for any reaction.

Nothing, no twitch, no hesitation, no darting eyes. He doesn't miss a beat before saying, "Yeah, I was there with a friend. I wasn't sure about the bright colours but they kind of grew on me. It has a real modern feel to it now, an injection of life. I'd say it'll do well."

It had to be an innocent, friendly lunch, she reasons with herself. Surely no one could answer like that without so much as a twitch or a pause, thinking they'd been caught out. Is it not even crossing his mind that she knows, or is he not worried because it was just lunch with a friend? Did she see them hugging, and put two and two together and get five?

Watching him peel a slice of Parma ham from its cover she asks, "What did you eat there?"

"We shared a few of the light bites, chorizo, Spanish omelette, that sort of thing."

"And, did he like it as well?" She holds her breath, looking at his long, dark eyelashes.

"He?" He looks up from her plate. "Oh, it was a she. Tracey, a friend from college, was down from Dublin. She did, yes. It wasn't a patch on the new proper tapas place, not authentic like that, but it was tasty. Not as tasty as you though." His eyes twinkle and he reaches across the table for her hand.

Tracey? She racks her brains, she doesn't remember any Tracey, but college was over fifteen years ago, and she only knew Thomas through Carla during their final year, she reassures herself. And plus, if he was up to no good, he surely wouldn't have told her that.

Standing up, she finishes the last of her wine and goes into the kitchen area to refill her glass with water from the tap.

"Do you want some?" she says, looking back over her shoulder, only to find him coming up right behind her.

"I want you," he says, nuzzling into her neck, "and I can't wait any longer." His deep, soft voice is like a drug to her body. "Come here." He turns her around. "Let me show you how I love you."

He drops to his knees.

48

Throwing leggings and a hoody in her bag along with a towel, Dawn is all set. Salthill is calling. She hears the radio playing in the kitchen as she goes downstairs; her mum mustn't have left for work yet.

"Morning, are you on a late shift today?" she asks, tapping the kettle on and putting a slice of bread in the toaster.

Looking up from reading the *Galway Advertiser*, her mum takes off her glasses and scoffs, "What are you wearing? Are you flying off to Ibiza or something?"

"It's going to be roasting today, I'm going to the beach in Salthill with Ruth and Samantha." Dawn pulls her shorts down a little.

"Oh. I'm off today. I thought we could go somewhere nice for the day together," her mum says. "I've made some couscous for a picnic."

"I … I didn't realise," Dawn says, "You never mentioned it last night."

"Well, I didn't expect the day to turn out so nice, did I? You can never trust the weatherman."

"Is Michael going?"

"No, he's gone to Cork. He's meeting up with some friends from college."

"Right. Well, if I'd have known, I wouldn't have made –"

"Cancel them," her mum cuts in.

Taking a deep breath, Dawn puts her hands on the back of a

kitchen chair. "I've made plans with Ruth and Samantha to go to the beach, we're celebrating handing our last assignments in." Seeing the all-too-familiar crease in her mum's brow, she adds "I can come back early though. We can go to Barna or Silver Strand and walk the beach and watch the sunset. How does that sound?"

"No, I'd planned a picnic. I thought we'd do the Cliffs of Moher walk. Ring the girls, tell them it's off."

Dawn has to look away. She's looking forward to today. It's rare that all three friends get the same day off, and rarer still that the sun shines in Galway. Her toast pops and she turns to it.

"We could do it tomorrow instead. Michael will be able to join us then. I'm working in the evening but not until six." Her stomach tightens in anticipation of her mum's response. *Please let her see this as a compromise and go with it.* Her mum doesn't say anything. Dawn butters the toast even though her appetite has vanished. She just wants to get out of here. Get on the bus and meet her friends. She glances at her watch; she could catch the earlier bus if she leaves now.

Her mum clears her throat, and Dawn waits.

"Tell the girls you can't make it, that you have other arrangements."

"No." The word is out of Dawn's mouth before she realises. Pushing the plate of toast away, she turns to face her mum.

"What did you say?" Her mum stands up and steps towards her.

"No, I don't want to cancel ..." Dawn's voice tapers off.

"What? You're going to leave your mother, on her own, on such a beautiful day. I had plans for us." She takes another step closer.

Dawn glances across the room to her bag perched on the arm of the settee – she needs to leave and quick. Looking back at her mum, she blinks furiously. "I didn't know about your plans, Mum." The words stumble out of her. "I must go now, I've got a bus to catch." She steps forward but her mum blocks the way and grabs her wrist tightly.

"*We have plans today, Dawn.*"

"*Let go of me. Please.*" Dawn tries to pull her arm away, but her mum holds on tight, squeezing her.

"You should change those shorts before you go anywhere. You look ridiculous, with your fat thighs sticking out of them," she says, pulling Dawn towards her.

Dawn can smell the bitter coffee on her mum's breath. "*Leave me alone.*" She yanks her wrist free, grabs her bag from the settee, and leaves. Slamming the front door behind her.

Her heart is pounding as she half runs out of their estate to the bus stop. Relieved to see other people standing there, she takes her hoodie out of her bag and ties it around her waist. *This is becoming unbearable. I have to move out. I am a grown woman. I shouldn't be treated like this.* The bus trundles towards her and she takes out her student pass. The sleeping tablets need to be used again and soon. For real this time, Dawn thinks, taking the first free seat she sees.

Gazing out of the window, Dawn realises that she doesn't have a clue what her scheme is after she moves out. Where will she go if she does manage to escape her mum? She needs to focus on this. They haven't found a suitable house to rent yet. She needs to ask Ruth if she stay with her family until they do find somewhere.

49

Emily's phone beeps and she clicks into a message from Carla.

Not seen u properly in ages. Come over 2nite. Thomas is out w/ clients at that new tapas place. Takeaway & wine??

Emily knows she has to go. Carla is going to start getting suspicious if she keeps avoiding her.

Great. I'll pick up Indian. 8 OK?

Perf. I'll have my usual.

She taps her fingers on the steering wheel as she drives, reasoning with herself that Thomas will be gone by the time she gets there. She can't be in the house when he is. There is a niggling doubt in her head as to whether Thomas is going for a client meal at all or is he actually meeting up with the curly-haired woman? Her previous experience with her ex's lies makes her suspicious. Does she one hundred percent believe what Thomas had told her, that he'd met a friend from college? Was it just a hug that she misinterpreted? She wants to believe it. He certainly made her feel like she was the only one the other day in the show house.

Waiting at the traffic lights she rubs the back of her neck and attempts to take some calming breaths. The lights change, and she drives on, breathing a sigh of relief when she turns into their cul-de-sac and there's no sign of his car.

Carla is there to meet her in the hallway, with her finger over her lips. "Dan is still awake. I think he thought Theo and Rosie were coming too. I told him they've gone to their dad's for the weekend but I have a feeling he'll be sneaking downstairs to double-check."

She follows Carla into the kitchen and, seeing the table set for dinner, remembers the Indian takeaway! She's completely forgotten to order it.

"I'm starving. I ate half of the kids' dinner earlier," Carla says as she turns around. "Where's the food? Did you leave it in the car, you dozy mare?"

"*Shit!* I drove right by it. I totally forgot to stop. God, I must have been in a world of my own." Emily laughs.

"Did you order it at least?" Carla asks, pouring a glass of Chardonnay for Emily.

"Yes, of course."

"Well, we'll just ring and ask them to deliver it."

"No, it's fine. I'll go and collect it, it'll be quicker. They'll be busy with deliveries. Here, give me a sip of that." She takes a big mouthful of her wine. "I'll be back soon."

She calls the Indian on the way to place the order and then, she can't help herself, she googles the tapas restaurant Carla said Thomas had gone to as she waits at the traffic lights, deciding to do a drive-by. The traffic all seems to be coming in the opposite direction, out of Galway city, but Emily knows she will never be in and out in twenty minutes for the takeaway. She'll just have to tell Carla that she bumped into someone and got talking. She has to see for herself what the heck is going on with Thomas.

She finds the restaurant easily enough and drives past it a couple of times. It's a small restaurant, not much bigger than someone's living room. There's a large window on either side of the door, with vines displayed down the edge of each of them. She slows as she drives past. She can see red candles stuck into bottles on each table and a huge painting of a traditional Spanish scene decorates one wall. It looks quite busy at the back of the restaurant, but a combination of the lighting inside and the traffic and pedestrians on the outside makes it difficult for her to see the diners clearly. A car comes up behind her and she drives on, parking a little way down the street. Looking at her watch, she realises she's been too long already. She can't do a walk-by, those windows are just too big. She has to get back to Carla.

Indicating to pull out, she checks her rear-view mirror and as she does, spots Thomas walking on the opposite side of the road, towards the restaurant. He is alone. Switching the indicator off, she shrinks down into her seat, making herself as small as possible and watches him approach the door of the restaurant before something catches his eye and he looks up. Following his line of sight, Emily sees that same blonde woman walking towards him. A shiver runs down her spine as the woman smiles and gives a little wave, her blonde curls bouncing with each step. Her tiny bird-like frame is dressed in a red flowery knee-length dress and a blue denim jacket. Emily reacts quickly this time, taking out her phone and snapping away as they greet each other with a kiss on the cheek and go into the restaurant. That was definitely a kiss, and not how you greet a client.

Emily straightens herself in the seat and starts the engine. She bites down on her bottom lip as she drives in the direction of the Indian takeaway. Surely, if he was meeting an old friend from college, he would have said that to Carla. Why tell her he was meeting a client?

What does she do now? Fuck. She is falling in love with him. Dumping him only briefly crosses her mind before she pushes it away. This has to work in her favour. Somehow. Emily has a chance of happiness here. She wants Thomas. Her head begins to pound. Going through the village, a speed sign flashes red at her, she is going too fast. She presses the brake and breathes in deeply. This other woman has to be edged out of the picture. But how?

Emily pushes her food around the plate, only half listening to Carla talk about the plans for Sinéad's fortieth birthday. Her stomach aches as she sips her wine and looks around the kitchen. Thomas's kitchen. He is everywhere she looks – taunting her. His gold cufflinks are on the breakfast bar, his trainers sit inside the patio doors. His shirts are peeking out from the utility room, hanging on the airer. Looking down at her lamb bhuna, she pushes the fork around the onions. She is sitting here with his wife while he is off gallivanting with another woman. Aware of the sudden silence in the room, she glances up at Carla and sees her waiting expectantly for some sort of response.

"That's great, Carla, she'll love that," she says, hoping that's what Carla is still talking about.

Carla reaches over to top up her wine glass.

"No more for me, thanks, I've got to drive home."

"Don't be daft, I bought two bottles. I assumed you'd stay over. It's been ages since we've had a girly night in." She refills Emily's glass. "I'd say Thomas won't be back for hours anyway." She fills her own. "I'll just check that Dan has settled."

Staying here for the night, something that would have been completely normal only a couple of months ago, is now unthinkable. Waking up in the house with her lover and his wife, watching him with his tousled bed head pottering around the kitchen making coffee and poached eggs, wearing his tartan pyjama bottoms and his old navy university hoodie, would be excruciating.

Emily looks down at the naan bread left in her hand, the rest of it torn into little pieces and scattered over the top of her dinner. Hearing

Carla on the stairs, she pushes the plate to one side.

"Don't you like the bhuna?" Carla asks, sitting down.

"I think I've gone past the hunger stage, that's all. It's late to be eating. You know me, I don't sleep properly if I eat late."

Leaning back in her seat, Carla says, "I've eaten too much, too fast. I feel like I'm going to burst."

Emily scrapes the plates into the takeaway bag and takes it outside to the bin. Taking a moment, she leans against the cool wall at the side of the house and stares up at the night sky. Despite the orange glow from the village, she can see thousands of tiny stars twinkling. There is no way she can stay here tonight, drinking wine with Carla, gossiping and giggling. Pretending everything is normal. Greeting Thomas when he comes home, sleeping in the spare room with her lover in the next room with his wife.

"Are you all right, Em?" Carla rounds the corner of the house. "You're not having a cigarette, are you?"

"No, I would though, if you've any stashed away."

Carla laughs. "No, you know me, I haven't smoked since college. Thomas hated me smoking. You're the lapser after a drink."

"Shame. It'd be nice to have one now looking up at the stars, wouldn't it?" *And not have to go back into the house with him everywhere.*

"Come on, it's freezing."

Leading her into the living room, Carla lights some candles and sits down at one end of the couch, tucking her legs up to the side. Emily takes the opposite end, and turns her body towards Carla, crossing her legs.

"So, what do you make of the summer concert idea for the school? Do you think it's a bit over the top?" she asks, knowing that Carla will talk for a while on the subject.

Zoning out straight away, her mind replays what she saw outside the tapas restaurant. It can't be a coincidence that it was the same woman and, although she was at a distance again, it certainly looked more than a client meeting. It was definitely a kiss this time even if it was on the cheek. After the heartbreak of her marriage, Emily should have been more guarded but, she trusted Thomas, she thought she knew him. Curling a strand of her hair around and around her finger, she lets it untangle. Reaching for her wine, she drains the glass. She needs to decide what to do, and she can't do that here, in his house.

When Carla goes to the bathroom, Emily switches a ringtone on and pretends to have a conversation.

"Look, I'm going to have to go," she says when Carla returns. "That was Chris, Rosie has some spots on her stomach, and she can't sleep, he's worried it might be chickenpox. You know what a hypochondriac he is. It's probably nothing but I'll call in on my way home and have a look."

"Are you sure you're okay to drive? I can call you a taxi," Carla says, tilting her chin down and frowning slightly.

"I'm fine." Emily swallows the lump at the back of her throat. "I only had a glass and a half."

A heaviness accompanies her every step out to her car.

She has to get home and figure out what the hell she is going to do about Thomas.

50

Emily notices the open bedroom window as she pulls onto the driveway. Damn, she thinks, the house will be freezing, the bathroom window is probably open too. Sighing, she wishes she wasn't going into a cold, empty house. She misses having an other half, someone to chat to at the end of the day, someone at home waiting for her. She's never adjusted to the kids being gone to Chris's every other weekend. They love going to their dad's and she doesn't mind the break from them sometimes – it can be pretty full-on during the week – but the quiet house is just strange.

She cradles the keys in her lap, running a finger around the outside of the unicorn keyring. She really thought there was a glint of happiness for her with Thomas. She knew it would take time. Something like this wasn't going to happen overnight. But now, this woman, again. She'd tried to convince herself what she thought she saw in the hotel carpark wasn't what actually happened. That it was a hug between friends or a goodbye kiss. She'd believed him when he said it was a college friend. He hadn't acted strangely, just said it matter-of-factly. She'd wanted to believe him. But, tonight, seeing Thomas with her again, she isn't so sure. Was that dinner tonight another innocent meeting? It did only look like a peck on the cheek outside the restaurant, but still, why would he tell Carla he was meeting a client if it was an old college friend? Why the secrecy?

Emily goes inside and lights the wood burner and a couple of candles on the glass coffee table before going upstairs to close the windows. Looking at her bed, part of her feels like curling up under the duvet and crying.

Why is this happening to her? Why can't she be happy and loved? Putting her pyjamas on, she tells herself, no, she will not wallow, she deserves to be loved. She must be strong and think things through, decide what to do. She needs a plan.

Settling herself on the settee with a blanket and cup of tea, she opens the photo gallery on her phone and zooms in on the woman greeting Thomas outside the restaurant. It is only a peck. Is that because she is a friend, or because they are in public together?

Emily tries to recall ever meeting this woman at college, but she doesn't recognise her. If Thomas was telling the truth and she was someone he's kept in touch with, she would surely be on his friends list on Facebook. Clicking onto his page, she scrolls through his friends. There are a few Traceys and she squints at all the blonde thumbnail photos and taps on the ones that might be possible. None of them are her. *Who is she?*

Emily thinks as she sips her tea. She checks out his company's website next and scrolls through photos of his colleagues and events, but again no luck.

She closes her phone case and rests her head back on the settee. Maybe this is a warning to stop seeing Thomas. To stand back and end things now, while she can, before anyone gets hurt. Watching the candles flicker, she twists her eternity ring around her finger. She takes a deep breath and opens the dating app on her phone and looks through her matches. Should she forget Thomas and focus her attention on finding happiness here instead? She reads through a few of the matched men. None of them are Thomas.

What's happened between her and Thomas wasn't planned, it was fate. She already knows him and loves him. With him, she sees a little light, a narrow ray breaking through the clouds, illuminating her; a tiny hope of happiness.

It's too late. She can't go back on what she's done. What they've done. Even if she stopped seeing Thomas right now, and went back to the way it was before, it would never be the same. The damage is done. The step too far has already been taken. Going back now isn't an option.

Sighing, she goes into the kitchen and takes the vodka from the cupboard, pouring herself a generous measure, adding a couple of ice cubes and some Coke from the fridge. She downs it in a couple of gulps and pours another to take back into the living room, grabbing a bag of Maltesers from the treat cupboard on her way past.

Pulling her knees under the blanket, Emily hugs them to her chest. She knows she's put all her eggs in this basket and must now see it through. She gulps at the vodka. Is Thomas seeing this other woman? How can she get rid of her?

Scenarios start whirling around her mind. What if Carla found out about the other woman? If Carla knew Thomas is having an affair, she can kill two birds with one stone. Carla will dump Thomas. She'll never forgive him for his infidelity. It doesn't matter that they have been married for ten years, there is no way she will stand for it. When Chris came out as gay, it wasn't the fact he had lived a lie about his sexuality for all those years, it was that he'd been unfaithful that outraged Carla.

Emily doesn't kid herself she'll be able to be with Thomas publicly straight away. No, they'd have to leave it a respectable amount of time before announcing they were together. Maybe even a year. She can be patient. She looks at the photo of Thomas and the woman again. It's only a peck. It isn't incriminating enough. She needs more.

She tosses the phone onto the settee next to her, and lifts the glass to her lips, hesitating before she sips, as an idea forms in her mind. She could go back to the restaurant now. Try and get more photos. Some evidence. An anonymous tip-off to Carla could be enough to make her doubt Thomas and confront him.

Replacing the glass on the coffee table, she realises she's had too much to drink to go now, hasn't she? Wine at Carla's, vodka here. But she's had a meal. She doesn't feel drunk – not even tipsy. A feeling of determination washes over her as she throws back the blanket and stands up. She deserves to be loved and if this is what she must do then so be it.

Emily blows out the candles and goes upstairs to get dressed.

It hits her as she drives that if it is more than friends having dinner, it's going to be a blow to her too. She's the one who wants him for herself. Has Thomas been seduced by an old college friend? While having the evidence might help to split Carla and Thomas up, how does she know Thomas will choose her?

Surely he will, she remonstrates with herself as she drives past the docks, towards Galway's west end. If his head's been turned by this Tracey, it's only because he's flattered. Hasn't he told her he loves her?

But really, she doesn't believe Thomas is having an affair, not another one. They are just meeting up for dinner and he doesn't want Carla to know for some reason. Maybe she was an ex-girlfriend. Someone from before Carla. Years have passed since they were in college. It doesn't mean anything now even if it was so. But Emily needs to make it work in her favour. All she has to do is get some photos, a hug that could be interpreted as more from a certain angle. That and a note could be enough to cause trouble.

She parks a safe distance away from the restaurant and pushes her arms into her dark green trench coat, twisting her ponytail on top of her head before pulling a cap over it. She moves quickly along the pavement, keeping her head low as couples pass. Her stomach sinks when she sees the empty restaurant. Only a couple of staff are in there tidying up.

Emily looks up and down the street. Now what? That's her plan ruined. She turns back towards her car, annoyed with herself for thinking this would work.

It's his laugh she hears before she spots them coming out of Keogh's pub across the street. Emily ducks into a doorway, out of sight, and watches as they make their way down the street away from her. They aren't holding hands, just wandering alongside one another. Emily stares after them. What should she do? What did she expect? To see them snogging in the street? They disappear around the corner. She has to follow them. She must if she is to gather evidence.

She strides after them but hesitates at the corner. What if Thomas sees her spying on him? He might think she's a nutcase and break up with her. She glances down at her long coat. In hindsight, this wasn't the best coat choice as she stands out amongst other people dressed up for a night out.

She urges herself onwards. She must take the risk. It is her chance for happiness.

Staying close to the buildings, she walks slowly around the corner, her eyes darting left and right. She spots them standing next to a blue Fiesta. The same blue Fiesta she'd seen leaving the car park of the House hotel. Emily shuffles along the buildings until she reaches a funeral home. There she ducks behind a low wall and takes out her phone. They are talking and their heads are close, almost touching. She clicks away on the camera as they lean into each other. She can't quite tell if they are kissing from this angle, but it certainly looks like it.

The woman gets into her car and drives off. Emily crouches lower behind the wall and waits until she's sure Thomas has gone.

She stands up and checks the photos on her phone. This is it. They are convincing. She has the evidence. Now to show Carla.

As she hurries back to her car, she pushes the hurting niggles about Thomas with the other woman away. Thomas loves her. He's told her so many times. This woman is just a distraction and Emily is going to deal with her.

Back at the car, she closes her eyes, resting her hands on the steering wheel. She knows she doesn't have to do this. She could keep quiet and see how things play out but, on the other side of the coin, she has a chance to be happy and she deserves to be.

51

Dawn closes the accommodation app and pushes her plate to one side. There are only two suitable properties listed to rent and they've been there for weeks. Samantha knew a girl who lived in one of the houses last year and it was a dump; the landlord was awful and he owned both houses listed. Dawn sighs – this search for a house is beginning to feel hopeless.

Her boss sticks his head around the staffroom door. "Five minutes, Dawn, a big group have just come in and we'll need your help. I put those flatpack boxes you wanted by the kitchen door."

"Okay. Thanks a million," she says, standing up and washing her plate in the sink.

Looking at her watch, she has three more hours left in her shift. She really can't face going home and watching Mum's fake personality with Michael. She's sick of it. Moving out is all she can think about. She has to get out and soon. Texting Ruth, she says: **What u doing? I finish @ 5.**

Leaning against the worktop, she thinks through the logistics of moving out. The sleeping tablet scheme seems like the best non-confrontational way to go about it, but she doesn't have anywhere to move to yet. She nibbles the skin around her fingernails – she needs to bite the bullet and ask Ruth if she can stay with her family until they find student accommodation. But, she thinks, how much can she tell Ruth?

Her phone pings

Have car. Collect u @ 5.

Dawn exhales. Great. She can avoid going home for another few hours.

Perfect. Will you park around the back of the restaurant? We can go for a milkshake at the new place.

Slipping into a red leather booth in the American-styled diner, Dawn decides she just has to come straight out with it.

"We're not having much luck with the house hunting, are we?" She sips her chocolate malt milkshake.

"No, but we'll find somewhere. It's early in the summer yet." Ruth thumbs the pages of the mini-jukebox on their table. "Oh my God, these songs are so old. I remember my grandparents singing them!"

"I think I need to move out of home sooner rather than later. That's what those flatpack boxes are for," Dawn says, stirring her milkshake.

"How come?"

What can I tell her? "I just need to get out. Mum doesn't want me to move out and it's causing an atmosphere." She adjusts her fashion scarf, twisting it around her neck. The red, blue, and green of the pattern rests brightly against the black of her work uniform.

"Okay, well, why don't me, you, and Samantha get together this weekend and blitz this house hunting. We'll have a place in a couple of months. What do you think?"

"Sounds good. I need to break free. I don't see why I can't. It's not as if I am asking her to pay for accommodation. I have the money myself."

"It's not me you have to convince."

"Yeah, well, I need to find somewhere."

"Good for you. She'll get over it."

"*Mmm.*" Dawn stares at her milkshake.

"Are you okay?"

"Kind of." Dawn keeps her eyes on twisting the straw around. "I might need to move out really soon. Could I stay with you for a while? Would your mum and dad mind?"

"What do you mean?" Ruth asks, sipping the last of her milkshake, making it gurgle.

"I don't know. I was kind of thinking of moving out without telling Mum. I'm not sure I can deal with all the drama that will come with me going." She lifts her head to meet Ruth's eyes.

"Oh right." Ruth raises her eyebrows. "Do you mean tonight?"

"No, not tonight. But soon, in the next couple of weeks. Maybe after my Uncle Michael has gone back to Australia."

"Mum and Dad will be gone on holiday to France soon. They're taking the kids out of school for the last week, so that'll be fine. They won't even have to know," Ruth says, noticing Dawn's eyes pooling. "Hey, don't worry, it'll be great. We'll have the house to ourselves. It'll be a dry run of us living together. Come on, let's order brownies, this calls for a celebration. We're going to be housemates!"

Smiling through her tears at her friend, Dawn feels a weight lifting off her shoulders, not all of it but some of it.

52

Emily has sent the photos and short note yesterday via courier, to be delivered before three. Before the kids came home from school, and before Thomas returned from his work trip tomorrow. Emily expected to hear from Carla almost immediately, but no call or message came. She'd kept refreshing the screen, using her tracking number from the parcel company, and it confirmed it had been delivered. So why hadn't she heard anything? Who else would Carla call? She's her best friend, for god's sake.

Emily yawns and stares at her laptop screen on her work desk. She'd block-booked imaginary viewings for all of yesterday afternoon, expecting the need to rush over to Carla's. She's done the same again for this afternoon. Sipping her coffee, she embraces the caffeine hit. She'd hardly slept last night. Instead, she'd lain in bed, going over and over scenarios of what could happen and what could go wrong with her plan.

She drains the coffee and looks at her watch. The school run was over hours ago. Carla would hardly have gone to Pilates after hearing news like that, would she? What if she's confronted Thomas already? What if they worked it out it's she who sent the photos and note. She gulps loudly. No, they couldn't. She'd typed the note and sent it from a post office via courier on the far side of the city. It can't point back to her, of that she's sure.

Her mobile shrills and Emily jumps. Carla's name flashes across the screen. *Here we go.* Her heart thumps loudly as she answers.

"Hi, Carla! I'm at work so I can't talk for long."

"Oh, I forgot you were working today." Carla's voice is quiet and wobbly, and Emily is in no doubt that her parcel was received.

"Are you okay? You sound, I don't know, quiet. Did Julia piss you off again?"

"No, no, I ... I need you. Can you come around?" Her voice breaks and a quiet sob escapes.

"Yes, yes, of course I can." Emily's voice shakes as the enormity of what she's done is dawning on her. "I can be there in half an hour." A short, sharp stab of guilt catches in her chest. This is it. What has she done to her best friend? "What is it, Carla? What's happened?"

"I just need you to come here …" Her voice tails off and it sounds like she is fading into the background.

"I'm leaving now," Emily says.

Putting the handbrake on, Emily turns off the engine and stares at Carla's house. A bouquet of roses and lilies sits in the bay window. She cradles the car keys on her lap. This is happening. It's going to devastate Carla and crush her. Rubbing her thumb along the rubber of her car key, Emily wills her hammering heart to quieten. She must do this; she has no choice.

A glimmer of hope flickers for her own happiness, but she pushes it to one side. That has to wait. She has to concentrate on Carla now.

"*Hiya!*" she calls as she steps inside.

There is no answer, but she can hear a clattering in the kitchen. She opens the kitchen door, startling Carla, and she spins around.

Emily can see the devastation she's caused etched on her friend's face.

"Oh my god, Carla, what is it? What's happened?" She instinctively moves towards her.

Carla puts the cafetière on the breakfast bar and Emily pulls her into an embrace. She inhales the familiar smell of the cherry and almond shampoo that Carla's used for years. The one she sometimes borrowed when they lived together. The fruity bouquet of Carla's perfume is mixed in with the scent. Emily bought her that perfume on her way home from holiday in Italy last year. She squeezes her, perhaps a little too hard, before pulling back.

"Is it your parents? Your dad's heart?" Carla's dad had a heart bypass last year. "Do you want me to ring Thomas for you? He's away, isn't he?"

"No. No, it's not that." Carla's voice catches in her throat.

The bell on the oven beeps and only then does Emily realise she can smell fresh scones. What the hell is Carla doing making scones at a time like this?

"Hang on. Let me just …" Carle turns away, reaching for the oven gloves and taking the scones out. She lifts each one onto a cooling rack.

Emily's hands are shaking. She reaches for the cafetière for something to do and pushes her hands down on the plunger. She looks around. She's always envied Carla her large kitchen with its sash windows and French doors overlooking the decking and the garden. The shiny cream porcelain floor tiles reflect the light from outside and the glass from the cupboards. Everything is so clean. There are more flowers on the dining table; tulips this time. Photos of Carla's boys decorate the pale-yellow walls and family snaps of the four of them are on the tall, mahogany sideboard. An informal wedding photo of Carla and Thomas wrapped around each other on the dancefloor stands in the middle of these, in a silver embossed frame. Emily took that photo and gave it to them on their first anniversary. Their faces are red and glowing, eyes and smiles so bright they leave you in no doubt how happy they are. A large knot tightens in Emily's stomach.

She watches as Carla puts the last scone on the rack and the tray back in the oven. Carla rests her hands on the kitchen countertop and the way her body hunches over makes Emily thinks this is the only thing holding her friend upright. She moves around the breakfast bar.

"Forget about all this. What's happened, Carla?"

Carla turns and almost collapses into Emily's arms.

"It's Thomas," she says. "Look." She glances over Emily's shoulder to the far end of the breakfast bar.

Emily turns, seeing the padded envelope she'd filled yesterday, seeing the address label she'd printed at work.

She guides Carla to a stool before reaching for the envelope. A strange shudder passes through her as she holds it, despite knowing exactly what it contains.

"Open it," Carla says, reaching for a tissue, keeping her eyes firmly fixed on the cafetière.

Emily slides out the photos and the note. She stares at them for a moment, remembering crouching behind the low wall, before she realises she must react. This must be a shock to her.

"Oh my god, Carla. What are these? Who is this?"

"I don't know, I don't know!"

Her sobs are like a whimper and Emily moves back to her, holding her friend as she quietly cries.

She rubs her hand up and down Carla's back.

"Did this arrive today?"

"No, yesterday."

"Did you confront Thomas?" She holds her breath.

"No, I haven't done anything. He's away anyway but I've been too stunned. I can't think straight."

Her quiet sobs continue, and Emily continues to rub her back, staring at the cooling scones. Carla will always associate scones with this day, Emily knows she will. When she found out about Chris, they had just finished eating pizza – goat's cheese, red pepper, and pesto. Now, whenever she even smells pizza or goat's cheese, she gets the same sinking feeling in her gut she had that evening when her whole world fell apart.

After a few minutes, Emily says, "Come on, let's sit in the living room." She leads Carla through the double doors. It's cooler in here at the front of the house without the sun shining in and Emily is glad of it. The perspiration inside her jumper is dripping down her spine. She steers Carla to the settee and they sit down.

Looking up, Emily regrets their positioning: on the wall opposite is a huge photograph of Carla, Thomas, and the boys from a photoshoot they had last summer. A pang of guilt hits as she sees Ben and Daniel's faces looking down at her. This is going to change their lives too.

Putting her arm around her friend, she leans back and Carla's body shudders into her, but no sound comes out. Emily realises she's still holding the note and photos. She pushes them down the side of the settee.

"Do you think it's true?" Carla's words wobble, no louder than a whisper.

Emily knows the pain and hurt that she's causing Carla. She's experienced it herself. But she also knows that there is worse to come. Much worse. But not now. Not yet. First steps first.

"I don't know. It certainly looks like it. Why would someone go to the bother of sending these if it wasn't?"

Carla pulls away. Her eyes widen and blink frantically.

"But you know Thomas. He's always been the touchy-feely type. He hugs everyone. It doesn't mean anything."

Emily takes Carla's hands. "This looks more than Thomas being over-friendly though." She tries to ignore the quick sharp stabs in her gut.

Carla pulls her hands away. "No, not my Thomas. I'd know. Surely I'd know."

"How would you? Sometimes people are very good liars. I mean, look at me – I never knew about Chris, did I?"

"This is different. This is Thomas. He wouldn't. Surely he wouldn't?" Carla's voice tapers off to a whisper and she stands up and walks over to the fireplace, staring at the family photos displayed on the mantelpiece.

"The photos are the evidence, Carla." The words come out more sharply than Emily intends, and she quickly adds, "I don't want it to be true either."

Carla turns around. Her face has paled and her eyes seem sunken in their sockets but her look is determined. "Look, I know you're sensitive to these things, especially after what happened to you, but Thomas wouldn't do that to me. He hated that his father treated his mother like that and despised him. He'd never do that to me."

"The photos say it all, and the note. It must be true," Emily says softly, standing up. She moves towards her just as Carla's body sags and leads her back to the settee. "I'm sorry, Carla, I really am." She squeezes her eyes shut tight.

Carla shakes her head. "No, no, it can't be true. We're going away this weekend, remember?"

Emily nods and pulls her friend tighter to her.

"It was meant to be a romantic getaway, just the two of us. No kids, no meetings, no big deals to look after, just the two of us walking, talking, an afternoon at the spa." She hesitates. "I can't believe it." Sitting back from Emily, she says, "Why would Thomas do this?"

Carla's eyes are pleading, and a small part of Emily wishes she didn't have to do this. Wishes that Thomas wasn't Carla's. "I don't know."

Carla stares across the room, her eyes focused on the family photo on the wall, her hand reaches for her pendant on the solid gold chain around her neck.

"I'm here, Carla. We'll get through this together. Me and you against the world. Haven't we always said that? Since we were thirteen." In Emily's head, the words sound hollow, and she hopes they didn't come out that way. She doesn't want them to be, she doesn't mean them to be. But inevitably, when everything comes out, they will ring hollow, and Carla will hate her even more for saying them.

Carla rests her head on Emily's shoulder and together they lean back against the settee.

Emily is surprised by her friend's lack of tears. It's so unlike her. She expected loud, snotty sobs. Carla cries at sad movies, at her children's school plays, at heart-wrenching stories in magazines at the hairdressers. Why isn't she sobbing loudly on discovering her husband's affair? She is sitting still, occasionally muttering quietly to herself but mainly silent on Emily's shoulder. Emily rubs Carla's hand. She must still be in shock. The knot in Emily's stomach slowly tightens.

After about twenty minutes of sitting in the quiet, Emily asks, "What will you do?"

Sitting up straight, Carla stares at the family portrait. "I'll still go away this weekend."

"*What? With him?*" Her voice comes out louder than she expected.

"No. I'll make up an excuse. I need to get away and think about what to do." Turning to Emily, she says, "Promise me you won't babysit for him this weekend, no matter what emergency he comes up with. I can't bear the thought of him being with her."

"Of course I won't. I won't give the bastard any opportunity at all. Are you going to confront him before you go?"

"No, I can't. Not yet."

"Come here." Emily folds her into her arms. "Just let yourself cry, Carla. It's okay to cry."

But no tears fall. She stays quiet in Emily's arms.

Pulling away, Carla scrapes back her blonde hair with her fingers and takes a bobble from her wrist to tie it back. She wipes under her eyes and checks her fingertips for mascara.

"We'd better go and collect the kids from school," she says, standing up and straightening her white shirt before going into the kitchen.

Emily follows.

"I didn't even offer you a scone, Emily – you must be starving." Carla starts to clear away the plates.

"You stay here. I'll go get the kids." Emily pours the coffee down the sink and rinses the cafetière.

"No, I'll go too," Carla says, going into the utility room. "I'd better switch on the tumble dryer – I forgot about it."

Emily stands staring, dumbfounded. Carla is carrying on like nothing has happened. As if they have just had a normal lunch date.

Putting their coats on, they head out to their respective cars.

Emily is about to reverse when, looking across at Carla in her car, she sees her with her head in her hands, elbows on the steering wheel. Going over, Emily opens Carla's door and drops down next to her, taking her hands in her own.

"You go back inside. I'll go and collect the kids. You stay here."

"No, I don't want to be in there. I don't know how I am going to face him later, how am I going to set foot back in our house. I just want to drive and drive until I am far away from here."

"We can do that. How about we collect the kids and head down to Salthill? Walk the beach with them and get fish and chips." Emily doesn't fancy coming face-to-face with Thomas either.

"Okay, yeah. Let's do that." Carla nods at Emily. "Thank you."

Emily focuses hard on putting one foot in front of the other and not crumbling with guilt as she walks back to her car.

53

Carla is oblivious to the fresh wind of the west coast blowing through her light coat as she steps onto the prom in Salthill. The children are delighted with the impromptu trip. She doesn't have a change of clothes for them or even a proper coat for herself, but she doesn't care. Uniforms can be washed.

The children run ahead as Emily and Carla walk along the prom. Salthill is buzzing with crowds of people. Although schools haven't yet finished for the summer, plenty of people mill about, walking, playing on the beaches, and sitting in the cafés. Music greets them from the fairground. The big wheel is turning and happy shrieks are coming from the waltzer. It's all a blur to Carla.

"My God, that wind is cutting," Emily says, rubbing her hands together. "Let's get coffee."

She calls the kids and they cross over to a takeaway window. Daniel nags Carla to buy buckets and spades that are on display next to the postcards. She sees from the look in Emily's eyes that she has given in too easily, but Carla doesn't care, she buys some for Theo and Rosie too. In the grand scheme of things at this moment, what's a few buckets and spades, she thinks, wrapping her hands around her coffee cup as they walk down the ramp to the beach. She sips it but can't taste it – her stomach is hollow.

Emily rattles on, trying to fill the silence between them. Her words float away on the breeze. Carla's gaze wanders across the beach at the waves turning over, and the people paddling towards them in their swimming costumes. She doesn't notice her teeth chattering. The children stop to carve their names in the sand with their shiny plastic spades. Ben adds MUM and DAD to the list, and Carla stops and stares at lines making up DAD written in the yellow-grey sand. Their family names: Mum, Dad, Ben and Daniel.

"Carla."

Turning to Emily, Carla knows she's been asked something.

"Are you okay?"

Carla barely nods her head and stares out across the beach again.

"Carla, look at me. Talk to me."

Carla nods but doesn't speak. She doesn't know what to say. Her voice has been silenced by this news. Her mind is still trying to absorb it.

"Will we get fish and chips and let the kids warm up for a while?" Emily says.

The kids reluctantly carry their buckets and spades over. Carla looks past them to a family walking down by the seashore. A mum, dad, and two boys, just like her family. A dog scampers between them. Not so much like us, she thinks, we don't have a dog and their family isn't falling apart. Her gut bubbles with bile and she turns away, tossing her full coffee cup into the bin.

She sips her glass of water in the restaurant, and the kids' chatter flutters about her as she stares out of the window at life continuing. Everything is normal. People are going about their business not realising her life and everything she believed in has disintegrated right in front of her.

Rosie reminds Emily about her ballet class this evening. "We can't miss it, Mum, it's the dress rehearsal for the show, remember?"

Emily looks over at Carla apologetically.

"Go on." Carla smiles. "We'll probably head home soon anyway."

After they leave, she buys the boys hot muffins and ice cream, and they beg her to take them back to the beach.

"Of course," she says.

"*Yipee!*" The boys giggle and shout as they leave the restaurant.

She feels like she never wants to go home.

Perching on the rocks, the cold seeping through her jeans, she watches the boys play. Watching them but not seeing them. How can this be happening to her?

The ringtone of her phone echoes faintly in her pocket and she takes it out, staring at Thomas's name and face lighting up the screen. She has to answer. She can't let on that she knows anything.

Not yet.

"Hey, you, I'm on my way home. On time for a change. Do you need me to pick anything up?" Thomas says.

Carla's heart soothes with his deep gentle tones and for a moment she wonders if it's all rubbish, a misunderstanding. This is her Thomas.

"We're at the beach. We came here after school with Emily and her kids. The boys are still playing so do you want to get a takeaway?"

"Okay, what d'you fancy?"

"Oh, we've already eaten fish and chips. Just look after yourself. We'll be home soon."

"I might pick up a Chinese so. See you at home. Love you."

And he hangs up. A perfectly normal conversation. Nothing seemed any different.

When Ben comes over to her with chattering teeth, she realises she can't put this off any longer. They have to go home. Strangely, she only feels the cold when they are back in the car. She tests the boys on their spellings and gets them to do their reading homework as she drives. Her fingertips turn white, her head pounds and she shivers as she sounds out Daniel's tricky words with him, her voice quiet and shaky.

Turning into their estate, her stomach lurches at the sight of Thomas's black BMW parked in the driveway. *Okay, Carla, you can do this*, she says to herself and her churning gut, as she follows the boys into the house.

Thomas is eating his takeaway at the dining table and the boys sit at the table with him, munching the left-over prawn crackers and telling him all about the channel they dug and what they found on the beach to build dams with. Carla potters in the background, watching the way Thomas listens intently to the boys. His hair keeps flopping forward and he keeps pushing it back. He needs a haircut. His hair is so thick, and it gets wavy when it gets longer. She loves running her hand through it, loves pulling his head towards her and smelling his hair. Watching as he asks Daniel questions about the dam, she can't help thinking about the other woman holding his head in this way. Her stomach heaves and she turns to the sink, swallowing quickly. Running the tap for a few seconds, she fills a glass and sips slowly, focusing on a tile behind the sink, the one with the hairline crack in it.

She collects up the takeaway boxes and starts to put them in the paper bag they came in.

"I'll do that in a minute, Carla."

"It's okay, you chat with the boys. This is your time with them." She is disgusted with herself as soon as the words are out. Why is she being kind to him when he probably spent the afternoon in the arms of that other woman?

She wanders around aimlessly upstairs, collecting laundry and folding towels away. Standing in the doorway of their bedroom, she can't bring herself to step inside. How crazy to think she'd woken yesterday morning thinking that they were a normal family. In the boys' bedroom, she lays out their clean uniforms for tomorrow, picks up a few toys, and takes some pyjamas out for them. Sinking onto the edge of one of the beds, she looks around. To anyone looking at them, they would seem to be a normal loving family. It's quiet up here and she lies back on her son's bed, closing her eyes. Everything had been going along just perfectly. Well, not perfectly; nothing is perfect. But she was happy; she thought they were happy. Maybe she should just ignore the note and photos. She hadn't noticed until it was forced in front of her. Should she just turn a blind eye, let him get it out of his system? That might be all he needs to do. It could be a mid-life crisis. He might get over it and they can carry on. It jars with her how he can behave so normally with her while living with such lies. He's being just as loving and kind as he always is. How can he be so deceitful at the same time? But what is normal? She doesn't know anymore.

On the wall opposite, there's a birth sampler of Winnie the Pooh and Tigger, stitched by Thomas's mother. Thomas hated his father's treatment of his mother. His mother put up with her husband's infidelities because she had no choice. Divorce was frowned upon; she didn't have the financial capability to leave either. She'd been stuck.

Turning on her side, Carla hugs Ben's teddy, a brown fluffy bear with a red bow tie and a blue grandad hat. Inhaling her son's smell, she closes her eyes. If this is a once-off, would she be able to forgive Thomas? The note called it an affair. Why would someone send these things if it was a one-night stand?

I can't turn a blind eye to an affair and I won't. I'm not going to allow history to repeat itself.

Hearing Thomas saying, "Bath time, you little sandboys!" to the kids as they bound up the stairs, she sits up, running her hands through her hair, and refolds the pyjamas on her lap.

54

Emily's finger hovers over Thomas's name before she presses the call button for the third time, her heart hammering in her chest. This is the next step – she has to do this. The voicemail kicks in again, she hangs up, and places the phone on her desk.

Staring at the computer screen, she allows a small smile to spread across her face. Carla had left this morning for the planned romantic weekend away, alone. Emily's plan is coming together. Hopefully Thomas will soon be hers. She doodles on the edge of her notes. She just has to get rid of one other stumbling block – that other woman. Who is she? If she's an old college friend, like he claims, surely he'd have told Carla. There's definitely something more to it, and it's up to her to deal with it, to move things along a little quicker. She's going to use this woman to cause more trouble. She picks up her phone again.

Call me. It's about Carla x

He can't ignore that message – he'll have to contact me.

She pushes back from her desk, grabs a folder and makes her way into the photocopying room. For a moment, she stands at the window, watching the trucks from the refrigeration company next door, the blues, reds, and greens, manoeuvring in the distribution car park. He has to ring her now, of course he does. She hasn't given him enough information to know what she's on about. Just a Carla-carrot dangle.

The phone shrills in the quiet of the small room, and its screen lights up along with Emily's face. She lets it ring for a few seconds before answering.

"Hey, I missed your calls, I was stuck in a meeting. What's up?" Thomas says.

"Sorry for ringing you so much. I thought I might catch you on your lunch break."

"I've not had a chance to take it yet. One of those days, you know."

"Look, I think we'd better meet up," she says. "Can you meet me in half an hour? I can get the key for the Westgate offices, say the third floor."

"Not today, unfortunately. I'd love to, obviously, but I can't."

"Did you not read my text? We've got to talk – about Carla."

"What about Carla?"

Emily holds her breath for a fraction of a second before saying, "There's something weird going on. Someone's watching her and, I think, following her too."

"What? What the fuck? "

"Look, we can't talk over the phone." She keeps her voice calm and steady.

"Okay. See you in about half an hour."

This is it. She pops into the bathroom, scrunching her hair in the mirror and reapplying her lip gloss. She's going to play it real cool and watch him carefully. This has to work.

55

Emily stands at the third-floor window watching Thomas walk across the car park. The lights on his car flash to say it's locked; he doesn't glance back. He looks around him and confidently strides towards the building. God, he is gorgeous. How had it taken her so long to realise it? They could have got together years ago. Before Carla. She could have snagged him first if she'd wanted to. Instead of wasting her time on a gay husband. Her life could have been so different.

The lift pings and Thomas appears. He walks past the empty reception desk and straight over to her.

"Hey." His dark eyes meet hers, full of concern. He puts his two hands on her shoulders. "What is it?"

Emily pulls away and steps back. "Someone's watching Carla," she says, not meeting his eyes. "A woman."

"What do you mean, what makes you think so?"

"I've seen her in the car park at school and on your estate. Are you having Carla followed or something?"

"What? No, of course not. Why would I?" Thomas backs away and leans against a pillar. He glances out of the window before looking at Emily. "You're being paranoid. It's probably another mother from school who lives on our estate."

"No, it's definitely not. I would recognise her. Carla's noticed her too."

"What?" He walks towards her. "Why the fuck didn't you just say that as soon as I walked in, or on the phone even? "

She winces at his bark.

"What did she say to you, Emily?"

She takes a deep breath. *Here goes.* "She thought a woman was watching her at school."

"*What do you mean, watching her? For fuck's sake, stop drip-dropping information and tell me the whole fucking thing!*" His shout echoes around the empty office space and bounces back at them in the pause.

"God, I will if you give me a chance to speak!" she snaps. "She says she's seeing the same woman around the place, and she feels like she's being watched. She's convinced."

"Why wouldn't she have told me about this?"

"I don't know. I'm scared she's suspicious of you. Maybe that's why."

"Who knows about us, who have you told?"

"I didn't tell anyone. Why would I?"

"What does this woman look like?"

Emily watches Thomas carefully as she describes the other woman to him. "She's short, very slim, with big curly blonde hair." She watches the realisation sweep across his face at her description and she continues. "Do you think it's someone who's seen us together and is going to tell Carla?"

She glares at Thomas staring at the floor. His face has paled. The tip of the one ear she can see is bright red, a siren against his waxy complexion.

"I'm probably being paranoid. We've been so careful. No-one could have seen us, could they?" she says.

He raises his head slowly and meets her eyes. "I don't know." He cracks each knuckle in turn on one hand.

Her fists clench and she wills herself to stay calm. The cheeky fucker. She wants to scream at him '*I know, I know!*' Her fingers relax.

"We need to figure out who it is. I don't think she's a school mum unless she's new because I would have recognised her and why would we be seeing her everywhere? We should probably cool things for a while and see what happens." She looks directly at him but he doesn't seem to be able to meet her eyes now.

He checks his watch and then takes his phone from his pocket and checks that.

"I've got to go." He straightens up. "Look, we'll talk soon. You're right, it's probably best to keep our distance from each other." Walking to the door, he turns and looks back briefly. "See you."

Emily leans against the window, shaken. That's it? That's all she gets? No hug, no squeeze? No reassurance that all will be fine? No kiss? Did she just make a mistake? Maybe it will backfire on her, and he will break it off with both her and the other woman and stay with Carla. *Shit.* And what if Carla doesn't confront him? What if she decides to ignore the note and photos and carry on as normal? She didn't think this through properly. *Fuck.*

She rushed into this at the thought of her own happiness. She should have been patient.

Looking out of the window she sees Thomas sitting in his car. He's on the phone. Emily takes a few steps back so that she is out of his sightline, but she can still see him. He throws the phone on the passenger seat and slaps the steering wheel. She thinks she sees him look up at the window and she steps back again quickly. His car engine roars into life and he accelerates fast around and out of the car park.

Emily walks out of the offices and turns the key in the lock. What is he going to do? All she can do is wait.

56

"Thank you," Carla says to the porter, closing the hotel room door behind him.

Wow, what a view! She steps towards the floor-to-ceiling windows that frame the dramatic cliffs and churning sea below. A moving picture that is difficult to tear her eyes from.

The smell of roses assaults her senses, and she turns to see a huge bouquet of red and cream flowers sitting on the dressing table, alongside two champagne flutes and a bottle of champagne resting in an ice bucket. Her hands begin to tremble at the thought of the romantic weekend they had planned.

She'd lied to Thomas yesterday. Told him her sister was sick, her husband away, and she needed help with the kids. She said she'd postpone the hotel. They could go another weekend.

He and the house were stifling her. She had to get out.

Unzipping her suitcase, she takes out her wash bag and takes it into the bathroom. The wall of semi-transparent glass separating the bathroom from the bedroom drenches the space in light. An oversized bath stands alone on a raised platform. She catches sight of her sunken eyes in the mirror.

In the bedroom, she sits in one of the wingback chairs that's angled to face the sea, tucking her legs up to her side. The dark clouds are scudding across the sea towards her. How could she have been so blind to it all? How had she not seen the signs? She supposes everyone views life through a different lens. She thought her marriage was a happy one; two kids, a nice house, lots of love and laughter. It wasn't perfect, nobody's is, no matter what they tell you. It's daft to think the thing she was most concerned about was convincing Thomas that her going back to teaching was a good idea.

She twists her engagement, eternity, and wedding rings until they come off, and places them on the mahogany coffee table beside her chair, closing her eyes. Now, it seems that her husband has kept the little wife at home, raising the children, having his dinner ready when he came home, while he played the part of a complete hypocrite. Just like his adulterer of a father. Rubbing her finger where the rings have been, the indents feel strange, her finger feels naked. The knot in her gut twists. How can everything she thought to be true come crumbling down so easily? A feeble wall of love exposed to be riddled with lies and deceit.

The sky is darkening as the grey encroaches ever closer. Rain pelts the windows, the wind blowing it in horizontal sheets, and violent waves churn beneath the cliff. Her phone beeps beside her. She glances at the message flashing up on the screen. It's Emily asking how she is and has she thought about confronting Thomas. She doesn't open it. She doesn't want to reply or invite conversation. She doesn't have the energy for her right now. Emily will understand. Carla needs to think.

What is she going to do? Part of her wants to scream, shout and hit Thomas, and the other part of her wants to walk into those thundering waves below and disappear. Hugging her knees to her chest, she knows she won't do either. She needs to find out more, but how? The sea mesmerises her and she watches as each wave curls and crashes onto the rocks below.

She needs to get out of this room and shake herself out of this despair. It's not an afternoon for walking the cliff top. Not unless she wants to end up in the sea. Wallowing in that beautiful big bath isn't going to help her head either. She'll go to the swimming pool. She hasn't swum in ages. She used to go most mornings before school before she had children.

Walking through the foyer of the hotel, she spots a couple sitting in the side lounge having afternoon tea. A small group of Americans pass by in waterproof clothing and hiking boots, chatting loudly. A young couple toast each other with glasses of bubbly, and Carla lowers her eyes. She shouldn't have come here. Her thumb rubs the finger where her rings usually sit. What in the world is she going to do to pass the weekend here? Maybe she would have been better at home, keeping busy with the children.

The pool is quiet. There are only two others here and the swim lane is free. Welcoming the resistance against her body, Carla starts off swimming breast stroke, building a rhythm, and picking up speed in her strokes, enjoying the pull on muscles she hasn't used for a while. No matter how she tries though, she can't blank her mind, it keeps coming back to Thomas. Is she about to lose him and the life they have built together? A memory of bumping into him in the college pool comes to her. They were just friends then. He stood out amongst the serious swimmers, wearing the most ridiculous pair of bright blue Bermuda shorts, decorated in oranges and lemons. He'd explained that he was playing a character in the drama society's next play who was a swimmer, and as someone who wasn't confident in the water, he was trying to get into the mindset of the character. Turning in the pool now and changing to front crawl, Carla wonders if that's how he has been able to live with all these lies and secrets – was he just playing a part? Which version was the real Thomas? She touches the other end and flips underwater. Is she reading too much into it all? Maybe it was a one-off.

Could she forgive him if it was? Everyone makes mistakes. A glimmer of hope rises from her gut as she pummels through the water. Maybe the woman threw herself at Thomas. Not many men can resist being handed sex on a plate. Perhaps the woman misunderstood Thomas's chattiness and touchy-feely friendliness as flirting? He might have been drunk or flattered. Maybe he regrets it now. Taking a mouthful of water instead of air, she has to stop and cough at the other end. Could she forgive him if it was only a one-night stand? Is it something they could work through, to save their marriage? Every thought is leading to more questions. She wants to hurl them at Thomas, to try and get the truth, but she can't, she needs to figure some of these answers out herself. But how? She keeps swimming, counting the lengths so that she has to focus on that and not think about Thomas.

On the way back to her room, she peeks into the House restaurant, its Michelin star proudly displayed. They have a reservation for tonight and she'd been looking forward to it. She thinks of the three dresses she'd bought for this weekend. She hadn't got around to returning the third one yet – she might as well return all three now, she won't be wearing them. And the underwear, well, she can't return those, she'll bin them. She won't be able to look at them without thinking of Thomas's betrayal.

A member of staff approaches Carla at the entrance to the dining area. "Can I help you, madam?"

"I have a reservation for eight o'clock tonight and I'm not feeling the best so I might just get room service. I'm in Room 206."

"Okay. Let me check the reservation list. Ah, I see it's for the eight-course tasting menu. Now, we won't be able to serve this to your room but if you'd like to choose a few things from it for yourself and your partner?"

"It's just me."

"Okay. Well, have a look at this and I'll give you a few moments." He turns to leave.

"It's fine," she says, quickly scanning the menu. "I'll have the roasted monkfish at around seven o'clock."

"Certainly, madam."

Back in the hotel room, she stands in the hot rainforest shower, blasting the pool chlorine from her skin. She needs to focus. She can't waste this weekend. She must have a plan to find out the truth. Rinsing the soap from her body, she dries off and wraps a fluffy white bathrobe around her, moving into the bedroom.

She needs help here; she needs a professional. Opening her laptop, Carla inhales deeply and googles private investigators.

57

Amanda slows her pace to a walk as she returns to the entrance gate of the woods. She puts a hand on the fence and stretches to cool down after her run. She has time to go home and shower before her doctor's appointment. Removing her AirPods and unclipping the arm belt holding her phone, she notices three missed calls from Thomas.

"Hiya, were you looking for me? I saw a few missed calls." She lifts her T-shirt to wipe the sweat from her forehead.

"Yeah, I'm heading over to your side of town, where are you?"

"I'm just out for a run in Barna. I must have been out of coverage in the woods. My phone only beeped now with the missed calls."

"Where are you running? I'll come and meet you."

"Don't be daft. I'm all sweaty and sticky. Let me go home and shower first."

"No. I need to see you. I'll come and walk with you."

She smiles at his insistence and laughs, saying, "I'll go straight home and I can meet you in an hour. But I don't have long, I have an appointment later."

"*Where are you?*"

She hears the urgency in his voice. He's keen, she thinks, leaning against the fence.

She tells him where she is and hangs up, grinning broadly. She hasn't seen much of him lately; he's been busy with work. She's tried to be patient but if she's honest, she's started to get a bit annoyed. With everything that's been going on with Michael and Dawn, she could have done with the distraction of Thomas and some positivity in her life.

Amanda takes her hoodie out of the car and, glancing around to make sure no one's in view, takes off her running top and slips the hoodie over her head. She sits in the car, reaching for concealer stick and tinted lip balm. She's not going to look perfect but it's the best she can do. She dabs concealer under her eyes and rubs it in with her fingertip. A shiver runs through her – her body is cooling down after the run.

She switches the engine on, turning up the heat, and rests back against the headrest, feeling the air warming from the vents. It's actually nice to get a bit of space from Michael. She can feel the questions about the fire and their parents bubbling beneath his surface all the time, and she's finding herself on tenterhooks around him, waiting for him to attempt to probe further. She can't help it; a surge rises within her and she snaps at him when he does. Why does he need to know? The fire was ruled accidental. There's no point in digging up old ground. It's only going to cause more upset.

Thomas arrives with a dust trail blowing up behind him in the gravel. Getting out, she smiles and waves to him, watching him walk towards her dressed in trousers, a shirt, and smart shoes. As he gets closer, she notices his red cheekbones, his normally groomed brown hair tousled and sticking up in places, and the top couple of buttons of his shirt undone.

"Have you come from the gym?"

She moves in to kiss him in greeting but he sidesteps, saying, "What? No. Let's walk."

Following him along the path, she sees beads of perspiration dotting the back of his blue shirt.

"You're hardly dressed for walking."

"We won't go far."

Amanda has to walk fast to keep up with his pace.

A couple pass them with a golden retriever on a lead. They both nod and say hello. Thomas's head turns and seeing a narrower path off to the left, says, "Let's go this way."

She follows his lead down a track. It's muddier here, the trees clustered and the pine scent intense. Watching Thomas stepping carefully around the puddles, she says, "Are you okay? You seem, I don't know, a little stressed. Is work crazy busy?" She reaches out and touches his arm.

"I'm waiting for you to explain what you've been doing." He spins around to stand in front of her.

"What?"

"What you've been doing," he pauses, looking straight into her eyes, "to my wife?"

"What are you talking about, Thomas?"

He steps towards her and stares down at her, their faces inches apart. "You've been watching my wife. What the fuck were you thinking?" His stale coffee breath lingers in the air between them.

Amanda puts her hand on his chest and lightly pushes him away. She steps back, putting her hands on her hips. "I don't know what you're talking about. I certainly haven't been watching her. Why would I?" Her voice is defiant. *What is he on about?* She watches him glance around and sees a protruding vein throbbing at the side of his head.

"You are lying." He looks up at the trees crowding the skyline. His Dublin accent sneaking out in his anger. "You are lying, I know you are. Were you that pissed off that I wouldn't meet your brother that you decided to take matters into your own hands?"

"No! Why would I watch Carla? *Why?*"

His face snaps back to hers. "Who knows what your crazy motives are, but you *have* been following her, watching her."

"No, I haven't. I've only ever seen her once, in town with you!"

"You've sometimes said it!"

Thomas rubs his neck with both hands and spits on the ground.

Stepping forward, she puts her hand on his bicep. He immediately recoils and takes a few steps back.

"Don't touch me."

"Whatever has happened, Thomas, whatever's upset you, I promise you, it has nothing to do with me."

He grabs her arms and shakes her. His words spitting in her face. "*You are lying. You're a lying bitch! Stay the fuck away from my wife! Stay away from my family or you won't know what's hit you!*"

He pushes her away and she stumbles backwards over tree roots and slips. She staggers, putting out her hands to try and regain her balance, but she's falling. She grabs at a thorny bush as she falls and the tiny spikes tear at her skin. Banging the back of her head on a tree trunk, she plonks down hard on the forest floor and watches as Thomas marches his way back through the woodland towards the carpark.

58

Turning off the engine, Emily looks around the supermarket carpark, her head pounding. Why she ended up here she doesn't know, but the next turn-off was for work and she can't face going back into the office. What has she done? Has she blown everything with Thomas? Should she just have left it at the note and photos to Carla? Left the marriage to implode. She wants to scream and roar at the people pushing trolleys full of shopping past her. Has she pushed her chance of happiness away?

She inserts her coin into the slot and reverses out of the trolley bay. The bar is sticky. She roots in her handbag for a small packet of wipes; every good mother carries wipes with her. A stab of guilt hurts her chest as she recalls laughing at Carla's *Mary Poppins* bag, as she calls it, prepared for almost any occasion with small children.

Emily automatically reaches into her pocket for her list before she realises she didn't write one, she hadn't planned on going to the supermarket. Wiping the perspiration from her top lip with the back of her hand, she pushes the trolley towards the entrance. She can't do anything about the line of it dripping down her back, her shirt is probably dotted with it but at least her jacket is covering it.

She hesitates at the salad section and stands staring. She had to make up something about the other woman so that Thomas would push her out of the picture. But now he wants to cool it, all because of something she made up. What was she thinking? *That's the problem,*

I didn't think it through. Putting lettuce and cucumber into the trolley, she drops a packet of salad tomatoes in a little too forcefully. An elderly lady looks at her so Emily pauses, pretending to browse other salad produce until the lady moves on, and then she swops the tomatoes for another packet.

Has her whole plan fallen apart? Emily had not been prepared for him agreeing to cool things. She'd wanted him to take her in his arms and reassure her that she was important to him. What if he decides it's all too risky or discovers she's lied to him and rejects her?

She stops abruptly when she sees one of the school mums further down the aisle, immediately turns her back, and continues in the opposite direction. She is not in the mindset to bump into someone she hardly knows and have a forced conversation about nothing.

Lowering her face and letting her hair flop down, she pretends to be interested in the cheese section. The conversation with Thomas replays in her mind; she saw the way his fists clenched, the way he wouldn't meet her eyes. He was angry. Throughout all the years she has known him, she has never seen him angry, never heard Carla telling her about him being angry. He is always calm and in control. Yet, this afternoon, she had seen a slip, she'd seen a sliver of rage beneath his cool exterior. And she was responsible for it.

Emily stops in front of the coffee shelves. She puts her capsules into the trolley, and the ones Carla likes. It is automatic. A whisper of betrayal sounds in her ear: *you are sleeping with your best friend's husband, yet you still think to stock her favourite coffee capsules.*

At the freezer section, she chooses some ice lollies for Rosie and Theo. They aren't going to the after-school club today. She only usually sends them when she is working long days but lately she finds herself leaving them there most days, even if it is only for an hour, just so she doesn't have to see Carla at the school gates.

She moves on, then stops and reverses back – she'll get ice cream for herself. She picks out a tub of Ben and Jerry's Phish Food. Ice cream, wine, and a soppy movie she can cry along to is what she needs tonight. She sighs. Why was he so quick in agreeing to pause their affair? If she was honest with herself, that is what's bothering her the most. It's grating at her with every step she takes. As soon as she'd told him, he distanced himself from her and that's what is making her angry. She stacks two bottles of Chardonnay into the trolley and joins the queue for the till.

There is no way to predict how it's going to play out now and no way to backtrack either. At the moment the only influence she has is over Carla. She needs to think very carefully about her next move if she is going to keep her man.

59

Dawn leans her shoulder against the door to click it shut, dropping her bag on the floor and resting the pile of folders on the side table. She exhales loudly, looking in the mirror; she looks as wrecked as she feels. Not long to go now until the exams are over.

"Hiya, where's Mum?" she asks Michael, going into the kitchen and taking the foil from her dinner plate to put it into the microwave.

"She went to bed early with a headache."

Dawn's relieved. She's too tired to deal with any snide comments from Amanda about the exams.

Flopping on the settee after eating, she flicks until she finds a TV show that will relax her. Michael is sitting in the armchair, reading the newspaper. They chit-chat about the TV and the news. She sees him glance at his watch and back at her, before taking his glasses off, cleaning them on his jumper, and putting them back on.

"Do you want to switch to something else?" she asks. "I'm not really watching this, just winding down after all the studying."

"No, no, it's fine. Actually," he crosses and uncrosses his legs, shuffling further to the edge of the settee, "can I talk to you about something?"

Dawn looks over at him.

"Something sensitive," he says.

She feels the hairs on her arms stand up. "What is it?"

"First of all. I haven't been snooping, I promise you that. You had already left for college. "

Oh God, what does he know?

She tilts her head and nods at him to continue.

"I went into your ensuite the other day looking for some toothpaste, and when I was putting the box in the bin, I noticed this." He takes out a tiny folded piece of paper from his pocket and unfolds it.

She frowns as she watches him. "What is it?"

"It's a medical leaflet from a box of sleeping tablets." He raises his eyes to meet hers.

Look normal, look normal! she screams inside her head as the breath is taken from her like from a punch in the gut. Her eyebrows curl in pretend confusion.

"Look, I'm not nosing but I just want to check that you're okay. These kinds of tablets are very strong and can be highly addictive. I wanted to give you a bit of free medical advice about them if you can humour your uncle."

Dawn waits until he glances down at the leaflet in his hands before she swallows the boulder-like lump in her throat. She takes a breath and smiles a toothy grin, willing her body to relax.

"I can suggest alternatives if that would help," he says.

"I haven't been taking sleeping tablets. I was cleaning out my make-up bags. Mum gave me the tablets during my Leaving Cert exams last year, but I didn't use them. I don't know where the tablets went to, I probably gave them back to her. That piece of paper was in the bottom of my make-up bag."

"Why would Amanda give you sleeping tablets?" He frowns.

"Oh, she was worried about me not sleeping but I was fine. I used to do some meditation each night. It was so calming," she says, looking across the room, uncurling her hands, letting her thumbs twiddle around each other. *How can he not hear her heart thumping?*

"Right. Your mum did say something about meditating. Okay. Well, sorry if I seemed nosy, I was concerned. My doctor hat came on." He tosses the leaflet onto the coffee table.

Dawn feels the blood drain from her face, and she grips her hands together as she turns back to face him. "Did you tell Mum you found it? Was she worried about me?"

"No, I didn't mention it. We were talking about you being calm during this exam season and she mentioned you meditating last year. That's all. I wanted to speak to you about this first."

The tension drops from her shoulders. *Thank God he didn't tell Mum. She would know, she would add things up and the scheme would be scuppered.* She sees Michael's expectant face looking at her.

"Please don't tell her. She'd use it as another reason not to let me move out."

"You don't exactly need her permission to move out – you are an adult, you know."

Dawn inspects her nails. "I know, but she'll hate me, and I really don't need that negativity in my life. She can be really cruel."

She looks across at the ski-trip photo of her mum, the grandparents she never met, and Michael.

Turning back to him, she asks "Was she like that when she was younger?"

"Like what?"

"Controlling." She watches him closely. Did Mum treat him the same way she did herself and Dad?

"A little maybe, but I think it was because we'd lost our parents and she was scared of losing me."

Looking back at the photo, she sighs. She'd wanted Michael to say yes, he'd been treated the same. So that she could tell him, and he could help her leave.

"You know that photo only comes out when you're visiting," she says, nodding over to the family photo. "And the same with the chain she wears, the Celtic locket. I've never seen her wear it any other time."

Michael's eyes narrow. He looks at the photo and back at her.

"Sorry, I shouldn't have said that. You didn't need to know," she says.

He pushes his glasses up his nose. "No, it's fine. Sure, there's no harm in her wanting to put it away. Everyone deals with grief in different ways. I know she tries hard to keep their memories alive for me, so when I'm back in Australia she might just want to keep them private."

"*Mmm*," Dawn says, holding her tongue. No need to mention how fake Mum is when Michael is here. She'll just have to wait until he's gone back to Australia before she can go ahead with her scheme. "I think I'll head to bed now. I've got another long day of studying tomorrow."

"I don't think I'll be long after you. Goodnight, Dawn."

Glancing back at him from the doorway, she sees he's still staring at the photograph.

60

The sun streams in the window of the playroom, highlighting Rosie and Theo sitting on the rug building Lego. Emily ignores the Sylvannian families scattered all over the floor and the monster trucks that look like they have created the carnage that surrounds the toy tree house and country lodge, and goes back to cleaning bathrooms and folding laundry. Sitting in the living room afterwards, she glances around. She should straighten the cushions and even consider washing the settee covers – they are getting very grubby. She pulls the navy blanket down further over the settee and sips her coffee, scrolling through her phone.

She's texted Carla several times since she left for the hotel. Asking her how she's doing, what's the hotel like, and if she's thought any more about confronting Thomas. Carla's replies have been short – she says she needs more time to think before confronting Thomas. Emily rereads Thomas's last few messages. She hasn't heard from him since they met on Friday. He is online now. Her fingers hover over the keypad. She wants to text him. She wants to know if he's done anything about the other woman. Tracey.

She cradles the warm mug in her hands and remembers the look on his face when she'd described the woman. What did he do after leaving her in the office building? Did he dump that woman? Emily hopes so. But if he has, why hasn't she heard from him? Picking up her phone again, she checks to see if he is still online. He is. Carla is still away. Would it hurt if she sent a text and asked how he was? She is staring at her phone when Rosie bounds into the room.

"Mum, Theo won't share the wheels and he has loads. I need some for my car."

Theo follows behind her protesting. "I've built a tyre centre, Mum; I need the wheels."

"Okay, Theo, but your customer, Rosie, needs some so why don't you help her out at your tyre centre? You could get her to put her car on the ramp while you affix the wheels."

"Okay."

They run back to the playroom.

Checking the clock on the mantelpiece, she reminds herself that she still has to iron their taekwondo kits before their session this afternoon. The session that Thomas's boys also go to. She breaks into a huge smile, having found the perfect excuse to text him.

Hiya, r u all set for taekwondo later?

He answers in seconds. He's obviously thinking about her too.

Hey you, can't find gloves. Must be in other car.

She reads it over and over. He hasn't mentioned anything about Friday. Should she?

Typing out a question, she deletes it and retypes. Her finger hesitates over the send button.

They'll have spare ones at the session. Any ideas about who it could b watching C?

Pressing send, she takes her coffee cup into the kitchen, and dumps it in the sink.

Immediately, she looks at their message thread again. There are two ticks next to her message, he has seen it. Clicking quickly out of it, she stares at her phone. Why isn't he responding?

Leaving the phone on the windowsill, she washes her cup and the kids' breakfast dishes. Shit. Should she not have asked him? Maybe she should have waited until taekwondo and asked him then, face to face. Sighing, she plugs the iron in. He wouldn't be able to dodge the question face to face surely.

Her phone pings a message. With her two elbows resting on the ironing board, she reads it.

Yep, figured it out. Can you remember that girl, who kind of got obsessed with me in college when I was in the play about the swimmer? Well, she was in the area and got in touch so we met for dinner. I didn't think for a minute she'd still be into me! I've dealt with her now. Don't think we'll have a problem with her again.

Emily does remember that girl. She was in the play too and had such a crush on him. She was like a lovesick puppy following him around. She remembers Carla being rather freaked out by the whole thing. Emily made a song up about her to diffuse the situation with Carla and they would sing it whenever they saw her. But as she thinks back, trying to recall the song and picture the girl, she can't remember her being called Tracey or having curly hair. But using hair straighteners was all the rage back then. People change their hairstyles, don't they?

Anyway, she smiles, it's his last words in the text that are the important ones. 'I dealt with her now. Don't think we'll have a problem with her again.' She exhales, and the tension releases from her shoulders. Everything's okay. It isn't an affair but Carla thinks it is so this could still work to be a win-win. The woman isn't important to Thomas. And it explains why he'd told Carla she was a client. She's pretty sure Carla wouldn't be happy about Thomas meeting up with that woman.

His black BMW is already there when Emily arrives at the taekwondo centre. Pulling down the mirror in her car, she checks her lip-gloss and runs her hand through her hair, scrunching the waves before she gets out. She adjusts her summer dress, the one with the flamingos on that he loved her in at the birthday party, before going in.

Inside the hall, her eyes scan the room for Thomas. Rosie and Theo see Ben and Daniel over at the benches and run over to them. Emily spots Thomas at the other side of the hall, talking to the female instructor. He must be asking about spare gloves for the boys. Watching, she sees the way the instructor throws her hair back and laughs at something he's said.

She adjusts the navy handbag on her shoulder, and glances around to see if there are any other parents she knows, who she could pass the time with for a minute or two. But there isn't, they've all gone. Going over to the kids, she helps them tidy their shoes under the bench.

"*Right, class, are we ready? Everyone into their lines, please!*" The instructor shouts.

Emily looks up quickly to see Thomas's back going through the double doors. Her stomach clenches as her mouth falls open. *Right then. Not even a hello.* Saying goodbye to the kids, she purses her lips together tightly and heads out to her car.

The bright sunlight blinds her for a moment as she steps outside, and she doesn't at first see Thomas leaning against his car with his arms folded, looking at her. Her face breaks into a wide smile at the sight of him, and the tension in her body dissipates.

"Hey, you, have you got anything planned for, say," he looks at his watch, "the next hour and twenty-five minutes?"

He grins as she replies, "I can think of something."

"See you back at yours then?" he says, turning to get into his car.

Emily has to stop herself from skipping back to her car.

61

Amanda stares at the phone on the kitchen table in front of her. Why hasn't she heard from Thomas? She was expecting an apology from him. It's Monday afternoon now. He's had plenty of opportunities. Okay, she reasons, he might not have wanted to contact her over the weekend, especially not if he believes someone is watching his wife, if he thinks their affair is about to be exposed. The last thing he'd be able to do is text.

She picks up her phone, checking for new notifications yet again but there's nothing. It's three o'clock. He's had all day. Surely he's cooled down by now and realised he got it wrong. That she's innocent of everything he's accused her of. Surely he'll want to apologise? Maybe he'll want to do it in person – they could meet tomorrow. They often meet on a Tuesday, although lately his work seems to have taken precedence.

She rubs her fingers over the back of her head. It's still sore to touch but it's healing. Thankfully she has such thick hair that the wound wouldn't be spotted, although it will take longer to scab over. Amanda examines her fingers and the backs of her hands – the scrapes from the thorn bushes are still there, but they aren't as red now. When Michael asked, she'd told him a half-truth, that she'd slipped when running and in trying to steady herself, grabbed on to spikey branches.

The doorbell rings, and she sits up straight. Could this be him? No, she corrects herself, walking towards the front door, he wouldn't just show up at her house, would he? She answers the door. It's a parcel for Dawn. Amanda's shoulders droop as she closes the door and leans against it. She should be fuming at him. She knows she should. He'd threatened her and then pushed her against a tree, forcefully, and walked away as she sat, hurt, on the ground. But, he had obviously being rattled by the thought of someone watching his wife. She's not angry with him, she's disappointed. Disappointed he's not apologised for his actions. Everyone can make mistakes, especially when they think they're protecting their family. She will forgive him if he says sorry. He will come back to her with his tail between his legs. She's sure he will.

62

Carla looks at Thomas next to her on the couch, his head lolling on his shoulder. She coughs lightly and he jumps.

"God, I'm falling asleep here. Will we go to bed?" He yawns.

"I'll follow you up," she says. "I'm going to try and finish this PA update about the success of the fundraiser."

"Okay, I'll wait with you."

"No, you're shattered. You go on up."

Thomas leans over to kiss her, but Carla quickly turns her head so that it's her cheek that he kisses.

She pats his hand. "I won't be long."

There is a bitter tang in her mouth as she listens to him locking the front door and going upstairs. She has to act normally and it's killing her. She's trying so hard, but she just wants to shrink away from him, especially when he touches her. The reason she has the laptop on her knees is so he can't snuggle up to her. The thought of Thomas being with another woman, reaching to kiss her like he does herself has consumed her all evening.

She's only back a day but already it's too hard to pretend. It's too hard to be normal. She closes the computer and wonders, not for the first time, how he's lived with himself while being so deceitful? She turns off the lamp on the coffee table. How the hell has she never noticed? Carla is so cross with herself for not seeing the signs of his betrayal. Is this an indication of how naïve she has been or how clever at deception Thomas is?

Going into the kitchen, she remembers the washing in the machine. She's been like a zombie, wandering around the house all day yet accomplishing nothing. Setting up the airer, she begins to hang the clothes on it. A vibration behind her makes her freeze. She half turns to see Thomas's phone, sitting, plugged in on the kitchen countertop. She stares at its black leather case; it is hardly noticeable against the dark granite. If it hadn't vibrated, she wouldn't have known it was there.

She steps towards the door into the hallway, and listens. Not a sound from upstairs. She walks back into the kitchen and closes the door softly behind her. With her eyes focused on Thomas's phone, she moves slowly towards it, her heart hammering so fast it's as if it's two paces ahead of her. Is she going to do this? In all their years together, Carla has never once snooped at his phone, never once opened his post. It had never crossed her mind to. She trusted her husband. Now, she needs to know.

Opening the phone case, the screen saver lights up with a photo of the four of them in Portugal at Easter. Their sun-kissed faces all squashed together and laughing. Her fingers hover over the screen for so long that it goes dark. She rubs her thumb across it, and it asks for a pin number. She tries his birthday, hers, the kids, and then it flashes up telling her to try again in twenty seconds. *Shit.* She can't risk getting locked out completely. Thomas will know. Carla racks her brains, the phone shaking in her hands. What does she do now? Try again? He can't find out that she's been trying to look at his phone. What can the pin be? His bank card pin? The date they got married? The numbers on the car reg? She can't risk it. If she locks him out of his phone, he'll ask questions, he'll know.

She closes the case, and replaces it where she found it. She steps away from the phone, towards the airer. And then stops. There is one more number to try. She turns back and taps in Thomas's mother's birthday 0911. The phone vibrates as it unlocks and Carla takes a sharp intake of air. Her whole body tenses as she sits on a stool at the breakfast bar and looks through his messages, reading some, scrolling through others, her eyes moving fast, skimming the texts. There are messages going back over a year, but nothing looks out of the ordinary. She clicks on names she doesn't recognise but there isn't so much as an inappropriate emoji. Next she checks his SMS messages and then his emails. The phone wavers in her hand. What is she missing?

His call log is the same, nothing suspicious. There are two numbers without names, so Carla picks up her own phone and googles the numbers. One is a tapas restaurant in town and the other is for a business taxi company. Nothing strange about that. He was at that tapas place with clients a couple of times recently. He'd told her all about it. And its usual practice for him to pay for the clients' taxis. Resting her phone next to his, her mind wanders. What if the photos are misleading? Yes, they look like kisses but maybe it's the angle. What if it was innocent between Thomas and the woman? Carla's heart lifts a little.

He *is* very touchy-feely with people; that's just what he's like. Maybe whoever sent the note and photos just had a suspicious mind that jumped to the wrong conclusion?

She leaves the phone exactly where she found it and finishes hanging the clothes on the airer, putting the basket back on top of the washing machine. Her step is a little lighter. It explains why she hadn't picked up any worrying signs from Thomas. There weren't any. He was just being him.

Carla hesitates in the doorway. No matter how much she wants the photos to be misleading, she knows that they show a side of Thomas that's more than being touchy-feely. The dread creeps back into her heart. She doesn't want it to be true. Anyone can delete messages and their call history, can't they? Especially someone wanting to cover their tracks. Someone who's having an affair.

Switching the kitchen light off, she goes upstairs, turning on the landing not to her own bedroom but towards her son Daniel's room. She'll snuggle in there with him tonight and tell Thomas tomorrow Daniel had a nightmare. She can't bear the thought of sleeping next to Thomas. She can't stand the thought of his skin touching hers.

63

Emily drives into the school car park. She is early. After putting the kids into afterschool on both Monday and Tuesday, she'd promised them she'd be here today.

Scrolling through her messages, she smiles to herself as she reads Thomas's latest text.

Can't stop thinking about you and yesterday.

Her heart warms at his words. A flash of white catches her eye, she looks up, thinking it's Carla's jeep. It isn't. Emily looks back down at her phone and deletes Thomas's message.

They've spent the last two lunchtimes wrapped in each other's arms in a show house. She knows she's going to have to be careful about using the show homes. Her job would be on the line if she got caught. Despite the risk, her body is aglow. Things are starting to go in her direction. She twists a strand of auburn hair around her finger. Now this other woman, Tracey, is out of the way, and Carla thinks Thomas is having an affair. Thomas will soon be all hers. The tiny ray of light, of hope for her, is pushing its way through the clouds, determined to shine on her.

She hasn't heard much from Carla. She'd been texting her a couple of times a day but then Carla abruptly said she needed some space to think things through. Maybe she was asking Carla too many questions about what she was going to do and when she was going to confront

Thomas. She should have been more of a listening ear for her. White flashes across her windscreen again and Emily looks up. This time, it is Carla.

Stepping out of her car, Emily pulls her red body-warmer tight around her, zipping it up as she crosses the school car park.

"God, this bloody wind is freezing, isn't it? You'd hardly believe it's June," she says, as Carla gets out of her car and pulls on a baby-pink hoody.

Emily notices the skin across Carla's cheeks is splotchy and she isn't wearing any makeup which is unlike her, even for a school pick-up.

"Have you just come from a gym class?" Emily nods at Carla's Nike leggings and baggy hoody.

"What? No, I swam this morning. I'm finding it difficult to concentrate on Pilates or yoga, I find my mind wandering. Swimming is easier, I just focus on counting the lengths, then I don't have to think." She stares down at her hands, examining them.

There is a crowd of parents with toddlers in prams, grandparents, and minders all waiting in a huddle at the gate, like penguins sheltering from the wind. Emily and Carla hang back.

Taking a sidelong glance, Emily takes in her friend's shoulders drooping, and slack expression. She sees her looking into the distance, her face blank. Emily stares at the ground. She is responsible for this.

"I didn't see you all week, work's been busy. Are you okay?"

Carla's eyes dart around them. "No, not really. I feel like a zombie." She rubs her hands together, blowing into them. "Is it just me or is it really cold? I can't seem to warm up these days."

"I take it you haven't confronted Thomas yet?" Emily sticks her hands in the pockets of her body warmer to steady them.

"No, I need to get my head around it all first. Decide what I'm going to do."

Turning to face Carla, Emily says "What do you mean? Can you stay with him, after what he's done?"

Carla's eyes well up and she frantically blinks them away. "I don't know. I honestly don't know."

"Carla, it won't go away if you pretend it's not happening. Don't let yourself be walked all over like his mother was."

"Look, I want to be one hundred percent sure before I tear my family apart. I'm going to keep a close eye on him for now and suss things out." Sniffing, Carla takes out a tissue.

There is a flurry of activity up ahead as the school's main doors open and a stream of children pour out, a sea of coloured coats covering the schoolyard. Emily and Carla walk towards the gates as the huddling crowd of adults disperse along the railings ready to wave and catch their child's attention.

Emily's mind is racing. What does Carla mean, keep a close eye on him? Why doesn't she just confront him? God, this is not going the way she expected. She should have kept her mouth shut until she'd figured out a fool-proof plan. Thomas assured her this other woman was gone. She'd been satisfied with that, but now Carla doesn't sound so sure about confronting Thomas. What if Carla turns a blind eye and doesn't act to get rid of him? Where will that leave her? It will all be for nothing. She will never have Thomas.

If Carla says she is going to keep a close eye on Thomas, then Emily had better warn him.

She doesn't see her daughter, Rosie, until she tugs on her arm.

"Mummy, can we go to the playground on our way home?"

64

The private investigator didn't say much when he rang. He was a man of few words as Carla was to find out.

"It's Mr Lane here. I have some information for you. We should meet."

She asked him could he not just tell her over the phone, and he said "That's not how I work. What day suits for me to come to the house?"

The house? She yelped internally. She didn't want him in the house. There was enough poison floating around the house without him adding to it. He suggested a coffee shop she'd never been to.

Standing across the road from Mary's Tearooms, Carla stares at the quaint window display of teacups on a three-tiered cake stand, and doilies on the outside tables. She's early. She'd tried to busy herself all morning, but this has been hanging over her like a guillotine since his call yesterday.

Forcing her lead-like limbs to step off the pavement, she shoves her hands in the pockets of her body-warmer and walks across the road. Does she want to know the truth? Wasn't everything just fine before she knew? Thomas treats her well – she's always felt loved and valued by him. She reaches the other side of the road and hesitates. Will she just go home and forget about this meeting? Turn a blind eye to Thomas's infidelity and hope it's a mid-life crisis, one that he'll come out of eventually? She stands at the door of the café, her hand on the handle.

"Excuse me, are you going in or coming out?" a lady with a pram asks.

"Sorry, here, let me hold the door for you." Carla opens the door and steps inside after the pram.

She spots the private investigator straight away. He's the only person sitting alone and he has a beige cardboard folder open in front of him. Not looking very undercover. He looks up as she stands at the door, closes his folder, and nods as they make eye contact.

"Hello, Mr Lane."

"I ordered us a pot of tea," he says, standing.

She nods and shakes his hand, wishing she'd wiped her clammy hands first. She sits down and he pours the tea. Not knowing what to do with her jittery hands, she clasps them together on her lap.

Mr Lane selects a sachet of white sugar and rubs the long thin packet between his thumb and forefinger before tearing it open and pouring it into his tea. He stirs slowly and sniffs.

As he raises his eyes to meet hers, she knows, at this moment, it is confirmation of bad news.

"Is it as bad as I thought?" Carla asks, barely able to hold his eyes. Her leg is vibrating incessantly under the table.

"Thomas is being unfaithful that is true. Only it isn't with one woman."

She zones out after the first few words and doesn't catch the end of what he's saying. Her eyes drop to the teacup. Her world closing into just this table.

"Sorry, what?" She has to fight the pain in her chest to get the words out.

"Thomas is having more than one affair. I believe he is seeing two women."

The pain pushes down on her shoulders and crushes her towards the table. She rests her elbows on the table-top and leans forward in an effort to support the force of the weight bearing down on her.

Mr Lane reaches methodically into his folder and slides across a photograph.

The tension flows out of Carla. It's a photo of Emily. Only Emily. A squeak emits from her, the sound a cross between a sigh and a laugh. Mr Lane looks at her with a sniff and a raised eyebrow.

"That's Emily. He's not having an affair with Emily. That's just friendship." The words come out fast with relief. "She's my best friend." She smiles in what she hopes is a reassuring way.

His face stays blank. *Does this guy have any facial muscles?*

"I am certain that she's also having an affair with your husband. You may find these photographs upsetting," he says in his monotone voice and pushes a couple more photos across the table.

She doesn't touch the photos. She can't. In one, Thomas has his hands in Emily's hair, and they are kissing. Emily is wearing a blue suit jacket. Carla remembers when she bought it, years ago. She was with her, had bought the same one in navy, and they'd agreed to swop whenever they needed to. In the next one, Emily's back is pushed against a window, the parrots decorating her white blouse are colourfully squashed against the glass. He is wearing the sky-blue shirt with the black trim and the red horse on the pocket. Carla's mum sent him that for his birthday last year. Emily's hands frame his face, touching the coarse stubble he's been trialling lately. She has her legs wrapped around Thomas's waist. The air gets stuck in Carla's lungs – she can't breathe. This can't be happening. Not Emily. Not Emily and Thomas. Her best friend and her husband. The café begins to spin and blur. She lifts her hand to pour some water, but it misses the jug and knocks the sugar pot to the floor. The brown and white paper packets scatter around their feet.

Mr Lane looks down at his hands.

Bile rises in her throat. Carla forces it down and swallows. She pushes the photos away. She's seen enough. Mr Lane sniffs and pours her a glass of water. She wants to scream at him to blow his nose. A waitress passes the table carrying a full Irish breakfast and this time she can't stop the bile from surging and she pushes back from the table, the wooden chair legs scraping on the floor. With her hand over her mouth, she dashes into the bathroom and splurges her disgust into the sink. It splashes up the porcelain sides.

"Oh God, you poor thing, are you alright?" A woman about her age hands her a couple of paper towels, putting her hand on Carla's shoulder.

Another lady comes out of a cubicle. "Crikey, I hope that isn't a review of the food here."

"Seriously, Jane, not sure that's necessary. Can I get you a glass of water?"

Carla looks in the mirror at these caring strangers and shakes her head. "No, I'll be fine, thanks. Sorry, you didn't need to see that."

The lady called Jane looks over sympathetically as she dries her hands. "Can we take you anywhere?"

"No, but thanks." She rinses around the sink.

They leave and Carla glares into the mirror. She pictures Emily in her mind. Her Emily. How can this be true? The surge rises once more, and she makes it into the cubicle this time, retching until there is nothing left inside of her. Closing the toilet lid, she drops down onto it. Her shoulders sag and the tears begin to fall.

The bathroom door opens, and a gentle voice calls out. "Carla, are you okay? Your friend asked me to check on you."

Her friend? Emily? Is she here? No, stupid, she means the sniffling PI.

"Yes, thank you. I'll be out in a minute."

Shuffling back to the table a few minutes later, she's grateful to see he's put the photos back in his folder. She looks around at the other customers to see if they are waiting for the next instalment of her life drama, but no one looks in her direction. No one has noticed her life crumble and collapse over the last few minutes. All of them are busy getting on with their own lives.

Mr Lane sniffs yet again and looks at her. She must have frowned at his annoying habit without realising it because he reaches into his pocket for his handkerchief. It's been a while since Carla has seen anyone who wasn't from her parents' generation carry a cotton handkerchief. She focuses on the embroidered pattern in the corner of it, a tiny navy boat, and tries to ignore the folder at his elbow containing the information that has irrevocably changed her life.

"Would you like some tea?" he asks as he tops up his own cup.

She shakes her head and glances around, taking small sips of water. A couple are sitting very close to their table. They probably heard every word if they'd wanted to. Her chest constricts, she needs to leave, it's too claustrophobic. Looking at her watch, she says, "Look, I have to go."

"But I haven't gone through everything with you properly, the photos, the calls, the –"

"No, no, it's fine. You've told me what I need to know. You've given me confirmation." She stands up.

"What about the other woman? I understand that you are shocked about your friend, but surely you want the full picture?"

She looks around. The room is closing in on her. She can't stay. She clicks the belt closed on her body warmer and pulls the strap tight around her waist. "Can you email it to me?"

"I have it here," he says, pushing the folder across the table. "Take this."

Feeling the surge threaten from her stomach, she can only shake her head at him. She can't take this.

She doesn't want this evidence of betrayal in her hands.

"Email will be fine, thank you. Include your bill as well and I'll settle what I owe." She shakes his limp hand with her cold one and turns to leave.

Outside, Carla gasps at the air. Pushing through the lunchtime crowd, she crosses the road and hurries back to her car. She sits, gripping the steering wheel, staring at her wedding ring. There is no excusing it all now, no chance of blaming it as a one-off weakness, as a temporary midlife crisis. Two affairs, not a one-night stand, but two affairs. What the hell?

It's only half-past twelve. She doesn't have to collect the kids until three o'clock. What is she supposed to do with her thoughts bouncing around her head until then? She can't phone Emily. The thought of her betrayal makes Carla gip again, and the whites of her knuckles shine through her gripped skin. She feels filthy, she needs to go home and shower, wash this betrayal off, and somehow work out what to do now that she knows.

65

Carla drives on autopilot until she reaches The Paddocks; her sought-after picture-perfect estate. Thomas called it their forever home on their second visit here with the auctioneer. With his arms wrapped around Carla's pregnant waist, he'd said "It's the big country house in an estate setting, Carla. It's perfect for us, for our family. You'll be able to walk to the village with the kids, and take them on adventures in the woods." She remembers flinching slightly at him implying that she would be at home with the kids, as she hadn't intended on giving up her teaching job at that point.

Looking at the windows of her home and its neat front garden, it's everything a family could want, everything she wanted. Apart from an adulterer for a husband. A beautiful bouquet of roses, snapdragons, lilies and chrysanthemums sits in the bright bay window of the living room. Whose husband buys their wife flowers all the time and not just on special occasions? Maybe she should have known. Her stomach heaves again. Maybe he bought them after every occasion he was unfaithful. The sour taste rises and she swallows. What is she going to do? She can't bear to be trapped inside the walls of this house, inside this pretence of a marriage and a family.

She's startled by a rap on her car window. It's the Tesco delivery man. She hadn't heard his van pull up. She smiles and tries to make chit-chat as he brings the groceries inside and she unpacks them.

Mangos and bananas in the fruit bowl, houmous and pickle in the fridge. Picking up the fresh chicken breasts and stewing beef, she falters, the room seems to spin around her.

"Are you okay, love? You look a little pale if you don't mind me saying."

Glancing up at his kind blue eyes, she briefly considers unburdening herself to this stranger. "Just a little under the weather, but thanks."

She smiles weakly as he collects the last of the empty green and blue crates and follows him out to the front door.

Back in the kitchen, she glares at all the groceries on the countertop and the breakfast bar. Is she just expected to put them away, make the dinner and carry on as normal? Emily and Thomas, how could they? Rage bubbles up through her and erupts as her arms flail and her fists fly. Fruit, milk, and chicken crash to the floor. Raspberries, couscous, sweet potatoes, flour, and castor sugar. Her eyes blur with tears as her arms swoop along the breakfast bar, swiping at the bottle of Thomas's preferred red wine of the moment. She watches it fall in slow motion, hit the newly polished cream porcelain tiles, and shatter in all directions. Like lava shooting out of a volcano, the red wine splashes back up as the glass makes contact with the tiles, droplets splatter across the bottom of the cabinet doors and up the side of the breakfast bar. A dark red pool encroaches across the tiles towards the spilt couscous and raspberries. Sliding down the cabinets, she sits beside the mess, resting her arms on her knees, and watches as the couscous soaks up some of the red wine and turns a purple colour. A sudden cold hits her core, and she hugs her knees to her chest, turning her focus to the wine dripping down the cupboards. Two drips race each other down, until they reach the bottom of the cupboard door and drop off into small dark red puddles pooling below.

The packet of flour lies sideways yet intact, soaking up the liquid, its paper packet crimson-dipped. Next to it, the castor sugar, just out of reach of the wine, has sprinkled its tiny sugar crystals around the base of the sideways packet like some bizarre art project.

Thomas loves red wine. Carla, she's a white wine drinker but she'll always share red if that's what others prefer. Always happy to go along, that's her. Look where that has got her. She's been walked over by the two people she loves most. *Why didn't I ever say no I prefer white?* Clenching her fists, her whole body tenses, the whites of her knuckles push through her skin. How dare they walk all over her like this? How dare they think they can get away with it?

Did Emily send the note and the photos? Is this why she keeps asking her about confronting Thomas? Why would Emily send them and risk her affair with Thomas being revealed? If she hadn't received the information, she would be none the wiser about either affair. Why involve her?

A lawnmower starts up outside and Carla stands up quickly. The gardener is trundling about on the sit and ride. Dizziness comes over her, her legs weaken and she has to steady herself with her hands on the countertop. The sweet spice and vanilla smell from the rioja is making her head hurt. She needs to get out of here. This house, these walls, are closing in on her. She needs air. Like the red wine spilt across the kitchen, she feels life draining out of her. She wants to walk out of that door and just keep going. But she can't.

The front door opens and Carla holds her breath. Is this Thomas?

"*Hello!*" Lena's voice rings out. "*Carla, are you here?*"

Shit. The cleaner. Surveying the mess, she knows there's no time to do anything. She wipes under her eyes.

"In here, Lena, I'm afraid I've had a bit of an accident."

Changing out of her wine-splattered cream chinos and white shirt, she wraps them in a towel and pushes them to the bottom of the washing basket before putting on sports leggings. She drives out of the village and to Coole Park. She won't bump into anyone she knows there. She hasn't run in years but she has to run this aching feeling out of herself. She needs to clear her brain of this deceit and think of what the hell she is going to do.

The cold wind nips her eyes. She fastens her headband over her ears and jogs slowly to the start of the woodland trail. Two women run past, chatting as they go, and Carla's reminded of the time she and Emily attempted to do the Couch to 5 km challenge. It didn't last long, with their red sweaty tomato faces, and the fact they couldn't run and talk, not if they wanted to breathe as well. Walking was much more sociable.

Increasing her pace, her thighs start to hurt and she dodges in and out of the tree roots and puddles. She has to concentrate on her footing, so she can't think, and for that she is thankful. She pushes herself harder and faster. Her legs are screaming at her to stop, and her head hurts but she keeps going. Coming to a fork in the path, Carla takes the opposite one to the two women ahead of her. Her path turns sharply left and goes deeper into the woods. The ground is squelchy, dead leaves mulch into the mud and disguise the tree roots. She doesn't bother to avoid the puddles now and the mucky water splashes up the back of her legs. Sweat drips down her spine and her head feels like it's a time bomb about to blow.

Emily and Thomas. How could they? The palms of her hands burn and she unclenches her fists; the heat is flushing through her body. She misses her footing around a tree root and stumbles and slips on the mud. Reaching out for a low branch to steady herself, she grabs it too forcefully and it snaps, landing her on her bottom in the mud.

Her body begins a shuddering that she can't stop, and she resigns herself to her despair and let the tears do as they wish.

The mud is soaking into her leggings and her legs are jerking with the cold. She shuffles backwards until she is sitting on a large root with her back against the tree trunk. Examining her hands, Carla sees dark red lines made by her own nails. Sinking her perfectly manicured fingers into the mud, she aimlessly draws circles round and round, watching as the dirt seeps under and around her rose-pink shellac nails. What is she going to do?

66

"Michael's going to pick up an Indian takeaway later, what do you fancy?" her mum asks.

"Me? Oh, I'm fine. I'm going out to meet the girls. We're going for pizzas." Dawn pulls her dress over the ironing board.

"Students out for dinner. I don't remember getting so much as a takeaway coffee when I was a student."

"It's only pizza. Besides, we all have part-time jobs, we're not asking anyone to pay for us," Dawn says, ironing the frilly trim of her orange and blue summer dress.

"I hope you've given up on that silly idea of moving out." Her mum puts the plates in the oven to warm.

Dawn freezes for a moment. She doesn't want an argument, she just wants to go out with her friends and enjoy the warm evening. Michael is upstairs on the phone to his family in Australia. Surely her mum's not going to cause a scene here and now.

Her mum doesn't wait for an answer, isn't interested it seems. "Well, I'll tell you this for nothing. If you move out, I won't be paying your college fees. See how far you get then." Her tone is casual as she lays the knives and forks on the table, as if she's discussing the weather forecast.

Steam rises from the iron and Dawn lifts it off her dress, her cheeks reddening in the heat of the moment. Looking up, she sees her mum standing at the other side of the kitchen table, waiting expectantly for her to speak.

Dawn nods. She doesn't know what she can say here without provoking her mum's temper.

"And, don't think about running to Daddy, Brad, for more money. He won't be able to afford both your accommodation and fees."

Dawn turns to switch the iron off; she doesn't hear her mum until she appears at her shoulder.

"Did you hear me? Don't you have anything smart to say about it? Another secret plan?"

Dawn's shoulders curl forward over the iron and her fingers tighten around its handle. She's afraid to breathe out. *Does Mum know about the sleeping tablet idea? How could she?*

Hearing Michael's footsteps on the stairs, her mum steps back, turning to fill a jug of water at the sink. Dawn hurries into the utility room with the iron, leaving it next to the cupboard to cool. Standing behind the door, she leans against the countertop, her heart threatening to burst out of her chest. Her mum said 'secret plan'. How could she know? Did Michael tell her about finding the sleeping tablet leaflet? Did Mum put two and two together, and work out that the night she was so keen to help with dinner, the night Mum was feeling tired and a bit dizzy was, in fact, her tinkering with the sleeping tablets?

She takes deep breaths in and out. No. Her mum couldn't know, she reasons with herself, she'd have exploded before now. There's no way her mum would have been able to react and speak so calmly as she just did in the kitchen. And, Michael had assured her he wouldn't tell. Dawn trusted him. He'd understood that her mum might overreact.

Going back into the kitchen, she sees Michael and her mum huddled together looking at the menu on his phone. Dawn tidies the ironing board away and grabs her dress from the kitchen chair.

"Do you want anything from the Indian, Dawn?" Michael looks up.

Dawn opens her mouth to explain but her mum beats her to it. "She's abandoning us for her friends tonight."

Michael meets Dawn's eyes, smiles brightly, and nods. "You enjoy yourself, it's a beautiful evening for it."

A look of understanding passes between them, and Dawn is certain at that moment Michael hasn't broken her confidence.

Upstairs, she gets changed and applies a small amount of make-up. She's relieved that she didn't react to her mum. That she didn't say anything at all. Her mum obviously thought she might rethink things if she threatened not to pay her fees. That she said nothing might lower her suspicious radar. Plus, Dawn knows, even if her mum did refuse to pay the fees when she moves out, there are grants available. And she is definitely moving out. She is absolutely certain about that.

67

Carla locks the front door behind her, carrying the A4 white envelope into the kitchen and placing it on the breakfast bar, lining it up with the granite corner. She stares at her name printed. **Carla O'Reilly.** She hadn't hesitated in taking Thomas's surname when they married. She knew lots of women who didn't. Emily, for one, kept her own name. Saying she wasn't changing who she was. To Carla, taking Thomas's name had felt like becoming a team. She loved having the same surname as their children, of the four of them being Team O'Reilly. Now, she realises, running her fingertip around the letters, that she changed more than just her name. She had moulded herself to be the wife Thomas wanted her to be. She had changed who she was.

She goes through the motions of making a cup of coffee she knows she won't drink. Anything to avoid opening the envelope. The poor private investigator, she hadn't given him the chance to go through his hard-earned evidence the other day. It came in the post this morning. He'd told her via email that he prefers his clients to have a hard copy. Carla glances back through the hallway at the locked front door, knowing that if Thomas should come home, he would have to ring the doorbell and she'd have time to hide the envelope. He won't come home. He never pops home during the day.

For the first couple of days back from the hotel, Carla had to focus hard on acting normal, reminding herself that nothing was sure until she heard from the private investigator. Until then she had to go through the motions of being the Carla that Thomas knew. She couldn't. It was too difficult not to react as she watched Thomas carry himself with such confidence and behave normally despite knowing what awful deception he was committing. She'd become quiet and withdrawn and blamed it on picking up her sister's bug. She'd stayed in bed, hidden under the covers, asking Thomas to drop the children to school. If she'd been honest with herself, a tiny part of her had been holding hope out that Mr Lane would come back and say he couldn't find anything. That Thomas was still hers.

Placing her hands on either side of the envelope, she questions whether she really wants to see its contents. She turns it over and breaks the seal, sliding out the beige file, her fingers resting on the edge. She's not sure she wants to know any more. She knows enough. Thomas is having two affairs, one with her best friend. Sliding the pages out, she sorts the Emily ones from the others and puts them face down beside her. She doesn't want to see or read any more about Emily.

Looking at the photo, at the same woman in the photos that she'd already received with the note, Carla realises she hasn't actually thought about this other woman since meeting Mr Lane. She's been focused on Emily and Thomas, and their deception. There aren't any photos of Thomas and Amanda together, just this one of her alone. She is surprised by how petite this woman is.

Carla raises the photo to her face: she has a slight gap between her two front teeth, like the female singer in Roxette, only not as pronounced. Why this woman? What is it about this woman that made Thomas decide that an affair was worth risking his marriage for? The PI has included an information sheet and reading it she feels she's reviewing the woman's credentials for a job. Her CV of betrayal includes her phone number, full name and address, her age, number of children, and her job. There are phone records and lists of hotel bookings.

Reading these facts makes this woman real. Knowing that she is called Amanda Williams, she's forty-four, and that she works as a librarian, makes her a real person. A real person with whom Thomas has been having an affair for six months, according to the PI's findings. Six months. Leaning back in her chair, Carla's fist rushes to her mouth and she swallows the sour taste back down her throat.

She squeezes her eyes shut and thinks back over the last six months, resting her head in her hands. Christmas, their holiday in Portugal during the Easter holidays, her birthday. And, not just the big events, but the family walks and adventures, in the woods, digging sandcastles at the beach, endless moments of love and laughter between them. Snuggling up on the settee after the kids had gone to bed, talking until late wrapped in his arms, making love. She opens her eyes. No, don't think of that, there is no way out of that quagmire.

She looks across the kitchen, her eyes landing on a framed photo of the four of them on holiday last year. A happy smiling couple with two lovely kids. Their sun-kissed faces, Ben's freckles illuminated in the sun, Daniel's dimpled cheeks. A snapshot of family life but not the real picture. She stares at the oak frame. What if she peeled away the photo? What lies beneath – what lies are beneath it?

Carla realises the truth now. That she became a version of a wife that Thomas required, not allowing her to be herself. Staying at home while he repeated family history with his marital infidelities. How could she have been so blind to his control for so many years? Convinced by his way of thinking, coming around to view things his way, and what was best for the family, as he always said. And, she thinks, with a sigh of disappointment that comes from deep inside her, she bought it all. She's an educated, clever woman; how did she not see him for what he was until now? Carla looks back at the photo, his dark brown eyes shining, not with love as she thought, but deceit.

Carla has always wanted to be more assertive like Emily. She twists off her wedding rings and, placing them on top of the file of deception, pushes it one side. Well now, she is determined to be assertive. From now on, Emily and Thomas are strangers to her, and she's no longer going to be defined by her loyalty to them, or anyone, except herself and her boys. She must figure out a way forward.

68

Emily switches off the radio. It's beginning to grate on her nerves. She's been sitting here for nearly an hour now and no sign of Thomas. His car is in the office car park. He must be inside. Surely he has to come out at some point, for coffee or lunch or a meeting of some sort. Please let him have a meeting, she wills, she needs him to leave the building. She must talk to him. When Carla said yesterday that she planned to watch him carefully for a while, Emily had to focus hard on keeping her voice normal so Carla wouldn't sense her panic.

She has to warn Thomas, tell him they have to be careful. Carla can't find out. Not now, not yet. She hadn't dared to ring or text him in case Carla's checking his phone. Emily allows herself a little smile. Her plan is working. There hadn't been another woman, just a deluded ex. Carla thinks he's having an affair and will soon dump him, and then Thomas will be all Emily's. They just have to be careful and patient for now.

She can't hang around for much longer. It's nearly half-past one – surely if he was going to go for lunch, he would have done so by now. How can she communicate with him? She twists her ring round and round her finger. Could she ring the office, pretend to be someone else to the receptionist? Googling his office number, her fingers hover over the call button, just as something blue catches the corner of her eye and she looks up.

A blue Fiesta pulls up a little way down the road at a bus stop and the driver puts the hazard lights on. Emily recognises the car. She's seen it once before. A wisp of air escapes her mouth and her heart drops as the driver's door opens. The woman's blonde curly hair bounces as she walks down the street and looks casually into Thomas's offices. Emily's eyes follow as the woman, dressed in grey skinny jeans, matching ankle boots, and a fuchsia pink blouse turns and walks past the office entrance again. They are both waiting for the same man, she realises. A bus approaches where the woman's car is parked, and she waves in apology as she half walks, half jogs back to it. Emily watches as passengers disembark the bus. What the hell is that woman doing here? She thought Thomas had put an end to that. Isn't that what he'd said? Maybe she didn't get the message clearly enough.

The car indicates and pulls out behind the bus. Emily sits up straight and stares as she drives past, hating every curl on her head. How dare she think she can have Thomas? Emily quickly starts her engine and indicates, waving out of her window to thank other drivers as she swings her car around in the road, stopping the traffic on both sides. She is going to have to warn this woman off. Fight for her man.

There is a car between them, and Emily sticks close to it. The traffic lights ahead turn to amber.

"Stop, woman, it's on amber!" she urges. She'll lose her if the blue car doesn't stop. It stops and Emily sighs with relief. She stares straight ahead, as if boring a hole through the car in front, and all the way through to the Fiesta. It's a crossroad junction and it feels like forever for the lights to change. *Fuck, this is ridiculous, what the hell am I planning on doing?* The lights turn to green, and Emily drives on.

Approaching the roundabout, the Fiesta changes lanes and she follows suit only to find herself directly behind it. *Okay, I have to see this through, I have to warn her off. She needs to be out of the picture.*

The woman in the car in front looks in the rear-view mirror and for a moment Emily feels they have locked eyes. At the next junction, the car turns left and left again into the library car park, and Emily follows before realising where she is. Panicking, she parks at the opposite end of the car park, facing inwards, and watches in the rear-view mirror as the woman gets out, puts an oversized navy handbag over her shoulder, and walks purposefully towards the building. The glass double doors stay closed as she approaches. She keys a pin into the keypad, the doors open and she disappears.

Emily gasps in disbelief. Didn't Thomas tell her that woman was visiting from Dublin? How then does she know the keycode for the library? She must work there. Why would Thomas lie to her?

What should she do now? Charge in there and threaten a librarian? Glancing at the clock, it's ten to two, the library will be opening at two o'clock. She can't leave without doing something. And she has ten minutes to work out what.

Over the next few minutes, Emily wavers between *What the hell am I doing?* and *I'm going to go in there to tell her what for.* She watches as an elderly lady walks around the corner leaning heavily on her walking stick. On her other arm, she carries a blue reusable shopping bag weighed down with books. Her long purple mac flaps around her knees, its hood tied tightly under her chin, in preparation against the darkening sky. As she reaches the glass doors, she sees a man approach from the inside, and the doors open. She watches him greet the old lady as she shuffles in. The doors close automatically behind her.

A young mother, hair scraped back, her face make-up free, pushes a double-decker pram past Emily's car. A baby is underneath and a toddler on top. The mother smiles and chatters away to the toddler as they approach the library.

What am I going to do? Doubt creeps into Emily's mind. This is silly. She rubs her finger over the small diamonds in her ring. She needs to make this woman understand that she has to stay away from Thomas. How in the world is she going to do that in the library? Whisper it menacingly? She stares in her mirror as more cars arrive and mothers with young children get out.

I have to do this. She gets out of the car, her legs stiff from all the sitting and walks towards the library entrance, hoping with every step for an idea to come to her. The doors open as she approaches and she hesitates for a second, tucking a strand of hair behind her ear. The man looks up from the library counter and smiles. She returns the smile and nods as she dips behind the first shelves she can. Her keys dangle and clink in her fingers and she quickly pushes them into her handbag. She doesn't want to draw attention to herself. Pretending to browse in the history section, she walks slowly along the shelves, stopping now and again to pick out a book, all the while trying to locate where the woman is.

"Can I help you find something in particular?" The tall mousey-haired librarian from behind the counter appears at her shoulder, holding a pile of books. He nods at the book Emily is holding, *Putin's Progress*. "That's a bit outdated now, it was published in 2004. There's a more recent book on the same subject by Angela Stent, *Putin's World*," he says in his quiet, gentle librarian voice. "It's just down here."

"Oh, *er*, thank you, that would be great," Emily stutters and follows him.

"It's on the display shelves around the corner."

Around the corner is toddler storytime, and sitting in front of all the mums and children is the woman Emily came to see, tortoiseshell glasses resting on her nose. Thanking the librarian as he hands her the book, she stands thumbing through the introduction, while listening intently to *The Tiger Who Came to Tea*, being read animatedly by the other woman, who according to her name badge is called Amanda not Tracey.

"And they also bought a giant tin of tiger food in case the tiger ever came to tea again, but he never did."

Amanda's curly hair shakes like springs as she smiles brightly at her audience, taking off her glasses and closing the book.

"Next, we'll read *Percy the Park Keeper.*"

Putting the Putin book down, Emily turns and walks behind the travel section to the front door, avoiding eye contact with the helpful librarian who is now back behind the counter. *This was a stupid idea.* She walks quickly across the car park, wiping the layer of perspiration from her top lip.

She googles it later that evening; the library shuts at eight on a Tuesday. She doesn't know if Amanda is working that late until she pulls into the car park and sees her car parked in the same place as this afternoon. There's five minutes until the library closes. She parks up, facing the library this time. She has no intention of going inside, she'll wait for Amanda to come out.

Earlier was a mistake. Well, it wasn't. It would have been a mistake to confront Amanda in the library, in the middle of storytime. It was too full of mums and children; the wrong moment. But she's learnt a lot from following her. She now knows Thomas didn't tell her the truth about this woman. She knows her name is Amanda, not Tracey, thanks to the name badge, where she works, and that the library shuts late tonight which suits her as Rosie and Theo are at their dad's tonight.

A couple of people walk past her car and along the road towards the supermarket. Glancing around her, she notices there are still a few cars here. What if Amanda comes out with a co-worker, how is she going to confront her then? *I can't be parked here. I need to move.* She moves the car and parks around the corner, pulls her hat on, and walks briskly back.

Amanda is locking the door of the library and Emily hesitates, standing close to a car, holding her breath, and watches as Amanda walks towards her car, pinging it open. *It's now or never, if I want Thomas this is what I have to do.*

"*Amanda,*" she says loudly, walking towards her.

Amanda turns.

"I just want a quick word before you head off." The words spill out of Emily before Amanda has a chance to reply.

Her brows furrow in confusion as Emily comes to a stop at the edge of her car.

"*Stay away from Thomas. It's over. Do you understand me?*"

"What? Who are you?"

"*If you know what's good for you, stay away from him,*" Emily says, stepping closer.

"You aren't his wife. Who are you?" Amanda's forehead creases.

"*I'm warning you to stay away. It's over, done, finished. Be very careful, you're being watched.*" Emily surprises herself with her menacing tone. She moves forward again, and Amanda takes a step back, banging into the wing mirror. Stepping towards Emily this time, Amanda's icy blue eyes stare into Emily's.

"I don't know what you're talking about." Her voice is calm and direct, and she turns to her car.

A tsunami of anger and desperation floods over Emily and she grabs Amanda's arm tightly and spins her around. Amanda's face pales as the colour drains from it.

"*You need to watch your back. Stay the fuck away from Thomas or else!*" Emily slams her against the car, and then turns and quickly walks away.

"*Mind your own business,*" Amanda shouts after her. "*This is harassment, you know, I could report you to the guards. Didn't you see the security cameras? I have proof!*"

Emily's back stiffens, but she doesn't look back. She continues striding back to her car. Her whole body is boiling with anger. Sitting in the car, she raises her shaking hands to her face, and rubs her cheeks, willing her heart to calm down. She takes deep breaths, in and out, in and out. "*Fuck, fuck, fuck!*"

69

An hour earlier

Carla can hear the murmur of the TV as she comes downstairs after putting the boys to bed. This house, with Thomas in it, makes Carla feel like she's in a crowded room, people shoulder to shoulder, pushing past her, putting physical pressure on her as they move. She has to get out. Standing at the door to the living room, she looks at Thomas watching *Grand Designs*.

He glances over. "Come and sit down, love, he's ripping right into their budget."

Carla turns away, carrying the boys' empty milk glasses into the kitchen. "I think I'll try and catch that new spin class at the gym. Julia was asking me to go with her."

She drives aimlessly around their city, trying to make sense of everything. It doesn't help, and she's tormented with memories of both Thomas and Emily. Finding herself on the other side of town, in Salthill, she parks along the prom and gets out, ready to let the wind blow these thoughts from her mind, if only for a while. The prom is breathing, living, through the sea, the waves continually turning over. Carla walks at a fast pace, weaving between people, feels her chest constricting, her breathing difficult to regulate. Thomas's deception weighs heavily. She can't make sense of it.

The picture of Amanda won't shift from her mind, the address of the library where she works is imprinted on her brain, and Carla finds herself turning back to the car before she reaches the end of the prom. She drives towards the library. She needs to visualise it; she needs to see where Amanda exists in real life.

Driving slowly past the signposted turn for the library, she sees the lights are still on. It must be late night opening. She wasn't expecting that. She hadn't thought beyond seeing the building. Her fingertips tingle as she grips the steering wheel and turns the car at the next chance she gets, sitting up straighter in her seat. Will she see the woman who has stolen her husband's attention for the last six months? Does she want to see her in the flesh?

She indicates to turn back onto the main road, towards to the library. Her hands are clammy on the steering wheel, her heartbeat thundering in her ears. On the opposite side of the road, she sees a woman striding determinedly along the pavement, her hands thrust in her pockets, a hat pulled tightly over auburn wavy hair. Carla would recognise that walk anywhere. What is Emily doing here, at Amanda's place of work?

As she slowly passes the library again, the light goes out. Watching in her rear-view mirror as Emily walks into the car park, Carla makes a split-second decision, indicates left, and turns into a church car park. She wraps her hair into a bun, and pushes it under her hat, zipping up her jacket. She hurries across the road, just in time to see Emily step out from behind a parked car and walk towards Amanda, calling her.

Standing in the shadows of a dark people carrier, Carla watches Emily confront Amanda. The exact words aren't clear, she's too far away, but the body language is, and she gasps loudly as Emily grabs Amanda and pushes her against the car. Ducking down behind the car as Emily turns her way, Carla shuffles backward and out of sight until she passes. She hears Amanda shouting after Emily, threatening to call the gardaí. She stays, crouching there, as she waits for Amanda to drive out of the car park. Her whole body is shaking as it dawns on her what exactly her best friend is up to. Emily wants Thomas for herself.

She moves to the edge of the car, and checks the coast is clear before standing up, and hurrying back to her car. Looking back across the road to the library, she plants her feet in a wide stance, pushes her shoulders back, and takes off her hat. Loosening the bobble from her hair, she shakes it down over her shoulders. Emily is not going to get away with this.

70

Why, oh, why didn't she check for security cameras at the library before she challenged Amanda? Emily stares out of the bedroom window. She hadn't intended to grab Amanda. Whatever came over her? She only meant to warn her off. Turning away from the window, she looks at the pile of washing on her bed. Who is she angry with here? Amanda? Thomas? Why isn't he telling the truth? This was not some friend from his college days, and she wasn't visiting from Dublin. She lives and works here in Galway, that much was obvious. Thomas had assured Emily that he'd dealt with Amanda, or Tracey, as he'd called her. That she wasn't to worry about it. The same day he'd whispered he loved her when they made love. Was he trying to protect her? What did Amanda want with Thomas?

Emily had thought the situation was under the control. She had been confident he was soon going to be hers. Now it feels like control is slipping through her fingers. Has following Amanda to the library and worse, physically confronting her, put her plan in jeopardy?

Sitting on the bed, she begins to pair socks. *What do I do now? I can't walk away, it's too late, I love Thomas. The plan has almost come together. Carla will leave him any day now.*

A nagging feeling sits in her stomach as she folds the kids' pyjamas. Amanda knew she wasn't Thomas's wife, that much was obvious. Shit. Emily rests the towel she is folding on her lap. At the moment, Amanda has the upper hand. This needs to change. She needs to be dealt with.

71

Carla paces up and down the kitchen. She needs to think.

She will not accept this.

She will not be walked over.

She knows they have always thought of her as easy-going Carla, happy to go along with whatever, never really pushing her opinion forward. Naïve, underconfident and unsure. Well, not anymore. They are going to get some shock if they think she's going to let them get off lightly. Do they think she is just going to say, 'Off you go then, be happy together, I wish you the best'? Not anymore will she play Nice Carla. No, this time she is going to take control. She is searching deep into herself to recover the Carla she used to be, the young woman who had plans and was excited by the future.

She leans against the breakfast bar, and glares at the strip of passport photos of herself and Emily as students that she'd found only recently and stuck on the fridge door. At college, Carla was never one who needed a man. Emily jumped from boyfriend to boyfriend, but Carla was never bothered. She had boyfriends and flings, but it wasn't everything to her to have someone by her side. Yet now, she realises, having someone by her side has stifled her plans and dreams. Instead of her other half sharing her dreams and encouraging her, he has muted her somehow and she didn't notice it happening.

Her cup of coffee stands cold in front of her, a thin skin across the top. The wrap she made half-heartedly sits uneaten. She doesn't seem to be able to eat anything these last few days. She has no appetite despite the hollow feeling in the pit of her stomach. Picking up the teaspoon, she breaks the flimsy film of the coffee and stirs round and around aimlessly.

They had bought a coffee machine each, Emily and Carla, a couple of years ago, in the Black Friday sales at the retail park. Emily picked out the red one, to match the backsplash tiles in her kitchen, and Carla went for cream. They'd got into a fit of giggles in the queue for the checkout and said how sad their lives were now that they were excited about buying coffee machines. Carla always keeps a box of Emily's preferred strong Columbian capsules in the cupboard and Emily keeps Carla's sweet and smooth Brazilian coffee in hers.

We have shared so much together, so many memories. She's known Emily since she was thirteen. She still remembers walking into secondary school on that first day of her first year.

Everyone looked the same in their school uniform, but they were all strangers to Carla as she'd recently moved into the area. Already, it was apparent who were the popular kids, who were the social outcasts, and who was somewhere in between. Sitting quietly next to a small group of inbetweeners at the end of a wooden bench, Carla had fiddled with her hands in her lap, praying that time would hurry up and they would be put into their form groups. She was better in smaller groups of people. "Hi, what school did you go to?" a girl with the shiniest auburn wavy hair asked her. Emily was sitting next to her and had turned towards Carla. They quickly became friends. They just clicked.

How could Emily do this? Did she think that Carla would confront Thomas about his other affair and that he would confess about Emily too? Is this why Emily is constantly asking her about what she's going to do? Does she think he would pick her if forced to make a choice?

Maybe he would but Carla doubts it. If she knows her husband, he will come crawling in regret, pleading for forgiveness. Glancing around the kitchen at all their family photos, she realises she doesn't know her husband, does she? She didn't know that he was cheating on her. She didn't suspect a thing.

Looking at the photos displayed here, she only half recognises her husband. The version he shows her, the version she now knows isn't the real him. She takes the teaspoon out of the cup and leaves it to drip on the granite. Thomas has obviously been able to compartmentalise his family and his affairs as if the two would never meet.

Well, now they have.

Why has he turned into his father? And why choose Emily, of all people, to have an affair with?

And why now?

Thomas has always been a charmer; he has the gift of the gab. He's the sort of person who can walk into a room and have everyone listening and chatting with him in minutes. And Carla, she would be hiding in his shadow, at least for the first while until she got to know people. When she'd met Thomas, in her final year at college, Emily hadn't warmed to him. It wasn't awkward, they got on fine, but they never really clicked with each other and that had always niggled Carla a little. Her two favourite people, she wanted them to like each other.

Oh God, how long has it been going on? Months, years? Was Thomas and Emma's apparent indifference towards each other a cover for a long affair? Maybe the other woman is the new girl on the scene and Emily's nose is out of joint. Is that why she was threatening her at the library? Did she send the note and photos to Carla so that the other woman would be forced out of the picture, and Emily would be able to continue as normal with Thomas?

Bile rises and so does she, in a mad dash to the downstairs loo. She is dry retching after the initial sickness with nothing left to give. She bleaches the toilet and washes her hands, looking in the mirror at her face, drawn, grey and ashen, her hair limp and lifeless. She wants to crawl upstairs, curl up under the duvet and wake up to find this is all a nightmare.

Sitting back down on the stool at the breakfast bar, she opens her laptop and logs into the bank. She has already started packing, only a few things, the kids' clothes and hers, returning the suitcases to the attic until she's ready. The toys will have to be packed on the day. She needs to put some distance between her and Thomas.

She keys in the security number, and looks back over transactions on their joint account. Nothing is out of the ordinary. A few clicks and the money is scheduled to be transferred into her own account on Friday. The day she plans to leave.

She hasn't been greedy, just taken half, that's what is legally hers, if not more. She also has the rental income from the house she bought after college, the house she shared with Emily until she moved in with Thomas. Carla could move back there with the boys. She'd have to give notice to the tenants and find somewhere else in the meantime. But she doesn't want to move there. There's too many memories in that house of her friendship with Emily. She glances at her nails, they are chipped and spoilt, they need to be redone. It's not something high on her list of priorities at the moment.

She can't move back to her mum and dad's. They will wreck her head with questions and suggestions. They still live in her childhood home, her bedroom is still as it was when she left for college, albeit with the *Smash Hits* posters taken down and neatly folded in a drawer.

Closing her eyes, she can see herself and Emily, slouched on the bed, doing quizzes from *Just Seventeen* magazine on their potential perfect partners. Jumping around the room singing into hairbrushes to the Top 40 countdown on Radio Two. Revising for their Leaving Cert, books piled up around them, her mum bringing mugs of hot chocolate to keep them going. She opens her eyes. No, she can't go back there.

She'll go to her sister, Grace, in Kinsale near Cork. She has space for them. It'll be a bit of breathing space until she works out what to do. She needs to ring her. She hasn't told her yet. She hasn't told anyone.

Clicking into Word, she opens the letter she typed last night. Looking at Thomas over the last few days, all she has felt is empty. A man like that won't change. She doesn't even know if he'll be upset when she leaves – he may just fall into either Emily or Amanda's arms. Carla doesn't want to know if he does. He's not the man she thought he was. Her heart aches for what was or what she thought was. Yet she doesn't want to fight for it. At the same time, she can't let him get away with it, not without punishing him. And, she knows exactly how to hit him. Carla clicks on the print button. This letter will explain what he's been doing with the money that isn't his. Let's see what a success he is then, she thinks, reaching for an envelope in the drawer. Let him feel that body blow.

She slides the envelope inside her handbag, and her mind returns to Emily. Carla's rage at her friend is intense. She wants to scream and pull her hair, throw her to the ground and hurt her.

Carla knows she can't let Emily get away with this either, and Amanda's given her the perfect idea.

72

Amanda glances at her phone as they wait at the crossing. No word from Thomas in nearly two weeks now. She needs to tell him about the woman challenging her at the library last night. Who was she? Was she the one watching Thomas's wife? Surely he must know by now that it wasn't her. The lights change and she follows Michael across the road to the coffee shop.

The windows are steamy and inside is busy with mums with babies and toddlers and loud with chatter. They navigate their way through the prams to a free table at the back of the room and order food. Amanda scrolls through her phone checking if Thomas is online.

She checks his work website too just in case that might show he's been too busy to get in touch.

"My head's still not right after that wine last night. I thought the fresh air might have shifted it. How's yours?" Michael asks, rubbing his stubble.

"Fine. Are you thinking of growing that into a full beard?"

"No, I'm thinking of shaving it off actually, it's getting too itchy."

A baby starts screeching in the pram at the table next to them and the mother stands up and rocks the pram until the child settles again.

"It's loud in here, isn't it?" Amanda says, glancing around, before looking back down at her phone. She can't text him. That would break the rules and she can't do that, not when he thinks she's been watching his wife. She has to be patient. There have been times when she hasn't heard from him but never for this long and they've never argued before.

"You ever thought about having more?" Michael asks, nodding at the toddlers playing at the table behind her.

"God, no. I'm too old. Anyway, one is handful enough for a single mum like me."

Their food arrives. Michael tucks in but Amanda ignores her wrap, and focuses on her phone, switching it off and then on again.

"I think there's something wrong with my phone, I don't seem to be receiving any messages or updates."

"Here, pass it over. I'll have a look."

"No, no, it's fine." She picks it up. "Just send me a text to check, will you?"

He texts her a smiley face, her phone beeps immediately. "There, it's working. Maybe switching it on and off again helped."

Amanda doesn't answer; she scrolls through the phone. No new notifications. Nothing. Is this it, is it over just like that? She didn't do anything. Why hasn't he realised that? The tears well up and she blinks them away furiously and blows her nose.

"So, are you going to tell me who he is?" Michael asks.

"Who?"

He nods at her phone. "The guy you're desperate to hear from."

"No one really. Just a bit of fun." She bites into her wrap, avoiding his eyes.

"Come on, spill the beans."

"Just a guy from the other side of town. Nothing serious." She twiddles with her napkin.

"Tell me everything. What's his name? How long have you been together? Are you going to introduce me?" He leans back in his chair, running his hand through his light brown hair, pushing it off his forehead.

Amanda looks around her nervously and it doesn't escape Michael's notice.

"What?" he asks.

"Nothing. There isn't much to tell. It isn't too serious." She glances down at her food. "I'm not looking for anything long-term."

"Is he married?"

Finishing her coffee, she pushes her half-eaten wrap to one side and stands up. "Come on, let's head off." She puts money on the table and turns to leave.

Michael takes the last bite of his sandwich, stands up, and drinks the rest of his coffee. She moves quickly to the door of the café and down the path towards home, hearing Michael's hurried pace behind her.

"Tell me you aren't seeing a married man, Amanda."

She says nothing, she just keeps walking.

"Why won't you answer me?"

Amanda swings around. "It's none of your business who I'm seeing. And, it's certainly not up to you, with your perfect marriage, to be judging me either."

"*Woah!* I wasn't judging. I'm just concerned." He takes a step back.

"Your voice is judgemental. Yes, he's married. No, I don't care. It's a bit of fun. I'm not planning on breaking up his family."

She swings off the path and into her estate, her fists clenched.

Later that night, after dinner, they take their wine into the living area. Michael settles himself on the navy leather settee. Amanda sits in the armchair, tucking her legs up and switching the TV on. She can feel her brother's eyes flicking over to her every few minutes and she focuses determinedly on the news programme. She can't face any more of his questioning, his probing into the past or future.

"Amanda, tell me the truth, did you know Dad was having an affair?"

"No," she says quickly, too quickly. She takes a breath before adding, "We've already discussed it, Michael."

"Do you think Mum knew?"

"I don't know. How would I know?" She stands up, walking over to the kitchen area. "Let's not go over this again."

"You were older, did you pick up on anything? I only remember the arguments. Do you remember those?"

"No, not really."

Opening the fridge, she takes out another bottle of wine and stands with her back to him as she uncorks it. Her hands shake as she tries to steady the corkscrew. She's tried so hard over the years to make up for the absence of their parents. She's kept them on a kind of pedestal for Michael, focusing on all their good memories and embellishing more than a few. She has to keep this up. She can't fail now.

Taking the bottle back into the living area, she refills their glasses and sits down. She gulps her wine, staring at the TV screen not hearing the presenter's words. Michael doesn't say anything but the silence between them is awkward, the air still. Amanda tries to tune into the TV programme so she can break this moment with a chat about something featured. She hears Michael take a deep breath and she holds her own.

"I think you knew about the affair, and so did Mum."

"What are you talking about? You don't know what you are saying, sure you were only a little boy then."

"There was a copy of the fire report in Uncle Seán's paperwork."

"What? Why didn't you mention it?" She stands up and lights a couple of candles on the mantelpiece, keeping her back to him. "I've never seen it. What did it say?" Her lip trembles.

"Did you ever wonder why they were found next to each other on the settee, in the living room? It was the middle of the night, why weren't they in bed?"

She turns back to face him. Her fingers are on her Celtic heart locket, running over the pattern.

"They most likely just fell asleep there." She shrugs, not meeting his eyes and sitting down again. "It was New Year's Eve – remember their infamous parties every New Year's? They were probably just shattered and fell asleep."

"Why did you wake up in the middle of the night and they didn't? No smoke alarms went off, remember, they weren't working, what made you wake up?"

"I don't know, probably the smoke. Do we have to relive this again?"

"In the report, it said the Christmas tree – the one in the snug – must have fallen into the fire somehow or else that it was very close. Well, we always knew that but now I'm puzzled. Wasn't it tucked into the corner between the window and the fireplace? And remember the metal stand – the 'stupid metal stand' Mum called it. Can you remember it wasn't adjustable to fit the tree into it? Dad always had to hack away at the tree trunk until it fitted into the stand. There's no way it could have come loose from that, surely."

This conversation has to be shut down. She downs her glass of wine and stands up. "Can we just stop this? You know I don't like talking about the night of the fire." Her voice slurs a little.

Going to the fridge, she stands staring into it for a second or two before she realises the bottle is already on the coffee table. Coming back to the living area, she leans over to refill Michael's glass, but he covers it with his hand – he hasn't touched a drop since she last filled it.

"Not for me, thanks."

"How many years have you been in Australia now? Eighteen, nineteen?" she says, sitting down in the armchair again. "We really should come and visit you."

She knows she is waffling, changing the subject, she can hear her voice wobbling with the wine. He keeps pushing it. She needs to make him stop.

"Do you think that Mum got Dad drunk that night? That she knew about the affair, got him drunk enough so that he collapsed on the settee, and then set the house on fire? That it was a murder-suicide. That if she couldn't have him, no one could?"

"No. Stop it. Don't say that about Mum." Her words slur into each other. "She wouldn't do that. That fire could have killed us all. Mum loved Dad; she wouldn't have wanted to kill him. It was an accident."

"If she was desperate, if she was drunk too, then she might not have been thinking rationally."

"*Stop it, Michael! Stop it!*" she puts her head in her hands. "Mum loved us. It was an accident. They weren't supposed to be downstairs."

"What do you mean, they weren't supposed to be downstairs?" He moves towards her, taking her hands from her head. "What do you mean?"

"Nothing. I just meant that it was an accident. I tried to find them, I tried to save them. They weren't supposed to be downstairs. I looked everywhere. I couldn't get downstairs, the flames … I tried to save them." The tears stream down her cheeks, her black mascara leaving dirt-lined tracks. Amanda sinks back into the armchair and her body is wracked with sobs she can't stop. "I thought I could save them. I thought I could save our family."

Michael kneels next to his sister and takes her hands. "You saved me from the house fire, Amanda. You saved my life. It's not your fault they weren't in bed. Any other night they would have been. You did the best you could."

Heaving with the weight of her tears, she curls to the side in the foetal position. Michael reaches for a tissue from the box on the coffee table and passes it to her. Blowing her nose, she follows his gaze to the family ski photo, and she knows by the way his face drains that he has finally realised where in their family home it used to sit. On the little coffee table in the snug.

She hears him whisper "The snug." He gasps, confused, stunned. He looks across at her and she averts her eyes. "But this photo was in the snug. The fire started in the snug. How did you get this?"

"I took it before the fire. I was just looking at it earlier and I took it up to my room."

Why? Why would you do that?"

She doesn't look at him but hears his intake of breath – it's so sharp it pains her that he is wounded.

"Was it you? Did you light the fire?"

Amanda doesn't look up. She buries her head in her hands and sobs loudly, her shoulders shuddering.

"Answer me. Was it you?"

"They weren't supposed to be downstairs," she whispers between her fingers.

"Amanda, look at me. Look at me!" Michael stands up and towers over his sister.

She doesn't move. He grabs her shoulders and tries to turn her to face him. "Did you deliberately light the fire that killed our parents?"

Her whole body is shaking as she says "I overheard them talking about splitting up. She said she knew about a woman called Deborah and that he was putting money in Deborah's account, and he said yes he was and he was leaving Mum for this Deborah! I thought if there was a fire, and everyone got out, it would shock them into realising what was important. I was supposed to save them," she sobs. "But they weren't in bed. They were asleep on the settee in the living room! I didn't see them in the dark when I went down to the snug. I couldn't reach them."

Michael stands up, facing the fireplace. He swipes across the top of the mantelpiece, knocking off ornaments and the two candles. The flames flicker and go out as they fall to the rug below. He turns and storms out of the living room. Amanda hears his hire car keys scraping against the dish on the sideboard, the front door slamming behind him, and she gives in to her sobs.

73

Dawn peeks into the spare room. Michael's suitcase sits neatly in the corner. His aftershave and electric razor are on top of the chest of drawers. He can't have gone far. Maybe he's visiting friends although she doesn't recall him mentioning it. She hasn't seen him since they made breakfast together a few days ago. She can't help feeling that if he'd gone to stay with friends, her mum would have been very vocal in complaining but she's been unusually quiet, and not snapping at all. It's as if something is bubbling underneath, Dawn can sense it. Like walking up a track leading to the core of the volcano, hearing it rumbling beneath your feet, not having a choice but to continue walking towards the uncertain peak. She is waiting for her mum to erupt.

Wherever Michael is, he's not here, and she's decided that instead of waiting for Michael to go back to Australia, she'll move out while he's here. Dawn can feel the small plastic bag of crushed tablets rub against the material of her trouser pocket as she goes downstairs. Tonight is the night to go through with the sleeping tablet scheme for real. The trial worked well; there hadn't been a movement from her mum's bedroom all night long. Dawn hasn't had a chance to do it again, she's been focusing on her exams and assignments. But now that they're finished, tonight could be the perfect opportunity. Ruth's family have left for France. Dawn told her that she plans to move out during the night when her mum is asleep. There was no need to tell her more than that.

It might even help to have Michael in the country, she thinks, as she makes a curry. Adding the chicken and onion to the sizzling pan, he can help her mum to see that moving out is a normal part of growing up. He can support her if she's upset. Dawn isn't a monster, after all, she just wants to live her life. She chops the mushrooms and the peppers while keeping half an eye on her mum. She needs to add the sleeping tablets without being noticed.

"Do you think Michael will be joining us? There's plenty of food."

"I've no idea but I doubt it at this stage," Amanda says, her shoulders hunched over as she rinses glasses in the sink. She doesn't look up, snap, or make a sarcastic comment. There is just a hint of resignation in her voice.

Dawn turns back to the curry. She needs to focus, she has a busy night ahead of her. Tonight is about Dawn and she is determined not to let anything stop her from moving forward. This is her chance to escape. The powdered tablets feel as if they're burning in her jeans pocket. She has to get out. Once she is out, she'll be free, and Mum can't force her to come back.

Putting the rice on, she checks the clock on the oven, it's three o'clock. They are having an early dinner as Dawn is working at six. She hopes the tablets will last as long as last time. Amanda will be getting them much earlier than on the trial night. She needs her to stay asleep until 2 am at the earliest. That'll give her plenty of time to move most of her things out.

When the rice is simmering, and the curry gently bubbling, Dawn adds the rest of the vegetables and sets the table, the cutlery clanging in her trembling hands. The time is coming close now to add the tablets. Putting her hand in her back pocket, she feels the plastic bag with her thumb and forefinger – could she add them now? She looks at Amanda at the washing machine in the utility room. No, not yet.

She takes her hand out of her pocket and says, "Mum, is that a white wash you're putting on?"

"Yes."

"I have a few bits in the basket at the top of the stairs. Hang on, I've just got to strain the rice."

"I'll get them. You serve up the dinner."

Smiling to herself, Dawn drains the rice and spoons some onto her mum's plate. Scooping some curry on top, she takes the packet out from her pocket and sprinkles the powder over the dinner. Hearing footsteps on the stairs, she quickly mixes it into the curry with a teaspoon, the stairs creaking as Amanda gets closer. Dawn carries the plates to the table just as she comes in.

"Dinner's ready," Dawn says, realising her now empty hands are shaking. She shoves them awkwardly into her jeans pockets.

She's thankful she's working tonight and that she won't have to nervously watch Mum all evening like with the trial. Thinking ahead, as she pours water for both of them, she'll need to pack as she goes, which is going to be time-consuming, and possibly a bit noisy. These tablets have to work. She needs Amanda to be dead to the world.

Taking the first few mouthfuls is an effort that takes all Dawn's attention. Her stomach is in bits; tiny balls of tightness colliding and sticking to each other, forming bigger, tighter balls of nervousness pinging around her stomach. Her mobile phone bursts into song, a duet by Ed Sheeran and Justin Bieber, 'I Don't Care'. It's her boss.

"Can you come in earlier tonight?"

"Yeah, no problem, 5pm?"

"If Gary was to collect you, could you come in sooner? He's coming in too. Would that be okay? I've got a restaurant full of a family birthday meal, and only one waiter. Jenny went home throwing up."

Looking over at her mum, relief washes over Dawn. She can go now. She doesn't have to anxiously wait and watch. "Yes, okay. He knows where I live. He's dropped me home before. I'll give him a ring. We'll probably be there in half an hour. Give them all a glass of Prosecco, that'll keep them happy for a while."

"I'll try that. Thanks a million."

"Are you going in early?" her mum asks, sipping her wine.

"Yes, they're short-staffed." Dawn puts her plate on the side and wraps foil over it. "I'll eat this when I get home."

Her mum doesn't answer. She drops her fork and stands to get more wine from the fridge.

Rushing upstairs to get her apron and name badge, Dawn doesn't have time to think of the tablets, if and when they'll start to work or whether they will last long enough. Quickly putting on some mascara and rubbing highlighter cream on her cheekbones, she brushes her teeth and comes back downstairs, just as Gary pulls into their driveway.

She puts her head around the door of the living room, and says "Bye, Mum. I'm off now."

"Bye." Amanda doesn't look up from her phone at the kitchen table.

Leaving, Dawn realises that could be their last interaction for a while, the last civil one anyway. She isn't under any illusion that Mum will take this news well. She can almost picture the steam coming out of her ears when she finds out Dawn has moved out without her blessing.

74

Carla sits watching people walking along the prom. She knows she'll miss Galway. Schools close for the summer next week, so her boys won't be losing out on much by finishing early. She has the whole summer to settle them into a new area and they'll have their cousins around. She'd kept things vague with her sister, told her she needed some thinking time, that she'd explain later. Looking at online rentals in her sister's area, she's seen a few options. They are expensive with it being the summer season but she's confident that she can get a good price for a long-term rental. She's survived the last few days by dealing with the practical issues, pushing all emotions to one side.

Thinking of Thomas only causes an empty feeling in her gut, a disappointment in him, in their failure of a marriage, and a wonder as to how it ended up like this. She posted the letter this morning after the school drop-off. It's the least he deserves. She knows she should challenge him about his infidelities but she doesn't want to. There is no point. He'll find out soon enough what she's done and he'll know it was her.

Emily is a different story. Carla can't leave without dealing with her. Tomorrow she will. Sitting in the car, she texts her.

Hi Em, do u fancy walk tomorrow? Tracht beach. Before school collection.

Emily replies straight away.

Tracht? OK. See you at yours. I'll bring flask of tea.

See you at beach 1.30, I have things to do b4.

OK xx

She deletes the texts. Emily's face on her profile picture makes her feel sick. Since seeing her confront Amanda, Carla is more convinced than ever of Emily's scheme to get Thomas for herself.

Carla examines the nail marks on her palms. She breathes deeply, exhaling slowly, and tunes into the presenters on the radio show, waiting for the monotonous chat about nothing important to calm her. But it doesn't. She stares at the sun setting over Galway Bay, like blood spilling across the horizon. It will be her last time for a while. This time tomorrow she'll be gone. But first, she has things to do. She turns the key and drives on.

Parking at the entrance to the estate but out of the pools of light from the lampposts, she stares at the house. The lights are on downstairs, the curtains drawn. She wants to go and knock on the door, but some invisible force seems to be holding her back. Amanda's car sits on the drive so she must be there. She isn't with Thomas anyway. He's at home with the kids.

She looks over the PI's notes again; Amanda has a daughter in college but there's no mention of a husband or partner. Carla reaches under Emily's peach woollen jumper to scratch her shoulder blades. She'd forgotten she had this jumper actually. It was only when she was sorting out clothes last week to pack she came across it. This, the stilettos and the light blue suit jacket Emily lent her for her romantic hotel trip with Thomas that never happened. Pushing her seat back, she kicks off her navy pumps and slips into the stilettos. They will come in useful now as will the auburn wig she'd bought in a party shop.

The light goes off, and the front upstairs bedroom goes on. Has she missed her chance, has she wimped out in doing this? Her hands shake, she rubs them together. *I've been sitting here for ages now. Thinking but not doing. Will I be like this tomorrow, meeting Emily? Will I back out then? No. I will not be walked all over.* She is determined to leave tomorrow with her head held high.

The bedroom goes dark. She must do this. Unclicking her seatbelt, she takes the keys from the ignition – the radio abruptly cuts off mid-tune. Rubbing the key fob, she thinks of this woman, Amanda, who's been having an affair with her husband for six months. Does she feel guilty? Is she aware he's married with children? Does she know he's having another affair? That the woman who confronted her at the library is also Thomas's lover. Will Amanda believe that she is Emily?

She bites her bottom lip, she's frozen to her seat. She wants to go and knock on the door but she can't. Gripping the steering wheel, she looks around the street. It's late now and lights are going out as people go to bed.

Another hour passes and still Carla sits here. A shadow passes under the street lamp and she watches as a young woman crosses the road and walks towards the red front door of Amanda's house. Carla starts to sink down in her seat. Is that the daughter? She enters the house. The lights go on and Carla sighs. Now what? Was this the excuse she was waiting for to duck out of this? Or is it the excuse she needs to push herself across the road? Does the daughter know what kind of a mother she has, a homewrecker? Maybe it's time Carla exposed the truth.

Movement at the door catches her eye and she cranes to see. Something is happening behind the door. Shadows. Is it Amanda? Is she coming out? Does she know Carla is here? Keeping her eyes on the frosted windows on either side of the red door, she sees shapes appear but struggles to see what's happening.

Bright lights illuminate her car as headlights swoop into the estate and swing around. She sits still as the lights flash over her. A small silver Clio reverses into Amanda's driveway. The young, female driver gets outs and opens the boot just as the door of the house opens and the daughter emerges, looking up and down the cul de sac. Carla watches as they step inside the house, revealing the shadows to be boxes and bags which they load into the small boot. The daughter turns and closes the front door. Another movement to Carla's right makes her turn her head. A man is walking away from a car, its locking lights flashing. He walks straight towards Amanda's house.

Carla reaches for her phone and photographs this man as he walks. Who is he? I'm in out of my depth here, Carla realises. I need to leave. But she can't, not now. She must wait for the street to be quiet again. She watches the man as he talks to the daughter. Who is he? Could he be Amanda's husband or the young woman's partner? Looking down at her phone, she zooms in on one of the photos. It's a hire car….

When she looks up again, the man has gone. He must have slipped inside the house. The girl paces up and down next to the car, looking up at the bedroom window. Carla follows her line of sight and watches as a light goes on, dim behind the curtains. The girl throws her hands up and gets into the car. Frowning, Carla can't take her eyes off the house. What's going on?

A minute passes, no more, until the man comes out of the house, with a suitcase, closing the door behind him. The girl talks to him before they hug, and she gets back into the car. Hands in his pockets, he looks to be in deep thought as he watches the two girls drive off. He returns to his hire car and leaves.

Carla should go too. Turning on the engine, her headlights come on automatically and the key left in the red front door glints across the road at her. She kills the engine and stares at it.

75

Dawn stirs, her eyelids fluttering in the bright light flooding in through the curtains. She checks her Fitbit, half-past eight; she's slept well. Reaching for her phone, she stares at it in her hands, weighing up whether or not to switch it on. She draws her legs up to her body, and pulls the covers up to her armpits.

She's reminded of the books in Hagrid's class, in the Harry Potter series, that screech at you when you open them. This is what she's expecting when she switches on her phone: her mum's voice screeching.

She looks around the spare room in Ruth's house; a small suitcase lies open on the floor, her bag of toiletries on top of the chest of drawers. Boxes and carrier bags are piled up around the bed. She didn't bring everything, but it looks like a lot from here. Shit. She remembers the blister packet of sleeping tablets. They are still in the cabinet in her ensuite at home. What if her mum goes snooping around her room once she realises Dawn's left? She'll find them and know.

She looks back at her phone in her hands. It doesn't matter what her mum says, Dawn is free from her clutches. Physically anyway. She isn't under any illusion that she'll be left alone. Her mum will try every which way to manipulate her but at least she has the advantage of not living in the house anymore, of not having to go home. She has almost a month until Ruth's parents come back and that is plenty of time to suss out student accommodation for herself and her friends.

Okay. Time for the reckoning. Dawn switches on her phone. It pings and beeps with snap chats, Instagram posts, WhatsApps from friends but nothing from her mum. No messages, no missed calls, no screeching voicemails. Dawn's eyebrows furrow, her forehead creases. *Strange, very strange. What game is she playing? It's after half-past eight in the morning, She'll definitely be up by now. Maybe she hasn't realised I've gone yet. I didn't leave a note and closed the bedroom door. Mum probably thinks I'm still asleep.*

There is a quiet knock on her door, and Ruth's head appears. "Morning, did you get any sleep?"

"Yeah, better than I expected to." Dawn shuffles over in the bed and Ruth climbs in next to her.

"Did you hear anything?" Ruth nods at the phone.

"Nope. Not a thing. She must think I'm still in bed." A small smile of relief flashes across Dawn's face as she realises she's actually done it. She's moved out.

Ruth giggles. "You are. Just not in your house! Is she going to go mad, or will she give you a look like my mum does when she's disappointed in me?"

"Oh, it'll be more than a look."

"Come on, let's go make some pancakes," Ruth says. "This is the start of a new beginning for you, me, and Samantha living together. It's going to be amazing."

By eleven o'clock, Dawn still hasn't heard anything. Her mum would never let her sleep in for too long; a waste of a day she would say.

The day passes slowly. *Whatever Mum is going to say, let her just get on with it.* The confrontation is unavoidable. This waiting is unbearable, and no matter what Ruth says to try and distract her, she is on edge, convinced at every beep from her phone that it's her mum.

Michael rings. "I called around but there was no sign of Amanda. Her car is still in the driveway so I didn't want to let myself in but she didn't answer the door. She must have gone for a run. I'm surprised I've not heard from her though, considering."

"Me too. I thought I'd have woken up to at least ten messages. It worries me that I haven't."

"Maybe she's digesting it; going for a run and thinking it through."

"I don't think so. She was working today at eleven."

"Well, let's wait and see. I left your key under the terracotta plant pot."

"Maybe I should pop around later." Dawn is starting to worry. She is equally scared of her mum's non-reaction.

"No, just leave it, let her cool down. I'll call around again. I need to talk to her anyway. Sort out the argument we had. I don't want to fly back to Australia on bad terms."

Dawn stares into space. This silence is not a good sign. She thinks of all the horrible things Mum did to manipulate Dad. *What is she going to cook up for me?*

Ruth goes to work, leaving Dawn sitting on the settee, flicking through the channels of daytime quiz shows. She switches the TV off in frustration after a few minutes. *I have to go home, this silence is driving me crazy. Mum should be at work by now, I can go home and get rid of the sleeping tablets and see if Mum has been into my bedroom. Then I'll be sure she knows I've left.*

At the entrance to their estate, she sees her mum's car still parked on the drive, and she stops for a moment. Did she cycle to work? Or is she sitting inside waiting for Dawn to come home or contact her?

Two guys from an internet company, the logo displayed across the back of their jackets, walk up the next-door neighbour's drive. Dawn hangs back. They knock and Mrs Mannion answers and sends them on their way. She isn't interested in their sales pitch. They tuck their clipboards under their arms and walk down the drive and up the next one. Watching as they ring her front doorbell, Dawn knows there's no way that her mum will entertain them, she will give them short shrift. Dawn steps closer to the laurel bush at the side of the path so that she's out of sight.

The internet salesmen get no answer. They knock again. Brave guys. Still no answer. One of them makes a note on his clipboard and they move on to the next house. *Mum must have cycled to work. The coast is clear, I can shoot in and out.*

She hurries across the road, her heart thumping in her ears. *I just have to get in and out quickly.* Her eyes dart up and down the road as she reaches for the key under the plant pot as if she expects her mum to come sprinting around the corner. She turns the key and steps inside, leaning her shoulder heavily against the door to shut it properly behind her.

Dawn turns and freezes. Her mum hasn't gone anywhere. She's lying in a twisted mess at the bottom of the stairs.

Rushing forward, Dawn drops to her knees, barely aware of her legs nudging into a pool of blood, the stickiness seeping quickly through the thin material of her black leggings.

Blood is clotted in her mum's thick, curly, blonde hair, and a congealed puddle surrounds the back of her head, soaked into the collar of her pink fluffy dressing gown, which is half off, exposing her shoulder.

"*Mum*," Dawn whispers, her breath catching at the back of her throat as she puts a hand on her mum's bare shoulder before quickly taking it away, gasping. The skin is cold to the touch. Lowering her head to her mum's mouth, she can't feel any breath and, pulling back, she sees the slight blue tinge on her lips.

"*Oh my God, oh my God!*" Dawn rocks back on her knees, feeling the perspiration prickle on her forehead. Bile surges into her throat and she swallows it down, the acidic taste lingering. She opens her mouth to take a breath and inhales the tangy iron scent of the blood in the air.

Running her fingers into the roots of her hair, she tries to think. What should she do? What does she *need* to do? Her whole body is convulsed by shudders, and she tries to steady her shaking shoulders. Shuffling back, the blood stuck to her knees smears across the tiles.

Shit. The blood is on her. Dawn has touched her mum. She shouldn't have.

Now she has to stay. Mum is dead. Dawn needs to act.

Standing up, a weakness tries to sink her, and her knees threaten to give way. Pulling her blue denim jacket across her body, she reaches her hand out to the side table to steady herself. Averting her eyes from the body, she glares at the tiled floor; tiny droplets of blood are splattered in her range of sight. Breathe, she commands herself. In and out. She focuses on a different square tile as she wills the dizziness to pass.

What is she going to do? The sleeping tablets are in her bathroom cabinet. She has to get rid of them. Checking the soles of her shoes for blood, she carefully steps around her mum. Hesitating at the bottom of the stairs, she slips off her shoes. She glances in the door of the living room and sees the empty wine bottle and glass on the table. Shit. Combining the tablets with all that alcohol wouldn't have helped. She tiptoes up the stairs and retrieves the packet from the cupboard.

At the top of the stairs, she averts her eyes from the body and stares at the front door. What does she need to do before she calls the police? Going into her mum's bedroom, she glances around. The purple and red striped curtains are closed. The white duvet cover decorated with pictures of huge red roses is cast aside as if her mum just stepped out of bed. The pale blue shirt and navy trousers her mum wore last night when they spoke for the last time, are hanging on a coat hanger through the handles of the oak wardrobe. On the matching bedside table, there's an empty blister pack of tablets on top of a small box. Dawn reaches to pick them up but then changes her mind and crouches down to read the label. Anti-depressants. Oh fuck. Dawn didn't know about these.

She is halfway down the stairs before she looks directly at the body. *This is all her fault. Mum has mixed her anti-depressants and alcohol unknowingly with sleeping tablets, and now she's dead.*

Mum's pale blue eyes seem to be staring at her, glossy and terrifying. Just as they could be in real life.

Dawn steps slowly down the last few stairs and kneels again, gently closing her mum's eyelids.

"Sorry, Mum."

With a calm that surprises her, she goes to the medicine cupboard in the kitchen, pushes the half-used blister pack into the back and shakes out a new pack of the sleeping tablets. She pulls her jumper down over her hand and pops out a few of the tablets and pockets them. Dawn goes upstairs and puts the packet on the bedside table.

Back downstairs, she pours herself a glass of water and stares out over the back garden. The house is so quiet and still, without the usual radio on in the kitchen, or the whir of the washing machine. But it's not eerie, it's a calm kind of quiet. Sipping the water, the cold slithers down her throat and shocks her into reality. It's her fault her mum is dead. Those sleeping tablets killed her. She gave her too many. Dawn has just managed to escape her mum's clutches and now this. Will she be charged with murder? Manslaughter? Her legs buckle underneath her and she half staggers to a chair at the table. She didn't mean for her to die, she hadn't wanted to kill her, she just wanted to move out, and live her own life. But who's going to believe that? Between the sleeping tablets, the anti-depressants, and the wine, her mum is lying dead only a few feet away from her, at the bottom of the stairs, and Dawn is going to be blamed for it. She's sure she is.

Trying to ignore her chest tightening, she bites the skin around her thumbnail and replays in her mind the moment she'd popped the tablets out of the packet and crushed them with the back of a teaspoon at the desk in her bedroom; she desperately tries to visualise how many she'd used. Moving onto her fingernails, she was sure it was the same as last time and her mum was fine then. Had she had some wine that night? Yes, Dawn thinks, she had.

Everyone is going to think she did it on purpose.

Ruth knew she was desperate to leave home, although Dawn hadn't mentioned the sleeping tablets to her. Michael knew what a contentious issue moving out was between herself and Mum, and he'd found the medical leaflet for the sleeping tablets in her bin. It's not going to take him too long to put two and two together, he's a doctor for God's sake. Fuck! Everything is going to be stacked against her. How is she going to explain this? The pain cuts across her forehead. Oh God, she can't breathe properly. Sitting there panting, her chest is tightening, she can't get the air she needs. She swings her legs around the side of the chair and she puts her head between her knees. She tries not to think of her mum's body lying close by, or of her almost certain arrest for her murder. She stares at the crumbs under the next chair and pants at the air.

As her breathing calms, she realises she needs to call someone, but who? The emergency services, the ambulance, the Gardaí, Michael? Lifting her head, she reaches for her phone in her jacket pocket. She can't delay any longer. Walking across the living room, she peeps through closed curtains and across the cul-de-sac. Any number of neighbours could have seen her coming home. If the guards view the death as anyway suspicious, they might do door-to-door enquiries. They will have questions if there is a time delay between her arriving home and ringing to report it.

Her fingers are shaking as she dials 999, and asks for the Gardaí.

76

Carla is early. She sits and stares at the waves barely turning over, as if in apology. The tide is out, exposing the limestone rocks jutting out to sea. Thick brown seaweed dotted with orange flecks sits in neat rows along the beach. The sand is grey and stony, and empty, bar a dog walker or two in the distance.

From inside the car, you'd be easily lulled into thinking it's a warm day. The sun is shining at intervals, peeking out from behind the scattered clouds which are moving fast in the wind. There's always a wind on this beach. A slate cloud blanket is visible across the bay in Salthill. It won't be too long before it reaches here.

Opening the window halfway, the truth of the cold outside seeps into the car. Carla gasps as it blows in. She needs this fresh air. The house is unbearable. All the lies and deception that are trapped within its walls make it difficult to breathe. It's suffocating her. Pressing on her neck and chest. Carla blinks away her tears. This is really happening. She's about to lose her best friend.

Despite what she knows, despite what she saw, could it all just be a nightmare? The truth is that she can't imagine her life without Emily in it. She's been her one constant for so many years. *We've shared everything. We've shared too much.* Carla looks at the bag on the passenger seat, containing Emily's peach jumper, stilettos, and blue suit jacket. The cold blue, dead eyes of Amanda flash across her mind and she shudders. This is the last thing she has to do before she leaves. Deal with Emily and then go.

The wind picks up and she closes the window. Carla doesn't like this beach; it isn't one she comes to with the kids. It's too exposed, there isn't any shelter from the elements. She chose to meet Emily here today, on the pretence of a walk, because she doesn't have any memories or associations with this place and, when she leaves here today, she won't ever have to come back.

A flash of silver glints in her wing mirror as Emily's car comes into view. The knot in Carla's stomach turns and tightens as she watches her friend's car glide down the hill towards her.

Taking the scrunchie from her wrist, Carla scrapes her hair back and ties it. She tucks her pendant chain inside her jumper. She gets out of her warm haven and stands staring at the sea. The breeze catches her dread and whips it around her body. She pulls her hat down over her ears. Hearing Emily's car door shut, Carla feels sick. The strong smell of the seaweed irritates her nose and the back of her throat, small flies buzz in their hundreds over it. Her jaw tightens as Emily approaches.

"God, it's easy to see why we never come here. It's always windy," Emily says as she curls her hair behind her ear.

"Here, these are yours." Carla passes her the bag.

Emily looks at the coat sticking out of the top of the bag. "I'll throw them in the boot."

They walk along the pebbles, over the seaweed, facing into the sun. Carla pushes her hands down into her pockets to keep them from shaking.

Emily starts rattling on about one of the mothers on the parents' association at school. "She is just so pushy. Why can't she understand that some of us don't have the time to attend every meeting? And, why do we need to have so many meetings? The fundraiser is over."

Carla's mouth is so dry that she can't respond with more than an "*mmm*". *How can Emily be talking about such mundane things when she's deceiving me in the cruellest way possible?*

"Are you okay? You're very quiet."

"I'm not sure," Carla says, her voice only slightly above a whisper.

"Sorry, I'm waffling on about the stupid PA when you're going through hell. I suppose I'm just trying to take your mind off it." Emily reaches to link her arm, but Carla pulls away, pretending to get a tissue from her pocket. "Have you made a decision about when you're going to leave him?"

"I'm not sure." *This is it; this is the moment when everything becomes real.*

"What do you mean you're not sure? Not sure when to leave, or not sure whether to leave him? Have you confronted him?"

Carla can't speak, her lips part but no words come out. She can't formulate them. She knows what she wants to say. What she has to say. She's practised them a hundred times in her head since she found out. But now, here with Emily, the words are stuck.

"You can't stay with him, Carla, not after what he did to you." Emily turns to walk on.

Carla's fingers tingle and she clenches and unclenches her hands to relieve the rage inside her. Watching the back of Emily's hair bounce on the collar of her navy waterproof jacket, she thinks of her husband's hands cupping Emily's face, in her hair, exposing the ear that she doesn't like, the longer ear lobe she likes to keep covered. The anger is shaken up like fizz in Carla's stomach and she feels it bubbling and rising. Taking a quick couple of steps, she catches up to Emily.

Watching her carefully, Carla says, "I hired a private investigator."

Emily pauses ever so slightly before righting herself and Carla sees her eyes twitch, the way they do when she is stressed.

"Well, that's good. Good idea. The more evidence you have, the less Thomas will be able to talk his way out of it. When does he start, the PI?" Her eyes twitch again, and she turns her head to look at the sea as she walks.

"He's already started. In fact, he started a while back."

Emily falters this time, and it takes her a fraction longer, a few seconds, to react and continue walking. Carla falls a step behind and watches her friend twiddle her eternity ring with her thumb as she walks. This is Emily's chance now. She's giving her a chance, a moment, to come clean, to be honest. After being her friend for all these years, Carla surely deserves that. Emily doesn't speak. Carla tucks the fronds of her hair under her hat and inhales deeply.

"Aren't you going to ask me what he found out?" She stops and stands still, waiting for Emily to react and turn around.

"What?" Emily glances back and half turns, her front teeth scraping her bottom lip before the wind catches her hair and blows it across her face, slapping her cheek. Like Carla wants to. "Did he get more evidence for you? Did he find out how long it's been going on? Come on, keep walking, it's cold."

Carla doesn't move. She stares at her friend's back. She wants to run at her, push her down to the sand, claw at her. Emily takes a few more steps before turning back.

"He got plenty of evidence," Carla says. "It turns out that my darling husband hasn't just been having an affair. He's been having two affairs."

She watches as Emily's eyes widen and whiten. Carla's whole body shakes and she folds her arms to steady herself.

"One with my best friend, apparently."

Emily's face reddens and her eyes drop to the dull, grey sand.

"How could you, Emily? My husband? Were there not enough men in the world for you to choose from that you had to take mine?"

"Carla, I'm sorry … I … Let me explain."

"*Explain? Explain? Don't patronise me with your shit!*" Carla is screaming at her now, drowning out Emily's words and the gusting wind.

Their eyes meet, Emily's brimming with tears.

Carla steps closer and starts jabbing her chest. "*My husband, Emily, my husband!*"

"I'm sorry, I'm sorry, I never set out to …"

Carla's rage takes over and, as if she is hovering above, she sees herself grabbing Emily's shoulders and shaking her, screaming into her face. "*My husband, you bitch, how could you? It was you who sent the note and photos, wasn't it? So, I'd leave him, and you could have him for yourself?*"

Emily staggers backward a step or two but Carla keeps a tight hold on her.

"I … I … wanted you to know what he is like."

"*No, you didn't, you wanted him for yourself!*" She shakes and shakes until Emily is limp in her arms. She doesn't fight back. "*I can't believe that you would do this to me!*"

Pushing Emily away and watching her stumble backward, Carla realises she doesn't want to hear what she has to say. She doesn't care. It isn't going to change anything. She has lost her best friend and her husband. Emily is looking at her feet, toeing the pebbles, arms limp. Carla needs to leave. Turning, she starts to walk away.

"*Carla, Carla, wait, let me explain!*"

Hearing the dry seaweed crunch behind her, Carla spins around. "*Don't you ever come near me again.*"

Emily stops and her shoulders hunch at the anger in Carla's voice.

Carla turns and keeps walking.

77

After ringing the gardaí all Dawn can do is wait. Closing the door to the hallway so that she can't see her mother's body, she wonders if she should cover her up, lay a blanket over her. But she doesn't. She sits on the settee and waits, pulling at the skin around her finger with her teeth.

She stares at the empty wine bottle and glass on the coffee table, and thinks about tidying it away. But the gardaí will need to know Mum was drinking. That in itself might have influenced her falling down the stairs. They might not need to know about the sleeping tablets then. She could hide the anti-depressants too, and then they would have no need to think it was anything more than a drunken fall down the stairs. She tears off a tiny bit of skin around her fingernail and a bobble of blood oozes from it. Sucking her finger, she remembers Michael. She must ring him.

"Michael, it's Dawn."

"Hi, did you hear from your mum? I've tried ringing her a few times, but it just rings out."

"I'm here now, at the house. I … I …" her voice wobbles.

"Are you okay? Is she angry with you? I can come straight away."

"It's not that." Dawn's tears finally begin to drip down her face. "She's not angry, she's … she's dead."

"*What?*"

Her tears turn into sobs. "I came to the house, and she was lying at the bottom of the stairs … dead."

"Oh my god. I'm on my way. Are you on your own?" he says over her loud sobs. "Dawn, are you on your own?"

She can hear him getting into his car, the engine starting and the radio automatically coming on. "Dawn, can you still hear me? I'm on my way. Will I ring the police?"

"I already have," she whispers. "Please hurry up. They're on their way."

"I'll be there in five minutes. Hold on."

Dawn hangs up. How is she going to be able to explain everything? To Michael, to the guards? Michael knows about the sleeping tablets, he will suspect her, and he might have known that Amanda was taking anti-depressants. She isn't going to get away with describing this as a drunken fall. What will she say?

The guards arrive before Michael and so does an ambulance. She doesn't know why they sent an ambulance; she had told them Amanda was dead. She opens the door to a male and female officer.

Speaking in gentle tones, the officers step inside and the female officer takes her by the arm and leads her around her mum's body and back into the living room. Dawn allows herself to be seated back on the settee. The officer sits in the armchair and leans forward.

"Shall I make you some tea?" she asks, glancing at the wine bottle and glass.

"No, thank you. They aren't mine." She nods at the coffee table. "I haven't been drinking. They were there when I came in. I wasn't sure if I should move them."

The officer nods. "Is there someone we can call to be with you?"

"I called my uncle, he's on his way."

"Will I call your dad?"

"No, he lives in America, not with us."

Dawn silently urges Michael to hurry up. She twiddles her thumbs in her lap and then entwines her fingers. Is she supposed to be crying? She doesn't know what to do.

As she looks over at the officer, the woman smiles gently. "You've had an awful shock – shall I get you a glass of water?"

When Dawn doesn't reply, she asks, "Can you tell me how you found your mother?"

"I – I came in the front door, and she was there. Just lying there. I tried to see if I could help her, turn her into the recovery position or something but she was dead."

"And, did you talk to her this morning before you went out? How did she seem to you? Was she her usual self?"

"I, *er*, I didn't see her this morning, I moved out .... yesterday." Dawn rocks back and forth in her seat. She regrets the words as soon as she speaks them. She notices the officer's reaction – it's only slight but she saw it. *Oh God, why did she say that? Now she is going to be viewed with suspicion. She has exposed herself. More questions are going to come now.*

"I know this isn't going to be pleasant, but would you accompany me into the hallway to identify your mum. You won't have to come to the morgue then."

Dawn clasps her hands tightly together as she follows the woman into the hallway. The paramedic slowly lowers the sheet over her mother's face, Dawn nods quickly, holding her breath, her ribcage tight, and turns away and goes back into the living room.

The doorbell rings. Please let it be Michael, I can't do this on my own. She hears his deep yet quiet voice followed by a painful wail that emits from him when he sees his sister's body. His voice is muffled through the half-open door, but she can tell from his tone that he is asking questions. The door swings open further, and he is accompanied into the living room by the other officer.

Rushing to Dawn's side, he pulls her into a tight embrace. "Oh Dawn, you poor thing!"

Resting her head on his shoulder, she wills the tears to flow like they did when she rang him, but her face is dry. Why isn't she crying? Her mother is dead, she should be howling. This non-reaction is surely going to go against her in the eyes of the law.

Michael pulls away and, taking her hands in his own, he turns to the male officer standing in front of the fireplace, and says, "So, she fell? Do you know what time approximately it happened?"

"No, not yet. When did you last see her?"

"Last night," he says, looking at Dawn. "About midnight. She was asleep in bed, a deep sleep. I went into her bedroom, but she was conked out."

"At midnight? And what time did you leave here?" He writes something in his notebook.

"Soon after that."

"And can anyone verify that for you?"

"Yes, I can," Dawn speaks up. "I was here with him, we left separately but at the same time."

The female officer looks over. "I thought you said you moved out yesterday?"

Dawn feels the heat rise to her face as both officers watch her.

"I did, last night. I was moving some of my stuff. My friend Ruth was here too, she can verify for both of us." The words rush out of her mouth, and she has to remind herself to take a breath when she has finished. "Are we suspects or something?" She makes eye contact with the female garda. "Wasn't it a fall?" she says, making a point of looking back at the empty wine bottle.

"We're just trying to establish her last known movements, that's all. No one's pointing any fingers."

"These are standard questions, Dawn," Michael reassures her, squeezing her hands between his.

A paramedic steps into the living room and beckons to the male officer. Putting his notebook back in his top shirt pocket, the officer excuses himself and leaves the room.

"Look, I should tell you she was on anti-depressants," Michael says.

Dawn looks at Michael. So, he did know.

"And, sleeping tablets too sometimes," Dawn says quickly but quietly.

Now, it's Michael's turn to look at Dawn. His eyebrows arch at her. Fortunately, the officer is writing in her notepad and misses the look between them.

"Okay. Right. Do you know what type?"

"No," they both mutter.

"She keeps them next to her bed," Michael adds.

"I can go and get them," Dawn says, desperate to escape the scrutiny. She feels so exposed.

"Not at all. We can look at them later."

"Will they have made her fall?"

"Possibly. Look, we are going to be here for a while." The female officer looks at Michael. "I'm sure we'll want to talk to both of you at a later time but do you want to take Dawn to your house for a while? You've both had such a shock. I'll need your phone number and address, so we can contact you later."

"I'm just visiting from Australia. I was staying here but now I'm staying in a local hotel."

"Oh. Right. Where are you staying?"

She writes down the name of the hotel in her notebook along with both of their phone numbers.

Dawn watches the officer carefully. *Why did Michael say that? Now he'll be under suspicion too. He might as well have told them he'd argued with Amanda too. Why didn't he just say he was staying in a hotel?*

A click of the door sounded behind her and both of them turn to see the garda coming back into the living room.

"Are they going to move her now?" Michael asks.

"Yes, soon."

Standing up, Michael holds his hand out to Dawn.

"Look, before you go," the officer says, "the paramedics showed me an injury at the back of Amanda's head which isn't consistent with this fall and looks older." The other officer walks around the living area until she is standing next to him, looking at them both. "Would either of you be aware of her getting a bang to her head lately?"

"No," Dawn and Michael say in unison.

"Okay, well, we'll be in touch. Do you need a lift somewhere? You've had quite a shock. It might not be the best idea to drive."

"Thanks, but my hire car's outside. The hotel isn't far away."

Michael grasps Dawn's hand and leads her out past her mum's covered body. Taking a deep, pained breath, Dawn averts her eyes, the guilt ringing through her ears. *She's caused this. Mum is dead because of her selfishness.*

78

The sound that came from Carla when she saw the truth on Emily's face had been more of a whimper than a cry. It pierced Emily's heart. *What has she done?* She's left standing on the beach watching Carla walk back to her car, knowing that their friendship is over. Emily turns and walks further along the beach, ignoring her tears.

The beach is empty of walkers. She sits on a rock, the cold wind blowing her hair back as she watches the sea tumble onto the shore. She's broken her best friend's heart. She feels as if the pebbles scattered around her on the sand are being forced into the back of her throat. *This is what she wanted, isn't it? So why does it feel so bad?*

It's going to be terrible for a while, she thinks, remembering how it was when Chris left, how awful it was. *It will get better in time.* Emily says these words in her head, but they are Carla's words. This is what Carla said to her when Chris left. *Why did Thomas have to be Carla's?* Emily toes the sand with her trainer, digging down until the sand cascades into her shoe. *This is my chance at true happiness.*

She checks her watch. Shit. She has to collect the kids from school. School. Carla will be there. No, that can't happen, Emily can't do that. She has to stay out of Carla's way, give her space. It's the least she can do. Ringing the afterschool club, she apologises for the late notice and asks if they can hold on to the children for an hour.

The sky darkens with grey clouds as she walks back towards her car.

She's got what she wants. *Why does it feel so shit?* Thomas will be hers now.

She must ring Thomas, tell him Carla knows about his two affairs. Emily wonders how he'll explain Amanda to her. He has, in theory, cheated on Emily too. She'd given him the chance to break it off with Amanda without stating that she knew about her. At least now he can start afresh. They can start afresh. Together.

Thomas doesn't answer the first time and she doesn't bother to leave a message. The rain begins to spot on the sand. Emily waits a minute or two before trying again. This is it, she thinks, as it rings. It'll be a relief for both of them that the truth is out, and they can finally be together.

"Hi Emily, it's not a good time, can I ring you later?"

"Not really. Where are you?"

"I've just arrived back at the office. I'll ring you later, I've got a lot on."

"No, wait, Thomas. Carla knows. She knows everything. About me and you. She hired a private investigator, she had you followed. She knows." The babble of words flies out of her.

"*What? How do you know?*"

"She confronted me, just now, on the beach. She said you've been having two affairs. One with someone called Amanda."

"*Oh shit. Carla knows. Oh my God. Oh no. Fuck. What am I going to do?*"

"Who's Amanda?" Emily asks, a little pissed off that he hasn't asked if she's okay after Carla confronted her.

"*Fuck*. This is a mess, a big mess. How did I fuck this up so badly? Where was she going, where was Carla going when she left you?"

"I don't know. She was fuming. It's school collection time soon so she'll be collecting the boys I imagine. What are you going to do? Will I go with you?"

"What? No, that will make it worse."

"Okay. Yes, I suppose it will. But who's Amanda? What's been going on?"

"Nothing. Amanda isn't important."

"Look, we should meet up before you go to Carla. Talk through everything rationally. Have a plan before you talk to her."

All the while she is saying this, all she can think is that Amanda isn't important to him. He doesn't care about her. Thank God. The path to her and Thomas being together is a little less cluttered now. It's not going to take too much to clear the path.

"What? No, that's not a good idea. I need to get to Carla quickly. Apologise and sort things out. I have to get her to see that I've been a fool, that I'm sorry. I have to prove to her that I love her."

Emily's breath constricts like a corset as she struggles to speak. "But what about us? Are you going to tell her about us? About us being together?"

"Us? There is no us, Emily. It was a bit of fun that has spectacularly backfired, that's all."

Emily opens her mouth, but no sound comes out.

"Now, I have to go to my wife. You'd do as well to stay away, from both of us." He hangs up.

Emily stares at his name on the phone screen as it disappears before dropping it on the sand. She staggers down the beach. The tide is coming in fast. She walks through lines of seaweed clumps, barely registering them. The rain is becoming heavier, a continuous downpour that quickly plasters her hair to her head, her makeup streaking down her face. Reaching the water, she doesn't stop, the foamy waves turn and ripple over her trainers and her toes squelch. She keeps walking. Her feet are like bricks as she tries to wade through the sea. The water's force pushes at her ankles and then her shins. Her tracksuit sticks to her legs, the cold of the sea goes unnoticed as she wades deeper. Knee-high now and Emily comes to a stop. She stretches her neck up to the sky and lets out a roar. A helpless ache of a screech echoes along the beach carried by the wind. Emily drops to her knees and lets the waves crash over her shoulders.

79

Bustling the boys in the front door, Carla says, "Okay, boys, this is a super-quick toilet stop and change out of uniforms. No messing."

Ben turns to her at the foot of the stairs. "Will we still have time to get our Friday treats in the shop?"

"Even better than that, we'll stop at the McDonald's drive-through and get Happy Meals. Now, quick, up you go!"

"McDonald's! *Yahoo*!" Ben bounds up the stairs.

"Can we get hot muffins and ice cream too?" Daniel asks, coming out of the bathroom.

"Absolutely." She smiles. "I left your clean clothes on your bed. Just throw your dirty ones …" She trails off – he's already disappeared, and she realises she doesn't care what the boys do with their uniforms.

They won't need them again, ever. She doesn't plan on returning to Galway.

She'd rung her sister, Grace, this morning, telling her what time she'd be arriving and not to answer the phone to Thomas.

Glancing in the hallway mirror as she walks towards the kitchen, she sees her mascara streaking her cheeks like dirt on a window, and rubs her fingers under her eyes. Thank God she didn't get out of the car at the school. She'd been too depleted of energy after the confrontation with Emily to be civil and make small talk at the school gates. Waving out the window and flashing her lights to the boys was all she could muster.

She shudders as she stands in the kitchen doorway. It's only the toys that are missing but it feels strange, empty.

"*Can we bring my Lego plane?*" Ben shouts downstairs.

"*Yes, I've already put it in the car!*" The car is packed with a suitcase of clothes and their favourite Lego box of the moment. Everything else went with the couriers this morning. "*Hurry up, boys!*" she calls, scanning the many photo frames displayed around her.

Her eyes rest on the silver-framed photo that Emily took of Carla and Thomas on the evening of their wedding. Carla loved that photo. It was so natural compared to the staged official photos. She feels her nails digging into her clenched hands as she is reminded of their betrayal once more.

The phone vibrating in her back pocket startles her, and she rushes back out to the hallway, ignoring the call tone, and calling the boys once again.

When she's safely strapped the two of them in the car, with story and stickers books at their fingertips to keep them entertained for the journey ahead, she starts the engine before abruptly switching it off again.

"I'll just be a minute, boys."

Standing inside the front door, her phone rings again. It's Thomas. He knows she knows. Emily must have told him.

She goes upstairs and stands in the doorway of their bedroom. It looks bare without her things in it. Taking off her wedding ring, she leaves it on his bedside table.

Her phone shrills again, blasting into the quiet of the house. Taking it out of her pocket, she sees Thomas's name and face flash across the screen. Carla silences it before turning it off completely.

That's the fourth time. He'll be panicking now. She knows he will. She can envisage the vein throbbing at the side of his temple. He might be on his way here, right now. She has to leave. She hurries down the stairs and closes the door.

80

At the sound of the doorbell ringing, Dawn comes to the top of the stairs at the same time as Michael emerges from the living room.

"It's the gardaí," he says, looking up at her. "They rang while you were sleeping. They want to talk to us again."

Seeing the wariness in her eyes, he says, "Don't worry, it's just an informal chat for them to double-check things, that's all. I'll go first."

He doesn't see her fists gripping as he moves to answer the door.

Dawn retreats to her bedroom. *Shit. What if they know? What if they know I killed her?* She leaves her door open. She wants to sit at the top of the stairs and listen but she can't risk looking suspicious. Between what she's already told the guards, and what Michael has told them about the clear signs of depression, she thought she was going to get away with it. But now, they are back.

She sits on her window seat, staring out at the rain, the never-ending drizzle that seems to have descended on Galway lately. *Please just let this be over, let us have the funeral. I need to say sorry to Mum.*

Her suitcase and other bags lie open on the floor. Both she and Michael have moved back into the house, but it feels weird, wrong somehow. Her bed is unmade, the covers in a heap. Despite it being after ten o'clock, she isn't out of bed long. She's been so sleepy the last few days.

Her teeth chatter with the cold and she blows into her hands before reaching for her navy college hoody. She can't seem to warm up lately.

They are going to want to speak to her next. She has to look normal. Well, as normal as a grief-stricken daughter should look. Just not guilty, she reminds herself. She brushes her teeth and runs her hands under the hot tap to warm them up.

"*Dawn, they're ready for you now, if you're up to it!*" Michael calls up the stairs.

No, no, I'm not up to it. What if they see straight through me? I could pretend to be too distraught to talk to them. She hesitates at the bedroom door. *They'd only come back another time. No*, she rallies herself, *better to get this over with*. Taking a deep breath, she shakes her wrists and goes downstairs.

In the living room, two officers await her. The female officer, who came to the house after Dawn found Mum, is sitting on the settee, and a tall, red-headed plainclothes male officer stands in front of the fireplace.

"Hello, Dawn, come in, sit with us. I'm sure we are the last people you want to see again," the female officer says. "We just have a few things we want to go over with you. It won't take long, I promise."

Dawn makes her way over to the settee, sits down, and rests her hands in her lap.

"Would any of you like a cup of tea?" Michael calls from the kitchen area.

"No, thank you. Actually, if you don't mind, we'd like to speak with Dawn on our own," the officer says, pushing his red curly hair across one side of his head.

"Of course, no problem. I'll be upstairs if you need me."

Staring at her thumbs twisting around each other, Dawn hears the door click shut before she raises her eyes to the plainclothes officer.

"I'm Officer Davenport. I'm sorry for your loss, Dawn. This is a terribly sad time for you, I know, and we won't keep you too long."

Nodding at him, the voice in her head is screaming at her – *they know, they know everything.*

"We noticed there's an old security camera outside the front door – does it still work?"

"No, that's been broken for ages. I think Mum just had it for show really, you know, being a single mum and all that," Dawn says.

The officer raises his eyebrows.

"But you're obviously welcome to look at it."

"Were you aware that your mum was on anti-depressants?" he asks.

"No, but I wasn't surprised to find out. She's had a tough life – I'm sure my Uncle Michael has filled you in." Her voice wavers over the words at first, growing in strength as she continues, "She was always a 'glass is half empty' sort of person. It didn't take much to get her down. I knew about the sleeping tablets though."

He nods for her to continue.

"She tried to encourage me to take them when I was studying for my Leaving Certificate exams last year. I was a bit anxious and wasn't sleeping well."

The female officer smiles. "It's a stressful time. I've got a son who is doing it this year. It's a lot of pressure."

"I didn't take them, though, the tablets. I used to meditate. I found that helped."

"You might like to know that the anti-depressants were prescribed by her doctor and had been for years."

"Right." Nodding, Dawn looks back down at her hands.

"The sleeping tablets were over-the-counter ones," he says.

Dawn holds her breath – she knows what's coming next. Should she just admit it now?

"We suspect that Amanda falling was a terrible accident. That the wine, mixed with the antidepressants and sleeping tablets made her stumble and fall."

And breathe.

"We won't know until we get the toxicology report back exactly what was in her system. That could take a few weeks."

Weeks? Dawn stares at him.

"So we can't have her funeral yet?" she asks quietly.

"Yes, you can have the funeral. We are ruling her death as accidental."

The tears well up behind her eyelids and she grips her hands together to stop them from trembling.

"Just one more thing – was there anyone else close to Amanda that you need to tell?" the female officer asks.

Dawn looks at her quizzically.

"Did she have a boyfriend or partner?"

"No. No one serious anyway. It was just me and Mum."

"Are you sure? Your uncle seemed to think she was seeing someone."

"No, I'm sure. She might have said that to him, to make him think she was happy. She had a habit of making the world seem perfect to him as I'm sure he's told you."

As she shuts the front door behind them, Dawn's shoulders sag with relief and her legs wobble under her. Putting a hand out to the side table to steady herself, she looks at Michael as he comes downstairs and walks into the living room.

"We can start to plan the funeral now," he says. "Do you want a cup of tea?"

"No, thanks. I think I'll have a shower."

She feels lighter with every step she takes upstairs. *Has she got away with this?*

81

Emily stands in the shower, the steam rising around her. She doesn't feel it. She's still numb. Not numb from the cold sea that she was dragged from by strangers on Friday, but numb from the realisation that she has fucked everything up. How could she have been so stupid? At no point was this ever going to end well.

Closing her eyes, she can see Thomas's face, laughing over lunch in the show house, kissing her in bed in the hotel, that first moment when he told her he loved her. And she'd believed him. The tears cascade down her face, mixing with the shampoo and body wash. She'd allowed herself to be swept off her feet by him. Why did she think it was love? It was lust, pure and simple. She spits the soap into the shower basin. She's disgusted that she believed in him, that she'd even considered him. She was nothing more than sex to him. Dropping the loafer, she touches her arms; they are rubbed raw of the last few weeks.

Emily has always been the protective friend, the more worldly of her and Carla. Carla is too nice, too trusting of people, she always looked for the good in people. Emily saw herself as a little more streetwise, less likely to be taken in. Well, the roles have certainly changed now. She rinsed out the shampoo.

Poor Carla, she doesn't deserve any of this shit. She'll never forgive me. She's rung her and texted, but she knows their friendship is over.

No friendship recovers from this. How did she allow herself to get so carried away, that she didn't realise what she was set to lose, what she was always going to lose?

The heat in the shower makes her feel light-headed, and she steadies herself, putting her arm against the wall. Did she really think she and Thomas could be a couple? Carla had confirmed he was having two affairs. Emily hadn't needed a private investigator to find that out, but she had deluded herself that Amanda was just a friend who was a bit clingy. When it dawned on her that he was probably having an affair, she naively thought he would choose her if she pushed him into a corner. Seriously, the words in her head berate her, as she switches off the shower and reaches for her towel, he was already having one affair, why wouldn't he be having two? She's been made a fool of by him. How could she have been so stupid?

Rosie knocks on the door.

"*Mum, Mum, Theo is annoying me. I'm trying to practise my spellings and he keeps shouting out letters!*"

"*Put the TV on if you like, we can do your spellings after dinner. I'll be down in five minutes!*"

She sits heavily on the edge of the bed, wishing she could just curl up under the covers and wake up tomorrow to find this was all a bad dream.

82

"I'll go and get some coffees," Carla says to her sister, Grace, turning towards the coffee truck.

She stands in the queue looking at the playground, watching Daniel and Ben playing with their cousins. They think they're on holiday. She hasn't told them about the separation. She can't, she wouldn't know where to start. How does a parent have that conversation? She moves along in the queue. Ben's infectious giggle floats across the playground and her heart surges. They'll be okay, she reassures herself for the hundredth time, children are resilient.

Carla orders coffee and watches as Ben tries to pass Daniel on the climbing frame only to have his path blocked by his brother. What if they turn out like Thomas? What if it's a hereditary thing? Can the cycle be stopped? What can she do to raise good, honest, loyal young men?

She adds sugar for her sister, and turns, coffee cups in her hands, catching Grace's worrying eyes watching her. She made the right decision coming here, her sister has been a rock. Held her as she sobbed, ranted and raged. She's made her shower and get dressed on days she's wanted to stay on the settee and cry, and fielded calls from their worried parents, keeping them at bay for now.

"Did you see this?" Grace says, holding her phone out as Carla sits on the bench, handing a coffee to her sister. She takes it and reads the

Galway News Facebook headline: **Dublin man arrested and charged at his Galway business for misusing client's money.**

"That didn't take long," Carla murmurs to herself.

"It's the least he deserves," Grace says, taking back the phone as Dan comes bounding over from the climbing frame.

"Mum, Mum, can we get ice cream? Please?"

"Of course. Let me drink my coffee first, and then we'll go over to the ice-cream van," she says with a smile.

Ignoring her sister's concerned look, Carla glances back at the children playing together. She knows that her sister expects her to move back to Galway eventually. Not to get back together with Thomas but to the familiarity of life there. But she won't. Of that, she's sure. Carla's set on making a new life here in Kinsale. She knows it's not going to be an easy path but she is confident that she's capable of doing it. She raises her face to the sun, watching seagulls swoop and soar in the blue sky, and the cotton wool, white clouds floating by. This is exactly what she needs right now.

83

Dawn sits on the bench in the back garden, tucking her black funeral dress beneath her, and watches the birds swooping in and out of their little bird boxes.

Yesterday she'd sprinkled sandwich crumbs on the bird table, a huge pile of them and they're all gone now. There's so much food. It's as if people around her have to keep busy. With all this waiting around for the funeral, people just keep buttering and filling and cutting. Everyone's tiptoeing around each other, being polite, exchanging banalities or talking about the weather.

She can hear the mutterings of voices coming from inside the house and glances over her shoulder. Her dad, Brad, is standing at the kitchen window. He looks up and their eyes meet. He tilts his head and she smiles. He came over with Maria a few days ago, as did Michael's wife, Sally and their two kids. Dawn knows they're all trying their best to support her, but the quiet is stifling her, the guilt pushing down on her rib cage. She needs to tell the truth but how can she?

The gardaí have ruled it an accidental death and only she knows the truth. *How can she live with herself knowing that she was responsible?*

The family thinks she's in shock; they don't realise it's guilt keeping her quiet.

Dawn watches as one tiny wisp of a cloud slowly floats across the sky. She hopes Mum is at peace.

"The cars are here, honey." Brad stands in the open doorway.

Sally is organising the children with their coats, and no one seems to be in any rush out to the cars, so Dawn sits on the settee, staring into the fireplace, twiddling her thumbs on her lap. Ruth and Samantha sit down on either side of her, and Dawn rests her head on Samantha's shoulder. She's grateful they aren't trying to engage her in mindless chatter.

She hears the bustle around her but it's as if she's underwater – their voices float over her. She must say something before they go to the church, before it splurges out of her at the graveside, and everyone hears it. The family deserves to know the truth. It was her fault.

Before she knows it, the room is empty apart from Michael. He sits next to her and takes her hand. A lone tear drips down her cheek. He wipes it with his thumb.

"It's okay, love, there's no rush. Take your time."

The front door closes, and her dad comes back into the living room, sitting on the arm of the settee, on the other side of Dawn.

"We'll get through today together," he says.

"I should have been here. If I hadn't moved out …" Dawn whispers.

"It would still have happened, Dawn," Michael says. "You wouldn't have woken until she fell. There's nothing you could have done to change anything."

"*I shouldn't have left her. I shouldn't have left her.*" She's crying in earnest now and she rocks back and forwards. She feels the lump loosening in her throat.

Brad rubs her back. "It's not your fault. You can't blame yourself. Mixing those anti-depressants with the wine was an accident. She didn't even know you were leaving, did she? It was a terrible accident, that's all."

Dawn stands up and steps around the coffee table. "You don't understand. It was my fault. I made things worse." She stares at the candles on the mantelpiece.

"How? By wanting to move out? You have to stop thinking like this," Michael says, trying to reassure her.

"*I spiked her food with sleeping tablets!*" She spits out the words, still staring at the mantelpiece, her back to them.

"What?" Brad says quietly, standing up.

Dawn turns around to face them, catching the confused look passing between the two men.

"I put sleeping tablets in her dinner so that she would sleep soundly. So, she wouldn't wake while I moved out. I didn't know she was on anti-depressants, I swear. The sleeping tablets combined with the anti-depressants killed her, I'm sure." Her shoulders sag with relief as the truth is revealed and tears stream down her face. "I just wanted her to sleep so I could get my things out of the house without any more confrontation. I didn't want to kill her."

"Of course you didn't." Her dad steps forward and wraps his arms around her. She crumples into his embrace.

Michael stands up. "Dawn, you're wrong. She didn't ingest them."

"I made a curry, mixed the tablets into it. I left her eating dinner when I went to work," she says, pulling away from her dad, her chest heaving with the sobs.

"Well, she mustn't have eaten much of it. Two almost full plates of curry were left in the fridge. I threw them out when we moved back in," Michael says, adjusting his glasses.

"*What?*" Dawn's voice catches in her throat. "Mum didn't eat the dinner?"

"No, she didn't."

It wasn't because of her. She steps back from Brad.

"It wasn't your fault," Michael says. "According to her doctor, Amanda had been on anti-depressants for a long time, probably since our parents died. You need to stop feeling responsible because you're not."

Brad leads her back to sit on the settee and Michael perches on the arm of it.

"Your mum became who she was as an adult because of what happened in the fire when we were younger. Now, I don't know all the details of the fire, but she felt responsible and that's why she was so controlling and manipulative with all of us." Michael nods at Brad. "She was scared of losing us, and she was probably trying to protect us from the big bad world too."

Brad's wife, Maria, pokes her head around the door. "They're waiting to go to the church if you are ready."

"Okay. We'll just be a minute," Brad says.

"Don't let this sad chapter be your whole story, like she did," Michael continues "Don't let it change the sweet young independent woman that you are. Learn from this, grieve, and in time you can move on." He passes her a tissue.

Brad stands up, taking Dawn's hand. "Come on, it's time to say goodbye."

84

The night it happened

Amanda pours herself another large glass of wine and stands the bottle in the cooler on the coffee table. She's finding herself tucking into a few glasses most evenings; more than a few glasses if she's honest. Mixed with her anti-depressants, her world fogs enough to cope with.

Just lately, everything has gone wrong. She can feel the hate oozing out of Dawn towards her but she is still determined her daughter will stay at home. She can commute to college from here no problem. She has done it for the last year.

She hadn't thought her daughter would abandon her after she has raised her on her own all these years. She'd expected her to feel some responsibility to stay. But no, she can't wait to escape, and now that Brad, the non-parent, has thrown money at her, she knows she's going to find it incredibly hard to keep Dawn. She needs to think and work out another angle to keep her at home. Maybe an illness would play on her daughter's heartstrings?

Taking a big gulp of wine, she allows the cold liquid to embrace her as it slides down her throat. She looks at her phone. Nothing. No texts, no missed calls from Thomas. She opens her call history. No phone calls at all today. Nothing since the day she saw Thomas in the woods. Amanda has no idea what has happened with him. She hasn't been anywhere near his wife. Not recently anyway. She might have stalked her a bit at the beginning of their affair, but she hasn't been near her in months.

She'd learnt very quickly that the affair was on Thomas's terms, but she'd been confident that over time she'd be able to make him hers. She was willing to play the long game, play by his rules for now. His children were young, he wasn't going to leave a young family. Patience was the key. But now this has happened, this bolt out of the blue. His face, his expression had been one of pure disgust and rage when he'd yelled at her. She'd never seen this side of him before and she was shocked. He'd always been caring and attentive and, although they didn't spend too much time together, she would have described him as loving and respectful towards her. Meeting him in the woods had been like meeting a completely different man. The accusations, the words he spat at her, the hate in his eyes. Did she really mean nothing to him?

Shuffling on the couch to get comfortable, she tucks her legs up under her. Her hip is still sore since she scraped it on the forest floor. She didn't scrape it. *He* did. She'd been taken in by declarations of love and his shows of affection. When he hadn't contacted her after the meeting in the woods, she'd realised she was the typical cliché of the other woman. To her, he might have been a future, to him it had just been a fling. When he thought the affair was threatened to be revealed he had rejected her in a second, desperate to save his own skin.

She dials his number now. She knows it's late and that he'll be at home with his wife, but she wants to hear his voice. He doesn't answer. She waits for his voicemail and then listens as he apologises for not taking the call. The pips sound. She doesn't speak, just ends the call.

Amanda leans forward to refill her wine. The turquoise photo frame sitting on the table next to the fireplace comes into focus and she rests her eyes on it for a moment. The white of the snow is glaring around her parents, herself, and Michael in their brightly coloured ski suits. Her fuchsia pink one matches her mum's. Michael and Dad are in identical navy salopettes and royal blue jackets. The sun is shining on their smiling faces. She has studied this photo hundreds of times over the years. A tear runs down Amanda's cheek. She didn't mean for them to die. She thought a tragedy like a house fire would bring her parents together. Make them realise their love for each other. She'd been trying to save them. To save their family. The guilt has tormented her, her whole life. All she has tried to do since is keep everyone close, to keep them safe. One of the candles on the coffee table fizzes and hisses as it goes out. Amanda watches the thin wisp of smoke rise and disappear.

Michael's betrayal hurts the most, more than Dawn wanting to move out, more than Thomas ditching her. It is Michael who's pierced her heart. She's been committed to him her whole life; she'd been a sister, a confidante, and a mother to him. Since the fire, she's loved and protected him as if he was her son. She shouldn't have slipped up, should have kept quiet. He'd been questioning and pushing her to talk. It had been when he'd accused their mother of setting fire to their home with them there, as a way of punishing their unfaithful father, that she had snapped and let out the truth. Michael had jumped and grabbed at her words when they were barely out of her mouth and flung them back at her. She'd tried to protect him for all these years but now he knew.

She hasn't heard a word from him. His suitcase and clothes are still upstairs, his passport too; she's checked. She's probably rung him ten times after he left, never once daring to leave a voicemail. Too scared she would say more than she should and make things worse. If that was even possible at this stage.

The wine bottle is empty now and she's tired. Standing up, she holds onto the back of the chair, turning away from the empty wine bottle. She'll clear it in the morning. What she needs now is her bed.

She feels lonelier with each step she takes upstairs. Dawn, Thomas and Michael, all abandoning her, neglecting her. How can they do this to her? It's not fair. After everything she's done for them. The anger bubbles up from her stomach. How dare they? Sitting on the edge of her bed, she picks up the box of tablets. She'll show them. She'll give them a taste of their own medicine. What if she was to abandon them? Then they'd be sorry. Sliding out the blister pack of tablets, she runs her finger over each tablet pocket. The doctor had refused to up her dosage, said it was high enough. If she took a few more, would that make her ill enough to be taken to hospital? She wouldn't do serious damage, maybe need to have her stomach pumped. That might work. It would give the three of them the jolt they need to realise how much she means to them. A little scare. She pops out the tablets and swallows them with some water from her bedside locker. Curling up under her covers, she smiles and closes her eyes, awaiting the love she's certain will envelop her when she wakes up in hospital.

Amanda turns over and her eyes flutter open. Where is she? Everything is blurred. She blinks and tries to focus. It feels like something is stamping on her head. Her eyes zone in on the glass of water on the bedside table and she reaches her hand out, knocking it to the floor.

"*Shit.*" She tries to sit up. She shuffles to the edge of the bed. It takes her three attempts. "Water, I need water." The words are as blurred in her mind as they are coming out of her mouth.

Staggering to the door, she grabs her dressing gown from the back of it. Struggling to get her arms in, she leaves the belt hanging loose.

The light in the landing is too bright and she lowers her eyes, her shoulders hunched against the pain in her head.

"*Water,*" she murmurs as she stumbles over the loose belt of her dressing gown and tumbles down the stairs.

85

Ruth links Dawn's arm as they kick through the autumn leaves along the river path. Samantha walks alongside, her arms full of books. "So, do you think the sale will go through?"

"I don't know. Dad's dealing with it but there seems to be a lot of toing and froing," Dawn says, trying not to picture the scene where she found her mum four months ago. The house has only been for sale for a short while but it's on for a good price and it's been snapped up.

Galway cathedral looms in the distance and although Dawn isn't a religious person, she likes to stand outside it at night and look at it all lit up and think of her mum. It's beautiful in the day time too, the fiery colours of autumn blazing all around them.

"Property law can be confusing and delays seem to happen at the drop of a hat. I doubt I'll be specialising in it," Samantha says. "I'd get too frustrated."

Dawn and Ruth make eye contact and a knowing smile passes between them that says 'Sam and her studies!'.

"It's my turn to make dinner tonight. How does spag bol sound? I can have it ready for when you come back from your counselling session," Ruth says.

"Sounds yummy. I'll pick up some garlic bread on my way back to the apartment." Dawn stops to rewrap her oversized maroon scarf around her shoulders. The three of them rent together near the college, only a stone's throw from the library, which Samantha loves.

"How are the sessions going?" Samantha adjusts her arms around the books.

"Good so far. These one-to-one sessions are more intense than the group ones." Brad and especially Michael had been worried that she might be overcome with grief, and they'd convinced her to attend counselling in the college. It helps with both her anxiety and self-blame. "I'm taking the booklet Mum's library sent me to the session." Her eyes fall on it sticking out of her bag. It arrived yesterday; a lovely booklet made by the parents and children who attended the story time in the library where her mum worked. She'd sat on her bed last night and opened it to find drawings of the children's favourite books and messages from the parents. She was surprised to read them; it showed a side of her mum that Dawn hadn't seen for a long time and had forgotten existed. One of the parents mentioned *The Tiger Who Came to Tea* and what a hit such an old story had been with the children. They said it was testament to Amanda's wonderful animated reading. She'd closed her eyes and the words of the story came back to Dawn. She could picture herself curled up on the settee, Mum's arm around her, reading and rereading that story. In her mind's eye. she could see other books next to them: *Mog the Forgetful Cat*, *Topsy and Tim*, *The Gruffalo*. She'd rested back against the bed frame, and remembered jigsaws on the coffee table and empty bun wrappers next to her cup of milk.

The tears had fallen then. Cascaded. The first proper tears of genuine grief since Mum died. Ruth found her curled up on the bed, and sat with her, not saying much just being there. Samantha came in with hot chocolate and they'd looked through the booklet together. Dawn told them about her mum. About the good times she'd forgotten about. Her mum had loved her, played with her, and read to her. It hadn't all been bad. Mum's controlling nature had increased with her anxiety of losing Dawn to adulthood.

Last night, she had dreamt of her mother. A trip to the beach holding hands with her mother, singing and laughing as they skipped across the sand.

"I hope it goes well. See you later." Ruth turns to hug Dawn, and Samantha is pulled in too.

"See you for dinner." Dawn continues along the river path. The water is flowing at a furious rate, and she feels for the rowers in the two boats trying to battle against the current. She has some time before her counselling session, so she sits on her usual bench for a few minutes and watches the rowers struggle and heave at the oars. One of them waves over at her. Squinting to see, she realises it's John from the bereavement group. She waves back. He lost his dad to cancer at the beginning of the year.

She toes a horse chestnut shell with her foot, rolling it towards her. Picking it up, she pulls it apart, discarding the spikey outer covering, and rubs the smooth, shiny conker in her hand. She didn't kill her mum. She's accepted that now. The toxicology report hadn't shown any sleeping tablets in her mum's system. She hadn't eaten the dinner just like Michael said. Her mum had been on her own self-destructive path, although neither Dawn nor Michael thought she'd intentionally taken too many tablets. It was an accident. Dawn stuck to that thought in her mind. Her life would be a slippery slope if she let herself think otherwise. And, as Michael said, she can't let this consume her. This was a chapter in her life, and she's determined not to let it define her.

Dawn watches as the rowers turn back downstream and speed up with the current before she continues along the riverbank. She wants to share this booklet with her counsellor and talk about the happier times with Mum. She wants to move forward.

As she wanders, her feet kicking through the leaves, she wonders how different life would have turned out for Mum, herself, Brad, and Michael, if Mum had had access to counselling after her parents died. Would it have made her less clingy, less manipulative? Would she have avoided her self-destructive path?

86

Gathering the maths sheets she needs to mark, Carla glances at the clock on the wall, she should have enough time to get through these before Ben and Daniel finish at the afterschool club.

It's been four months since she left Thomas and, in some ways, she's still finding her feet in Kinsale. Her parents had wanted her to stay with them in Limerick, but she didn't have the heart to. Too many memories of growing up with Emily there. Not that she can escape the memories, they're still around her all the time.

She was lucky to get this temporary job in the boys' new school. Although it's not ideal to be working in her own children's school, it makes childcare easier and she's loving teaching again. She uses the fact that she's a teacher in the school as an excuse not to get too friendly with the other mums. She's not ready for any close friendships. Polite and pleasant is all she can muster at the moment.

The boys are settling into their new life without too much upset and thriving at school. They spend a lot of time with Grace and her family. Carla's heart nearly broke yesterday when they were coming home from their cousins and Ben said "That den we made today was almost as good as the one we made with Rosie and Theo. Can you remember, Mum? When we went on that wood trail and Emily found all those big branches and we made a den against a tree trunk."

She'd felt a pang for the life she'd lost – for the husband she'd loved and a best friend she'd adored. Thomas had rung her a lot at the start. She'd ignored the calls and never listened to his voicemails. In the end she'd bought a new phone number, hired a solicitor and instructed her to deal with Thomas's constant contact. There isn't any point in speaking to him. Nothing he can say can undo what he has done.

He's still in her life because of the children. She doesn't stand in the way of him seeing the boys. He is their father after all. Her brother-in-law does the handovers. He meets Thomas in Limerick, and that works for now. She's not under any illusion that it can continue long term. She will have to be in the same room as Thomas at some point, but for now it's all she can handle. She's heard he is due in court in the New Year for his dodgy financial dealings. Unless he can charm the judge like he manages to charm women, he could be facing a sentence. Carla doesn't know if he realises it was she who reported him but, in a way, she hopes he does.

Her plan to leave Emily at war with Amanda hadn't worked out – tragically – but she didn't care anymore. Looking back, it had been a knee-jerk reaction to hurt her friend in some way. She still misses her. So much sometimes it hurts but she will never speak to Emily again.

Yawning, she sits at her desk, tucking her new, shorter bob haircut behind both ears. She takes out her red pen and pulls the maths sheets towards her.

She didn't sleep well last night. She still has nightmares about Amanda's body lying there, of the blood surrounding her head, the weird twisted way her legs were. Carla often thinks about what would have happened if she didn't drive away earlier that night, if she'd found Amanda sooner and rung for an ambulance. That Amanda could have been and was saved. That night has replayed in her mind and dreams many times over the last few months. The guilt sometimes pushes so hard on her ribcage that she thinks it might crack.

* * *

That night, she'd waited a few minutes after the man in the hire car had driven off before starting the engine. Then she'd spotted the key. Glinting in the red front door.

She killed the engine and stared at it.

She told herself to go over there and confront Amanda. After sitting in the car all evening, here was her chance. But she couldn't move. She stared at the key and then put her car into gear and drove away.

A belt of tiredness hit her as she drove. Just one more day, she thought to herself, as she rubbed her eyes at the traffic lights. I have to get through tomorrow and then I am done. The key shone at her from inside her eyelids. She opened her eyes, blinking furiously, and drove on.

She drove aimlessly around the city before she eventually pulled over down at the Claddagh and closed her eyes for a while.

She'd woken with a start and looked at her watch. It was 3 am. Shit. She checked her phone. No missed calls from Thomas wondering where she was. He must have gone to bed early. Squeezing her eyes shut, the mascara cracked on her eyelashes. The key blinked across her mind again. She had to go back. She had to see this through. Turning the engine on, she drove back towards Amanda's house and parked at the entrance to the estate where she couldn't be seen, beside a high hedge of laurel bushes.

Carla stepped out of the car, straightened Emily's peach jumper, pinged the boot open, and took out the light blue suit jacket. She didn't fasten it; the evening was warm, and between the coat and the jumper, a line of sweat had already formed and dripped down her spine.

The stilettos tapped the tarmacadam and echoed around her as she stepped across the road. She looked up nervously at the bedroom windows in the surrounding houses, expecting to see faces peeking out. But it was late, and no lights were on. She turned back to face the house and focused on the front door as she strode towards it. This is going to be very straightforward, she reassured herself, she'll be in and out in a few minutes. Her heart thumped so fast and loud it was as if it was a couple of paces ahead of her.

Carla tucked in a stray strand of blonde under the auburn wig. She and Emily don't look alike, but they are the same height and have a similar build. It was dark, and wearing her clothes and confronting Amanda in the same menacing way as Emily did in the library car park, she hoped Amanda would follow through on her threat to report Emily to the gardaí. She had to think it was Emily threatening her. Carla imagined how good it would feel to walk away the next day with the two women at war with each other. A small win in the overall scheme of things.

As she reached the car on the driveway, she faltered and stared at the wilting viola pansies in the window box before she urged herself forward. This had to be done. She hoped to catch a sleepy Amanda at the door, to hiss threats in a whisper that she'd practised, for Amanda to be sleepy enough not to react quickly.

A New York City keyring in red, white, and blue hung from the lock. She reached for it and then hesitated. It's not on to barge into someone's house, even if it is someone who's been sleeping with your husband for the past six months. She rang the doorbell and stood back. Nothing. Again, she rang the bell, once, twice, and a quick double press. Hurry up. She wanted to get this over with.

Carla peered into the frosted window next to the door, looking for movement. An upstairs landing light was on, casting a dim light down to the entrance hallway. She could make out a coat stand and a sideboard of some sort. The stairs were right across from the door so she would have a good view of Amanda coming down.

Seconds passed and her teeth started to chatter despite the June evening, still no movement from the house. *Okay, maybe this wasn't going to work. Amanda must be a very deep sleeper.* She rang one last time, put her hands against the glass, and peered through them. *There was something on the floor, at the bottom of the stairs. Did the daughter leave bags behind her? No, it isn't bags, what is it? A washing basket?*

She turned the key, pulled down the handle, and stepped inside. She will confront Amanda, even if she has to drag her out of bed to do so. A metallic scent scraped at the back of her throat at the very moment Carla raised her eyes to see the shape at the bottom of the stairs. There lying in front of her, in a twisted mess, was Amanda, in a pink dressing gown. She gasped, stepped back, and put a hand out to steady herself on the doorframe. What the hell? She took a quick look behind her to the driveway and shut the door, having to push her shoulder firmly against it. She moved forward on the tiptoes of Emily's stilettos as if the noise of the heels would disturb the crumpled heap. Amanda's blonde curls fanned out, and framed her head on the tiles, bloodstained on one side. What the hell has happened? Was Carla sitting in her car watching the house as a murder was committed? Who did this, the daughter? The man? Both of them? Instinct kicked in and she dropped to her knees and shook Amanda's arm.

"*Amanda, Amanda, can you hear me?*"

Amanda's eyes, pale blue and cold, stared up at her. There was no reaction. She was dead. Carla double-checked the pulse on her wrist. Nothing. She sat back on her knees and stared at Amanda, what should she do now? Should she ring for an ambulance? It dawned on Carla, slowly yet very clearly, that she had to get out and quickly. She couldn't ring for an ambulance. She was the wife of the man Amanda has been having an affair with. It wouldn't take long for the guards to implicate her in all of this. A woman scorned and all that. She had to get out.

Carla stood up, looked down at Amanda's twisted body. No one deserved this. She left the key in the lock, pulled the door firmly behind her, and then stopped. The blood in her ears pounded. The sweat was pooled at the base of her spine. Was the house locked or unlocked when she arrived? Her hands shook as she reached for the key. It was open, wasn't it? No, I turned it to open the door, didn't I? She thought, yes, I did, I'm sure I turned it. Okay, breathe. Lock the door and walk away. Was she leaving a dying woman on the floor of her house? No, she was already dead. There was nothing she could do. It wasn't anything to do with her, and Carla left before it became her problem.

THE END

Acknowledgements

This story began as a very different idea in February 2020. Then Lockdown arrived and I began to treat my writing as an office job. As my children sat down to homeschool, I sat down to write. I signed up for an online week's writing challenge run by Writer's Ink. That was to be my doorway into the writing world. I became an Inker (as we like to call ourselves) immediately after. I had found my tribe! Thanks to Vanessa Fox O'Loughlin (aka author Sam Blake) and Maria McHale who run this fabulous group. I can't begin to put into words how much these two women have done for me. They are two incredible powerhouses of knowledge, experience and kindness. They don't stop giving to the writing community, both within our tribe and outside it. As for the mighty tribe itself, Writer's Ink, well, where do I start? You are all wonderful. I feel like I've known some of you forever. The motivation, the support, the sharing of ups and downs in our writing, the being there, day in, day out. I have learnt so much while being in your company, so thank you.

To Clo, Ronan, Anne, Valerie, Mary and Sharon, whom I met through Writer's Ink and have gone on to be the most amazing writing buddies. I see you all as the matriarchs (sorry, Ronan!) (And nothing to do with age!). You have guided me from the very early drafts of this story to where it is now, and I appreciate every bit of critique. Mary, you very kindly read the full manuscript and gave me detailed feedback. With that feedback, I produced yet another draft and that was the one Poolbeg liked. So, thank you.

To my in-person writing group, Gráinne and Karen. We met eight years ago at a writing class in Clarinbridge and, although these classes and other people came and went, we stuck together – becoming The Purple Pens. Your support and advice, on life and writing, have made us firm friends. We've sat on hillsides in the Burren writing next to fairy trees, weekends away in Doolin, scribbled in warm pub snugs, and each other's houses. You have always been there for me to sound out ideas, fix plot holes and find inconsistencies. Thank you.

Thank you to my fact checkers: Tom, Marie, and Ollie for their expert Garda knowledge and for being over the fence, or on text message for me to check the most random things. To Ian, in Clarke's Pharmacy in Kilcolgan, for answering all my medical queries and not once (I hope) thinking I was about to bump someone off. People like this are so helpful when it comes to writing a novel and I'm very grateful to them.

To Paula at Poolbeg who received my story on a Tuesday and emailed me on a Wednesday looking for more. You restored my faith in the Irish postal service! Seriously, I'm thrilled you liked my story and put the wheels in motion for it to be published. You have always been at the end of the email with any of my queries, answering promptly and with great humour. To Gaye, my editor at Poolbeg, wow, you did an amazing job! From bouncing off section rewrite ideas to fixing the holy mess that I sent back to you – you truly are fabulous! Thank you.

Now to the family. To Mum and Dad, who nurtured my love of reading and writing from a young age. I can't remember ever going to bed as a child without a bedtime story. And I may have been turned down money for various toys, or designer clothes growing up, but in a bookshop money was always handed over. I wrote my first story with my dad, 'Arthur's Arm', when I was about eight, and have been writing since. Thank you for being you.

To my siblings, Mark, Elizabeth and Suzanne, spouses and offspring. Although we are separated by the Irish Sea, when we are together the laughter and stories flow. I'm not sure you get my writing world any more than I understand your working worlds, but you humour me! I say humour me – I mean 'laugh at'. Not so long ago, while I was on a car journey with Elizabeth and Suzanne (and Mum too), a writer friend rang, and we proceeded to chat about our writing. My sisters creased themselves laughing at our talk of first-draft vomits, getting the story down, and you can't edit an empty page. When I hung up the phone, they had tears rolling down their cheeks and now love to throw these phrases into various conversations and text messages. But still, you're the best.

To all the O'Callaghans, and there are a lot. Gráinne, Pádraig, Gráinne (Jnr), John, Éadaoin, Dearbhail, and Fergal, spouses and offspring. Thanks for all the support. The O'Callaghans are a family who love a good story and are probably wary of what may be in this book. Don't worry, I have stored it all for the next one!

Now to the most important people in my whole world. My people. Niall, thank you for understanding I needed to give this journey a shot. Thank you for your love and patience. To Patrick, Alexander, and Aoife-Lily, you are my everything. I am the luckiest mum in the world to have you in my life. And although you are growing up and away from me, starting your own adult lives, always know there is a place for you in my world. And, yes, I will always interrogate you about your lives. Just for story material, of course!

Lastly, to the reader, thank you. These journeys don't happen without you. I hope you've enjoyed the story and that you'll follow me on the journey to the next story.

You can find me on Facebook: Lucy O'Callaghan Instagram: lucy.ocallaghan.31

X: @Lucy COCallaghan